JAKE
BUCHAN

SECOND
SIGHT

CAN JOHN STEADMAN FIND THE LINKS BETWEEN A
TRAIL OF BIZARRE AND MACABRE MURDERS?

JAKE
BUCHAN

SECOND
SIGHT

CAN JOHN STEADMAN FIND THE LINKS BETWEEN A
TRAIL OF BIZARRE AND MACABRE MURDERS?

MEREO
Cirencester

Mereo Books

1A The Wool Market Dyer Street Cirencester Gloucestershire GL7 2PR
An imprint of Memoirs Publishing www.mereobooks.com

Second Sight: 978-1-86151-721-0

First published in Great Britain in 2017
by Mereo Books, an imprint of Memoirs Publishing

The address for Memoirs Publishing Group Limited can be found at
www.memoirspublishing.com

The Memoirs Publishing Group Ltd Reg. No. 7834348

The Memoirs Publishing Group supports both The Forest Stewardship Council® (FSC®) and
the PEFC® leading international forest-certification organisations. Our books carrying both the
FSC label and the PEFC® and are printed on FSC®-certified paper. FSC® is the only
forest-certification scheme supported by the leading environmental organisations including
Greenpeace. Our paper procurement policy can be found at
www.memoirspublishing.com/environment

Typeset in 11.5/16pt Plantin
by Wiltshire Associates Publisher Services Ltd. Printed and bound in Great Britain by
Printondemand-Worldwide, Peterborough PE2 6XD

I Delyth
Dymuniadau gorau.
John 'Jake' Buchan x

John ('Jake') Buchan was born in Aberdeen, Scotland and moved in 1981 to Mid Wales, where he worked as a family and hospital doctor for over thirty years. This is his second novel featuring DI John Steadman, the blind detective.

ACKNOWLEDGMENTS

Although writing is a fairly solitary occupation, I have been reliant on many others for information, help and encouragement. My grateful thanks go specially to retired Detective Sergeant Terry Parkhouse, Paul Nally (vet), Nick Randall-Smith, Susan Rimmer (now sadly passed on), Jo Wolfenden and, by no means least, Nick Passmore and his red pen.

Robbie, my retired guide dog, is no longer with us. However, he did lie at, or more usually on, my feet during most of the writing. Both Robbie and his former owner have been a great inspiration.

Thanks also to Chris Newton of Memoir Books for his professional editing and wise advice.

Without the love and support of my wife Trish and my children Emma, Jo and Nick, this book would never have been completed.

ACKNOWLEDGMENTS

To Robbie

Undoubtedly the best guide dog the world has ever known.

CHAPTER ONE

The phone rang, breaking the silence of the small hours. Detective Inspector John Steadman rolled over, brought a hand out from under the duvet and felt for the receiver. He didn't switch on the light; Steadman no longer had much use for light.

'Have I got a case for you!' boomed the voice of the irrepressible Dr Frank Rufus, the Home Office pathologist. 'You'll love this one – both hands screwed to the desk and a copper wire neatly threaded through his neck holding his head on to the back of the chair. It was several hours before his housekeeper even realised he was dead. Impressed so far?'

It was the "so far" that roused Steadman's curiosity.

'Go on,' he replied. He knew his friend was desperate to say more.

'It was blooming clever, mind you. From the door, you would have sworn the old boy was simply poring over a book. Somebody knew what he was doing.'

Steadman waited. 'And?'

'And, as you quite rightly deduce, there is an "and". Someone had gone to the bother of squirting whisky into both lungs. Filled the buggers almost to the top. But, and here's the rub, it was done after he was dead. So put your detective's thinking cap on, if it's not too dusty, and figure that one out!'

Steadman pressed the button on the side of his watch. A metallic voice informed him that it was one thirty a.m. precisely.

'Who's leading the investigation?' he asked.

'None other than your former protégé, Alan Munro.'

Steadman bit his lip. It was all very well being a close friend of the pathologist, but technically he was no longer working. He was stuck in limbo, somewhere between long-term sick leave and retirement, and could only be brought into an investigation by special request. He tried to suppress a burst of excitement at the possibility of being involved in another case. For the last week or so he had been feeling particularly low, with nothing but his own bleak thoughts for company in his grey world.

'Have I got clearance?' he asked.

'From the top, otherwise I wouldn't be phoning you.'

Steadman heaved a sigh of relief. 'You do know, Frank, that it's half past one in the morning?'

'It's what?' Time meant little to Dr Rufus when he was working. 'Well, it's nice chatting with you, John, but I really have better things to do at this God-awful hour. Munro and I will be with you at eleven. Make sure you get a plentiful supply of coffee and cakes sent up.'

Steadman didn't like to remind Rufus that it was he who had instigated the call. He was awake now, and he knew it would be at least a couple of hours before sleep returned. Since he had lost his sight in the shooting incident that had killed Holly, his wife, the radio had become his constant companion.

He switched it on. Scarlatti on the harpsichord; what could be a better accompaniment to the start of a case? Gently he felt his way along the short corridor towards the kitchen and carefully poured himself some orange juice. He would have preferred something hot, but the effort at this time of night was too great.

He had lived in a safe house for a time, but now occupied a flat above Lloyd's café, an establishment not far from Helmsmouth Police HQ, otherwise known as the Eyesore, for it was an abomination of 1960s architecture. The café was the local watering-hole for his police colleagues. Marco Lloyd, the owner, and his family had taken Steadman under their wing. The only challenge in providing coffee and cakes would be getting Marco to accept payment.

The bed was still warm. As he lay down a voice inside his head whispered:

'Anything interesting?'

It was Holly's voice, clear and unmistakable. She had known before their wedding that Steadman was already married – to his work. Being woken in the night was part of the job. She had also known the rush of adrenalin he got when his sleep was interrupted, his anticipation, almost childlike, if the call proved to be worthwhile and his disappointment if it was unnecessary. For years all she had ever asked was, 'Anything interesting?'

Steadman was fully aware that the voice was of his own making, but it did not stop him stretching out an arm to the empty, cold side of the bed.

At two forty-five he lifted the receiver. Navigating his fingers from the raised blip on the 5 button, very carefully he called Frank Rufus's number.

'This had better be bloody good,' growled the voice on the other end.

'I've been thinking,' Steadman started.

'Oh, it's you. What hellish hour is it?'

'Almost three, did I wake you?'

'Touché. Well, let's hear it.'

'The immediately obvious reason would be to try and fool the pathologist into thinking he had drowned. By the way what sort of whisky was it?'

'What sort of damn fool question is that? I'm not a blasted sommelier, or whatever the whisky equivalent is. Anyway, I know how he was killed and it was actually quite subtle. Now bugger off and let me catch up on my beauty sleep. God knows, I need it. I'll see you at eleven.'

Steadman smiled and shook his head. 'Goodnight, Frank.'

Dr Rufus might have slept soundly, but Steadman tossed and turned. He no more believed that whisky had been pumped into the victim's lungs to fool the Home Office pathologist than that his late wife was lying beside him. It was a bizarre thing to do and not likely to be a random act. His mind raced down one avenue then another, each time finding a dead end like a maze with no solution. What little sleep he had was disturbed by nonsensical nightmares. In these Holly was riding a steam-driven machine bristling with spikes that spurted whisky each time she pulled a large brass lever. In a voice that was not hers she kept asking, 'Is this interesting enough for you?' Then she would laugh; a braying, mocking laugh, throwing her head back to reveal a mouth full of shark-like teeth.

Steadman woke, still mumbling, 'You're not my wife, I know you're not my wife.'

He swung his legs around and sat on the edge of the bed. The images and sounds faded rapidly, like the first frost of autumn in the morning sun. Yet somewhere in the deep recesses of his mind, as in the shade, a little of the coldness lingered and his body gave an involuntary shudder.

His watch informed him that it was just after eight. Better a get a move on, Frank and Alan would be here in no time. Blindness had slowed down his life, frustratingly so. Everything from washing and dressing to preparing food seemed to take an age.

He felt his way towards the sitting room and pressed the intercom. Marco Lloyd had insisted that this was installed so that he could ask for refreshments, or help if needed. Marco himself answered.

'*Buongiorno*, Mr Steadman. Ready for your morning coffee?'

'Encourage my laziness, Marco. May I have a croissant as well? Dr Rufus and DS Munro are coming at eleven and I'm running late.'

Marco hesitated. He wanted to ask if that meant another case for his friend, but he knew that it would be indiscreet, and anyway he would soon get to hear about it. Policemen, like every other group of professionals, love to gossip. If there was something in the offing, he would surely find out by the end of the day.

'Will you want coffee at eleven as well?'

'Please – and some cake, you know what DS Munro is like.'

Detective Sergeant Alan Munro was a very large rugby-playing Scot with a degree in physics and a tendency to go red in the face at the slightest provocation. Maureen, his wife, tried to mother Steadman, and their two little daughters, Melanie and Annie, adored their adopted Uncle John.

An odd sort of murder, Steadman thought as he ate his breakfast. Assuming it was murder. But it had to be; why else would Dr Rufus be calling him in the middle of the night? What sort of person would you have to be, or what would you have to have done, to deserve – no, deserve was the wrong word – cause, would be better. Yes, cause someone to kill you, screw your hands to a desk, wire you up so that you looked like you were busy reading then fill your lungs with whisky? Bizarre, he thought. And a terrible waste of whisky.

He seldom wore a suit but today, as he was working for once, he made an exception. The hand-held colour scanner assured him in a monotone that it was his grey suit and helped him select a white shirt and red tie, although which red tie it was, he hadn't a clue. No matter, his sister Linda had made sure his Father Christmas tie was safely rolled up and tucked at the back of his sock drawer.

He sat down at his piano. In his youth, he had played well and with lessons, was slowly regaining his skills. His bony fingers ran up and down a few scales, and then it was Bach. It was always Bach when he wanted to think; methodical, logical and deeply satisfying. The crime was a statement, he mused, possibly revenge, but revenge for what? He needed to know a lot more about the victim. And why whisky of all things? Why not milk or water? Bach could not help him. He closed the lid of the piano just as the doorbell rang.

'My, but you're looking smart! Going anywhere special?' enquired Dr Rufus, whose way of coping with the awfulness of his work was to make light of everything else.

'I'm glad you appreciate the effort, Frank,' Steadman replied. 'Is Alan with you?'

'I'm here, sir.'

Were it not for Steadman's blindness, the massive bulk of DS Munro filling the door frame would have been impossible to miss.

'Come in both of you. Marco will be bringing us coffee at any minute.'

'I see you've been persuaded to cheer the place up with a few pictures,' Munro ventured. It had been a long-fought battle between Steadman and his sister Linda. 'It's so stark with bare walls. It looks like nobody loves you,' she had pleaded. Steadman had tried to argue that they would do nothing for him but present a hazard for, as likely as not, he would knock them off and cut himself on the broken glass. Of course Linda had won, but Munro noted that the pictures were all screwed firmly to the walls like paintings in an art gallery.

'I'm surprised she allowed you to put up nudes,' Dr Rufus remarked.

'I know they're all Pre-Raphaelite prints and the closest to a nude is Millais' Ophelia, although I have no idea which it is.'

There was a rattle of crockery at the door.

'Here comes Marco with the coffee,' said Steadman.

'Mamma has been baking,' said Marco, entering. 'She says if you force money on me, Mr Steadman, she will never cook for you again.' That settled any debate.

'Bloody hell, this is good!' Munro exclaimed as he helped himself to a second slice. 'I'm surprised you're not as fat as a barrel.'

Munro looked at his old boss, who was still very thin, too thin almost. His clothes seemed one size too big for him. The dark glasses didn't help.

'Down to business,' said Steadman. 'Alan, why don't

you start, then Frank can dazzle us with his forensic findings.'

It was a slightly mean trick, as John Steadman knew Dr Rufus was desperate to tell him what he had discovered. It could wait, Steadman thought. The story had to be told in the correct order. DS Munro loosened the top button of his shirt before it gave way under the strain and pulled out his notebook.

CHAPTER TWO

Munro cleared his throat. 'The call came in yesterday afternoon from a Mrs Juliet Winterby, housekeeper to the late Mr Crenshaw Tipley.'

Steadman frowned. He knew that name; it was a hard name to forget. His fingers drummed on his thighs.

'Wasn't he the theatre critic?'

'Theatre critic, art critic, music critic, literary critic – you name it, he would review it and usually give a damning opinion. His pieces were renowned and feared – acerbic, I think, is the word.' Munro fumbled in his pocket and retrieved a scrunched-up piece of paper. 'I found this one in last week's *Echo*,' he said, smoothing out the cutting with his enormous hands. 'Listen to this.' He read aloud.

'One wonders why Helmsmouth Operatic Society really bother – or do they? This year's offering, and by that, I mean sacrificial, was Gilbert and Sullivan's 'HMS Pinafore' – a work I have always felt should be sub-titled "a piece for the less discerning." But even amongst that hardened bunch who braved the performance, the interval was more anticipated and

welcomed than the all too familiar ditties. In the entire theatre, I only counted twenty people who appeared to be enjoying themselves. Sadly, all of these were on the stage.'

'Ouch! Not one for the scrapbook,' said Dr Rufus.

'Oh, they are pretty much all like that,' Munro continued. Delving into his pocket he produced another newspaper cutting.

'I was intrigued by Mr Breneski's sculpture. Intrigued, because I initially thought it was something left behind by the builders.'

'A man with lots of potential enemies,' Steadman said wistfully. 'What else do you know about him, Alan?'

'He was in his late fifties, lived alone, estranged from all his family. I'm told he only sent one Christmas card and that was to his housekeeper. He lived in Upper Bridgetown – I expect you know it.'

'Yes, a pretty little village - fairly upmarket if I recall. Isn't there a nice inn there – The Three Grasshoppers?'

'That's the place. His house is very old, quite small and set in what I believe is called a cottage garden. According to Mrs Winterby, his housekeeper, the garden is the only thing that gave him pleasure, that and his writing.'

'Apart from unpleasant reviews, did he write anything else?' asked Steadman.

'He had a book published last year, a psychological Cold War thriller, apparently – sounds a bit highbrow for me.'

'I bet it was panned by the critics,' suggested Dr Rufus.

'On the contrary, it was well received and was runner up in some major competition,' Munro replied.

Steadman bit his thumb nail. 'Mrs Winterby says his only pleasures were his gardening and his writing – no significant others in his life?'

'Probably bent as a four-pound note. These arty types are all the same. Drug fuelled parties, naked people all cavorting about – I can just imagine it.'

'What a booming generalisation, Frank. And I worry about your imagination.' Steadman shook his head. 'Go on, Alan, what did Mrs Winterby tell you?'

'Despite the rumours, she says that to the best of her knowledge he had no interest in sex – male, female or otherwise.'

'I find that hard to believe,' Dr Rufus muttered.

'Well, she's known him ever since he moved to Upper Bridgetown and that was over twenty years ago.'

'Tell me about yesterday. How did she find him?' asked Steadman.

'It was all rather sad. She arrived in the morning as usual. He was an early riser and it was not uncommon for him to be in his study. He was not a man given to chitchat and days would go by when no more than two or three words were exchanged. Anyway, she made him a cup of tea and placed it on the edge of his desk, then tiptoed out of the room. At noon, she crept back in to remove the cup and saucer and offer him some lunch. He seldom ate more than a sandwich. She was surprised that he hadn't touched his tea. Only then did she notice that he had drooled all over his papers. She asked him if anything was the matter. As she got no reply she gently touched his hand. It was stone cold. Worse still, a flap of skin peeled off the back of his hand, exposing the head of a large screw. Mrs Winterby is of the vintage that doesn't distress easily. She sat down, counted to ten, then dialled 999.

'Forensics reckon the killer entered by the back door, which is invariably unlocked. Very little appears to have been disturbed and nothing taken. Whoever it was wore rubber gloves.'

'What was his study like? Can you describe it?' Steadman asked, trying hard to visualise the scene.

'Very neat, despite being crammed with books. There is only one door into the study and that faces the desk. The desk is at right angles to a small window overlooking the back garden. There is another door behind the desk that leads into a tiny lavatory. What else would you like to know?'

Steadman was about to say "everything", but thought better of it. He would have liked to have known the colour of the carpet, whether it was an old desk, were there curtains on the window – all the countless little things a sighted person takes for granted. He merely shrugged.

'Was his desk tidy?'

'Pretty much so. There was an old, large glass paperweight, an antique ink stand, an ivory paperknife,' Munro paused, 'and of course the book he was reading – *The Old Curiosity Shop* – a very nice leather-bound edition.'

'Come on then, Frank. Dazzle us with your expertise!'

Dr Rufus leaned forward in his chair. He had found it

very hard listening to his young colleague without interrupting him.

'From the doorway, it really was convincing. He was fully clothed and looked as though he was engrossed in a book. The copper wire may have come from an electric cable. It had been skewered through his neck and through the back of his leather chair. The ends were neatly twisted together, holding the head at just the right angle.'

Steadman rubbed his chin, trying to form a mental picture. It was difficult.

'What did he look like?'

'Thin, but not in the least athletic, clean shaven with light brown receding hair, greying at the temples and a bit on the long side. He was wearing a cardigan, a mauve shirt and a ghastly maroon cravat with horseshoes on it.'

Steadman's brow furrowed as he painted the canvas in his mind's eye.

'Frank, I know you are itching to say more. The immediate thing that is puzzling me is why there was no blood.'

'Well spotted! The reason is quite straightforward. Whoever killed Crenshaw Tipley waited for several hours, I would say, before screwing him to the desk and wiring him up, let alone filling his lungs with whisky.'

'You hinted last night, Frank, that how he was killed was quite ingenious. Let's have a summary of your pathology report.'

'I thought you would never ask. Despite his sedentary lifestyle and being a heavy smoker, he was reasonably healthy. He drank very little and ate mainly vegetables, which could account for his miserable outlook on life, but I'm no psychiatrist. He had sustained a blow to the back of his head that would have knocked him out but not killed him. You know about the hands. Each lung had been punctured three times and copious amounts of Scotch pumped in. Here, I've brought you a sample.' He pressed a small specimen bottle into Steadman's hand. Although Steadman was on the whole fairly abstemious, he had become something of a whisky connoisseur.

'Good grief, man!' Munro exclaimed. 'You're not expecting Inspector Steadman to taste it?'

'Quite right, Alan. I will resist the temptation. Let's see if my nose can tell me anything.' He unscrewed the lid and sniffed once. He thought and sniffed again. 'Well, I can tell you it is not a single malt, it's a blended whisky. But there is a hint of something else, possibly rum and... I'm not sure. I suspect this is one of the new-fangled whiskies produced to attract the younger generation.'

By the look on Steadman's face, he didn't think much of it.

'Doubtless forensics will be able to give a full analysis,' he went on. 'How did the whisky get into his lungs?'

'With a bicycle pump, that's how. The other smell may be bike oil – I think there is a small drop floating in the sample I gave you. Kim Ho from forensics identified it without much difficulty. When you were at school, were you ever given the task of blowing up the footballs?'

Steadman nodded. A particularly sadistic games master would boot about a dozen balls as far as he could over the playing fields. Whoever had irritated him that day was handed a bicycle pump that had a small spike attached with the instructions to retrieve all the balls and inflate each until it was as hard as a brick. Any that didn't meet his exacting standard were similarly redistributed about the field. The whole process always ended in tears and humiliation.

'But you said it wasn't the whisky that killed him.'

'No, and if I'm honest I missed it at first. As I extracted the wire from his neck I noticed a small mark just below the base of his skull, partly hidden by his hair. I thought it might have been a graze from whatever was used to thread the wire through his neck. When I examined it further it proved to be a small stab wound that had gone, as neat as you please, in between the vertebral bones at the top of his neck, and severed his spinal cord.'

Steadman looked a bit puzzled. 'Go through what you think is the scenario.'

DS Munro took up the story.

'As we read it, we think someone came into the house through the back door and hid in the small lavatory off the study. Crenshaw Tipley came in, sat down at his desk and became absorbed in his work. The radio was probably on, he may even have dozed off in the chair. The attacker approached him from behind, knocked him out, forced his head on to his chest, thrust a small sharp object into the top of his spine and, for good measure, gave it a wiggle.'

'Death would have been almost instantaneous,' added Dr Rufus.

Steadman was still having difficulties visualising the scene.

'What sort of weapon was used?'

'Something quite small and very sharp,' Dr Rufus replied. 'A sharpened screwdriver perhaps, but I favour something like an upholsterer's needle. You know the thing I mean – sharp, hard and with a flattened, slightly curved end. I think the same needle could have been used to thread the wire through his neck.'

'When do you think all this happened?'

'Probably about six pm,' Frank replied. 'Having killed Tipley, I think he simply waited for a time. At some point he removed Tipley's shirt and then, using the pump, filled his lungs with whisky, dressed him and propped him back in the chair. Once he was certain that he would not bleed, he peeled back flaps of skin from the backs of his hand, screwed them to the desk and replaced the flaps. Either before or after, he wired up the neck. Rigor mortis would be setting in by then to hold the body rigid.'

'This must have taken several hours. Didn't anyone see the light on?'

'No. The study is at the back of the house and is not overlooked. Besides, he often read until very late.'

'Wouldn't the killer have had to carry a lot of stuff with him?'

'Probably no more than a tool box or a small rucksack.'

'All very strange – quite bizarre in fact,' Steadman

mused. 'What sort of person do you think we're looking for?'

There was an awkward silence.

'What is it? Have I said something?'

'Go on, Alan, you tell him – you're the investigating officer.'

Munro was less than encouraged. 'As well as your skills, DCI Long wants to bring in a forensic psychologist,' he said quietly.

John Steadman groaned. He had only once worked with a forensic psychologist and it had been a complete disaster. The psychologist had been an opinionated man with greasy, lank hair, a beard and bad breath. His glasses were invariably covered in dandruff. To top it all he invariably wore open-toed sandals regardless of the weather and seemed to find everything vaguely amusing. He had insisted that the culprit was a middle-aged man who had probably been beaten by his parents with a kipper in a plastic bag or some other such nonsense. In fact, the culprit proved to be the ex-girlfriend, something Steadman had suspected from the start.

'I can only hope that it's not the same idiot I worked with last time.'

'I doubt it, sir,' Munro replied, 'although I don't know who it will be as yet.'

'So long as he doesn't have a bad breath and an annoying laugh or you might end up with another murder on your hands.'

Just then, Munro's mobile phone rang. He pressed the phone to his ear.

'What? Where? Do we know who... no? DS Fairfax is on the scene... yes, Dr Rufus is here. We are with DI Steadman... OK, we'll be right there.'

He put the mobile back in his pocket and stood up.

'He or she has struck again, it would seem. An old lady this time, but the appearances are very similar.'

'I will need to collect my bag from the police mortuary,' said Dr Rufus.

'Don't let me detain you,' Steadman mumbled, trying hard not to let his frustration turn into anger.

'Detain us!' exclaimed Munro. 'You're coming with us – DCI Long's orders.'

Munro bounded down the stairs two at a time to fetch the car.

'I'm not sure what the rush is,' Dr Rufus remarked. 'Dead bodies, in my experience, seldom run away.'

'Is it cold outside?' Steadman asked.

'Wet and windy – real autumnal weather. Have you got a coat?'

'There's one in the cupboard by the door. And there should be a hat of sorts there too.'

His sister Linda had bought him the hat and insisted that he wear it if it was cold. It was a rather unfashionable green felt fedora. He put it on.

'You look like something out of an American gangster movie,' Dr Rufus commented.

'Don't mock. It hides my bald patch.' Steadman's hair

had never fully re-grown over the patch of reconstructed skull.

The two men went down the stairs. Without thinking, Steadman counted off the steps. A thin, watery light played through the stained glass by the front door, casting pretty patterns on the wall. Dr Rufus was about to say something, but not wishing to cause his friend distress, he bit his tongue. He shouldn't have worried. Steadman wouldn't have been in the least upset, in fact, quite the opposite. He wanted other people to be his eyes and describe what he could not see. In that way he could still try to imagine his surroundings. It lessened his feeling of isolation.

'Ah, here's Munro with the car,' said Dr Rufus, rather too obviously. He guided Steadman into the seat and passed him the seat belt.

'Will you manage?'

'Yes thanks.'

Steadman fumbled with the buckle. As he brought his hand back he touched the knob on the gear lever.

'They're still letting you loose in the Audi,' he observed.

'They have to prise the keys away from me. It's a cracking motor and it can shift like b...' Munro stopped himself just in time. Whenever he got enthusiastic his Scottish accent became more pronounced and his language more choice.

'What colour is it? I've completely forgotten,' Steadman asked.

'Bottle green.'

Steadman vividly recalled an image of the car and nodded as they sped down the road.

'The call was from DCI Long,' Munro continued. 'The victim is an elderly widow who ran a small antiques shop. She was found this morning by her niece who helps with the business. It was only when the niece tried to rouse her that she noticed the copper wire through her neck.'

The shop was in the older part of Helmsmouth. Cobbled streets fronted a delightful marina that had become the haunt of the town's well-heeled. Munro had to do a small detour to the police mortuary. In the silence Steadman tried to think of anything that could link the two killings. Forensic psychologist or no forensic psychologist, he remained convinced that it was only by understanding the victims that the murderer would ultimately be found.

The lane outside the antiques shop was cordoned off with blue and white police incident tape. Uniformed officers stood at either end. A small crowd had gathered. Dr Rufus was first out of the car. He grabbed his bag and barged his way through.

'Do you mind?' cried an indignant onlooker.

'No, do you?' Dr Rufus retorted without giving her a second glance.

Steadman unfolded his cane. The cobbles were damp and slippery. He took Munro's arm. There was the flash and click of a camera.

'Damn, the press are here already,' Munro grumbled.

'Are you going to be involved in the investigation,

Inspector Steadman?'

'Hello Jack,' Steadman replied, recognising the reporter's voice. 'I don't know yet.'

'Is it true this is similar to the Tipley case?'

'You know, Jack, you're wasted as a reporter. DS Munro is leading on the Tipley case and DS Fairfax is on the scene here. If they have no objections, I'll give you a statement within the hour.'

The crowd of onlookers parted before the imposing bulk of Alan Munro as he gently steered Steadman towards the shop. A voice at the back whispered, 'Isn't that John Steadman, the blind detective?'

DS Fiona Fairfax was waiting for them at the door.

'Same scenario, I'm afraid. Neck wired up to look like she was dozing in the chair. Hands screwed to her cross-stitch frame. Cause of death not immediately obvious. Dr Rufus is in there now along with the forensics team and the photographers. It's more than a little crowded,' she explained.

'Any trace of whisky this time?' asked Munro.

Steadman could have told him there wasn't. The only smells were beeswax, leather and the vague mustiness that seems to emanate from all antique shops.

'There doesn't appear to be. The niece is with Dr Rufus. Then if I can find somewhere quiet I am hoping to have a word with her.'

'You stay here, sir,' Munro said to Steadman. 'I'll fetch the Audi and we can all sit in the car. It will at least be a little warmer than standing out here.'

A cold wind was blowing in from the sea. Steadman was making a determined effort not to shiver.

'What have you found out so far, Fiona?' he asked.

'The victim is a Miss Velda Meemes, a sprightly eighty-two-year-old spinster who has been running this shop for over thirty years, well before the marina was all tarted up. Everybody round here knows her and nobody has a bad word to say about her. It's all very bizarre.'

Bizarre: that was the word that had described the Tipley case. Things were only described as bizarre, thought Steadman, when they couldn't be explained.

Dr Rufus interrupted his ruminations. 'Smothered, I would say, with one of her own cushions. Kim Ho, our beloved forensics expert, has bagged it up and should be able to confirm later. The victim is sitting in a puddle. Not whisky – I would guess it's sparkling mineral water.'

'Definitely not urine?' DS Fairfax asked.

Dr Rufus gave her a quizzical look. 'No, take my word for it. Killed last night I reckon. I'll be able to tell you more after the post-mortem.'

Two vehicles were easing their way through the crowd and past the police cordon. The first was Alan Munro in the Audi. The second was a dark blue van discreetly marked 'Private Ambulance'.

'I'll get a lift back to the mortuary in the van. You don't need me any longer, do you, Fiona?'

DS Fairfax shook her head. 'Thanks, we'll speak later.'

Munro parked a little way beyond the shop, leaving the engine running.

'I'll go and fetch the niece,' said DS Fairfax. 'I don't want her to see them moving her aunt's body.'

Munro led Steadman to the waiting car.

'Alan, tell me what the niece looks like when you see her.'

'They're coming now. Small, about five foot two, early sixties I would guess. Probably would have been quite dark but now grey. Dressed – how shall I put it? – a wee bit extravagantly, bright colours and lots of beads.'

DS Fairfax made the introductions. 'This is Doreen Meemes. My colleague, DS Munro,' she continued pointing to Alan Munro, who was doing his best not to tower over the diminutive figure. 'And this is…'

'Aren't you Inspector Steadman, the blind detective?' Doreen exclaimed.

Steadman removed his hat and held out his hand in what Munro thought was a touching, rather old-fashioned gesture. The hand that clasped Steadman's was shaking, but the grip was firm. There must be rings on every finger, Steadman thought.

'Please accept my condolences,' he said.

Inside the car it was warm and a bit stuffy, not helped by Doreen Meemes' cloying perfume. DS Fairfax and Doreen sat in the back, Munro and Steadman in the front.

'I'm very sorry about your aunt,' said DS Fairfax. 'I know this will be distressing, but I do need to ask you some questions.'

'I understand,' Doreen replied in a husky voice. 'When I last saw her alive, and how I found her – that sort of thing, I suppose. I've seen it on the telly but never thought for a moment…' She choked slightly and dabbed her eyes with a lace hanky. 'I left her last night at about half past five. We don't have fixed hours. We open around ten in the morning and close at six, or whenever we feel like it. It's a quiet time of year. The tourists have gone and nobody is thinking of Christmas yet. Most days we have no more than a dozen customers.'

'Was she alone when you left her?'

'Yes – I left her doing her cross-stitch almost exactly as I found her this morning.' Doreen let out an enormous sigh. 'Who would want to do that to a harmless old lady?'

DS Fairfax gently touched her hand. 'Take your time. Did your aunt live above the shop?'

'Oh yes, she was fearfully independent – did all her own cooking and cleaning. I don't know if you've been up to her flat, but it's spotless. And she was sharp – knew far more about antiques than I did. I have a good eye, but Aunt Velda knew the value. I live in a small flat in town. On Saturdays I go to car boot sales, auctions, house clearances and the like. Aunt Velda would take a taxi over in the evening. We would have a meal together and she would price up what I had bought. She was very kindly, you know. If I had bought tat, she just laughed and told me to take it to the charity shops. My flat is full of tat… I'm sorry, I'm just wittering on.'

'Not at all, we need to build up a picture of your aunt. This is very helpful,' DS Fairfax reassured her. 'Did you notice if anything had been stolen?'

'No, that's the odd thing. We seldom have anything of much value in the shop. That's not where the market is. I would say that most of our stock items are worth less than a hundred pounds. The odd bit of furniture is a bit more. All the jewellery is costume or Victoriana. The most valuable item in the shop just now is the ornate French clock in the window. It's worth about a thousand pounds, but it's still there.'

'Did she have any enemies that you know of?'

'Enemies? No! I don't believe she ever had an angry word with anyone in her life. Or at least... I just can't believe it...Do you think she suffered much?'

'The Home Office pathologist believes she was smothered – I'm sorry. We will have more information after the post-mortem examination.'

'Oh, poor Aunt Velda – a post-mortem. She would have hated that. Why would somebody wire her up like that? It seems so bizarre.'

That word again, thought Steadman. Bizarre, yes; but also unnecessary. Would knowing why someone had decided to go to that lengths lead to discovering the culprit? It would surely help, he thought, but he was not entirely convinced. So far both killings appeared motiveless. Somewhere there lay a strand that linked them together.

'When did you get here this morning?' asked DS Fairfax, once Doreen had regained her composure.

'Shortly after ten. I thought something was odd as the shop was silent. Aunt Velda always had Radio 3 playing in the background. Also, the lights weren't on. I went through to the back shop and… well, there she was, just sitting with her cross-stitch in her hands. But she didn't seem right, if you know what I mean. I touched her cheek and she was quite cold. I knew she was dead. Her hair had fallen over her face. I pushed it back and it was only then that I noticed the wire sticking out of her neck. I may have screamed – I can't remember. I knew I had to call the police and not touch anything. I think that's how you found me. It was a dreadful shock.'

'Do any of your customers go into the back-shop?'

'Yes, quite often. Sometimes we're asked to put things by so that rooms can be measured, colours checked, wives consulted and so forth. But I can't think of anyone who would have done…' Her voice trailed off.

'I notice there's a small CCTV camera in the shop. Was it on last night?'

'On? Oh dear me, no. It's just an empty box really. I bought it at a jumble sale. All it's good for is providing a home for Boris, a large spider that Auntie wouldn't let me get rid of. There, I'm wittering on again.'

The strain was beginning to tell. DS Fairfax patted her arm gently.

'Inspector Steadman, Sergeant Munro… do you have any questions?' she asked.

Alan Munro half raised a hand as though he was still at school.

'Who will inherit the shop?' he asked.

'I suppose I will,' Doreen replied. 'I've never really

thought about it. Aunt Velda was so fit it hadn't ever occurred to me that she would die.' She paused and dabbed her eyes again, then looking up quite sharply, she added, 'You are not suggesting that I...'

Munro turned vermilion.

'No, no – not for a moment,' he stammered. 'It is simply routine to find out who might benefit in the case of any suspicious death.'

'I have one question,' Steadman interjected. 'Did your aunt have any hobbies besides her sewing?'

'Yes, she was a quite gifted artist – watercolours mainly. She must have painted the marina a hundred times or more. We sold a lot of her pictures in the shop. She even had postcards made of the best ones.'

Steadman nodded; that was where he had seen the name Velda Meemes before, on the bottom of a postcard.

'She would paint every Sunday. In fact, only last month she came second in the annual competition run by the *Helmsmouth Echo*.' She sighed again, heaving her bosom and causing the beads to jangle. 'When do you think I will be able to organise the funeral?'

After DS Fairfax had explained the formalities, the four of them got out of the car and walked back to the shop. Most of the crowd had dispersed but Jack, the reporter, was still there.

'What about that statement, you promised me?' he asked.

'Is that OK?' Steadman asked his two colleagues. Both were more than happy to let him speak with the press.

'He won't interview me, will he?' Doreen asked in a pleading voice.

'Leave it with DI Steadman,' replied DS Fairfax. 'I'll arrange for a car to take you home.'

Steadman was as honest as he dared to be with the reporter. 'It's very early in the investigation, Jack. Promise me you'll not pester the niece – and do put in the usual request for anyone with information to contact the Eyesore.'

'What do you want to do now, sir?' Munro asked as he wiped the condensation off the windscreen.

'Would you take me back to my flat? I've arranged to see a man about a dog this afternoon.'

CHAPTER THREE

That was true; Steadman was seeing a man about a dog: a guide dog. He had been on the waiting list for several months. The flat and the garden at the back of Lloyd's café had been inspected. He had been interviewed extensively and had even had his height measured. Apparently the dog had to be matched for size as well as temperament.

For the last eight weeks he had been walking increasing distances with the long cane, counting the paces between each landmark, memorising the various smells, noises and doorways. It was all too easy to get distracted and become disorientated. His detective skills helped. The ticking of a large clock and he knew he was outside Eldon's jewellery shop, the sulphide smell of setting lotion and he was passing Upper Cuts, the ladies' hairdressers. Yet it was exhausting and terrifying, and more than once he tripped over pushchairs or walked into lamp-posts. Two black eyes in one week, and Linda was all for banning him going out unaccompanied, but he persevered. Dr Rufus would walk with him when he started a new route. Although grateful, he also felt he was being a nuisance. He craved his independence. It was the speed or lack of it that really irked him. What would have taken him fifteen minutes when sighted could easily now take the best part of an hour. Most people were helpful, but not all. Despite the dark glasses and the white cane, one cyclist had shouted at him after a near miss, 'You should watch where you're going!' If only, he thought.

Of all the places he wanted to be able to walk to alone, the Eyesore was top of the list. True, he had been back several times, but he had always been driven there and helped, usually by DS Munro.

He pressed the side of his watch. The tinny voice informed him it was two fifteen; they should be here by now. He was as excited as a school boy on the last day of term.

The doorbell rang. Cautiously he made his way to answer it, for it would not do to rush and fall on this day of all days. Mr Barnes introduced himself. They had met before during one of the interviews. Steadman was disappointed that he didn't seem to have a dog with him.

'I've got two in the car,' he explained. 'I'll bring them in one at a time and we'll see how you get on with each other.'

The first was Fifi, a Labrador bitch. Steadman was not sure how he felt about a dog called Fifi. Somehow he couldn't hear himself standing in the park shouting, 'Fifi, come here, there's a good girl!' He put his reservations to one side.

He need not have worried. From the outset it was clear they were incompatible. When Steadman held out a hand, the dog backed away and growled quietly, but in an unfriendly manner.

'I didn't think she would suit,' Mr Barnes reassured him, 'but you can never tell. Let's see how you get on with Robbie.'

Robbie was a large, black flat-coated retriever. Again Steadman held out a hand. This time the dog walked straight over to him, sat at his feet and put his large head on Steadman's lap. Steadman stroked the top of his head and his big floppy ears. If only he could have seen, Robbie was looking at him with his soft brown eyes in a questioning way as if to say, 'OK boss, where shall we go?' His long hairy tail was thumping happily on the floor.

'It looks like you've found a friend,' remarked Mr Barnes. 'Now the fun begins! Let's go for a little walk.'

They went downstairs and out through the front door. Mr Barnes put on Robbie's harness. Steadman folded up his cane and slipped it into his pocket. For a moment he stood there feeling quite naked.

'Now take the harness in your left hand and give Robbie the command to go forward.'

It was both exhilarating and frightening, like a roller coaster ride in the dark. The dog led and Steadman followed, feeling the slight tug of the harness as Robbie steered him along.

'Know where we are?'

'Yes,' replied Steadman, 'I've been counting the paces.

We're just about to come up to a crossroads.'

'Spot on! If there's a pedestrian crossing Robbie will take you there and, with his nose, point to the buttons. If not, like here, he will take you down the road so that there's not traffic coming in all directions.'

Steadman knew all of this, but it was scary putting so much trust in an animal. Robbie sat on the kerb.

'Now give the command to go. He'll disobey if there is a vehicle coming.'

A huge smile broke over Steadman's face as they reached the other side. The harness twitched and he high-stepped onto the pavement without stubbing his toes. They made it back to the flat safely and practised the stairs.

'That's enough for today. Take off his harness and let him out in the garden.'

The moment the harness was off Robbie scampered out, sniffing the grass and the bushes like any other dog.

'He'll come back once he's done, but you've got the whistle if he doesn't.' Steadman nodded.

'I've got his basket and food in the car. Won't be a tick.'

Robbie came back and nuzzled against Steadman's legs.

'I think this is going to work out just fine,' he said, giving the dog a stroke.

Mr Barnes went over the instructions again and with a cheery, 'I'll see you tomorrow at nine, any problems just call,' he was off.

Steadman sat down with Robbie at his feet and was

beginning to doze when there was a loud knock at the door. It had to be DS Munro; he was the only person who knocked that loudly despite there being a perfectly serviceable bell. Robbie was on his feet before Steadman got out of his seat, and dutifully stuck by his side as he made his way down the corridor.

'I didn't know you were getting a dog. You kept that very quiet!' Munro exclaimed. 'Is it a guide dog?'

'He most certainly is,' Steadman replied with pride.

'What's his name? May I stroke him?'

'He's called Robbie and if he's not in his working harness you can give him a pat.'

'Wait till Maureen and the girls see him. He's a beauty!'

The two men went into the sitting room and again Robbie took his place at Steadman's feet.

'What news?' asked Steadman.

'Dr Rufus has completed the post-mortem - death by suffocation. The fibres from the cushion matched those in Velda Meemes' airways. No other injuries apart from the copper wire through her neck and her hands screwed to her sewing frame.'

'What about the puddle she was sitting in?'

'Dr Rufus was right – it is sparkling mineral water. Kim Ho is running some tests. She says it will be easy enough to trace once she's analysed the mineral content.'

'Why mineral water, do you suppose? Not quite as glamorous as whisky but interesting nonetheless.'

Steadman started humming, a sure sign that he was deep in thought. The dog looked up. Seeing that his services were not needed, he lay back down and closed his eyes.

'Would you mind if I made myself a cup of tea?' Munro asked.

'No, not at all, I'll join you.'

'Oh, by the way you were right about the whisky – Debantry's Deluxe Blend, matured in rum casks.'

Steadman pulled a face. 'I'm glad I didn't have to taste it.'

'The manufacturers suggest serving it with cola and ice cubes.'

'Dear God, is nothing sacred? Does it get us any further?'

'Not so far,' Munro replied, 'unless our killer is a barman. Maybe the whisky and the mineral water are made by the same people and a disgruntled employee... nah! That doesn't make sense.'

'No, but these were not random killings,' Steadman said. 'They were well planned and executed, if I can use the word. I don't believe the victims were chosen by chance and unless we can find a link...'

'Do you think he or she will strike again?'

Steadman spread out his bony hands and shrugged. 'Who knows? However, I fear the worst.'

The dog was on his feet before either Steadman or Munro heard the faint tapping at the door.

'Are you expecting anyone?' Munro asked as he heaved his bulk out of the chair. Steadman shook his head.

The lady at the door let out a sharp gasp and took half

a step back at the sight of DS Munro filling most of the door frame.

'Oh! I'm sorry. I thought this was where Inspector Steadman lived.'

'It is, Miss Meemes. Come in, we were only having a little chat. The kettle's just boiled – would you like a cup of tea? Follow me – Inspector Steadman is in the sitting room. Do you take milk and sugar? There may be some cake, however I suspect I ate it all this morning.'

Doreen Meemes had become quite flustered.

'Tea? Oh, yes please – milk and one sugar, but only if it's not too much trouble.'

Steadman stood up to meet his guest and again held out a gentlemanly hand. He didn't ask why she had come. It was obvious she had something to tell him.

'What a charming apartment, and the view is...' She broke off, embarrassed. 'I'm sorry. I suppose I shouldn't mention the view.'

'On the contrary,' Steadman replied, 'tell me what you see. Not the boats and the rooftops – tell me about the sky.'

Doreen Meemes was taken aback, but a glance at John Steadman told her he was serious. 'Well, it's blue. That's not much help, is it? I'm sure I can do better.' She paused, and looked intently out of the window as if only noticing the beauty of the sky for the first time. 'This morning's rain clouds have blown away. The only clouds now are those stripy ones. My father used to call it a mackerel sky.' Steadman nodded appreciatively. 'I said the sky was blue but that's not strictly true. At the horizon it fades to a very pale yellow where the sun is going down. The only other things of note are two vapour trails from aeroplanes. I would guess they're on their way to America. Do you know, when I was a little girl, I used to think they had cut the blue of the sky and were letting the clouds tumble through.' She blushed as she realised what she had just said. 'How did I do?'

'Thank you – you painted the picture very well. Here comes Alan with the tea.'

'I was right – the cake's all gone, but I found some biscuits.'

Before Doreen could stop herself she said, 'You're not what I expected, neither of you.' She sipped her tea. 'I know I should have gone to the police station but... and I'm sorry - I eavesdropped on your conversation with that reporter. That's how I found out where you lived and also what prompted me to buy the first edition of the evening paper. I never really bother much with the news. It's so depressing. I only get a paper at the weekends to find out where there is an auction or a car boot sale. Oh, what a lovely dog! I've only just noticed him. Is he a guide dog?'

'Yes,' Steadman replied. 'I've only had him a few hours.' He was warming to this rather talkative spinster.

'And here I am bothering you with something that's probably of no relevance at all.'

Alan Munro finished his biscuit and unobtrusively slipped his notepad out of his pocket.

'I didn't know anything about the Crenshaw Tipley

murder. Tipley is not a common name round here, and I only know of one.'

Both detectives knew there was no point in hurrying her.

'As it was, when I read the newspaper I realised it was the same person. I was shocked to find out that he had been killed just like poor Auntie.' She paused to dab at her eyes again.

Very gently, Steadman asked, 'How do you know Crenshaw Tipley?'

'Oh, I don't know him, as such. Of course, I know of him. But... and I'm sure you would have found out soon enough.' She gave Munro a meaningful look. 'His housekeeper, Juliet Winterby, is my cousin.'

'Your cousin?' exclaimed Munro.

'Yes - let me explain. Auntie Velda had two older brothers, both now passed on. Daddy was the older of the two, and the younger was Juliet's father. That's how we are cousins – there are only the two of us.'

'And what does Juliet Winterby say about the murder?' Steadman asked.

'I have no idea. We haven't spoken in years. It's all very sad and unnecessary. I honestly don't want to make life any harder than it is for Juliet, and as to her being a killer – well, that's out of the question. I just didn't want you to find out and then ask me why I never told you, that's all.'

'I take it you and your cousin don't get on,' said Munro.

'Not now. She always was a bit doleful really. You know, "my glass is half empty", that sort of thing. Her parents weren't wealthy and what little she was left, her wretched husband spent at the bookies. He died leaving her fairly destitute. The only thing she had of any value was what she described as a Sèvres china dinner service left to her by her mother. Seeing as Auntie and I were in the antiques business, she asked us to sell it on her behalf. Well, even I could see it wasn't Sèvres but only "in the style of", as we say in the trade. We did what we could and got her a reasonable price. Of course, she accused us of robbing her blind, or at the best, being completely incompetent. She was very bitter. Yes - bitter, but not twisted. I'm sure you have spoken with her, Mr Munro – how did you find her?'

Munro gave her a dreamy, far-away look.

'Silly me! Of course, you can't answer that,' said Doreen.

'Would you say that she's still quite poor?' Steadman asked.

'Unless she's found a pot of gold somewhere, I suppose she must be. I don't think for a moment that... It must just be a coincidence.'

The room was beginning to get dark. Munro stood up, stretched and switched the lights on.

'I hope you didn't mind me coming. As it is, there is nothing I can do until...'

'Not at all,' Steadman replied. 'Did your cousin ever visit the shop?'

'Not since the sale of the dinner service, and that must be at least five years ago, possibly longer.'

'Was the layout of the shop the same?'

'Yes - why? What are you getting at?'

'Whoever killed your aunt had carefully planned what he or she was going to do. I would be willing to bet anything they had been to your shop before.'

Steadman drummed his fingers on the side of the chair. Robbie sat up and was rewarded with a gentle stroke of his head.

'What do you think, Robbie?' It was the first, but not the last time Steadman would consult his dog.

Munro leafed through his notes. 'You said that you sometimes kept goods in the back shop for customers – are there any items there now?'

Doreen thought for a moment.

'Probably four or five – no more.'

'Would you be able to tell me who the customers are?'

'Yes, that would be easy. They're all labelled.'

'Did your aunt have many visitors?'

'No, only a couple of old dears like herself. I could give you their names and addresses, but...' Again she gave DS Munro a meaningful look. 'It might be better if that nice lady detective... Now, what was her name? I'm sure it began with an "F".'

'DS Fairfax.'

'Fairfax – of course. It might be better if DS Fairfax were to call. I don't mean anything nasty, Mr Munro, but a man of your size knocking on their doors – well, they would have a fit!'

'What about tradesmen?'

Doreen Meemes closed her eyes and tried to remember.

'We had an electrician in last month – a bit of a rough diamond. I rather liked him but Auntie didn't. She always said I had poor taste when it came to men, and that was why nobody would have me.' She sighed.

'Can you remember his name?'

'Let me think – it was an odd name.'

'A foreign name?'

'No, it had something to do with fish... Eeles, that's it! Harry Eeles. I've never seen anybody with so many tattoos.'

Munro started to say something; Steadman raised a silencing hand.

'Do you know him?' Doreen went on. 'Oh dear, I seem to be landing all sorts of people in trouble.' She dabbed her eyes again. Robbie, as if sensing her sadness, nuzzled his head against her thigh. She brightened up and gave him a pat. 'I say, Inspector, have you found someone to walk your dog for you? Because if you haven't, I know just the person.'

Steadman confessed that he hadn't.

'Well, I'm sure Tim Warrender would be keen to. He's a lovely boy – more than a boy really, he's twelve or maybe even thirteen now– such an awkward age, don't you think? He looks as though he's been stretched and his feet are too big for him. His father has been restoring furniture and picture frames for us for years – an exceptionally gifted man. Tim has been coming to help since he was able to walk. I know they have recently lost their dog. Tim would like another, but his mother has gone back to work.'

'He sounds ideal and, of course, I would pay for his services.'

'That's settled then! I'll give them a call. I suspect he may pop round this evening, especially if I tell them it's urgent.'

As if she suddenly remembered the enormity of her tragedy, she let out a soft moan. Munro patted her dainty ringed fingers with his shovel-like hands.

'I should go now,' she said as she eased herself on to her feet. 'You will tell me, Sergeant Munro, when I can start organising things, won't you? Please don't let on to my cousin what I've told you, unless you really must. You will find out who has done these awful things. I just can't believe that somebody...'

Both men stood up and DS Munro escorted her to the door.

CHAPTER FOUR

Munro closed the door gently and walked back to Steadman's sitting room. Already there was a dark mark at waist height along the length of the corridor where Steadman had trailed a guiding hand.

'She's quite a character,' Munro remarked.

Steadman didn't answer at first. Munro was not sure if he had heard him.

'I'm not convinced,' he said at last.

'What do you mean? You don't think Doreen Meemes...'

'No, no – I'm sure she's as honest as the day's long despite the fact that she too is linked with both murders.'

'I'm not following you.'

'Well,' Steadman explained, 'Juliet Winterby could argue the facts that link her would similarly apply to Doreen. She is, after all, the niece of the second victim, and likely heir as well as being cousin to the first victim's housekeeper. It would be interesting to know who Crenshaw Tipley has left his money to. No, what I'm not convinced about is Juliet Winterby's involvement. Of course, I've never met her, but if she wanted to bump off her employer why not slip something into his coffee? And why go on to kill her aunt? We have to follow it up, though.'

'And what about Harry Eeles?' added Munro. 'I thought he was still in the clink. Wasn't it you who arrested him last time?'

'Yes, it must have been three years ago. GBH, if memory serves me. Ah well, at least he didn't waste his time in prison. Harry Eeles, a qualified electrician, who would have thought it?'

'I'll need to contact DS Fairfax and put her in the picture. We seem to be gathering a lot of loose ends.'

'Better than none,' Steadman replied, although he somehow doubted that any of them would lead anywhere.

The doorbell rang again.

'Your day for visitors, sir,' Munro commented.

A thin lady stood at the door. Behind her and half in her shadow, was a young lad with his hood up, staring closely at his feet.

'I'm Ann Warrender and this is my son Tim,' she said. 'Doreen Meemes asked us to call.'

Munro ushered them in.

'Pull your hood down, Tim,' murmured his mother.

Reluctantly the young man pulled his hood back to reveal a shock of red hair. He looked up at DS Munro.

'How tall are you?' he asked.

'About six foot five,' replied Munro.

'I wouldn't mind being that tall.'

'It has its advantages until you sit down, then I find there is never enough room for my legs.'

Tim grinned.

'Did Doreen say you were only thirteen? You're quite a big lad yourself.'

At this, he turned bright red.

'Let me introduce you to Detective Inspector Steadman and his dog, Robbie.'

Ann shook hands, rather nervously, and tried hard not to stare at DI Steadman. Tim was already on his knees playing with the dog, who, judging by the ferocity of his wagging tail, appeared to be enjoying it enormously.

'I'll take him out now, if you like?' Tim volunteered. 'We could go and see my sister, couldn't we Robbie?'

Robbie's tail thumped the table in appreciation. Ann explained that they only lived around the corner. It was agreed that he would call in the morning before school and again in the evening when he came home. Steadman insisted on paying.

'He seems a nice boy,' said Munro after they had left, 'although I'm never sure what to call a boy of that size. I see what Doreen means about an awkward age.'

'It certainly has solved a problem for me. Hopefully he will say a bit more when his mother's not with him. When are you intending to speak with Crenshaw Tipley's housekeeper?'

Munro looked at his watch.

'Too late to do it this evening. I'm planning to go back to the Eyesore, check that nothing new has cropped up, liaise with DS Fairfax, then grab a bite to eat – most important! I'll pay her a visit tomorrow morning. Care to join me?'

'I'm going out with Robbie and the trainer first thing. Any time after ten would suit me,' Steadman replied. It felt good to be back working.

★ ★ ★

The door opened only as far as the chain allowed.

'Oh, it's you again,' said Juliet Winterby drearily. 'I thought you would be back after I read the papers. What's my cousin been saying about me?'

Munro pretended not to hear her question. 'May we come in and have a little chat?'

'I know your "little chats". And who's the "we"?' she asked, her voice heavy with suspicion.

'This is Inspector Steadman and his guide dog, Robbie.'

She cast a wary eye at the thin man in dark glasses who was standing behind DS Munro.

'I have heard about you – you're the blind detective, aren't you? I don't know what we're coming to – the blind leading the blind,' she muttered. 'I suppose you'd better come in. I hope that animal is house trained.'

There was an unpleasant smell in the house, a mixture of fried food and bleach. Steadman wrinkled his nose. Robbie led him through into a cold sitting room and Munro helped him into an armchair. It was lumpy and uncomfortable. The fabric on the arms was threadbare. Steadman could feel small holes where the stuffing was poking through. He snapped his fingers and Robbie spreadeagled himself at his feet.

'He seems well enough behaved,' Juliet Winterby admitted grudgingly. 'So – what do you want with me now?'

It was more of a challenge than a question. Her voice was as dry as chalk and her manner simmered with barely-concealed hostility. Like Doreen she was diminutive, but unlike her cousin, she was stick-thin. She wore none of the frippery that Doreen was so fond of. The only note of gaiety was a vivid floral nylon housecoat that appeared remarkably out of place. It was Steadman who spoke first.

'Mrs Winterby, as you've no doubt read, we are now investigating not one but two bizarre murders.' That word again, thought Steadman to himself. 'The murders are sufficiently similar that it seems reasonable to conclude they were perpetrated by the same person. Up until yesterday evening we knew of nothing that linked the two...'

Juliet Winterby interrupted him. 'Ah – that's it, I'm guilty of murder now, am I? It's not enough to be cheated out of my inheritance. I'm being made out to be a double murderer! Let me tell you a thing or two about Velda and Doreen Meemes before we go any further.'

Patiently the two men sat through the saga of the Sèvres dinner service, how the valuation had been faked and the pieces sold without her knowledge.

'Next time you see Doreen Meemes, you ask her how she and her aunt paid off their mortgages.' She almost spat the words out at the two men.

'How long ago did all this happen?' Munro ventured to ask.

'Six years and three months,' she replied without hesitating.

'And when did you last see your Aunt Velda?'

'Six years and three months.'

'And your Cousin Doreen?'

'Six years and three months. No – that's not strictly true. I have seen her out and about on a handful of occasions but not to speak to, if you know what I mean.'

'Do you think Velda Meemes will leave you anything in her will?' Munro stared at her with his innocent blue eyes. Juliet Winterby was not taken in.

'Look around you – you can see that I'm poor. Well, *you* can't,' she added as an afterthought, glancing at John Steadman. 'Even if she did leave me anything, I wouldn't touch a penny of her money with a barge pole. You didn't know her. Listen – she had no conscience did that woman, none at all. And Cousin Doreen is just the same. Don't be fooled by her jangling beads and simpering voice. She's as hard as flint! Doreen will get the lot, mark my words. If you thought for a moment, Sergeant Munro, that I would gain by her death, you're sadly mistaken.'

Munro wanted to ask who Crenshaw Tipley had left his money to, but thought better of it.

'I know you've spoken to my colleague, Mrs Winterby,'

Steadman said in a conciliatory tone. 'Would you be kind enough to tell me how you came to be housekeeper for Mr Tipley?'

Juliet Winterby eased herself back into her chair, folded her arms and stared hard at John Steadman. His face was expressionless and the dark glasses unsettling.

'I was out of work and needed the money,' she answered bluntly. 'He put a postcard in the newsagent's window shortly after he arrived in Upper Bridgetown. I applied and got the job.'

'How long ago was that?'

'Just over twenty years.'

'I take it your husband was still alive then?'

'That's another thing you don't want to believe, if Doreen's been telling tales. My Ron had a heart of gold. His only problem was that he could never keep his wallet closed. Help anybody, he would.'

'We were led to believe that he spent all his money in the betting shop,' Munro interjected. Juliet Winterby gave him a venomous look and he turned bright red.

'I thought that's what Doreen would have told you. He had the occasional flutter, that's all. What's wrong with that?'

Steadman hastily changed the subject.

'Out of interest, what did you do before you became Mr Tipley's housekeeper?'

'I worked in the Purdie's factory.'

Purdie's – a name from the past, thought Steadman.

'I remember them,' he said. '"Mattresses by Royal

Appointment" – that was their slogan, wasn't it? Way before your time, Alan, I'm afraid. If I recall correctly, there was a little crown above the "P".'

'It was all nonsense,' replied Mrs Winterby. 'There never was a royal appointment, at least not to our Queen. The story goes that some exiled African king had an extra big mattress made for him and all his wives. That's about as near to royalty as Purdie's ever got. Mind, it wasn't a bad place to work.' She smiled wanly. A far-away look came into her eyes and Munro could see a glimmer of a family resemblance. 'It was old fashioned. Mr Purdie senior had us all in teams and we would compete against each other to see who could make the most mattresses each month. But they had to be right! He checked them himself and heaven help you if a spring wasn't stitched in properly.'

Steadman shook his head as Munro began to say something.

'Doreen worked there as well. We were in different teams. I guess we were rivals even then,' she said with a sigh. 'Of course, I was the better seamstress. Then old Mr Purdie died. Neither of his sons was interested. He was hardly cold when they sold the factory. We were assured our jobs would all be safe.' Bitterness returned to her voice. 'Barely six weeks later, and the place was closed. They razed it to the ground and built some swanky houses in its place. I was very grateful to get the job with Mr Tipley even though the pay was paltry.'

'What do you know about Mr Tipley?' Munro asked.

'What is there to tell? He was a solitary man, kept himself to himself, wrote all day or visited exhibitions and the like. Some evenings he would go to the theatre or listen to a concert. Occasionally he would have a meal out.'

'Did you ever read any of his reviews?'

She made a noise in her throat, like water going down a drain. Her eyes gleamed malevolently. 'Oh yes! He cut those smug, arty types right down to size.'

'He must have made some enemies,' Steadman commented.

'Mr Tipley didn't care. His waste paper basket was full of hate mail. He used to have a saying about it – now what was it? "Full of sound and fury, signifying nothing" – good, isn't it?'

'Macbeth, act five, scene five – Shakespeare,' Steadman responded without thinking.

'Oh? I thought it was one of his – just goes to show.'

'Did he ever speak about his family or where he lived before?'

'No. He was a man of very few words. He made it quite clear from the start that questions and idle gossip were not welcome, and that suited me.'

'Didn't you think it odd that he never received any birthday cards or Christmas cards?'

Juliet Winterby shrugged her bony shoulders.

'None of my business.' She hesitated, cast a wary glance at the two officers and, with a resigned shrug, said, 'I'll tell you one thing that was odd and it's stuck in my mind. Shortly after I started working for him, he received half a dozen letters addressed to a Richard Armstrong. I offered to take them back to the Post Office, but he said they were for the previous owner of the house and that he would deal with them. Now, I've lived in Upper Bridgetown all my life and to the best of my knowledge no Richard Armstrong has ever lived there. And he never took them back to the Post Office – I checked, I know the postmistress.'

She sat back in her chair and looked defiantly at the two officers. Steadman tapped his fingers gently on the side of the chair. He could hear Munro scribbling furiously in his little notebook.

'He never had any friends?'

'No.'

'So other than you and Mr Tipley no one ever set foot in his house,' added Munro.

'I never said that. You must have noticed, Sergeant Munro, that the house was full of books. In fact, it was more like a library than a house, if you ask me. Although he wasn't generous with his money or his conversation he would happily lend out his books.'

'What kind of people borrowed his books?'

'I don't know how you would describe them. College types, I'd say – intellectuals, scholars – people with long hair that used big words.'

'What sort of books did he have?'

'They were mostly about arty things – paintings, sculptures and the like. There was a section all about the theatre and another with nothing but poetry. Oh yes – sections on military history and politics, as well. I know that because I had to dust them. I never read any of them – they were all above me.'

'Would you know which books were taken?'

'Not the titles,' she retorted scornfully. 'He did put a slip of card in when a book was taken out. He always wanted them back.'

'Do you know if he kept a list of who had borrowed his books?'

'I expect so, though I've never seen one.'

Munro continued to scribble feverishly. 'Would you recognise any of the borrowers?'

'No. I took no notice and besides, most of them came in the evening when I wasn't there.'

It was clear that she felt she had said enough.

'So how did you know that people had called?' asked Munro.

'Dirty cups, muddy footprints and fingerprints on the bookcases, all of which I had to clean up. I'm not stupid, you know!'

Poor Munro blushed again.

'Apart from those visitors, do you know if anyone else has called recently?'

'Oh yes,' she said huffily. 'We had a ne'er-do-well of an electrician in. I expect you know him, Inspector Steadman, Harry Eeles and his hatchet-faced son. They were there last week putting in a new fuse box. I thought Harry was in the nick?'

'Do you know Harry Eeles?'

'We were at school together. Even then he would pinch

your dinner money when you weren't looking. I did try to warn Mr Tipley, but he waved me away without saying a word.'

'Do you know who will inherit Mr Tipley's estate?'

'Not me, if that's what you're implying.'

'Do you know who his solicitor is?'

'Why should I care?'

Munro's stomach rumbled loudly as a clock somewhere in the house chimed eleven.

'I would offer you a cup of tea but I've run out of milk,' said Juliet Winterby.

Steadman wondered why she should choose to lie quite so blatantly. Was she naturally difficult? Was she depressed, or was she trying to hide something?

'That's not a problem,' he said. 'I don't think we have any further questions. You've been most helpful.'

She sniffed, as if to imply that that had not been her intention. 'Odd though that someone would want to string him up like a puppet, then do the same to Velda Meemes. Quite bizarre, in fact.'

Exactly, thought Steadman.

The two men returned to the car. Robbie snuggled into the footwell and curled up into a surprisingly small ball for a large dog.

'Well, well – both seamstresses in a mattress factory. Didn't Dr Rufus suggest that Tipley could have been stabbed in the neck by an upholsterer's needle? Who's your money on, sir?' said Munro as he pulled out into the traffic.

'Neither of them,' Steadman replied in such an off-hand manner that his colleague's face flushed yet again.

'Doreen Meemes gains nothing by Tipley's death other than putting one over on her cousin, and she doesn't strike me as vindictive. Juliet Winterby, on the other hand does, but why wait six years and three months to kill her aunt? And why not kill her cousin as well? And if she wanted to bump off Tipley, for whatever reason, why go to all that bother when she could have just as easily laced his food with poison? No – I'm more interested in why Richard Armstrong changed his name to Crenshaw Tipley.'

'Do you reckon they're the same person, sir?'

'Without a doubt. Why else would he have kept the letters and not taken up his housekeeper's offer of handing them back at the Post Office? I wonder if Velda or Doreen Meemes ever knew a Richard Armstrong.'

'I can ask Doreen, and it may be worth asking the elderly spinster friends.'

'Check if Velda had an old address book. I have one somewhere that still has the names of my school friends. Old address books can be a source of valuable information, but they're often overlooked.'

They stopped at a set of traffic lights. A white estate car pulled up beside them in the nearside lane. Suddenly Munro became aware that the driver was staring intently at John Steadman.

'You've got an admirer in the car next to you, sir.'

Automatically Steadman turned as though to look at the car. There was a small flash.

'He's taken a photo of you, sir!' Munro exclaimed. 'We'll see about this.'

He undid his seat belt and opened the door as the lights turned green. The estate car sped off and turned so sharply to the left that Munro failed to note the number plate. The driver behind him started beeping his horn. He cursed as he got back into the car.

'What was that all about, do you think?'

'I have no idea,' replied Steadman cautiously. 'Did you manage to get a good look at the man?'

'No. He was wearing a baseball cap that hid his face. I'm fairly certain he was clean shaven – sorry.'

Munro felt angry with himself for being outsmarted, as well as feeling uneasy that somebody had, quite deliberately, photographed John Steadman.

'Let's get something to eat at Lloyd's café. And I think Robbie could do with a stretch of his legs.'

'Did that young lad Tim Warrender come around this morning, sir?'

'Yes. He didn't say much. I think he's naturally shy,' Steadman replied. And terrified by a scrawny old man with dark glasses and part of his skull missing, Steadman mused to himself. Munro was thinking exactly the same.

They lunched at Lloyd's. The double murder was the sole topic of conversation among the other officers. Pleas for more information from Munro fell on deaf ears.

'Can't a man have a quiet bite to eat?' Munro responded peevishly. 'I'm fading away to a shadow!'

As if to add to his annoyance, his mobile phone rang.

'It's DS Fairfax for you, sir.'

Steadman held out his hand and Munro carefully passed him the phone.

'Yes... I'm sure Alan can take me to the Eyesore after lunch... I'll be there within the hour.'

'What's up, sir?'

'Fiona has got Harry Eeles and his son in for questioning. Apparently they're refusing to speak to anyone but me.'

CHAPTER FIVE

Munro swallowed the remains of his sandwich and wiped the steamed-up window with the sleeve of his jacket.

'It's stopped raining and the wind's dropped a bit, sir. What had you in mind?'

'Would you be willing to walk with me and Robbie to the Eyesore?' Steadman asked hopefully. 'I realise it will mean you coming back to fetch the car.'

'No problem, sir. The exercise will do me good. Maureen's been telling me I've put on a bit of weight.'

Robbie appeared more than willing, and was on his feet before Steadman had time to put on his hat and coat. It was still quite chilly and the weak autumnal sun cast long shadows as the two officers strode towards the Eyesore.

'You know, sir, daft as it sounds, I still like shuffling through fallen leaves.'

'So do I,' confessed Steadman. It reminded him of long walks he and Holly used to take. It seemed a lifetime ago.

'There's a big pile of dry leaves just under a horse

chestnut tree on our left. Fancy a little detour? If anyone sees us, I'll say we're looking for evidence!'

'Go on, why not?'

Munro led Steadman over and the two men kicked and scrunched their way through the mound of leaves, grinning like naughty schoolboys.

'Are we at the junction with Compass Road?' asked Steadman.

'We are indeed,' replied an impressed Munro.

'I've been counting the steps as we went along,' Steadman explained. 'The next part is unfamiliar, at least it is since I lost my sight. I need to concentrate and try to memorise the number of paces. Can you tell when we pass any significant landmarks and when we're coming up to a crossroads?'

The two men walked on, the silence only broken by the occasional comment from Munro and command from Steadman to Robbie. At last they reached Helmsmouth Police HQ. Even in the afternoon sunlight it looked ugly and unwelcoming.

Sergeant Grimble, balding and rather fat, was on desk duty, the only job he ever did. No one knew exactly how old he was, but rumour had it that he was well past retirement age. His appearance was deceptive, for he was brilliant at his job. His finger was constantly on the pulse of all the comings and goings at the Eyesore. Every officer, uniformed or plain clothes, realised very quickly if you needed to know something, you asked Sergeant Grimble.

Although his desk was always a complete shambles, he would look aghast at any person foolish enough to point this out to him. With a wag of his finger, he would invariably reply: 'This is the famous Grimble filing system. I ought to patent it – now, be a good police officer and bugger off.'

Grimble looked up from the desk as Steadman and Munro entered. 'So this is the famous Robbie.'

Steadman knew there was no point in asking him how he had found out about his guide dog so soon. Grimble waddled out from behind his desk to take a better look.

'My, but he's a cracker. I love dogs. If you like, I'll take him for a little walk round the car park while you're in with Harry Eeles.' Grimble had no need to ask why Steadman had come to the Eyesore.

Steadman declined the offer. 'I'll keep him with me for a bit. It's important that he gets used to being at my side, even when I'm not going anywhere. Maybe before I go home you would take him out for me?'

That was agreed. DS Fairfax came through the swing doors.

'I thought I heard you, sir. I'm sorry to bother you, but Harry Eeles was adamant.' She looked at the dog with some uncertainty. 'Goodness! He's a very big dog, and very black. Is he...?'

'I am assured he is of a very gentle disposition, Fiona,' Steadman replied as she led him through to the interview room. Munro made his excuses.

'I'll go and collect the car. I'd better write up today's fun and games while it is still fresh in my mind.'

* * *

'Well, well, well – Inspector Steadman, this is just like old times! I don't think you've met my son, Maurice.' Eeles gave the long-haired, spotty young man sitting beside him a poke with his elbow. 'Oi, Maurice, where's your manners? Stand up and shake the Inspector's hand.'

Steadman was all too familiar with Harry Eeles' affected affability and incessant chatter. Behind the smiling, almost cherubic, face was a hardened criminal with a string of convictions, mainly for robbery, sometimes with violence. He was the only person Steadman knew of who had "HATE" tattooed across the knuckles of both hands.

Reluctantly Maurice stood up and held out a sweaty hand.

'Say something, you great pillock. He can't see you – he's blind!'

Maurice mumbled something that could have been 'Pleased to meet you'. With DS Fairfax's help, Steadman found a chair. Robbie lay down at his side.

'Why wouldn't you speak with DS Fairfax?' he asked.

'I don't trust women, begging your pardon, miss. And besides, you know me, Mr Steadman. I ain't no killer.'

'Your last offence was grievous bodily harm, if I remember rightly.'

'It was an accident!'

'You hit a man in the face with a golf club.'

'A man's got to have a hobby, hasn't he? It was unfortunate that he disturbed me while I was practising.'

Maurice sniggered, earning himself another dig in the ribs.

'Harry, you hit him five times.'

'I was putting in a lot of practice that day, Look, I'll admit, things did get a bit out of hand, but I've done my time. I've turned over a new leaf. I'm a qualified electrician now.'

'So I've heard. Why an electrician, of all things?' Steadman asked.

'On account of my name. We were given a choice and I thought it would be amusing to be an "electric eel" – do you get it?'

'The subtlety is not lost on me. Better than your other moniker, I suppose. What was it that people used to call you? "Slippery", wasn't it?'

'Mr Steadman, I'm surprised at you bringing that up. Maybe I would have been better talking to the lady.' He tried looking hurt, but failed abysmally.

'You're incorrigible, Harry.'

'I don't know what that means. I'll take it as a compliment.'

'Comedy half-hour over, Harry. Listen closely. We're investigating two vicious, calculated murders. You've read the papers. Both victims were wired up after they were dead. One sat reading a book - the other, a harmless old lady, doing her cross-stitch...'

'There are some sick people out there…'

'Don't interrupt. The killer used thick copper wire, possibly a stripped electrical cable. Guess what? We found out that Harry Eeles, the electrician, and son had recently been doing work in both houses. Coincidence perhaps? You know me, Harry, I don't like coincidences. Now it's your turn – I'm listening.'

'You may not believe me, but I'm a reformed character – a respectable member of society.'

Steadman rapped his knuckles on the desk. Eeles relented.

'You're right - I've worked at both places. At Tipley's house, Maurice and me put in a new fuse box. I don't think Tipley ever spoke – a right arrogant bastard, if you want to know. Maurice didn't come with me to Velda Meemes, though I wish he had. Her blooming niece was all over me like a rash! It was a small job – replacing a cooker socket.'

'Where was Maurice?'

'He had other plans that day.'

'He was appearing in the juvenile court on a charge of handling stolen goods,' said DS Fairfax.

Steadman smiled. 'Like father, like son, eh, Harry?' Turning to DS Fairfax, he continued:

'Has Maurice got any other offences to his name?'

'All small stuff – shop-lifting, possession of cannabis, driving without insurance.'

'So, Maurice, what do you have to say for yourself?'

'Nothing. Dunno what you're on about.'

'Where were both of you on Monday and Tuesday night?'

Father and son looked at one another. Maurice said he couldn't remember. Steadman suspected that he wouldn't remember his name unless constantly reminded. Not surprisingly, Harry had been "down the boozer" with his mates. Grudgingly, he supplied a list of names.

'Inspector Steadman, you don't believe that Maurice and me had anything to do with this, do you? We ain't a couple of angels, but you know what it's like to bring up a kid on your own.' Harry's wife had run off to London with a drug dealer when Maurice was barely out of short trousers. 'I've got an honest business now, and it's going well. For once in my life I'm doing something I'm proud of. I've been working really hard. Why would I kill a couple of old codgers and then wire them up? Come to think of it, why would anyone? I mean to say, that's bizarre, that is.'

That bloody word again, thought Steadman. He sunk back in his chair; his fingers were tapping out a melody on his thighs.

'You're right, Harry. You've got an evil streak in you, and a temper, but I don't think you would kill anyone, at least not deliberately.' An image of a man's face pounded with a golf club flashed up in Steadman's mind. 'Maurice, you're very quiet, and I don't like that. I wonder if you would be more talkative with DS Munro.'

'That Scottish bruiser!' exclaimed Harry. 'I know him. He belted one of my mates in the nuts.'

'Surely not,' Steadman replied. 'He plays rugby and was probably just practising. As you said yourself, Harry, a man's got to have a hobby. But you're probably correct. I don't think your son has much to say for himself.'

He paused. The drumming of his fingers got faster and louder. Eventually he slapped his hands on his thighs as though slamming shut the lid of a piano.

'I'll tell you what's bothering me – it's the copper wire. Fiona, may I suggest that we impound Harry's van and get forensics to go over it with a fine-tooth comb. I take it you came here in your van, Harry?'

'What about my work? I need my van. It's people like you that make criminals out of the rest of us.'

'Give it a break, Harry. It will only be for twenty-four hours. DS Fairfax will arrange transport to take you home and if your van is clean, we'll even deliver it back to you tomorrow. Have an afternoon off – you've been working so hard, you deserve a break.'

'I don't suppose we've got much choice. Don't you go putting things in the van that weren't there before. I know what you coppers are like, bloody crooks, the lot of you.'

DS Fairfax led the two men away. Harry Eeles was still protesting, but nobody took any notice. She came back to the interview room carrying a tray with tea and mugs on it.

'Thanks for coming, sir. Do you believe them?'

'On balance, probably. If the two victims had had their heads smashed in with a four iron and all their valuables stolen, then I might have a different opinion. That would be more Harry's style. No – there must be something linking Crenshaw Tipley and Velda Meemes, but I don't think it's "electric" Eeles. Who are the exhibits officers, Fiona?'

'DC Lofthouse at both sites. I don't know what to make of him. He's either utterly brilliant, or utterly useless. I can't decide which.'

DC Will Lofthouse was one of life's dreamers. His thinking was never entirely logical. He went by intuition, sometimes with remarkable results; on other occasions, he was miles off the mark.

'I've got him looking for any old address books and Alan Munro has got him checking for library lists,' said DS Fairfax.

The door opened. 'Is someone taking my name in vain? Oh good, I thought I could smell tea!' Munro exclaimed. 'Grimble is desperate to take your dog out for a walk. Would you mind, sir?'

Steadman took off Robbie's harness and handed Munro his lead. The dog scampered off quite happily down the corridor, which was lined with the photographs of long-retired police officers. He could hear Grimble making a fuss of the dog through the open doors.

'I wouldn't have put Sergeant Grimble down as a dog lover. Babies, perhaps but not dogs,' said Steadman.

'Oh, he's much the same with babies or little children. Apparently when he was on the beat, kids would follow him like the Pied Piper. His pockets were always stuffed with sweets,' DS Fairfax replied.

Steadman started beating a tattoo with his fingers again. His brow furrowed.

'We're missing something, Fiona. Not only do I not know what it is, I don't know where to start looking. There's someone out there who is evil. I worry that he or she may strike again.'

'You're looking a little tired sir,' said DS Fairfax gently. 'I'd be happy to take you home now, if you like?'

'I am worn out,' he admitted. 'I have never regained my stamina since I was shot. A lift back to Lloyd's would be appreciated.'

DS Munro came back with Robbie. 'He's found another friend,' he said. 'Grimble had even bought a packet of doggie treats.'

'Fiona is going to take me home, Alan, if that's all right. I haven't the energy to walk back.'

'That's fine sir. I'm going to spend the rest of my day looking for missing Richard Armstrongs.'

Steadman nodded. 'Young Tim Warrender will be coming around after school to give Robbie some decent exercise. I'm hoping Tim will start to relax and talk a bit more. Doreen Meemes was right, he is at an awkward age.'

CHAPTER SIX

Steadman had barely time to take off his shoes and undo his tie when the doorbell rang. One long ring followed by a short ring, then two long rings – the Morse code for "TW", Tim Warrender's secret way of letting Inspector Steadman know he was at the door. The boy stood there waiting anxiously. He had come straight from school and looked even more ungainly in his uniform. His trousers were too short and his shoes were scuffed. He had doodled on the back of his hands and there was a smudge of ink on his freckled nose.

'Come in, Tim. There's blackcurrant squash in the fridge and Kit Kats in the biscuit tin. I expect you're hungry.'

Tim slipped off his trainers and ambled through to the kitchen. 'How's Robbie today?' he asked, more to the dog than to Inspector Steadman.

'He's good, although I expect he could do with a walk.'

To Steadman's surprise, Tim offered to make him a cup of tea. It was a bit weak and milky, but no worse than if

Steadman had made it himself. The two sat down with their drinks. Robbie lay on his back and Tim tickled his stomach with his stockinged feet.

'How was school?'

Tim shrugged. 'OK, I suppose.'

Steadman tried to remember how his own son, Ben, had been at this age. He pushed his dark glasses up on to his forehead and rubbed his eyes. Tim stared, shocked at the spectacle of Steadman's eyes revolving round in their sockets, each following its own course, oblivious of the other's path. Before he could stop himself, Tim blurted out, 'Your eyes – I didn't think you had any! They're weird!' Realising what he had just said, he blushed so deeply that his freckles disappeared. 'I'm sorry, I didn't...'

'No, no – it's fine. I should have warned you. It's the back of my brain that was damaged by the bullet – the bit that develops the pictures, if you like. Although I still have my eyes, they're pretty useless. I can just make out bright lights in the darkness. I gather they swivel about of their own accord in a most alarming manner. And you're right – they must look weird.'

Tim was becoming fascinated as he watched the random movements of Steadman's eyes. As if to put an end to the topic, Steadman slipped his dark glasses on again.

'Tell me about school. What are your favourite subjects?'

Without hesitation, Tim answered, 'Art and drama. Maths and physics are OK, I suppose, but they're hard.

Mr Skinner's my drama teacher. He's really cool. He wears an earring and reckons I should become an actor. He's my head of year. He doesn't get on with the art department. But I like art best. Mr Haribin, he's my art teacher, is entering one of my pieces in a national competition. He says I could come second, if I'm lucky.'

Steadman thought that was a rather odd thing to say, but let it pass.

'Is it a painting or a drawing?'

'No, it's a sculpture. I do wood carvings. My Dad taught me. He's wonderful with his hands. Mum and my sister both draw really well too. I have my own carving tools and everything!'

'I'm impressed. What sort of things do you like to carve?'

'Animals and people mainly. I'm going to try and do one of Robbie. Mr Haribin wants me to use clay like he does, but I prefer working with wood.'

'If you like carvings, you might be interested in my netsuke collection.'

Steadman went on to explain about the intricate carvings: how they had started off as simple pouch toggles worn by Japanese men in the seventeenth century and evolved into objects of great craftsmanship. He didn't say that it was Holly who had started his collection, adding to it on each of their wedding anniversaries.

'Can you see the little glass-topped table in the corner?' he said. 'It's not locked. They are all in there. Take them out and tell me what you think.'

Tim walked over to the table and lifted the glass lid. 'Wow – these are amazing! Are they very old?'

'Some are. The little rat is two hundred years old. That was my first one and he's still my favourite.'

'What are they made from?'

'Ivory or boxwood, for the most part. The little frog on the lily pad is carved from a mammoth tusk. Which do you like best?'

After a thoughtful pause, Tim replied, 'The little man with the revolving face – one happy, one sad. How do they do that?

'Years and years of practice, I would guess. Even without my sight, I can still appreciate them. They are so lovely just to touch. Would you bring me some of your carvings round?'

'If you like. They are not as good as these.'

'They are different. I don't think good or bad comes into it. It's all a question of what you like.'

'That's what Mr Haribin says. He's always bringing me books and showing me pictures of sculptures. I like *some* of the modern stuff, like Antony Gormley. I can't see why people get excited about Henry Moore. I reckon anybody could carve a hole. Mr Haribin says I'm too young to appreciate it. Anyway, I've upset him.'

'How was that?'

'I told him I wanted to be a detective when I leave school. He wants me to be an artist, like him. I saw him driving out of school at first break and he never came back all day. Maybe he was visiting a gallery or something...'

Tim's voice faltered. Did children still have "crushes" on their teachers as part of growing up, Steadman wondered, or had Mr Haribin said something more?

'Did you tell him about walking Robbie for me?' he asked the boy.

'Yes, and about Sergeant Munro. Do you think I'll meet him again? I like him. He's big, isn't he?'

'He certainly is. And he could help with your physics homework, and probably your maths. He's got a degree in physics.'

'Cool! Come on Robbie – let's go down to the park before it gets too dark.'

Steadman heard the door slam and the boy and dog racing down the stairs. It wasn't cold enough to put the heating on, but there was a chill in the air. Steadman rummaged through his jumper drawer. He was trying to find his favourite, an old blue woollen jumper that was thin at the elbows. For a moment he wondered if Linda, his sister, had thrown it out. She hadn't; it was tucked right at the back of the drawer. Steadman took off his glasses and pulled the jumper over his head. Immediately he could feel the stresses of the day dissipate as he snuggled into its faded comfort.

He sat back in his chair and relaxed. It had certainly been an eventful day, he thought as his eyelids drooped and his head nodded gently in time with his breathing.

★ ★ ★

A bright spotlight shone on a pair of faded maroon velvet curtains. Particles of dust shimmered in the beam. With a flourish the curtains parted and in his mind's eye Steadman saw before him Punch and Judy. Even as a child, he had never liked Punch and Judy shows with their surreal mixture of violence and comedy. What unsettled him even more was the fact that these puppets remained motionless and silent. They simply stared at him with unblinking eyes from the safety of their little theatre.

He was about to turn away when both puppets let out a soft moan. The moaning grew louder as each puppet simultaneously bent double. Now, they were no longer glove puppets but had strings attached, and as he watched the strings became copper wires that wound tightly round their necks. The moaning became a muffled gargle that eventually ceased as the puppets were pulled upright. The wires melted into their throats leaving only twisted, macabre tails poking out from the back of their necks. The puppets stared again at John Steadman. Mr Punch's hands clasped a book, while Judy's were fixed to a cross-stitch frame.

'That's the way to do it!' shrieked a voice that was undoubtedly Juliet Winterby's.

'Nah – smash them with a golf club! That's the way we'd do it, isn't it, son?' Harry Eeles responded.

Maurice sniggered and shouted, 'Fore!'

Punch and Judy vanished in a flurry of falling autumn leaves. From behind a tree a small white-haired lady appeared wearing an enormous number of beads and bracelets. She pointed a camera at Steadman. There was a flash and a click. He could clearly hear Doreen Meemes saying, 'Well, I don't know anyone called Richard Armstrong. But if you do find him, let me know if he's single!'

She turned as if to leave. A boy with bright red hair was sitting in her way whittling a piece of wood.

'Why, Tim, you gave me such a fright! What are you doing?'

'I'm making a new leg for Robbie. Mr Haribin wants me to make it in clay, but I think wood is better,' Tim replied.

'How will you fix it on?'

'With copper wire, of course!'

'His legs all look perfectly good to me. How do you know he needs a new leg, Tim?'

'Us boys, at an awkward age, know all sorts of things. I even know the Morse code for T and W, my initials. It goes...'

A bell rang; one long ring followed by a short ring then two more long rings. It rang again. Steadman woke, confused and disorientated. Tim rang a third time. Bending down, he shouted through the letter box, 'Are you there, Inspector Steadman?'

The fragments of Steadman's dream slipped away like the last grains of sands trickling through an hourglass. 'I'm fine,' he shouted back as he made his way to the front door. 'Sorry, Tim, I must have dozed off. I was sound asleep when you rang.'

There was an old towel behind the door and Tim dried Robbie's paws. He looked up at Inspector Steadman, who was silently shaking his head.

'Are you sure you're all right?' he asked.

'Yes, yes – I've just had a very odd dream, that's all.' He could still hear Juliet Winterby shrieking, 'That's the way to do it!' And Harry Eeles replying, 'Nah, smash them with a golf club. That's the way we'd do it, isn't it son...' He gave his head a final shake.

'How was your walk? Did Robbie behave himself?'

'Robbie was great. He seems to understand everything I say to him! The park was a bit spooky. I thought I was being followed.'

Steadman stopped patting the dog and frowned. 'Come in. Sit down. Tell me exactly what happened.'

The change in Steadman's tone alarmed Tim. 'I don't think it was anything. It was getting dark and I probably just imagined it,' he replied in a tremulous voice.

Steadman felt very uncomfortable. He even contemplated contacting DS Fairfax. She was far more experienced at interviewing children.

'Listen, Tim, it probably was nothing, but I want you to try and recall precisely what you saw and heard – not what you imagined, only what actually happened. Try and think like a real detective.'

Tim screwed up his eyes and thought hard.

'Well, we were playing with the ball on the grass at the far side of the boating pond. The lamps around the pond started to go on, so I thought we'd better be getting back.

There were only a few people in the park – one or two with dogs, others just taking a short cut home, I would guess. Anyway, we started to walk down one of the long avenues. There was definitely something rustling in the leaves behind me. I thought it might be a blackbird or even a fox. I turned round. The noise stopped. I'll swear there was a man standing in the bushes.'

'Can you describe him?'

'Not really – it was getting dark and I could only see his outline. I think he might have been wearing a hat.'

'Go on.'

'I called Robbie over and put him on the lead. I know he's a softie but he is big and black. If you didn't know him, you might think he would bite. Well, the shadow began to move towards me, so I started running. I'm not making it up, Inspector Steadman, and I don't think it was my echo – I'm sure someone was running behind me. I ran as fast as I could. At the main gate, there's a burger van. Some people were standing in the queue. I ducked behind the van to get my breath back. I was hoping to catch a glimpse of the man, but nobody ran past me. That's why I thought I might have imagined it all.'

Steadman was about to say something about "never making assumptions", one of his maxims; however, he could sense that the lad was terrified.

'You did a good job. I reckon you'll make an excellent detective.' He paused and drummed his fingers on the side of the chair. Trying to keep the concern out of his voice, he continued, 'I don't know if someone was following you or not. Regardless, I want you to keep your eyes and ears open and let me know if anything like this happens again. Do you have a mobile phone?'

'Yes. It's a pay-as-you-go, but I've run out of credit.'

Steadman fished his wallet out of his pocket and handed Tim a note.

'Here's twenty pounds. As long as you're helping me I want you to keep your phone topped up, and with you at all times.'

Tim took the money. His hand was shaking.

'Can I ask you a question? How did you know it was a twenty-pound note?'

'Simple – it's slightly bigger than the ten pound notes. Before I put them in my wallet I fold down one of the corners.'

'That's clever. Did you think of that yourself?'

'Not me, I'm afraid. Tell me something, Tim. Is Robbie completely black? He could be striped like a zebra for all I know.'

It was only then that Tim realised the enormity of being blind. 'I suppose you wouldn't know, would you?' he said pensively.

'No. He might even have spots like a leopard. I know he doesn't have a hump like a camel, I would have felt that.'

'Robbie is completely black except for his eyes, which are the colour of chocolate,' Tim replied with a chuckle.

There was a loud knock on the door and DS Munro called, 'It's only me. Can I come in? The door's open. Did somebody mention chocolate?'

Tim was delighted to meet him again. 'Can I give Sergeant Munro one of your Kit Kats?' he asked.

Steadman nodded.

'I must go to the toilet first,' said Tim.

'Quick,' said Steadman to Munro, as soon as he was sure the boy was out of earshot, 'I'm not sure if someone didn't follow Tim when he was out with the dog in the park. Will you walk him home? It's not far. I've said you might help him with his physics homework. You can use that as an excuse.'

Tim returned from the toilet via the kitchen and handed DS Munro a biscuit.

'I just wanted to check you were not too tired, sir, but I can see that young Tim here has been looking after you,' said Munro. 'Tim, Inspector Steadman tells me you might be wanting some help with your physics homework. Why don't I walk home with you and you can tell me all about it?'

Tim grinned. 'That would be really cool!'

CHAPTER SEVEN

Steadman closed the door, safe in the knowledge that no harm would come to Tim with Munro by his side. He could hear the gentle rumble of Munro's voice fading as he descended the stairs and could imagine Tim, with his mouth slightly open, hanging onto every word. Munro had never lost his Scottish accent. Even this Steadman found reassuring. His was a trustworthy voice, quite unlike the nasal twangs of Harry Eeles or the viperish asides of Juliet Winterby. 'Foolish to make assumptions,' he muttered to himself.

'Come on, Robbie,' he said aloud. 'I'm going to treat you to a little Schubert, if I can remember the notes. Impromptu number 3 in G flat major – here goes.'

The piece was delightful, and as he played his mind drifted over the events of the past few days: the phone calls, the crimes, the interviews and, of course, the acquisition of a guide dog. Odd, he thought, how this time last week Velda Meemes was just the name on the bottom of a postcard, Crenshaw Tipley only a name in a newspaper and now... Harry Eeles was only too familiar, and although Steadman knew of the existence of a son, he had never met him. He smiled at the thought of young Tim Warrender trying to keep pace with Munro's great strides. Munro would have made a good teacher, he reckoned. Would he have liked a son? He had two little girls. Steadman and Holly had only one son, Ben. They would have liked a daughter: it was not to be. Munro would surely be at Tim's house by now. Why was he so certain that they would be safe? True, Munro was a formidable physical presence, but it was more than that. It was something to do with who was behind the two murders.

His fingers wandered effortlessly over the keyboard, his thoughts turning cartwheels with the music. He kept coming back to Tim's follower in the park. Was it the same person, or yet another coincidence? The murders were cold and calculated; they were, however, the work of a coward.

That was it! For what sort of person other than a coward would plan to take the lives of two defenceless people?

He finished the piece, but something was still niggling him. He started from the beginning again. Perhaps it was the sweetness of the music that counterbalanced the bitterness of the acts. In his imagination he conjured up the scenes as best he could. Tipley sitting bolt upright, supposedly reading a book, with his hands screwed firmly to the desk. And poor Velda Meemes similarly strung up with her cross-stitch. Similar, yes – but not the same. Wasn't the second killing less well executed than the first? Severing the spinal cord was, as Dr Rufus put it, "subtle"; smothering an old lady was by comparison, crude. And Tipley's hands – hadn't the screw heads been concealed with flaps of skin? He was willing to bet that they weren't in the case of Velda Meemes.

He stopped playing. Robbie lifted his head and raised a questioning eye as he closed the piano lid. Something was missing; some detail was being overlooked. As a boy, he had found an old musical box in a junk shop. Some of the pins on the drum were bent and some of the teeth on the comb were missing. He treasured it nevertheless and it still played a tune after a fashion. He often wondered what it would have sounded like had all the parts been in place. These two crimes, like the musical box, were part of the same mechanism. Somehow they didn't play a tune, as yet. It was more than the odd pin or broken tooth that was missing.

★ ★ ★

Steadman was about to embark on his second coffee of the day. He felt he deserved it. Patiently he had listened to Tim, who couldn't stop talking about DS Munro.

'He knows everything, I mean, absolutely everything! He can even do really hard sums in his head. I wish he was my teacher.'

And so it went on until, reluctantly, Tim dragged himself off to school.

Mr Barnes couldn't have been more fulsome in his praise, stating that he had never seen a dog and owner work together so well so quickly. 'It's like you've known each other for ages,' he said.

The kettle had just boiled when two things happened. Firstly, he remembered that he had promised to have coffee with Mr and Mrs Lloyd senior, who lived in the flat below his. Secondly, the phone rang. Steadman carefully swept his hand over the table and having found the receiver, gently felt for the right button. It was all too easy to cut off a caller.

'Do you want the bad news or the bad news?' Dr Rufus bellowed.

'And a cheery good morning to you too, Frank. Isn't it supposed to be the good news or the bad news?'

'I could make it the bad news or worse news, if you're going to be picky.'

'Frank, I don't like the sound of any of this - out with it.'

'DCI Long has called a lunchtime meeting to review the two murders, and...'

'And what?'

'And introduce the forensic psychologist assigned to the investigation.'

Steadman groaned. 'If it's the same fellow as last time I'll... I'll...'

'Are you still there, John?'

'Sorry, Frank, I was just wondering what I would actually do, if it was the same person. Is there worse news?'

'Oh yes!' replied Dr Rufus, a little too gleefully for Steadman's liking. 'You've been nominated for 'Helmsmouth Citizen of the Year' by the *Echo*. There's a nice piece about you, complete with photograph, in this morning's paper.'

Steadman's mind was immediately cast back to the incident at the traffic lights. That would explain it, he thought. But Rufus' next words told him he was wrong.

'I don't know where they dug it up from, you look about twenty-five! There are three other nominees and readers are invited to phone in their votes,' Dr Rufus continued.

Steadman swore. 'Please, Frank, tell me you're pulling my leg.'

'Afraid not, old man – that's what you get for being too nice to our colleagues in the press over the years. Do you want me to pick you up just before lunch?'

'If you have the time, would you be willing to walk with me to the Eyesore? I need the practice. I'll introduce you to Robbie.'

At the sound of his name the dog got up and stood expectantly at Steadman's side.

'Ah yes, your guide dog - Grimble has told me all about him. If he is to be believed, Robbie even makes breakfast for you in the morning.'

* * *

Mr and Mrs Lloyd senior had seen the morning's paper. Instead of gushing with dreaded enthusiasm, they displayed remarkable understanding. 'Given what you've been through, I imagine the last thing you want would be any more publicity,' said old Mr Lloyd.

Mrs Lloyd clucked in agreement and forced another piece of cake on him. 'What you don't eat now, you'll have to take home with you and give to that young lad who comes to walk your dog. He could do with a bit of fattening up – he's like a long drink of water.'

They talked enthusiastically about the dog and, as always, how nice it was to hear Steadman playing the piano. The clock on the mantelpiece struck noon.

'Good grief, is that the time! I must go,' exclaimed Steadman. 'Dr Rufus is walking with me to the Eyesore for a working lunch.'

* * *

Steadman stood on the pavement patiently waiting for Dr Rufus. He was glad of his hat, for there was a definite nip in the air. His nose tingled and he turned up the collar of his coat. Robbie sat panting at his feet, wreathed in vapour like a small steam train.

A screech of the brakes announced Dr Rufus's arrival. The fact that he was wearing a ghastly striped woollen hat with a bobble didn't stop him from commenting on

Steadman's fedora.

'That's right – mock the afflicted! And I thought you were my friend,' said Steadman.

Dr Rufus duly admired Robbie, but like DS Fairfax, he was none too sure about dogs, especially big black ones.

The two men linked arms and set off.

'I've been thinking, Frank,' said Steadman. 'The second murder, it wasn't carried out with the same rigour as the first, was it?'

'No, now you come to mention it. Apart from the cause of death, the wiring wasn't nearly as neat and whoever did it had made several attempts to screw Velda's hands to the cross-stitch frame. Maybe it was easier to screw Tipley's bony hands to the desk. Do you think it's significant?'

Steadman took his time in answering.

'It smacks of desperation, loss of control perhaps, even enthusiasm. That worries me. And, for the life of me, I can't figure out why these two should have been selected. And why wire them up?'

'Maybe our forensic psychologist can shed some light,' Dr Rufus suggested.

Before Steadman could give a withering reply, a boy raced past on a skateboard.

'Out of the way, you fucking gays!'

'Has that foul-mouthed youth got very dark, curly hair?' Steadman asked.

'Yes,' replied Dr Rufus.

'Charlie Withers, come here!' Steadman shouted.

Immediately the clattering rumble of the skateboard

stopped. 'How do you know my name?' Charlie Withers asked in a voice that was more of a challenge than a question.

'Because you sound just like your feckless father. He wouldn't recognise a guide dog if it came and bit him on the backside.'

'You're blind? I thought you were...'

'You made it perfectly clear what you thought, Charlie.'

'I know you – you're Steadman, the blind detective!'

Steadman did a quick calculation in his head. 'Your father must still be in prison.'

Charlie grunted.

'How is your mother? She deserves better.'

'Mam's OK.'

'She won't be when she finds out her son is shouting homophobic insults at strangers and skiving off school.'

Charlie was about to protest, but Steadman interrupted him. 'Listen son, if you don't want to end up like your father, get yourself back to school. You'll never earn an honest living if you're just streetwise.'

'I don't often skive – it's just that we've got games today and the teacher is always picking on me, he's a right bast...'

Steadman held up a hand. 'I sympathise, but it is only for an hour or so a week. If you don't turn up, he wins and you lose. Start turning up and I'll bet he'll stop picking on you.'

'You reckon?'

'Go on now. Tell your mother I'm asking after her.'

Charlie Withers didn't need to be told twice. He

dropped his skateboard and with a deft flick of his ankle, raced off.

'Do you think he'll take any notice?' Dr Rufus asked.

'No,' Steadman replied sadly. 'His father never did.'

The two men walked on.

'Do you know where we are?' enquired Dr Rufus.

'Yes, we've just passed the hairdresser's salon. Even you must be able to smell it.'

Dr Rufus confessed that he couldn't. Years of dissecting corpses in varying stages of decay had rendered his nose immune to all but the most pungent of aromas.

'I've also been counting the steps in the back of my head,' Steadman continued. 'I'm sure it helps if you're musical. It's rather like keeping time. You do it without thinking.'

At each crossing Robbie led them away from the junction and sat resolutely at the kerb until it was safe to cross. Dr Rufus was amazed.

'How on earth do they train a dog to do that?' he asked.

'A bit like Mrs Beaton's recipe for jugged hare – "First catch your hare." The dogs are bred for intelligence, then it takes hours of work with lots of rewards. I can't tell you what a difference it has made to the quality of my life already – greater independence, speed – not to mention the company. Isn't that right Robbie?'

The dog looked up without breaking his stride.

It was starting to drizzle again when the two men reached the Eyesore.

'I'm ready for dog walking duties whenever you like,'

said Sergeant Grimble, surreptitiously slipping Robbie a biscuit.

'Don't think I didn't notice that,' Steadman responded. He pressed the button on his watch and the metallic voice informed him it was twelve twenty-eight. 'Come up about one, if that's convenient, but not too many of those doggie treats.'

DCI Long was waiting for them in the small conference room. After Kim Ho, Will Lofthouse and Alan Munro had finished making a fuss of the dog, he called the meeting to order.

'Help yourself to some lunch, then we'll begin,' he said.

Dr Rufus led Steadman to seat. 'What do fancy?' he asked discreetly.

'Anything that's not likely to fall apart. I wouldn't mind a drink, but don't fill the glass too full.' Steadman could sense Robbie looking up expectantly. 'Don't mooch! I suspect Sergeant Grimble will be spoiling you despite my protests.'

DCI Long rapped his glass with a spoon.

'Thank you for coming. Dr Griffiths, our forensic psychologist, has been delayed – a flat tyre, I believe. In the meantime, I think it would be useful to go round the room and get an update on everyone's thoughts and findings. Ladies first, we'll start with Kim.'

Kim pushed her jet-black hair behind her ears.

'Only two things to report, sir. The wire is definitely from an electric cable. There are traces of insulation and scratches where the plastic has been stripped off. Secondly,

Harry Eeles's van is as clean as a whistle. With your permission, I would like to hand it back to him later today.'

DCI Long nodded and turned to DS Fairfax.

'Your turn, Fiona.'

Steadman had been unaware of her presence. She was unsure of the dog and had kept in the background.

'I've spoken with Velda Meemes' spinster friends. They can't help. However, DC Lofthouse and I have been looking at the reserved items in the back of the shop with Doreen, and we may have turned up something.'

DCI Long turned to DC Will Lofthouse, who looked as though he had just woken up.

'It's a possibility, sir. All of the stuff that's been put aside in the back shop has been labelled with the name and address of the potential customer along with the date. Velda and Doreen would hold items for two weeks, although they tell the punters it will only be for one. Trick of the trade, you might say. We've traced all bar one of the names. Whoever reserved a small bronze Buddha, for some reason, gave a non-existent address. Kim's being checking it for fingerprints.'

Kim gave a nervous giggle.

'The only clear prints are those of Velda Meemes, I'm afraid.'

'I don't suppose Doreen remembers the customer?' asked DCI Long.

'No – she thinks it may have been a man, as the name on the label is Reg Butler. I doubt if Velda would have written that name if it had been a woman.'

Something sparked in Steadman's brain. That name, Reg Butler – surely it was familiar.

'Anything else, Will?'

DC Lofthouse continued, 'We have found an old address book, but no Richard Armstrong. Doreen has a good memory and could account for all the names.'

'Has anything turned up at Crenshaw Tipley's house?'

'Well, there are at least a dozen books missing or lent out. Each space has been marked with a card. There's no pattern to the books taken out – anything from poetry to politics. He did keep a ledger of who had borrowed what. His writing is tiny and difficult to decipher. We've traced all bar one. Again, that person appears to have a given a false address.'

'It would be too much to hope for that it was the same address given to Velda Meemes,' said DCI Long.

'No, sir, different address,' DC Lofthouse replied. 'And the name this time was Gordon Greig, I think. I can't be sure as the writing is so small.'

Again, something lit up in Steadman's brain. He had definitely heard that name before, or at least a very similar name.

'Better get forensics to have a look at it. Alan, what have you been up to?'

DS Munro moved awkwardly in his chair, which groaned in protest.

'Well, sir, I've been chasing Richard Armstrongs. I drew up a list of every Richard Armstrong whose birth was registered within plus or minus five years of Crenshaw

Tipley's alleged date of birth. There was a surprisingly large number. Fortunately, nearly all were alive and working. Ten were reported as dead. None of these were in suspicious circumstances, but I've asked the local forces to confirm tactfully in each instance. Two have gone abroad. One is living in the south of Spain.'

Will Lofthouse and Dr Rufus both snorted.

'Go on, Alan,' DCI Long interjected.

'The other went to Washington about thirty years ago, and appears to have vanished without trace. The Spanish Richard Armstrong made a mint as a builder, quite legitimately apparently, and is still living as Richard Armstrong, enjoying the sunshine by all accounts. The American Richard Armstrong, if I can call him that, is more elusive. His parents are both dead, he may have a sister but that's about as far as I've got, sir.'

'Very interesting – do you know how old he was when left this country?'

'Twenty-six, sir,' DS Munro replied.

DCI Long fixed his gaze on John Steadman. He must be finding this very hard, he thought.

On the contrary, Steadman was thoroughly enjoying himself. His mind was shuffling round each piece of information trying to fit it into some sort of pattern, so far without much success. Why did he feel that investigating Crenshaw Tipley's past would lead nowhere? Could it be that it was too long ago, or that it would open up a hornet's nest? What was familiar about the two aliases? Should he share his concerns? No, he thought, he would mull that one over himself.

'Anything to add, John?'

'One thought struck me, sir, and Frank will bear me out. I don't believe the second murder was carried out as meticulously as the first. There is, if you like, an art in killing someone by severing their spinal cord. Velda was simply smothered. Tipley was injected with whisky, whereas second time round our killer merely pours sparkling water over the victim.'

'And the wires and screws were not nearly so tidy,' added Dr Rufus.

'Haste, do you think?' DCI Long asked.

'No, not haste – desperation and callous disregard,' Steadman replied. 'And that makes me feel very uneasy. I think he will try again.'

The room fell silent.

Grimble's voice could be distinctly heard chattering away and getting louder as he walked down the corridor. Whoever he was talking to was getting little chance to reply. The only other sound was a hurried clip-clop of somebody trying to keep pace with him. Steadman turned to Dr Rufus.

'Good grief, even worse than open-toed sandals – he's wearing clogs!'

Sergeant Grimble knocked on the door and walked in. All Steadman could hear was DCI Long welcoming someone, but he couldn't catch the name or the reply as

Grimble had trundled over and was making a fuss of Robbie.

'Have you been a good boy? Is your Uncle Bertie going to take you for a nice walkie? Your Daddy says I mustn't give you too many treats, but we won't tell him, will we?'

'The man's gone mad,' said Dr Rufus after Grimble had left. 'Completely mad! I mean to say, "Uncle Bertie" and Robbie's "Daddy." It's not healthy.'

'He means well,' Steadman replied. 'Mind, it's just as well I have a strong stomach.'

DCI Long called the room to order.

'This is Dr Sam Griffiths, forensic psychologist. Dr Griffiths has been working with the Met for almost fifteen years, and on my request has joined us, initially for the bizarre murder of Crenshaw Tipley, but now also for that of Velda Meemes. I think it easiest if I go round the room and make the introductions.'

Even DCI Long is calling the crimes bizarre, Steadman mused.

'Dr Rufus, our Home Office pathologist – you've already met, of course.'

Steadman's ears pricked up. Frank had never mentioned anything to him. What the hell was going on?

'And sitting next to him is DI John Steadman, whom I have also brought into the investigation.'

Steadman gave a cursory nod.

'Oh, I've heard all about you from Dr Rufus. I'm sure half his stories can't be true!'

It was a female voice: soft, gentle with more than a hint

of a Welsh accent. Steadman got clumsily to his feet, knocked over his chair and extended a hand. His cheeks were burning.

'I'm so terribly sorry... My former colleague completely failed to mention... It may be the fumes in the mortuary or more likely his warped sense of humour. I just assumed... Well, all I can say is that I have been well and truly hoist with my own petard.'

Dr Sam Griffiths clasped the outstretched hand and pressed it gently. Her hand was soft and warm.

'I gather you were expecting a man with greasy hair, halitosis and outlandish footwear? Well, I can assure you I washed my hair this morning and I hope my breath is minty fresh. I should have been wearing Italian ankle boots but I broke a heel changing the tyre. These are an emergency pair of black patent leather mules I keep in the car,' she said looking down at her feet. 'Stylish, but they don't half make a noise on your wooden floors.'

Steadman let go of Dr Griffiths' hand and smiled weakly. Munro had righted the fallen chair and guided him back into it. DCI Long continued going round the room making the introductions.

'Would you like to be cremated or buried, Frank?' Steadman said under his breath. 'After this, I fear I may well have to kill you!'

'Completely slipped my mind,' Dr Rufus lied unconvincingly. 'You should have seen your face.'

With the introductions over, Dr Samantha Griffiths took the floor.

'Everything I know about the case so far is based on my conversations with DCI Long and my apparently clandestine meeting with Dr Rufus,' she said pointedly. That's put you in your place, Frank, thought Steadman. Dr Rufus beamed back at her like an innocent child.

'So rather than just tell you what I think, I propose we develop an offender profile as a joint exercise with everybody chipping in or challenging what is being said. I would like to use the white board, if that's all right? Inspector Steadman, if I forget to read out what I've written or you wish to be reminded, please let me know.' She picked up the marker pen. 'Because nothing in life is definite, I will divide everything into four columns – "almost certain", "probable", "possible" and "uncertain".' She wrote each heading on the board in neat block capitals. 'Right then, what about sex?'

DS Munro blushed, looked awkwardly at his enormous feet and tried hard not to smirk. Dr Rufus opened his mouth but before he could say anything Sam Griffiths caught him in her steely gaze.

'Don't even think about it. Fifteen years with the Met – I can assure you, I've heard all the smart answers.'

Dr Rufus closed his mouth. The only male in the room unaffected was DC Will Lofthouse who, in his own dreamy way, had already mentally undressed and seduced Dr Griffiths. Even John Steadman had felt a sudden lurch in his stomach. He could not recall having thought about sex since the death of his wife. Why should Sam Griffiths' remark feel so provocative?

'I have no doubt the perpetrator is male,' she continued unabashed.

'Why not a woman?' asked Dr Rufus meekly, like a naughty boy trying to get back into teacher's good books.

'A woman might do something like this once to a man as an act of vengeance, but to two people, one of them a harmless old spinster... No, only a man would be so stupid.'

'We also have two possible false, male names,' DC Lofthouse added, explaining about the borrowed book and the reserved statue of the Buddha.

There was no further discussion and she ticked the box in the "almost certain" column.

'What about age? We know that most violent crimes are committed by the under twenty-fives, however, I don't see this as a young person's crime. Nothing was stolen and although the acts were in themselves violent, the violence was very controlled. That suggests to me a man in mid-life, thirty to forty-five, say.' She looked round the room for any dissenters. 'No? Let's give that a "probable", then. And I also have a feeling he's divorced, or single at least. He spent at least eight hours at each victim's address, maybe longer.'

'Perhaps his wife was away,' suggested Munro.

'What about their children? It's not school holidays.'

'Maybe they don't have kids.'

Sam bit her thumb. 'I would still like to give it a "probable". I think this character is a bit of a lone wolf.'

John Steadman remained silent. This was a different way of working for him. He liked to get to know the victims first, perhaps because it was easier. If you know the victim then you can work out the motives, he reasoned. So far, the motives remained obscure. However, without thinking about it he had already come to much the same conclusions as Dr Griffiths. Maybe they could work together.

'I think we should consider "occupation" next,' she continued.

Dr Rufus cleared his throat.

'The first murder definitely suggests he had medical knowledge. It wasn't luck that led him to sever Crenshaw Tipley's spinal cord. Could be a doctor, or a nurse - or even a vet,' Dr Rufus concluded in the derisory manner that medics invariably adopt when referring to their veterinary counterparts.

Sam Griffiths listened intently.

'You could add physiotherapists and osteopaths to that list,' suggested DS Fairfax.

'There's something troubling me...' Sam's voice trailed away.

'Perhaps,' said Steadman, 'it would pay to broaden the field. I think the killer's action showed, not so much medical knowledge, as anatomical knowledge.'

'Who are you suggesting then,' said Dr Rufus gruffly, 'morticians?'

'Possibly, Frank, but all sorts of other people know about anatomy – archaeologists, anthropologists for example. And even some more remote from your beloved medical field – slaughter-men for one.'

Dr Rufus's face brightened at the thought of a wild slaughter-man on the loose.

'No, I think our villain is well-educated,' Sam interjected. 'Crenshaw Tipley lent him a book from his private library. He was a man who would not tolerate fools gladly, I'm led to believe.'

The room fell quiet. All that could be heard was the tapping of keyboards in the neighbouring: officers no doubt typing up the endless reports that nine times out of ten nobody would ever read. Thank God, I'm at least spared that, thought Steadman. Another idea crossed his mind.

'There is one group that we haven't considered,' he said, breaking the silence. 'What about artists?'

He remembered, with embarrassment, accompanying Holly to a life drawing class without realising what this entailed and being quite taken aback when presented with a buxom naked model spread out on a chaise-longue instead of the anticipated bowl of fruit. Holly had become very enthusiastic and had bought all sorts of books on drawing the human form, including one on anatomy.

'I agree,' said Sam. 'By the same token, you could add elite athletes or ballet dancers. Are we agreed that the murderer is probably well-educated and leave it at that?' She scribbled on the white board. It was an odd squawking sound. Steadman thought he must have heard it a hundred times before, but had never noticed it.

'Do we think this man has a past criminal record?'

It was DCI Long who answered.

'Nothing similar has been recorded in Helmsmouth. I've been through the archives. We have only had ever had one serial killer. A man named Alfred Sheridan who murdered three parlour maids in the 1920s.'

'So what would turn a man to murder in mid-life?'

'Failure,' replied Steadman carefully. 'Men behave oddly when they realise they will never fulfil their life's ambitions.'

Sam Griffiths nodded then hastily added, 'I think you're right,' realising that her nod would have gone unnoticed.

'I also think he is a coward,' Steadman continued. The room listened intently to his theories. 'And that, I think, makes him all the more dangerous,' he concluded.

There was a knock on the door and a young constable poked his head in.

'Urgent message for DCI Long.'

DCI Long frowned, mumbled his excuses and left the room.

Sam Griffiths had written "place in society" on the white board and then read it out for Steadman's benefit.

'What do we think? – Outcast, misfit, life and soul of the party?'

'I think he must have some social skills,' said DS Fairfax. 'He persuaded Tipley to lend him a book and Velda Meemes to put aside an antique statue of the Buddha. He's probably a plausible liar as well.'

John Steadman was only half listening. The room was warm and it was hard for him to concentrate. In his mind's eye he kept seeing two people wired up meticulously and methodically.

'I think he's somebody local,' suggested Munro.

'Most serial killers are,' Sam Griffiths responded.

Steadman already knew that.

'I think he must be good with his hands.' It was the first comment Kim Ho had offered. 'The wiring was very neat and skilfully done.'

The image of the wired marionettes in Steadman's dream floated back into his mind.

'What sorts of people are skilled in manipulating wires, apart from electricians, that is?' she asked.

'Florists, basket makers,' someone suggested. It could have been DS Fairfax, but Steadman's thoughts were elsewhere. He played each crime over in his head in slow motion – the murder, the wait, the arranging of the scene. It was like a stage setting or a tableau, but why? And what could possibly link Velda Meemes and Crenshaw Tipley.

'There's got to be a reason,' he said, far more loudly than he intended.

'Inspector Steadman, you wanted to say something?' Dr Griffiths enquired.

'I'm sorry, I was miles away – thinking out loud. It's just that I can't conceive of a possible motive that links these two killings. No robbery, no sexual gratification. I'm sure lots of people wished Crenshaw Tipley dead and his killing was more carefully planned and carried out. Having realised how easy it is to kill someone, has our murderer simply turned his attention on the next person that's annoyed him? If so, who is next?'

'Has he made any possible contact with the police?' asked Sam Griffiths. 'Many serial killers do.'

'I'm not aware of any,' DS Fairfax replied. 'What about you, Alan?'

DS Munro shook his head.

Dr Griffiths continued raising various character traits. The white board was getting more and more crowded. Most of the topics she raised fell unhelpfully into the "uncertain" column.

'I think we've come as far as we can for today. I'll write this up and circulate. Inspector Steadman, I can do an audio version if you like?'

'I think I've remembered most of it. Thanks anyway.'

'Well, I hope you have found it helpful. At least I've not mentioned kippers in plastic bags!'

Dr Rufus and DS Munro smiled. The rest of the room looked puzzled.

'An in-joke, I'm afraid,' Sam responded. 'Has anybody got any questions?'

DC Will Lofthouse raised a hand.

'Yes, I have. What's a "petard" and how can you be hoisted with it? I've always imagined it to be some sort of flag, but that doesn't make any sense, does it?'

'I worry about him sometimes,' Dr Rufus whispered to John Steadman as they left the room.

CHAPTER EIGHT

'Before you ask, I've given him barely any treats. Besides, he's had a nice bit of exercise. He doesn't like playing "fetch", does he? Too intelligent, I suppose. I threw a stick once and he brought it back. The second time, he just looked at me as if to say, "If that's your attitude, go fetch it yourself". Didn't you Robbie?'

If Sergeant Grimble had one fault, it was that he did like the sound of his own voice.

Steadman called Robbie over and buckled on his harness. The dog stiffened, gave one wag of his tail and looked up, waiting for a command.

'You wouldn't know what the urgent call for DCI Long was, would you?' asked Dr Rufus.

'His brother has had a heart attack and is in intensive care,' Grimble replied.

'Where? In Helmsmouth General?'

'No, his other brother – the one that lives in London. His wife called for him and they went off together.'

'How does that leave the force?' Steadman asked. 'Is there an inspector who can act up?'

'I doubt it,' said Grimble. 'What with the spate of break-ins and trying to hunt down the drug cartel, I can't see who would be available. If you ask me, I reckon they'll get somebody in from a neighbouring force. I'll let you know.'

'How was your afternoon? Dr Griffiths seems very pleasant even if she's Welsh. Only joking!'

John Steadman tried in vain to put a face to the lilting accent. Why was he afraid to ask what she looked like? Would it appear unseemly, or maybe he didn't want to appear too interested? Or was it that he worried that others might think it didn't matter what people looked like if you were blind?

'It was good,' he replied carefully. 'I think I had come to most of the same conclusions myself, but not in any focused way. She did raise one question that you might be able to answer. You haven't had any odd calls that could be from the killer?'

Grimble scratched his head and shuffled round the papers strewn over his desk. It was deceptive. To any casual observer it looked chaotic, but Grimble fished out one sheet of paper from the mess with apparent ease.

'It's not been public knowledge for that long. Here we are – two calls both claiming to be the murderer, both female, although I presume we are looking for a man. I recognised the first voice as "Not-quite-with-it Nora", who pleads guilty to everything. So much for care in the community. I didn't recognise the second, but it was similarly barking. In fact, it could even have been Nora trying out a new funny accent.'

Steadman pressed the button on the side of his watch. 'Four forty-five,' chirped the metallic voice.

'We'd better be going. Are you able to walk with me, Frank?'

Before Dr Rufus could open his mouth, Harry Eeles burst through the door.

'I knew it, thieving bastards the lot of you! There's nobody with stickier fingers than a bunch of plods. Here I am turning my back on a life of crime, and you lot... Oi, Grimble – where's that bloody Fairfax woman? I want a word with her!'

'It's DS Fairfax to you, Harry,' replied Steadman. 'Now, calm down and tell us what the problem appears to be.'

'Problem! I'll tell you what the problem is, Mr Steadman. I had my van taken from me and when I gets it back there's a brand-new roll of heavy duty electrical cable missing. Cost me fifty quid – look, here's the receipt. The copper wire must be worth at least half that in scrap alone.' He brandished the paper in front of Steadman's face. 'Oh, sorry – I forgot. Here, Grimble, you can read it.'

'Is your van outside, Harry?' asked Sergeant Grimble.

'No, it's under my bleeding arm! Of course it's outside.'

'Can I suggest we see if Kim Ho is still about,' Steadman said, trying to ease the tension. She was, and Steadman explained the situation.

'I'll come right away,' she said. 'There's a detailed inventory - I'll bring it with me.'

'And maybe your finger print powder and brushes,' Steadman added.

The inventory confirmed that there had indeed been a brand-new roll of heavy duty cable in the van. Kim dusted the door. The only prints were those of Harry Eeles. The van had been parked at the back of the Eyesore. Grimble checked the CCTV footage. Nothing. The two officers who delivered the van were summoned. One had driven the van, the other followed in a squad car.

'Did you lock the van before you handed over the keys?' asked Steadman.

'I locked the driver's door – I just assumed that all the doors would lock automatically.'

'Nah,' interrupted Harry, 'you've got to lock the back door separately.'

Neither officer could recall seeing anyone hanging about or acting suspiciously.

'Harry, you aren't just trying this on, are you?'

'What sort of person do you take me for, Grimble?'

'A low-down, petty crook and an opportunist of the first order, Harry. I've known you since you were a nipper nicking sweets on the way home from school. I wouldn't put it past you.'

'You believe me, don't you, Mr Steadman? Like I said, I'm trying hard to earn an honest living.'

Steadman took out his wallet and took out two twenty pound notes and a ten. The corners of the larger notes were neatly folded over.

'Actually, Harry, I do believe you. Here's your money. We should have checked that all the doors were locked.'

Harry didn't hesitate.

'I always knew you were a gentleman,' he said as he pocketed the money. He left hastily in case Steadman changed his mind.

'You know we could have given him an incident number and let him claim from his insurance,' said Sergeant Grimble.

'Harry Eeles, with insurance? Don't make me laugh,' Steadman replied.

'Sir.' It was the nervous voice of Kim Ho. 'It's only a thought, but the wire that Mr Eeles alleges was stolen is the same gauge as that used in the two murders.'

'Probably coincidence,' said Dr Rufus.

Steadman drummed his fingers on Grimble's desk.

'You know I hate coincidences, Frank.' The drumming stopped. 'I think we should go, Frank. Thanks Kim. Let's hope that Dr Rufus is correct.'

★ ★ ★

It was almost dark when the two men left the Eyesore. A sea mist had rolled in and lay over the town like a damp blanket. The glow of the street lights hung like hazy orange balls suspended in mid-air, barely penetrating the gloom. In the distance, the foghorn moaned.

'Pity all poor sailors on a night like this,' said Dr Rufus. 'I can hardly see my outstretched hand.' It may not have been very tactful, but John Steadman found his quality of unguarded openness refreshing.

'Well, John, what did you really think?'

'About the foul trick you played on me, or about Dr Sam Griffiths?'

Frank Rufus laughed. 'You're right, I should grow up and I should apologise, but I'm not going to lie. The look on your face... no, no – I meant, what did you make of our forensic psychologist?'

Steadman thought for a moment. 'I think she is very clever,' he said cautiously.

'Clever can mean all sorts of things, from an insult to a compliment. What exactly do you mean by "clever"?'

'She knew she would be met with suspicion, possibly even hostility. The charade with the white board was well orchestrated. We all felt we had helped and contributed somehow. I doubt if anything we said fundamentally altered the profile she had already worked out from her dealings with you and DCI Long. Now that's what I call "clever".'

'Ah, but do you think we are any further forward?'

The two men walked in silence. Steadman was deep in thought and Dr Rufus knew his friend too well to interrupt. Eventually he spoke.

'Let's round up the figures for ease of calculation. The local population the Helmsmouth Police Force deals with is about 200,000. Half are male, so that's 100,000, and we're looking for someone aged between thirty and forty-five – say fifteen percent of the total. I would guess that half of them would describe themselves as professional. We're now down to seven thousand five hundred, but we think this man is single. What do you reckon? One in five? Still leaves us with fifteen hundred potential suspects. Even if we knock off all those with a previous significant conviction, we're talking about over a thousand.'

'So not really much further on,' Dr Rufus said.

'Not statistically, but we are in other ways,' Steadman replied. 'We're all thinking about the crimes differently, and that is positive. However, there was something else that somebody said that intrigued me.'

Before Steadman could recall what it was, a police car with flashing lights and wailing siren screeched to a halt beside them. The wailing tailed off and a fresh-faced officer wound down the window.

'I'll have two ice cream cones and a broken wafer for the dog,' said Dr Rufus.

The officer looked puzzled. 'Aren't you Dr Rufus?'

'No, I'm the King of Siam. Of course, I'm Dr Rufus. What do you want?'

'Inspector Crouchley has asked if you can come down to the railway station. Someone has jumped in front of a train and he's had to close the station until what's left of the body is removed.'

'Did he ask nicely?' Dr Rufus said as sweetly as he could. Inspector Crouchley was renowned for his bad language, rudeness and scant regard for regulations. 'Or did he say,' continued Dr Rufus, 'you two effing layabouts, go and find that effing Rufus and tell him to get the eff down here, now!'

'Something like that, yes,' replied the young constable.

'Oh, you mean it was worse. Some are born with a silver spoon in their mouths, I fear that Inspector Crouchley was born with a dog turd in his. Well, who was it? A drunk or a broken-hearted lover?'

'No, it's a boy. Possibly not even a teenager.'

'Damn it,' said Dr Rufus softly, more to himself than to anyone else. He straightened himself and scratched his forehead.

Steadman knew that Rufus was completely unperturbed by the grossest of mutilated, decaying bodies - corpses that would give any normal person nightmares for the rest of their lives, provided, that is, they were adults. But children were different. They got to him. Maybe, thought Steadman, it was because he had never had children of his own. His wife had drowned on their honeymoon. Her body had never been found and he had never remarried. Did he imagine that these could have been his children? Steadman knew that big fat tears would be rolling down his cheeks as he carried out the post-mortem examination.

'You had better go, Frank,' said Steadman. 'Robbie and I know the way from here. It's not far – in fact I could even tell you exactly how many steps it is.'

'If you're sure, John. I ought to go, especially if it's a kid.'

Dr Rufus climbed into the back seat. The young officer

switched on the lights and siren. The last thing Steadman heard was Dr Rufus shouting, 'Switch off that bloody racket, I've got a sore head as it is.'

Steadman turned up the collar on his coat. 'Go forward, Robbie, let's go home,' he said.

The dog dutifully set off and Steadman started to count. They reached the next junction four paces sooner than Steadman had anticipated. It was difficult to keep an accurate tally with so many other things to think about. Robbie stopped, circled and led Steadman a little way down the street, away from the junction. The dog sat at the kerb edge, waiting for the command to cross. Steadman listened: no sound of any vehicles.

'Go forward.'

Robbie paused, moving his head from side to side. Only when he too was satisfied did they both set off. Steadman wondered how long it would be before crossing a road no longer terrified him. He felt a slight twitch of the harness and with a smile of satisfaction, high-stepped onto the opposite pavement.

Neither of them was aware of the cyclist until it was too late. Robbie gave a small yelp and fell sideways, knocking Steadman off his feet.

'What the...?'

But all Steadman heard was the distinctive scrunch of gears changing, then silence.

'Are you all right, Robbie?' he said gently, patting the dog. His coat was warm, wet and sticky. The smell of blood on Steadman's fingers was unmistakable.

'The bastard!' he said under his breath as he unwound his scarf. He folded it haphazardly, forming a large pad. It was impossible for him to tell exactly where the dog was bleeding from, but he did his best to staunch the flow. Fumbling in his pocket, he retrieved his mobile phone. It was difficult at the best of times not to make a mistake. Now he was trying to find his way one-handed using his thumb to press the keys. The keys were deliberately large and the raised blip on the 'five' easy enough to find. 'Don't panic,' he muttered to himself, 'take it slowly – get it right first time.'

A distant phone rang. 'Fingers crossed, Robbie. You'll be fine,' he said soothingly. The dog remained motionless.

'Helmsmouth Police Station, how may I help you?'

'Thank God it's you, Grimble. There's been an accident.'

Sergeant Grimble recognised Steadman's voice straightaway.

'An accident? Are you hurt?'

'Please just listen. I'm fine, but a cyclist has hit Robbie. He's bleeding badly and not moving. We're on the corner of Fitzroy Avenue.'

'Alan Munro is still here. I'll get him on the other line.'

Grimble flicked a second receiver off its cradle, caught it and with a podgy finger called Munro's extension.

'Is there anything else I can do?'

'Yes – you can alert the vet. Robbie is registered with Mr Martindale at the Marina Practice, you know, the same one used by the police dogs.'

'I'm onto it. Hang on, Munro has just answered... are you still there, Inspector Steadman? Munro will be with you in ten minutes – faster, judging by the speed he's ran out of the door.' Grimble hesitated. 'Is Robbie still breathing?'

'I think so, but there seems to be an awful lot of blood.'

'Didn't the cyclist stop?'

'No.'

'The bastard!'

'My sentiments exactly. Listen, I better go, Robbie's getting restless.'

Steadman pocketed the phone and tried to rearrange the makeshift bandage as best he could.

Despite the fog, Munro arrived in Fitzroy Avenue in well under ten minutes. Steadman and Robbie were huddled under a street light. If Munro had not been looking for them, he could easily have mistaken them for a couple of sacks of rubbish.

'Christ, he's bleeding badly!' Munro exclaimed. He fetched a towel and a blanket from the boot of the car and wrapped the dog up carefully before placing him on the back seat. He helped Steadman to his feet and manoeuvred him into the car beside Robbie.

'Hold tight!'

The veterinary surgery was situated a little way down the hill from the Eyesore. Mr Martindale himself was waiting for them. Munro carried the large dog effortlessly in from the car and placed him on the vet's couch, then returned for Inspector Steadman.

'I don't know who's got more blood on them, you or the dog,' said Munro. He went back to the car and returned with a large tub of antiseptic wipes. 'Let's get you tidied up a bit first, then we'll see how Mr Martindale is getting on.'

In the treatment room, the vet and his assistant were busy. Robbie had been sedated, some of his fur had been clipped and the wound had been cleaned. Mr Martindale's assistant was gently stroking Robbie's head while the vet injected local anaesthetic before closing the gash with staples.

It took Munro some little time to get Steadman even half-presentable. 'You'll have to do,' he said as he shook his head and knocked gently on the treatment room door.

Before Steadman could speak, Mr Martindale asked, 'How do you think this happened?'

Steadman explained about how he had just crossed the road and how the first thing he was aware of was the dog's yelp.

'I'm certain it was a cyclist. Probably just didn't see us in the dark and the fog. Robbie is as black as the night and I've got a dark coat on. I think he must have clipped Robbie with his pedal. I don't understand why he didn't stop.'

Mr Martindale raised his eyebrows and shook his head.

'No – the cut is over a foot long, straight and clean. A pedal tends to cause a ragged tear, whereas this' – he paused to close the last staple – 'was almost certainly caused by a very sharp blade – a Stanley knife or a large craft knife, I would say. Fortunately, your dog has a thick, shaggy coat and that's what has probably saved him.'

'Are you saying this was deliberate?' Steadman asked.

'Beyond any shadow of a doubt.'

'Apart from anything else,' added Munro, 'you were directly under a street light. Even in the fog, he couldn't have missed seeing you.'

Steadman pushed his dark glasses onto his forehead and rubbed his eyes. He was weary, annoyed and above all perplexed. He knew that attacks on animals were sadly on the increase, but would anyone really want to attack a guide dog? He found it very hard to believe, despite what Mr Martindale had said. If it was true, was it because it was his dog? Surely it must be. If so, it meant someone was watching him, following him, trying to intimidate him. Why? He was damned if he was going back to living in the confines of a safe house. But was that fair on Robbie?

He let his dark glasses fall back over his sightless eyes and sighed. There was just too much to think about, too many alternatives, too many possibilities. He was teetering on the brink of self-pity, something he loathed.

The dog started to stir and, with a jerk, he pulled himself back into the here and now.

'How badly is Robbie hurt? It seemed as though he had lost a lot of blood.'

'I suspect he was quite stunned by the initial blow,' Mr Martindale replied. 'He has lost some blood but his coat was already wet from the fog and I can imagine that it would have seemed worse than it actually was. Nevertheless, given your circumstances, I would like to keep him here overnight.'

'What for?' Steadman asked.

'Someone to check him, make sure the wound isn't starting to bleed and that he is generally well.'

'So nothing too technical?'

'No, not really but...'

'You don't need to remind me that I'm blind. My sister could come and stay. She's very good with animals and desperate to meet Robbie.'

At the sound of his name Robbie stood up, rather uncertainly, but reassuringly wagged his tail.

'I could stay over at your place, if you like,' Munro offered.

'Thanks, but you have a wife and children who don't see enough of you as it is. I'm sure Linda will require no persuasion.'

Mr Martindale grudgingly gave way. 'Use the phone in the office. Mobile reception is not reliable unless you stand in the middle of the car park. I'll write out some instructions for your sister.'

Linda, as anticipated, readily agreed to come. Munro had promised to call Sergeant Grimble, who was as worried as an expectant father. For all his shortcomings he was no fool. After Munro had explained the circumstances, he said, more to himself than to Munro, 'I fear someone's got it in for Inspector Steadman.' Munro glanced briefly at his colleague standing in the doorway, bedraggled and bloodstained. He made no reply.

'Anyone else we should call, sir?'

'We had better have a word with Mr Barnes and Tim Warrender, of course.'

Mr Barnes insisted on speaking with the vet. It wasn't Tim Warrender who answered the phone, but his mother. The distress in her voice was obvious.

'Is it about the boy? We know already. It's awful, isn't it? Just too awful for words. He was Tim's best friend at school. Tim's shut himself in his room and won't speak to anyone. We should have called you but he couldn't face leaving the house.'

Steadman was so absorbed in his own predicament that he had momentarily forgotten about the incident at the railway station.

'No, it wasn't about that. I only know that a young lad was killed by a train. I have no idea who he is and, of course, I was unaware that Tim knew him. I'm so sorry. I'm phoning to say that Robbie has had an accident. He was hit by a cyclist and I had to take him to the vet.' No point in giving any details, he thought. 'He's fine now and we're just about to leave to go home. My sister is coming to give me a hand. I don't know whether it would be a good or bad thing to tell Tim. You'll be the best judge of that. I'll phone tomorrow, if I may.'

Steadman handed the receiver back to Munro. 'Do you know about the boy killed at the station?'

'Not a lot, sir. Crouchley's down there making himself unpleasant to everyone as per usual.'

'An odd character is our Inspector Crouchley,' Steadman replied. 'The boy was Tim's best friend and not surprisingly he has taken it very badly.'

'Poor lad, bursting with hormones, trying to make sense of it all and now his first brush with life in the real world. Or should that be death? Do you think it would help if I went to see him, sir?' Munro asked.

'I think that would be really helpful. Perhaps tomorrow – let him sleep on it. See if you can get the latest information before you go, Alan. The best person would be…'

'I know – Sergeant Grimble.'

The door of the treatment room swung open and a slightly unsteady Robbie walked towards Steadman and sat at his feet.

'Are you sure you'll manage?' Mr Martindale still looked doubtful.

'You don't know my sister, otherwise you wouldn't have asked.'

Munro opened the door of the Audi and gently placed Robbie on the back seat before helping his former boss into the car.

'Martindale might not know Linda, but I do. I wouldn't like to be in your shoes when she sees the state of your clothes. The only thing that hasn't got blood on it is your fedora, although it looks like it's been put through a mangle.'

Steadman smiled. He hadn't heard the word 'mangle' for years. A device with rollers for squeezing water out of laundry, he recollected.

'Never mind my hat, I feel as though I've been put through a mangle myself.'

They drove in silence back to Steadman's flat. True to her word, Linda was waiting for them. She cast a sisterly eye over her brother.

'Look at the state of you!' she exclaimed. 'Alan, you're not much better, however you've got a wife who can sort you out.'

Munro turned bright red and took this as his cue to leave. 'I'll keep in touch, sir.'

'So this is the famous Robbie. Well, you look equally disreputable. You also look hungry, in fact you both do. Where do you keep the dog food? Don't worry, I see it. Now you go and get a shower. Leave all your clothes outside the bathroom door and I'll see what I can do. Then I'll have to see what I can do to clean up Robbie. They have made a reasonable job at the surgery, but his paws are still matted.'

She was like a human whirlwind. Steadman knew his best option was simply to do as he was told. Dutifully he went and had a shower.

'Make sure you scrub your nails. I have left your pyjamas, slippers and dressing gown by the door.'

Steadman let the hot water cascade over him. The events of the day milled around in his brain in apparent confusion. He needed to put things in order, but try as he might they still got jumbled – a suicide, the Eyesore, Robbie, the cyclist, something somebody said, DCI Long's departure and Dr Sam Griffiths. At the thought of Dr Griffiths, he felt an odd sensation in the pit of his stomach.

'Better scrub my nails again,' he muttered, trying hard not to think too much about Sam Griffiths.

Linda had not only fed the dog but had managed to sponge Steadman's coat and trousers. She had taken one look at his scarf and confined it to history. His shoes were polished and a wash put on. In between all that she had somehow also managed to prepare a hot meal, lay the table and even light a scented candle. Robbie was sound asleep on his mat. After dinner, she vowed she would clean his paws too.

'This is really lovely,' Steadman said between mouthfuls.

'Of course it is, I made it myself,' Linda replied. 'Do you want to tell me what reckless escapade you've got yourself involved in this time, or is it still top secret?'

Steadman paused. Everything was in the public domain, he concluded, and it might help put his own thoughts in order.

Linda was a good listener. She had brought in a basin of warm water and disinfectant, and with a torn-up old towel she gently bathed Robbie while Steadman recounted in detail the events of the last few days.

'I wouldn't trust that Harry Eeles,' she said during a lull in Steadman's narrative.

'Neither would I, but I don't think he's capable of premeditated murder,' Steadman replied.

Linda nodded as she gently brushed Robbie's coat until it was nearly dry.

'Do these names mean anything to you – Reg Butler, and possibly a Gordon Grieg?' Steadman asked.

'No – should they?'

'They are the two aliases used – one to reserve an antique statue of the Buddha, the other to borrow one of Tipley's books. They are vaguely familiar, but I can't place them.'

Linda made coffee while Steadman continued with his tale.

'I thought you didn't like forensic psychologists,' Linda interrupted.

'This one is not the same,' Steadman replied. 'No, in fact she's quite different.'

'She? You never said it was a woman, John,' Linda said teasingly.

Steadman could feel his cheeks burning.

'Well, it is a woman and she's Welsh and quite charming. Dr Rufus had already met her. Of course, he didn't tell me. I made a proper fool of myself, much to his amusement.' Steadman paused. 'Poor man, he won't be laughing now.' He went on to tell Linda about the death at the railway station. 'Apparently, the young lad was Tim Warrender's best friend at school. Tim's very upset.'

Linda bit her lip. 'I can imagine,' she said under her breath.

'I still find it hard to believe that somebody deliberately slashed Robbie with a knife. It doesn't make sense. I don't think I'll tell Tim; it will only distress him further. He is, as Doreen Meemes says, at an awkward age.'

'He might like to help me in the garden in the summer if he's short of pocket money. Did you say he has a sister? Maybe they would both like to come. I could give them their own plot and teach them how to plant seeds and...'

Linda didn't have children of her own. Steadman had never asked why. He knew it was a taboo subject. He let his sister finish.

'I'm sure you'll meet them soon enough. Is that one of your own candles?' he asked, changing the subject. 'What's the scent? I can smell lavender but there is something else.'

'Lavender and jasmine. I made it myself. The aroma is meant to be relaxing. I thought that after what you've been through it would do you good. It certainly seems to have soothed Robbie, he's fast asleep. I'm going to tidy up. Would you like me to put on some music?'

'There's a new CD by the player. I haven't listened to it yet. You could put that on for me.'

Linda stood up. Robbie half-opened an eyelid.

'Is this the one – Canzonas and Sonatas by Giovani Gabrieli?'

Linda looked at the cover doubtfully. It was certainly not her kind of music.

'That's the one. I haven't heard it for years.'

It was early music, fragmented yet in its own way rich and satisfying. It was as if the composer had only just discovered harmony and was experimenting with all the different combinations, weaving them together, then unravelling them as though trying to find the hidden melody. A bit like this case, Steadman thought.

The candle started to gutter and immediately his thoughts turned to Holly. She loved playing with lighted candles, getting the wax to dribble in rivulets and eventually, to Steadman's consternation, licking her thumb and forefinger, then pinching the flame out. She knew it upset her husband and she did it to torment him ever so slightly. He, on the other hand was only concerned in case she hurt herself. And now she was gone. The same gun that had taken her life had snuffed the light out of his.

'What is it all about? What the hell is it all about?' he said softly to himself. Pondering the improbable only made him more depressed.

'More coffee?' Linda shouted from the kitchen.

'No thanks. I know it's early, but would you mind if I went to bed?'

'Sure. I'm almost finished here. I'll take Robbie out to the garden, then turn in myself. His wound looks fine. The vet's instructions state he should rest for a few days, but I expect you and Robbie will ignore them.'

CHAPTER NINE

Steadman refused Linda's offer of help to get into bed. His routine was fixed and he knew if he stuck to it he wouldn't stumble or fall. He was tired, but it was an odd sort of tiredness. Thoughts and noises kept jangling in his head, whirring around and making no sense at all. He lay back with a sigh and concentrated on his breathing, very gently drawing air in, then releasing his breath softly and silently. Within a few minutes he felt his body starting to relax, despite the continuing clamour in his head.

And now he was walking towards the noise; a cacophony of loud music with people laughing, shouting and screaming. The smell of the fairground wafted along on the night air long before he saw the lights. It was unmistakable; that familiar odour of candy floss, popcorn, hot dogs and onions. Burnt sugar and burnt grease – he never could see the attraction. Couples brushed past him holding on to helium balloons or carrying ridiculous oversized inflatable hammers or dying goldfish in plastic bags. It all seemed so pointless, so unnecessary. Yet his feet continued to march towards the lights, drawn inexplicably like a moth to a flame. They shimmered red, green, blue and yellow, bright and garish against the soft night sky, and the noise was deafening. Each ride was blasting out its own distorted tune with added bells and klaxons. They were tacky and crudely painted with cartoon characters. Steadman stared. Even the people manning the rides appeared two-dimensional and half-finished.

The 'Waltzer' came to a creaking standstill and disgorged its passengers. A girl in her late teens teetered towards Steadman on enormously high heels. Her skirt was hitched up way too high and her tights were laddered. The black make-up round her eyes was streaked down her pale cheeks. She lurched forward, took one look at Steadman, grabbed hold of the barrier rail and vomited at his feet, speckling his shoes with flecks of partly-digested food. Her friends brayed with laughter.

Steadman walked on. He saw only young people, for it was well past the time for families to be at a funfair. Groups of disaffected youths stood huddled in the shadows. Some were shouting, struggling to make themselves heard over the infernal racket. Others stood silently smoking scrawny roll-ups and spitting at their feet. A few were drunk and hurled abuse at Steadman as he passed. He was too old and knew that he must look ridiculous in his suit and tie. He felt out of place and threatened.

Something was drawing him on. He shook his head at the 'Hook a Duck' man and declined the offer of 'Three

Darts in Any Card'. He stopped for a moment by an amusement arcade. It was pathetically sad. Bored old women were relentlessly feeding coins into fruit machines. It didn't matter if they won or lost, their expressions never changed, not even when their buckets of cash inevitably became empty.

At the edge of the fairground was a large, almost deserted arcade. There were a few out-of-date pinball machines, an air hockey game and two table-football tables. At one of these some youngsters were quietly and conscientiously taking turns to play against each other. Steadman stared, mesmerised. They played with consummate ease, deftly flicking the ball from one rack of plastic figures to the next as fast as the eye could follow until, with a final flick of a wrist, it went clattering into the back of one of the goals. The achievement was barely acknowledged before the ball shot back into play.

'You should have a go at this one, Inspector Steadman.'

Steadman spun round. He recognised the voice instantly. Standing behind him was a grinning young man. His hands were thrust into two blue canvas pouches that hung from his belt. These were full of change and as he spoke he let the coins chink softly through his fingers. Round his neck hung a large bunch of keys.

'Maurice Eeles? What are you doing here?'

'A little bit of moonlighting. Don't tell the old man or he'll want half. This is the game for you, Inspector – look, behind you.' Maurice indicated with a nod of his head.

It was the oddest game Steadman had ever seen. It

appeared to be based loosely on one he had played with his son, Ben, some years ago, called 'Whack the Mole', a simple game in which molehills randomly popped up on a large green table, the aim being to whack them with a big mallet before they disappeared back into the table top. Chained to the front of Maurice's game was the same oversized rubber mallet. However, the table appeared to be covered not in green but with a giant sheet of writing paper.

'What is this, Maurice?' Steadman asked.

'Simple – it's called 'Whack the Alias'. Have you got a fifty pence piece on you?'

Steadman fumbled in his pocket and handed Maurice the coin.

Suddenly the machine sprang into life. Lights flashed and music played. Steadman recognised the tune: Peer Gynt's 'In the Hall of the Mountain King'.

'Here, I'll show you,' said Maurice. He grasped the mallet. A bulge appeared on one of the lines with the name 'Dr Frank Rufus' written on it. Maurice whacked it with the mallet. A bell chimed and the words 'Home Office Pathologist' flashed up on the screen in front of them.

'Got it? It's dead easy! Go on – you have a go.'

Steadman took the mallet. Another bulge appeared. This time it was Sergeant Grimble's name that appeared. Steadman hit the bulge. The bell chimed again and 'Uncle Bertie' flashed up in front of him. The music was getting faster. Two bulges swelled up simultaneously. Steadman ignored the one that had DS Munro written on it, but whacked the one saying 'Crenshaw Tipley'. 'Richard Armstrong' blazed across the screen.

'That'll help you,' Maurice suggested.

More bulges kept appearing and disappearing. Steadman found it hard to keep up. He tried not to whack the names he knew. Up sprang Juliet Winterby's name, but all the machine said in response to Steadman's blow was 'Tipley's Housekeeper'.

Now there were two bulges, both with DS Munro's name on them. Steadman hit one and the screen read 'Scottish Bruiser'. Maurice sniggered.

The tune was reaching its crescendo. Feverishly Steadman scanned the bulges that were popping up and down. He hit one that said 'Dr Sam Griffiths'. The machine gave a wolf-whistle. Maurice nudged him in the ribs and gave him a salacious wink. Tim Warrender's name appeared. As he brought down the mallet Steadman noticed a bulge in the top left hand corner with Reg Butler's name. The machine chimed again and next to Tim Warrender's name the word 'VICTIM' flashed in bold, red letters. Steadman blanched, the mallet suspended in mid-air.

The music was reaching its final bars. He looked back down only to see Reg Butler's name disappear. He scanned the table top desperately. Three mounds appeared – Velda Meemes, DI Steadman and Gordon Greig. Without thinking he hit his own name. The bell chimed repeatedly and in large letters 'The Blind Detective' blazed before his eyes.

Too late, Steadman realised his folly. With one final blast of music the lights died and all the bulges disappeared.

'I want to play again,' he said.

'Nah! It's closing time,' Maurice replied, jangling his keys as he slipped through a door at the back of the arcade.

The boys playing on table football had already left. The fairground became disconcertingly silent as one by one the rides closed for the night. Maurice reappeared with a pushbike.

'I didn't know you cycled,' said Steadman.

'The old man won't let me have the van. Reckons I'm not to be trusted. Cycle everywhere, I do. Amazing what you can get up to on a bike, Inspector Steadman.' An unpleasant leer crept over Maurice's face. 'Know what I mean, inspector? All sorts of things.'

Steadman looked down at Maurice's bike. The frame was spattered with blood. Before he could say anything, Maurice Eeles jumped on the bike and pedalled off.

It was quite dark now except for the small lamps that marked the path out of the fairground. Steadman joined the revellers who were leaving. More people joined them until quite a throng was jostling and pushing to get out. From the corner of his eye he saw Maurice standing by his bike grinning malevolently.

'Hey! Maurice I want a word with you – come here,' Steadman shouted as he tried to push through the crowd. Someone was holding him back, tugging at his shoulder.

'Get off, leave me alone!'

Whoever it was, was not giving up easily. 'John, John – wake up, it's almost ten o'clock. I've brought you a coffee.'

It was as though a brightly coloured Christmas bauble had fallen from the tree and shattered. The crowd vanished, the noise stopped and all that was left in Steadman's mind were tiny fragments of images. Only one remained clear, a picture of Maurice Eeles standing by a bike waving, and that too was getting fainter.

'Have you been dreaming again?' Linda asked. 'You were shouting at one point.'

Steadman sat up in bed, struggling to recreate the dream. He could only recollect scraps – a silly fairground game, something about Tim Warrender being a 'victim', a blood-spattered bike.

Linda put the mug in his hand.

'Is it really ten o'clock?' he asked.

'Not quite, but almost. Mr Martindale has called along with a dog welfare officer and checked Robbie. The dog is fine.'

At the mention of his name Robbie dutifully came and planted a wet nose on the edge of Steadman's bed.

'I'll wait until you're dressed before I go. My dear husband Dominic, divine though he is in many ways, would struggle to find the fridge in our house without appropriate instructions. Shall I make you some toast?'

Steadman nodded, drained his coffee and slowly got up. He had laid out his clothes before falling asleep and dressed without mishap. The dream still haunted him. Suddenly he recalled a girl vomiting at his feet, then an image of an old woman feeding coins into a fruit machine, then a tall gangly man with keys and a money belt. Was it really Maurice Eeles? He had no idea what he looked like in real life, yet it was unmistakably his voice. 'Whack the Alias' - what a stupid game! And why didn't he whack the only two names he couldn't place? 'All nonsense,' he said to himself.

'Are you sure you'll be all right?' Linda asked as she handed him his toast.

'Quite sure. Thanks for everything.'

She gave him a quick hug and Robbie a pat. 'That's what a sister is for – I'm off.'

The silence was suffocating. Steadman switched on the radio and caught the tail end of a chat show. It didn't hold his attention. His mind kept turning over the events of the last few days. Could someone really have slashed Robbie deliberately? Very gently he reached down and stroked the dog. His long bony fingers caressed the wound: twenty staples. He counted them twice. The scar was as straight as a ruler. This was no accident, and he knew it.

'Damn them, Robbie, damn them all to hell. Let's go for a walk. We'll show them.' He ruffled the dog's neck and stood up.

The doorbell rang as he was fastening Robbie's harness. Steadman made his way down the corridor, lightly trailing a guiding hand along the wall. Robbie trooped behind him. Only for a moment did he have second thoughts about opening the door. He shrugged. What the hell difference would it make, he thought.

'Inspector John Steadman?' It was a harsh New York accent.

'Yes – who wants to know?'

The man standing in the doorway looked puzzled and ran one hand through his short spiky hair. In his other hand he held an ID card which he thrust forward. His eyes flicked from Steadman's face, impassive behind the dark glasses, to Robbie, who had just poked his nose through the door. Steadman reached down and grasped his harness. Clearly the newcomer didn't care much for dogs and took a step back.

'That's a guide dog!' he exclaimed. 'Jeez, you're blind. Christ – why does nobody tell me anything? We need to talk, but not out here.'

Steadman hesitated, then said, 'Wait there a moment.'

He turned and went back down the corridor. This time Robbie insisted on leading. By the kitchen door there was an intercom. Steadman traced his fingers up the wall until he found the button.

'*Buongiorno*, Mr Steadman. How may I help you? A nice cappuccino and some cake? Mamma's been baking again,' said Marco Lloyd.

'No thanks, Marco. I have an unknown visitor and could do with some company,' he replied.

Marco picked up immediately. 'I'll come now or... Sergeant Munro has just walked through the door...'

'Yes, send Alan up straight away – perfect.'

He released the button. The dog nuzzled his leg.

'What do you think, Robbie? Should we wait here or

would our mystery guest think we are being impolite?' Good grief, he thought, if I'm not careful I'll turn into Sergeant Grimble.

Already he could hear the thunderous pounding of DS Munro's feet racing up the stairs. Steadman moved cautiously back to the apartment door, arriving at the same time as DS Munro reached the landing.

'Good morning, sir.' Despite his size and effort, he was not in the least out of breath. 'Now, what have we here?' he said, plucking the ID card out of the stranger's hand.

'What the...! That's the property of the US Government.'

'Is it really? Calm down or you'll steam up your Ray Bans. I only need to find out who you are, then you can have it back.'

'Can we just step inside?' the man pleaded.

'I think we'd better, sir. He's some sort of US agent. Just a moment...'

DS Munro handed the man back his ID. As he was about to put it into his pocket, Munro flicked the man's arms up in the air and patted his jacket, none too gently.

'Oh dear, he's carrying a pea-shooter, sir. Do you want me to relieve him of it?'

Before Steadman could reply, the American butted in.

'Look, big guy, it's not even loaded. I wear it out of habit, I guess.'

'We Brits are allergic to guns, Inspector Steadman in particular. They're the reason he's blind.'

'I didn't know,' the American stammered.

'I think we'd better move indoors,' Steadman said.

He led the way and flopped down into his favourite armchair, Robbie spreadeagled at his feet.

'Please take a seat, only don't move any of the furniture.'

The American glanced round the room. It was sparsely furnished – no photos, no books and most apparent, no television. His own living room was dominated by an enormous flat screen.

'I'm sorry about the confusion. I'm Arnie Yateman. I work for the US Government.' He held out a hand to Steadman. Realising the futility of his gesture, he continued, 'I keep forgetting that you're blind...'

To cover the man's embarrassment, Munro grasped his hand in his shovel-like mitt and gave it a vigorous shake.

'I'm DS Alan Munro. And just to show there's no hard feelings, here's my ID.'

'Great, two birds with one stone. You were next on my list.'

'As long as it's not a hit list, Arnie. I'm still not happy about that gun. Let's be clear, my wee man, if you make one move for it, I'll pull your head off.'

Arnie Yateman glanced at Munro's massive hands. 'I guess you probably could,' he replied.

Steadman broke the awkward silence. 'Alan, would you order us all coffee?'

'And some cake?' Munro replied hopefully.

'If you like. Now, Agent Yateman, I am sure you didn't come here to have coffee or have your head pulled off.'

Munro blushed. 'I assume you want to talk about Richard Armstrong.'

The American squirmed in his seat. He took a large breath. Clearly what he was about to say had been well rehearsed.

'I'm here informally, if you like. It has come to our government's attention that enquiries have been made about a certain gentleman who may or may not have been working for us some years ago. I am here to request that all further investigations in this area cease.'

Munro scratched his head and pulled a face. He disliked pussy-footing talk.

'You mean Richard Armstrong, also known as Crenshaw Tipley now deceased, was working as a US spy?'

'I am not at liberty to confirm the person's name or occupation.'

'What a load of bollocks!' Munro retorted.

Steadman raised a hand.

'You do realise that we are investigating a murder – two murders, in fact. So far they appear motiveless. I'm sure you can understand our interest in Crenshaw Tipley's veiled past.'

'We do not believe, if we are talking about the same man, that the two are in any way related. Further enquiries will only jeopardise security.'

'Yours or ours, Arnie?' Munro asked pointedly.

Steadman could sense his colleague's irritation. Fortunately, Marco arrived with the coffee and cake.

'What would happen, Arnie, if we simply ignored your informal request?' Munro asked between mouthfuls of cake, adding, 'Blimey this is good, you should have a piece.'

The American waved the cake away.

'Let's say the informal request would become a formal demand. My government would talk to your government. Your Home Secretary would start talking to your police chief or whoever and so on down the line until you are summoned and told, in no uncertain terms, to cease the investigation. I would guess that you would be taken off the case, and when it became known that you didn't play ball with us from the outset, you might find yourself on permanent traffic duty or similar.'

'You reckon you have the authority?' Munro asked.

'Not me, my friend. I'm only a tiny cog in the machinery – the messenger. However, I do know how the system works, trust me.'

Munro was about to argue, but Steadman interrupted him.

'I think it is likely that Crenshaw Tipley's former life is irrelevant, but we can't ignore it. We are also investigating a second murder, undoubtedly committed by the same person. The lead investigating officer is DS Fiona Fairfax. I don't know if she is on your list.'

Arnie Yateman shook his head. Steadman took his silence as a no.

'I believe that DS Fairfax and DS Munro would be more willing to play ball, as you put it, if we could be reassured that the second victim, Velda Meemes, had no connection with the US Government.'

'If you give me details I can check.'

'Is that acceptable, Alan?'

DS Munro took out a notepad which looked ridiculously small in his enormous hands and scribbled down Velda Meemes' details.

'Today is Sunday,' Steadman said. 'Alan, if you are agreeable, let us say we will make no further enquiries regarding Richard Armstrong until Wednesday morning. That gives you two full days, even allowing for the time difference, to confirm Velda Meemes' status. If you do not confirm within that time, we will make our own decision as to how we proceed. In fact, we will make our own decision anyway exactly as the police force in your country would do if the situation were reversed. I would doubt if anyone, even the Prime Minister, would consider putting Sergeant Munro on perpetual traffic duty.'

Munro beamed at his old boss's defiance.

'I'll see what I can do, gentlemen,' Arnie replied without much enthusiasm. 'Don't say you haven't been warned, that's all.'

Munro escorted the American to the door.

'I wouldn't have really pulled your head off,' he said reassuringly, 'just broken your arm.'

Arnie Yateman was not reassured.

'What a prat!' Munro exclaimed as helped himself to a second piece of cake.

'He's only doing his job. At least we now know who

Crenshaw Tipley was without having to dig further. More to the point, what have you been up to?'

'I've been to see young Tim Warrender. And thereby hangs another tale.'

CHAPTER TEN

Steadman scratched his head and frowned. He had not forgotten about the tragedy at the railway station, or that the boy had been Tim's best friend.

'Did you get the post-mortem report on the young lad? Do we know his name?' Steadman asked.

'Yes. He's called George Bremner. Dr Rufus left the report with the duty sergeant at some ungodly hour of the morning. I did try phoning to thank him but he's not answering.'

'No. I think I know where he has gone to.' Steadman ran his fingers through his hair. 'Despite his gruff exterior, Dr Rufus has an Achilles' heel. He always gets very distressed about anything to do with children. I remember some years ago investigating a suspicious house fire in which three children died. I knew he was upset so I called on him as he was finishing the last post-mortem. I offered to take him home with me but he said he was off to the hills. I had a day's leave and suggested that I went with him. He didn't say anything; in fact, I wasn't sure he had even heard me. Well, I raced home, grabbed some things and met him as he was about to leave. He hardly acknowledged my presence as I clambered into his car. It was barely seven in the morning and he had been working all night, yet he didn't appear tired.

'I tried making conversation. After twenty minutes of a monologue, I gave up. I had no idea where we were going. We got on to the motorway and headed west. Before the Severn Bridge I forced him to pull into the services. He didn't want anything; in fact, he never even switched the engine off. We drove on through Wales into the heart of Snowdonia until we arrived at a remote farmhouse. Either they were expecting him or they were used to him turning up unannounced. The old lady's only comment was, "I see you've brought a friend, I'll make up the other room." I had just managed to change into walking boots when we were off. The old lady, Mrs Lewis I believe she was called, thrust some sandwiches and a flask into my hand. "Make sure he eats something."

'We walked without a halt for twelve hours, uphill and down dale as they say, through marshes and across streams. At one point the rain was torrential, but he never stopped, never spoke, never even checked if I was keeping up. I reckoned I was fit back then, but Frank had the measure of me.'

Steadman paused, and DS Munro could tell by the look on his face that he was vividly recalling the escapade.

'Eventually we arrived back at the farmhouse,' Steadman continued. 'Mrs Lewis had prepared a huge meal. Frank ate for both of us, then sloped off to bed. He was up before me the following morning and tucking into a hearty breakfast when I entered the dining room. He looked up, dropped his cutlery and said, "Good God, John, what are you doing here?" Now although he has no recollection of our journey or of our tramp in the mountains, if you ask him he will recall every detail of the children found in the fire. It's as though he stores the information in a box and only opens the lid when necessary. Yet every detail is still there. It's his way of coping, I guess. So if you really want to speak with him, I think that's where you'll find him – somewhere up a Welsh mountain.'

DS Munro didn't answer straight away. He had never really thought much about the actual business of doing a post-mortem. He just received the report, scanned the text, read the conclusion and that was that. Of course it was far more complicated. Someone, in this case Dr Rufus, had to open up the body with a large knife, examine all the organs one by one, weigh them and goodness knows what else. Even the brain, except that in this instance there was not much of George Bremner's brain left as he had dived straight into the path of an oncoming freight train. The buffer had clipped the side of his skull. Death, at least, had been immediate.

'No, I don't need to speak with him,' DS Munro replied at last. He relayed the gist of the report to his colleague. Steadman could picture the scene all too clearly.

'We are definite that it was suicide?' he asked.

'The CCTV footage couldn't be clearer. He came to the station by himself, walked down to the end of the platform and took a running jump as the train came into the station.'

Steadman was not happy. 'Have we any idea…?'

'Apparently not, sir. Nice happy lad, good pupil, popular with his mates, not into drugs, sex or rock 'n' roll. Very good at art – took his work very seriously by all accounts. There was, however, some trouble at school yesterday.'

'Does Tim know what it was about?'

'I think so, but he's not saying much. Poor boy was lying in bed, fully clothed with his hoodie pulled over his face when I saw him. All he wanted to talk about was Robbie and whether he was OK. I think maybe if the two of you went round…'

Steadman thought for a moment. At the mention of his name, Robbie had stood up, keen to be working.

'Yes, I suppose I could go, but I am not that good with children and it wouldn't be by the book. Could we find out who the family liaison officer is?'

'Grimble will know,' Munro replied.

Of course Sergeant Grimble knew. 'WPC Rosie Jennings is back from sick leave and has taken on that role for the meantime,' he responded. 'I've got her number here.'

It took Steadman several minutes to pluck up the courage to call her. He remembered only too well that awful night: Rosie driving like a woman possessed, desperately trying to shake off an armed man on a motorbike. A man who had killed Steadman's wife and robbed him of his sight. A man who was intent on finishing the job properly but who at the last moment had shot Rosie in the shoulder instead. Steadman's guilt was enormous, and nothing that either Rosie or her parents said eased his shame. Still, she was back working; that was something to be thankful for.

Rosie was expecting the phone call. Sergeant Grimble had already forewarned her. He was like the oil in the machinery; imperceptible, but vital for the smooth operation of the force.

'I'll phone Tim's parents to make sure they are happy for us to call this morning,' said Steadman. 'I can't see any problems. Would you be able to meet me here in about twenty minutes? Then we can walk round – it's not far. And you can meet Robbie.'

'If Sergeant Grimble is to be believed, that dog makes you breakfast in bed each morning!' Rosie replied.

'I'll be off then, sir,' said Munro. 'I promised Maureen and the girls I would go swimming with them today. Let me know how you get on.' He gave Robbie a friendly pat and left.

Steadman sat down at his piano. Bach – always Bach when he had to think. The music flowed and his thoughts drifted. He recalled his grandfather once taking a television set apart and realising, only too late, that he had forgotten to label where each of the valves and other components had come from. Was it really that similar? It was possible to put all the parts together to make a working television. Indeed, his grandfather had done so, eventually. But looking at all the parts of this case laid out before him in his mind, it was difficult to see where any two fitted, let alone to make something complete.

His fingers glided up and down the keyboard; notes formed chords and melodies, the chords split apart and the melodies subtly shifted. At each key change, pause or twist and turn Steadman arranged and rearranged the pieces of information. Two murders clearly related, but how and why? Tim Warrender pursued, an attack on his dog, a ghastly suicide – no, it was all too much, just coincidences. But he hated coincidences.

And then two things struck him. Firstly, the time frame: all of these events had happened in such a short space of time – a few days, less than a week. They were linked in time, if nothing else. But there was another link – himself. He had been asked to help investigate the two murders. It was his dog. Tim was tied to him and now Tim's best friend... And somebody had taken a photo of him in the street before speeding off. At least his grandfather knew he was building a television. Apart from Dr Sam Griffiths' forensic profile, he had little to go on.

The doorbell rang, saving him from any further thoughts about Dr Sam Griffiths.

* * *

Rosie Jennings had changed. If Steadman could have seen,

he would have noticed that she looked much older and more weary. Her left hand now hung at a slightly awkward angle and when she walked her shoulder was held rigid. Her voice, however, remained bright and cheerful.

'You're looking well, sir.'

'You mean I've put on weight. Little wonder with Mamma Lloyd's cooking, but thank you. You sound well – how's the arm?'

'Shoulder's a bit stiff. Not much pain now. I can do most things.' Rosie knew how Steadman felt about the shooting and was determined to play it light.

'You're obviously driving again.'

'Yes – an automatic. It encourages my laziness, not that it needed any encouragement.'

'I doubt that. Come and meet the dog.' Robbie didn't have his harness on and was quite happy to be fussed over.

'How do you like your new job? I've always thought that being a family liaison officer would be one of the worst jobs in the force – child abuse, juvenile crime and now this. All grief and no glamour. And pretty isolating, I would imagine.'

'It's not easy, sir, but at least I have a job. With Dad being a vicar I've seen my share of human suffering. I think I can handle the emotional side better than most.'

'How are George Bremner's parents?' Steadman asked.

'Completely wrecked, sir, as you would expect. Both desperately looking for answers.'

Rosie had no need to elaborate. Steadman could well imagine the gruelling hours she had put in – the tears, the anger, the incomprehensibility, and this morning the visit to the mortuary.

'Tim Warrender was his best friend at school. Tim walks Robbie for me twice a day. Sergeant Grimble has no doubt told you that Robbie was slashed with a knife last night. He's fine. Apparently saved by his shaggy coat. Tim has taken a shine to Alan Munro, who popped round to see him this morning. Well, there was an incident at school yesterday involving George Bremner, and Tim knows something about it. However, all he wanted to talk about with Alan was Robbie. If you're agreeable, I thought we could walk round together. Once he's seen that the dog is all right maybe you'll be able to get him to talk about what happened at school. My forte is hardened criminals, not distressed adolescents.'

'Sounds good to me, sir. You'll need to wrap up warm. It's bitingly cold and the fog is still down.'

Linda had put his coat and hat back in their rightful places. She had even laid out a new scarf.

'What colour is this, Rosie?' Steadman asked, holding up the scarf.

'Dark green and blue, sir. It will go with your hat.'

'One of the many curses of being blind. I would hate to look any more ridiculous than I do already.'

An image flashed into Rosie's mind of a dashing, younger Steadman, always impeccably turned out. In that image his eyes, now concealed behind his dark glasses, were twinkling.

They walked down the stairs. Rosie opened the door onto the street; the damp chilly air caught in Steadman's throat and he gave an involuntary shudder.

'Robbie always walks on my left. Can you take my right arm or would that be uncomfortable?'

'Only one way to find out, sir.'

That was so typical of Rosie Jennings's attitude, thought Steadman; never give in, no matter how great the adversity. It made him feel even more guilty about the shooting.

It was only a ten-minute walk, even at Steadman's pace, to Tim's house.

'I can't get him out of bed, let alone eat anything,' his mother said. 'Maybe if you had a cup of tea and a biscuit he would join you. His room's upstairs – excuse the mess.'

Steadman stood in the hallway, completely lost.

'You'll have to guide me, Rosie,' he said quietly, 'I've not been here before.'

He slipped off Robbie's harness and the dog made a beeline for Tim's room.

'I think you would have been better with the dog than me, sir. He seems to know where he's going.'

They manoeuvred the stairs after a fashion and Rosie gently knocked on the open door. Tim's room mirrored his own troubled stage of life. Cartoon character wallpaper now had posters of football teams and rock bands plastered all over it. There was even a raunchy picture of a scantily-dressed lady that almost certainly would not have met with his mother's approval. Clothes and books lay in a jumble on the floor. More clothes poked out of half-shut drawers. All this was lost on Steadman. All he was aware of was a stale atmosphere and the pervasive aroma of adolescent socks.

Tim barely acknowledged the two officers' presence. He was too busy playing with Robbie.

Suddenly he turned to Steadman. 'Why would somebody do that to a guide dog?'

It was clear even to Tim's untrained eye that this was no accident.

'I have really no idea, unless to get at me,' Steadman replied.

'A warning, you mean?'

'A warning, or a challenge. It's impossible to say. Whoever it was didn't want to kill the dog, otherwise why not just stab the animal? Then again it takes a particularly nasty sort of person to deliberately hurt an animal... I'm sorry, Tim, this is Rosie Jennings. She's the family liaison officer working with George Bremner's family.'

Before Rosie could say anything, Tim's mother bustled in with a tray.

'Where's your manners? Clear a couple of chairs while I put the tray on the end of your bed.'

Once they were settled with their mugs of tea, Tim's mother left. 'Shout if there is anything you need.'

'I gather you might fancy becoming a detective yourself, Tim,' Rosie suggested.

'Might do,' Tim replied hesitantly.

'Well, I'm trying to help George's parents come to terms with what happened. I'm not here to blame anybody, but it might make some sense if I knew what happened at school yesterday. Now, I know it won't be easy for you and I'm not going to force you to say anything if you don't want to, and I certainly don't want you to make anything up.'

'Why would I do that?'

'Because you might think it's what I want to hear or you might want to protect someone.'

Tim turned a pleading eye to DI Steadman. As he got no response Rosie intervened

'What do you think, sir?'

'Tim has already proved himself to be a reliable witness. He was pursued in the park the other night and was able to give me as detailed an account as a fully trained police officer. I'm sure if Tim can help, he will.'

Tim blushed bright crimson. He never looked up, just continued stroking the knobbly crown of Robbie's head between his ears.

'It all started in the art class,' he began. 'Mr Haribin's been ratty all week, making us write essays about other artists – never letting us do any real art work. He says it will improve our creative flow, whatever that is. Anyway, GB, that's what we call George Bremner, GB had a moan and said something like, how will he ever become a great artist if he isn't allowed to draw? And Mr Haribin says he's never going to be great because he hasn't got enough talent, which is really unfair because GB is amazing. I'll show you.' He paused and scrambled under his bed, emerging with a picture and holding it up for Rosie to see.

'Wow, that's incredible! Go on, Tim.'

'Well, GB was having none of it, so he says to Mr Haribin, "You're only saying that because your drawings are shit…" Sorry, but he swore, "…your drawings are shit compared to mine." Mr Haribin was furious and told him to repeat that. So he did! The next thing he gets hold of GB and says, "Let's see if you'll repeat that in front of your head of year", and he marches him out of the classroom. Mr Skinner's our head of year. He teaches drama but he doesn't get on with Mr Haribin. They've both applied for the deputy head post. Mr Skinner's really cool – he makes amazing stage sets and stuff. Anyway, GB is my best friend and I didn't like the way things were looking so I followed them. I couldn't go into Mr Skinner's room so I listened at the door. GB repeated what he said and Mr Skinner said it was wrong to swear at a teacher. GB said he wasn't swearing at a teacher, just describing his work. Mr Skinner said he shouldn't criticise another artist and GB said Mr Haribin had started it by saying he would never be great. Mr Haribin denied it, which was a lie, and Mr Skinner said GB had to apologise. GB refused twice then shouted, "I'd rather kill myself than apologise to him." The door burst open and GB ran out, then he shouted over his shoulder, "I mean it, I'd rather kill myself than apologise." Mr Haribin and Mr Skinner had a terrible row afterwards. Mr Haribin said he would leave the school if Mr Skinner got made deputy head. Mr Skinner said that Mr Haribin had better start looking for another job as there was no way he was going to get it. I sneaked back to the classroom as the bell was about go.' Tim paused to catch his breath.

The images in Steadman's mind were vivid and disturbing. He could almost see George stifling back the tears and the two adults behaving no better than two children.

'Did anyone else hear what George said?' Rosie asked.

'Mr Wilkes, the RE teacher, was in the corridor with two of the sixth form girls, Wendy and Julie I think they're called. They surely heard everything.'

'Did you see George again?'

'No. He must have got back to class because his jacket and bag were gone. I never saw him again.'

'And what about in the next class?'

'There wasn't a next class. That was the last lesson of the day.'

'Are you sure that's what George said?'

'Sure I'm sure. I don't tell lies, do I, Inspector Steadman?' There was a waver in his voice; it was all becoming too much for him.

'No Tim, you don't tell lies,' Steadman replied soothingly. 'And before you ask me, there was nothing you could have done to prevent the tragedy. George walked straight to the railway station and jumped in front of a train. He was killed instantly. I'm so sorry.' Steadman was aware of Tim stifling a sob.

'I can still hear him, Inspector Steadman – "I'd rather kill myself than apologise to him."'

* * *

Rosie linked arms with John Steadman and they walked slowly back to his apartment.

'Poor lad, I doubt he'll still want to be a policeman,' Rosie remarked.

'I don't know. He's observant, with excellent recall. I bet he was playing at being a detective when he followed George out the classroom.'

'The two teachers don't come out in a good light, sir. Bickering and squabbling in front of a pupil – not very professional.'

'I agree, and they didn't pick up on George's distress. I doubt if either of them will get the coveted deputy head post. They may not even keep their present jobs.'

'I'm speaking with the headmaster tomorrow. Then I'll interview the two of them and see if I can corroborate Tim's version of events. He'll have to give evidence at the inquest. That will be tough for him.'

Steadman didn't reply. Something was niggling him, an undercurrent - a fragment of speech perhaps? Two events that seemed unrelated had briefly fitted together, but they were stuck in his subconscious. A passing flicker that had come and gone so quickly that he had missed it. He knew if he tried to catch it again it would elude him. All he could hope for was that it would return, sooner rather than later.

'Are you OK, sir?'

'Sorry Rosie, lost in my own thoughts. Let me know how you get on at the school. I hope Skinner and Haribin aren't stupid enough to cook something up between them. If they're honest, maybe…'

'I doubt I'll be able to keep Tim out of it, sir, if that's what you're implying.'

An image of a preposterous fairground game came into Steadman's thoughts. The word 'VICTIM' was flashing in bright red lights next to Tim Warrender's name.

'No, you're probably right, Rosie. I just hope… well, we'll have to wait and see.'

CHAPTER ELEVEN

The room had become too warm. It smelled of damp clothes and wet dog. There was a distinct uneasiness in the air.

Dr Rufus had called for John Steadman earlier that morning and the two men had walked to the Eyesore together in the fog.

'Well, it could have been worse,' Dr Rufus had said on the way to the meeting. 'On second thoughts, no it couldn't. DI Beaky Nesbitt standing in for DCI Long – I can't believe it.' He shook his head sadly. 'You don't know him, do you?'

Steadman confessed that the name was only vaguely familiar. DI Nesbitt worked for a neighbouring force.

'I've had dealings with him and he is the most arrogant, pig-headed detective I've come across. Jumps to conclusions and hates being challenged. You won't like him, or at least he won't like you. Nobody must steal his thunder or be in the limelight other than him. A blind detective and contender for Helmsmouth Citizen of the

Year – no, he definitely won't take to you. He doesn't like women either. You'll see – he will side-line DS Fairfax at the first opportunity and ignore Kim Ho.'

'What about Dr Griffiths?'

'Very formal, aren't we today? Now that might be fun. She's used to working with the lads in the Met. I doubt if she'll let him get away with much. It will be interesting to see if the sparks fly.' There was a hint of glee in Dr Rufus's voice.

'Why Beaky? That's not his name, surely?'

'No, no – Walter is his first name. When they were handing out big, ugly noses he was well up in the queue – he may even have been first. I expect you'll want to know what he looks like.'

Steadman did, but what he really wanted to know was what Dr Griffiths looked like. He dared not ask; he knew his friend would only tease him. Steadman nodded and mentally got out a blank sheet of paper.

'He's a short-arse for one thing, but you wouldn't notice,' said Rufus. 'He struts round with his chest stuck out and his chin poked in the air like a cockerel, or a small boy spoiling for a fight. It's a wonder he can see over that enormous hooter of his. His constant pugnacious attitude endears him to no one. I bet they were keen to get rid of him for a bit. Oh, he also has a habit of twitching the side of his top lip. I don't know if it's a tic or an affectation. Whatever it is, he always looks scornful, or as though that outsized nose of his has detected an unpleasant odour.'

As he sat in the meeting room, Steadman ran over Dr

Rufus's description again in his head. Well, he'll be right about one thing, he thought, ruffling his fingers through Robbie's moist and decidedly pungent coat.

The door was pushed open and a quarrelsome-looking man marched in with over-large strides. He was closely followed by a very disgruntled Sergeant Grimble. The latter was about to say something, but Beaky Nesbitt shooed him away with the back of his hand.

'I'll take over from here, Sergeant,' said Nesbitt.

Did Grimble make a decidedly rude gesture as he headed for the door? DS Munro certainly thought so.

Nesbitt cast a theatrically wary eye round the room before hoisting himself onto the desk. He sat there for a moment relishing the silence, swinging his short legs back and forth.

'Good grief,' Dr Rufus whispered to Steadman, 'he's wearing two-tone brogues!'

'Right then, I'm Nesbitt. I will be your DCI since Long has taken an unexpected jolly.'

There was a stony silence broken only by some shuffling of feet.

'A cracking start, don't you think?' whispered Dr Rufus. Steadman didn't respond. Nesbitt gave the Home Office pathologist a withering look. Dr Rufus smiled innocently at him.

'Rufus, I know,' he continued without any warmth. 'Who's the chap on your right in the dark glasses?' He nodded in Steadman's direction. 'Are the lights a bit bright in here for you, sonny?'

As though sensing something was amiss, Robbie got up and settled himself a bit closer to Steadman's feet.

'Christ! Is that a guide dog? Are you blind?' Nesbitt spluttered.

'Ten out of ten, Beaky! No wonder they've made you an acting DCI. Don't tell me you've never heard of DI John Steadman. Well, he's here at DCI Long's request, and with the blessing of the Chief Constable, no less. Sighted or not, he has the finest analytical mind I've ever worked with,' Dr Rufus retorted

Steadman turned to where he thought Inspector Nesbitt was sitting.

'If my presence here is an embarrassment to you, I am quite willing to leave,' he said.

Nesbitt ignored him and rallied on the Home Office pathologist. 'It's DCI Nesbitt to you, Rufus.'

'And it's *Doctor* Rufus to you. You'll get respect from me when you've earned it, not before.'

The two men stared at one another. Everyone else in the room felt awkward except for DC Lofthouse, who was thoroughly enjoying the verbal exchanges.

The introductions continued round the room. Nesbitt passed briefly over DS Fairfax, but asked DS Munro a few questions. Clearly Alan Munro was what Nesbitt thought a proper detective should look like.

Throughout all of this Steadman was aware of an annoying squeaking noise that he could not place. Try as he might, it was impossible to ignore.

Nesbitt frowned at Kim Ho and reluctantly accepted a

hard copy of Dr Sam Griffiths' psychological profile. 'I'll read it after the arrest and see how close to the mark you were, dearie,' he said. The tone could not have been more patronising.

'What a waste of taxpayer's money!' Dr Griffiths exclaimed.

'I couldn't agree more,' Nesbitt said tapping the report.

'I was not referring to my involvement,' Dr Griffiths replied.

'One nil to Sam Griffiths,' whispered Dr Rufus.

The introductions were over.

'Who's the lead investigating officer for Crenshaw Tipley's murder?' asked Nesbitt.

'I am, sir,' said DS Munro.

'Well, laddie, let's have it.' Beaky Nesbitt's lip twitched.

Munro outlined the scenario succinctly. 'Dr Rufus can give you a better account of the pathology than I can, sir,' he concluded.

'I can always read it later if I have to. Sounds like Tipley was a right unlovable bastard,' Nesbitt concluded.

'Takes one to know one,' muttered Dr Rufus.

'Are you leading on the Meemes case as well?'

'No, I am, sir,' replied DS Fairfax.

'Oh,' Nesbit said with some disappointment. His lip twitched again.

Fiona Fairfax's résumé was as good as that of Alan Munro. Despite this, Nesbitt interrupted and challenged her repeatedly and unnecessarily.

'So, two people killed and strung up. What bizarre, sick

people you have living in Helmsmouth. And clearly you haven't found the culprit yet. What links the two of them?'

DS Munro answered. 'We have several possible leads, sir. Tipley's housekeeper, Juliet Winterby, is also Velda Meemes' niece. She is a dry old stick and not very pleasant with it. She used to sow mattresses and it is possible that the murder weapon in the Tipley case was an upholsterer's needle.'

'Well, why haven't you arrested her?'

Dr Rufus nudged Steadman. 'Typical - what did I tell you?'

'DI Steadman and I have interviewed her. Other than spite, she has no motive. Tipley was worth more to her alive than dead. She did not strike us as a murderer.'

'Maybe I should interview her properly myself.'

Alan Munro turned scarlet, but wisely he remained silent.

It wasn't only Nesbitt's attitude that Steadman found irritating; the persistent unexplained squeaking was getting on his nerves.

'There are a couple of other unusual things, sir,' Will Lofthouse ventured.

'Speak up then, laddie.'

'I'm sorry, sir, can't you hear me?' Lofthouse replied in all innocence.

'I can hear you perfectly well.

'Oh, it's just that you said... never mind.'

Oblivious to Nesbitt's outraged gaze, Will Lofthouse recounted the details of the borrowed book, the set-aside

Buddha and the spurious aliases. Again a light pinged on in Steadman's brain. Where had he heard these names before?

'And that gets us precisely where?' asked Nesbitt. 'I'll bet there's not a person in this room who hasn't used a bogus name at some time or another to book a table or reserve tickets if there's a chance you're not going to show up.'

I haven't, thought Steadman, and I doubt if anyone else here has either.

'I repeat, where does that get us?'

'I'm not sure, sir, but you've got to admit it's interesting,' Lofthouse suggested.

'Talking of aliases, sir, it appears that Crenshaw Tipley started out life as Richard Armstrong,' Munro added.

'Why didn't you mention this before?'

Poor Munro was vermilion. 'It is a wee bit awkward, sir. We think he was working for American intelligence. I've been unofficially requested to back off.'

'Who by?'

'A US Government agent.' Munro thought it best not to mention Steadman's involvement. 'I have asked if they would check if Velda Meemes is known to them. I'm waiting for a reply. If Tipley has worked for the US, it was a long time ago and it doesn't seem likely that it is relevant.'

'I'll be the judge of that. Did this agent say anything else?'

'Yes. Basically, if I didn't desist from my enquiries,

official representations would be made to the UK Government and there would be hell to pay at a local level.'

Nesbitt sensed trouble and backed off immediately. 'I agree – not relevant, move on.'

'One other person is common to both crimes, sir.'

Nesbitt stared derisively at DS Fairfax.

'Yes?'

'Both victims have had electrical work done recently by the same electrician.'

'And the wire used in both murders is definitely stripped-down electric cable,' Kim Ho added.

'What the hell other type of wire is there?' Nesbitt said dismissively. Kim Ho started to answer, but he interrupted her. 'I want to know about this electrician.'

'He is called Harry Eeles and he has a string of convictions for burglary. He has just done a three-year stretch for GBH.'

'Are you lot telling me that you have two murders where the victims were wired up with electrical cable, that a known violent offender has been working in both houses and you haven't arrested him? It's as obvious as...'

'The nose on your face,' Dr Rufus said under his breath, but loud enough for Nesbitt to hear. He glared at the Home Office pathologist.

'He has been questioned, sir' said DS Fairfax.

'Oh, by you?'

'No, sir. He refused to speak to anyone except DI Steadman.'

'So he hasn't been interviewed by a proper police officer.'

Steadman could sense Dr Rufus's outrage. He stretched out, grasped his colleague's arm and shook his head.

'DS Fairfax was present throughout the interview, Inspector Nesbitt. I have known Harry Eeles for many years. Our paths have crossed on numerous occasions.'

Nesbitt's top lip curled. 'You've gone soft on him.'

'On the contrary,' Steadman replied, 'I have been the officer responsible for his two most recent convictions. My investigation led to him spending the last three years behind bars. No, I wouldn't say I had gone soft on him. I would suggest, however, that I know him better than any other officer in the force. These crimes are not Harry's style.'

'People change,' Nesbitt retorted.

'Yes, he's now a qualified electrician,' said Dr Rufus.

Nesbitt ignored him. 'Once a criminal, always a criminal, I say. Learnt more than how to wire a plug in the nick, I'll wager. Criminals like him should never be let out.'

So much for offender rehabilitation, thought Steadman. He never could stand a policeman who wanted to be judge, jury and executioner. Dr Rufus was right; he was not going to like acting DCI Beaky Nesbitt. And that damned squeaking was incessant.

'Who, in this place, is responsible for arranging an interview with the press?'

'Sergeant Grimble would be your best bet, sir,' Munro suggested.

'The fat, old fool behind the desk? I suppose he's got to be good for something. Leave that with me.' His lip twitched and he stuck his chin in the air. 'Right, I want Harry Eeles arrested and brought in. Fairfax, that's your job. I'll ask my friend Eric Crouchley to provide some uniformed muscle.'

Steadman pursed his lips. He had never known anyone admit to being a friend of Inspector Crouchley; he didn't think it was possible. He tried to imagine the looks on the faces of the people in the room and what they would be thinking. Would Dr Rufus be staring at the ceiling? Probably, and trying to will a chunk of it to fall down on Nesbitt's head. Alan Munro would be red-faced and tight-lipped, clenching and unclenching his huge hands. DS Fairfax would undoubtedly be gazing impassively into the distance and, as always, displaying little emotion. Will Lofthouse would have a dreamy, far-away look in his eyes. He would, as likely as not, find Nesbitt's antics quite entertaining, or possibly he was thinking about some woman or other. Lofthouse spent a lot of time thinking about women. And what about Kim Ho? She was nervous at the best of times. She had been publicly humiliated. Steadman imagined she would be looking at the floor, possibly even holding back a tear. And lastly there was Dr Sam Griffiths. Of course, he had no idea what she looked like, but had decided that she must have dark hair and brown eyes for no other reason than it seemed to go with her voice. At least she had stood up to Nesbitt. No, he thought, he would not like to get on the wrong side of Dr Sam Griffiths. Perhaps he would like to…

Damn, he had lost his concentration. A heavy thump brought him back to earth as Nesbitt slid awkwardly off the desk. Thank goodness the infernal squeaking had stopped.

'That's settled, gentlemen,' he said. Dr Griffiths cleared her throat loudly. 'Oh… and ladies,' added Nesbitt dismissively. 'DS Fairfax will make the arrest and bring Harry Eeles here for questioning by me. I will arrange a formal press release. That's that – any questions?'

The room was silent. Steadman raised a hand.

'You have a question?' said Nesbitt.

As no one else answered, Steadman assumed the remark was directed at him.

'Not a question, Inspector Nesbitt, an observation. You are making a big mistake. Harry Eeles murdered neither Crenshaw Tipley nor Velda Meemes, of that I am certain.'

Nesbitt started to say something, but Steadman was not to be interrupted. It was clear where the authority lay.

'I have the advantage over you of knowing Harry Eeles. As I said earlier, I have interviewed him for hours on end over the years. Harry is, or was, a thief with a vicious temper that spilled over into violence. However, his victims were all of the criminal fraternity – people who had come on to Harry's patch or tried to put one over on him. He has just finished a prison sentence for rearranging someone's face with a golf club. He never denied it. His defence was that his victim was a thug and a crook, and that he was doing society a favour by keeping him in his place. Naturally, the jury were not convinced and Harry went down. Interestingly, the subject of his assault was convicted for manslaughter, among other things, only four months later – a point that Harry made most strongly at his appeal. He is now well into middle age and apparently has a reasonably good business. I would happily let him re-wire my flat. I wouldn't leave my wallet lying around and I certainly wouldn't give him a dud cheque.

'From what I gather, these murders were premeditated and well-staged and nothing was taken at either location. That is not the Harry Eeles I know. And what about the whisky and the sparkling water that Kim Ho has so diligently identified? And the false names used to borrow a book and reserve an antique? And finally, apart from being male, Harry Eeles does not match Dr Griffiths' profile.'

It took a lot of self-control to stop Dr Rufus from clapping. All eyes turned from Steadman to Nesbitt.

His lip twitched. 'If you're quite finished. That's where you lot have been going wrong - overcomplicating things. What is clear to me is that we are dealing with two simple murders. Eeles may have learnt how to change a light bulb in the last three years, but I bet he's learnt all sorts of other nasty tricks like wiring up innocent people and defiling their bodies, probably in an attempt to confuse the police. Well, I can see right through him, something I'm afraid you can't.'

Dr Rufus was on his feet. 'That's a cheap jibe, even for you, Beaky!'

Nesbitt glowered at the Home Office pathologist.

'Leave it, Frank,' Steadman said in a soft voice. 'How does the proverb go? "There's none so blind as those who will not see." Time will tell which one of us is correct.'

'I know who my money's on,' Dr Rufus muttered as he regained his seat.

'Well, that's settled. I look forward to interviewing Harry Eeles after lunch.' Nesbitt stuck his chin in the air and strutted out.

There was an immediate buzz of angry conversation. Steadman put a finger to his lips and pointed to the door. It opened a crack. Nesbitt poked his head in. He had an odd expression on his face; a combination of smugness and hostility.

'I'll be in DCI Long's office, Fairfax,' he barked.

DC Lofthouse was standing near the door.

'He's gone this time,' he said after checking the corridor. 'How did you know he would be listening at the door, sir?'

Steadman raised an eyebrow. 'He stomped out of the room, but I didn't hear his footsteps in the corridor. Also, he struck me as exactly the sort of man who would listen at a door. I was half expecting it, to be honest.'

'Are you all right, John?' That really was an offensive remark.' It was Dr Griffiths. She had just called him 'John'. He was hard pushed not to smile and unable to prevent his cheeks from burning.

'You can only be truly offended by someone whose opinion you respect. I am not offended; disappointed maybe. I think it's going to make my future involvement awkward for him – I don't suppose Harry Eeles will give him the time of day.'

'I think I'll offer to sit in with Inspector Nesbitt,' Lofthouse said. 'It sounds like it might be quite entertaining.'

DS Munro looked at Will Lofthouse and shook his head. 'I worry about you sometimes, Will.'

★ ★ ★

The cold, damp air hit Steadman like a wet flannel as he and Dr Rufus stepped out of the Eyesore into the fog.

'Are you sure you've got time to walk back with me? I guess Robbie and I could manage by ourselves,' asked Steadman.

'No, you're fine. I need to cool down after that debacle anyway. What a pompous moron!'

'Tell me something, Frank – right the way through the meeting something was squeaking. Any idea what it was?

'It was Nesbitt's shoes. He sat on the desk swinging his little legs back and forth. Why would anyone in their right mind who wasn't a jazz singer wear two-tone brogues, do you think?

Steadman did not answer straight away and his friend wondered if he had heard him.

'If his nose really is as grotesque as you make it out to

be, I suspect he wears shoes like that as a visual distraction,' Steadman replied at last, although he was imagining a very different pair of shoes: a pair of black patent leather mules and a shapely ankle.

CHAPTER TWELVE

Helmsmouth Merchant Comprehensive School rose out of the mist like a scene from a Gothic horror film. It was an old sandstone Victorian pile that had fallen into disrepair before being taken over by the local council. Rosie Jennings parked her car in the bay marked for visitors. She looked at the gloomy building and wondered if 'Merchant' was the name of the founding philanthropist or his occupation. Doubtless there would be a plaque inside explaining it all in great detail.

She entered by a door that still had 'BOYS' carved over the lintel. The corridors were seething. In deference to its illustrious past the pupils all wore old-fashioned blazers and ties. She had arrived just as morning assembly was finishing. There should have been a lot of noise, high-pitched voices mingled with breaking and broken voices, giggles and shrieks, but today there was only a subdued silence.

For a moment or two Rosie stood there like a small island in a flowing river of humanity. Possibly because she was in uniform, she was neither jostled nor buffeted. She was looking for a sign to the headmaster's office but failed to see one.

A large youth with braid on his sleeves and a lapel badge proudly declaring he was a prefect materialised from the throng.

'May I help you?'

'I'm trying to find Mr Rotherhyde, the headmaster.'

'Follow me.'

He moved through the crowd like an Arctic icebreaker. Rosie followed in his wake. The mass of pupils thinned and disappeared as the classrooms filled. Only then did Rosie have a chance to take in the surroundings. Artwork hung on the walls. What was it with angsty teenagers, Rosie thought? Here they were on the brink of life, yet they all seemed to have a morbid preoccupation with death. They passed a large glass cabinet full of stuffed exotic birds and animals. They were dusty and looked sad. Out of the corner of her eye she noticed a small maggot crawl out of a fox's nose. She turned away in disgust.

'You'll have to get past the dragon first.' The prefect was now walking by her side.

'The dragon?'

'Yes, Mr Rotherhyde's secretary. Her name is Miss Smythe, although we all suspect it is really Smith and she changed it to make sound posh. Don't worry, she's usually benign on a Monday. It's only on a Friday that she breathes fire. Here we are.'

Rosie knocked on the heavy oak door.

'Enter,' a curt voice answered in a tone sounding more like a declaration of war than a welcome. A sour-faced woman with tightly curled hair and half-moon spectacles glanced up from the papers on her desk. She gave Rosie Jennings a disapproving look.

'Yes?'

'I have an appointment with Mr Rotherhyde at nine-thirty.'

Miss Smythe looked at her diary. 'There's nothing down here. Mr Rotherhyde is extremely busy. Can I take a message?' She closed the book and placed her mottled hand firmly on the cover, but not before Rosie had seen that today's page was entirely blank.

Their eyes met. Miss Smythe's stare was defiant. Rosie felt sorry for her. There's no point in you trying to protect him, she mused.

'I'm sure you know why I'm here. I spoke with Mr Rotherhyde briefly, at home, yesterday and he suggested that I come here this morning. I can wait if he's busy.'

Miss Smythe pursed her lips and gave a little snort. To Rosie's disappointment, there was neither smoke nor fire.

'I'll see if he's available.'

She tapped Mr Rotherhyde's door and slipped in. There was a brief muffled conversation and an indignant Miss Smythe returned.

'Mr Rotherhyde will see you now.' She glanced at her watch. Clearly there was going to be a time limit.

A cup of coffee would be nice, Rosie thought; she didn't dare ask.

In contrast to the secretary's pristine, starched-white office, that of Mr Rotherhyde's was in complete disarray. Files and folders were strewn across his desk, spilling on to the floor and lay in untidy heaps on the shelves. In amongst the folders were old yearbooks, sporting memorabilia and the odd trophy. Black and white photographs of cricket, hockey, rugby and netball teams covered most of the walls.

Mr Rotherhyde was much older than Rosie had expected. His white hair was sparse and his face care-worn and lined to the extent that his mouth had collapsed into a permanent frown. He had thick spectacles; one of the legs was held on with sticky tape. Even his suit and shoes had seen better days. He looked startled, as though a spectral apparition, and not a police officer, had walked into his study.

'Ah! Yes... Miss... Miss?'

'Jennings, Rosie Jennings. We spoke yesterday.'

'We did? We did, of course we did.' He held out a clammy hand. 'I wasn't expecting... you know...' He fluttered his fingers in Rosie's direction. 'The uniform. Don't want to draw attention, you see. A bit, how can I put it...' He spoke not in sentences but in short bursts, as though no one was listening.

'Manners, my manners – really! Please, do take a seat.' He cleared a chair by tipping its contents on to the floor.

It was evident that Mr Rotherhyde was incapable of speaking and physical activity at the same time. Rosie took advantage of the lull in conversation.

'I need to talk with you about George Bremner.'

'Ah yes, the boy Bremner. Tragic, sad… what is there to say?' he shuffled some documents on his desk. 'I could have been retired by now, you know.' He peered over the top of his glasses at Rosie. 'Yes, you mightn't think it, but I am seventy – well, a little over, to tell the truth.' He paused, expecting Rosie to comment, but was disappointed. In fact, Rosie had thought he must be at least eighty.

'George Bremner, sir. What can you tell me about him?'

'Not a lot. Can't be expected to know all the pupils – big school, you see. But I've managed it. All these years without a blemish or stain. And now this. Bound to reflect badly.' He was staring at the wall. 'Maybe I should have retired when I had the chance. Wouldn't have had to deal with all of this… bad business, really. But, and this is important…' He turned to peer over his glasses again at Rosie. 'It didn't happen on school premises. We must remember that.' He tapped his desk and looked almost triumphant.

The idea of slapping his face did occur to Rosie. She resisted.

'No, sir. It occurred in the railway station, not long after school finished. He was still in uniform.'

Mr Rotherhyde's face fell back into a frown.

'In uniform? Our uniform?' He groaned. 'I can just imagine our chair of governors… Difficult man, very difficult…'

'Mr Rotherhyde, there was an incident in the school

immediately beforehand. Apparently George had been rude to his art teacher and was taken to Mr Skinner, his head of year. He appears to have been very distressed by the whole thing.'

'I couldn't possibly comment. You know what children are like. Up one minute, down the next. I don't know who told you this nonsense. I wouldn't put too much store by it. Ignore it... yes, that's what I would do, ignore it.'

And hope it goes away, that's what you would like, Rosie said to herself.

'Mr Rotherhyde, I am liaising with George's family. I am simply trying to gather the facts in order to make some sense of what happened. Things cannot be ignored. I am told that the altercation was witnessed, or at least overhead, by another member of your staff and several pupils.'

'Which member of staff?' he asked innocently. It was obvious that he knew.

'Mr Wilkes, the religious education teacher. He was in the corridor talking with two sixth form girls.'

'In the corridor, you say. In that case, he probably didn't hear anything.'

'I need to ask him that myself. Where can I find him?'

A look of relief spread over Mr Rotherhyde's face as he realised his present ordeal might be over.

'Miss Smythe,' he shouted.

The door opened.

'Yes, headmaster.'

'Is Mr Wilkes teaching at the moment, do you know?'

'No, headmaster. He has a free period.'

Did she know the timetable off by heart, or had she been listening at the door? Rosie was willing to bet it was the latter.

'Can you find someone to take Miss Jennings? I think we are finished.' He beamed at her.

'Thank you, Mr Rotherhyde. You will probably be required to give evidence at the inquest. The Coroner's Court will be in touch.' That will wipe the smile of your face, Rosie thought. And she was right.

The same prefect was still hovering outside the office. Rosie was grateful for his help. She would never have found Mr Wilkes' room in the maze of passages and stairs. A shaft of watery sunlight briefly shone through a skylight window and dust sparkled and danced in the air. Rosie could smell chalk, but didn't everyone now use whiteboards and computer screens? Did anyone still use chalk? Evidently, Mr Wilkes did.

He was sitting bolt upright behind his desk. To his left was a blackboard covered with neat writing detailing the parable of the prodigal son, a subject very familiar to Rosie, who had debated its meaning for hours with her father. Mr Wilkes stood up as she entered. He was tall, thin, prematurely balding and, despite his efforts, was finding it difficult not to show his distress.

'I taught him. Bright lad. Always asked really interesting questions. His parents will be...' He gave Rosie a pleading look.

'In a state of shock and disbelief. I gather you were

there when he came out of Mr Skinner's room?'

'Yes, I was talking to two of our sixth form girls. I could hear raised voices but I couldn't make out what they were saying, not until the door was flung open. George rushed past me but not before shouting over his shoulder. He was saying, "I'd rather kill myself than apologise to him." I deeply regret not pursuing the boy. It's just that…'

'I don't think anyone thought he was serious, Mr Wilkes. Did you hear what followed between Mr Skinner and Mr Haribin?'

'Some of it. The door was still open and the two of them had a frightful set-to. I thought it most unprofessional so I moved away, taking Wendy and Julie, the sixth form girls, with me.'

'Do you know where I could find them?'

'They'll be hanging about the sixth form common room, painting their nails or talking about boys. They are inseparable. I would be surprised if either of them was engaged in anything academic. For the time being at least, learning is the last thing on their minds. That's what we were discussing in the corridor when…' Again, Mr Wilkes choked and Rosie felt sorrow for him.

'Would you show me the way? I'm quite lost.'

They traipsed in silence along the dusty passages and stairways. Rosie wondered what John Steadman would make of all of this. She thought he might enjoy walking through the school, for each part had its own unique smell and sound. They passed a home economics class with its enticing aroma of baking, then a gymnasium with shouts, the thump of feet and a bouncing ball. There must be a swimming pool nearby, for the smell of chlorine was now distinct. Someone was practising scales on a clarinet. Stale urine, bleach and running water; without looking Rosie knew they were passing a boys' toilet. Now they were in a new block that still had a distinct whiff of fresh paint and vinyl. Up another flight of stairs. A sign on a door read 'CHEMISTRY 2'. There was a new odour that Rosie couldn't place. Was it bromine or iodine? There was a slight breeze from an open door and on it wafted stale cigarette smoke. Whether it was a pupil or staff member having a sly puff was impossible to say.

'Here we are at last,' said Mr Wilkes. 'And there are Wendy and Julie. If it would help,' he added, 'I would be willing to speak with George's parents. Let me know.'

Wendy and Julie had struck up an unlikely friendship; an attraction of opposites. Julie was petite, plump and bubbly. Wendy was tall, heavily built and sullen, and she oozed distrust. It was Julie who did most of the talking. She was excited by the prospect of being interviewed by a real police officer, in uniform no less!

They added little to what Rosie didn't know already.

'Skinner and Haribin were having a right go at the poor little sod,' Julie said. Her eyes were flashing and her hands were waving in all directions.

'Did you hear it as well, Wendy?' Rosie asked.

The big girl shrugged. 'Yeah. Whatever.'

'Then he burst out of the room. Gave old Mr Wilkes a right fright, especially when he stopped and shouted what he shouted. Is it true the train knocked his head off?'

'You're gross, Julie,' Wendy muttered. 'Too gross for words.'

The drama department was not far from the sixth form common room. Mr Skinner was busy on the stage assembling scenery for the school's latest production. If it had not been for his pale, worried expression he would have been quite handsome, Rosie thought. He barely acknowledged her presence.

'I'm here regarding George Bremner's death,' she said in an attempt to open the conversation.

'I would never have guessed,' he responded sarcastically.

Rosie sensed that he was one of those people who always referred to the police as 'the filth' or 'pigs'. She wondered if he had a criminal record. Possession of cannabis probably, she hazarded.

She tried again. 'Your stage set is really impressive. How do you make rocks that look so real?'

Mr Skinner thawed a little. 'Chicken wire, fibre glass, dried moss and grass – that sort of thing.' He turned the 'rocks' round and Rosie could see how each was formed separately, then held together with twisted wire loops.

'Ingenious,' she said. 'Was George Bremner good at drama?'

'Not particularly. He was a gifted artist. If only Haribin wasn't so conceited, he would have been a great talent to nurture – every teacher's dream. But sometimes the system kills off talent.' He snipped a stray piece of copper wire with a large pair of pliers and moved the scenery back into its rightful place.

'About Friday?'

'You tell me what you know and I'll tell you if you're right.'

'That's not how it goes, as I suspect you're well aware. I've been told several versions – I want to hear yours.'

Reluctantly Mr Skinner recounted the events. They were sketchy, but broadly similar to what Tim Warrender had told her and DI Steadman yesterday. Was it only yesterday, she asked herself?

'Bremner had a point,' Mr Skinner continued. 'Haribin is shit at drawing compared to him.'

Rosie didn't like the look in Mr Skinner's eyes or his seeming lack of compassion. She couldn't resist.

'You didn't think to stop him?'

'Nobody thought he was serious,' he said with a shrug. 'He chose to jump in front of the train. Nobody pushed him.'

Rosie was taken aback.

'And there are other things going on that you don't know about. All sorts of rivalries and petty jealousies, dreams and desires that children of that age have. You only know about one incident. And don't think I don't know who told you. I genuinely believed I could make an actor out of Tim Warrender that is, until the police, or at least that blind detective and his sidekick, got their claws into him. Helmsmouth Citizen of the Year? I don't think so. He won't be getting my vote, that's for sure. Now, if you'll excuse me.'

Rosie strode out of the school theatre with as much self-control as she could muster. How could he have known about Tim Warrender? She tried to picture the scene. The door bursts open. George Bremner bolts, he stops and shouts before running off closely followed by… that must be it, the only boy in the school with such a shock of red hair.

She had walked a fair distance and was now lost. She asked a passing girl where she could find the art department. The girl looked at Rosie as though she were stupid and pointed to the door behind her clearly marked 'ART DEPARTMENT'. Taking a deep breath, Rosie knocked and went in.

It was not what she was expecting. The narrow, high Victorian windows had been replaced with large panes of glass to form a series of open-plan studios. The department was a hive of activity. Children were drawing, painting and making collages and incomprehensible models that Rosie believed were called 'installations'. In one studio there was a potter's wheel, a kiln and a printing press.

Rosie was directed to the last of the studios. The theme here was mainly photography. Black and white images of derelict buildings were hung next to pictures of dead animals and out-of-focus photos of flowers. There were some pieces of sculpture and two beautiful wood carvings that Rosie recognised as the work of Tim Warrender. She was admiring a clay model of a man standing in a pose that suggested he was looking out to sea. It was rather a sad composition. Rosie got the impression that the person would never find what he was looking for; it was quite moving.

A man had walked into the room. Rosie didn't notice him until he was standing right beside her.

'This is very good. Is it by one of the pupils?' she asked.

'Thank you. No, it's one of mine. I'm Mr Haribin. I believe you want a word with me.'

Rosie turned to face the man. Mr Haribin had a boyish face and a mass of curly hair. His eyes were steely blue and Rosie thought that here was a man she would not like to cross.

'I'm PC Rosie Jennings. I've come about George Bremner. I'm the family liaison officer.'

Mr Haribin's face betrayed not a flicker of emotion. His eyes barely blinked.

'I believe you had words with him in the last lesson.'

'Yes. The boy swore at me – repeatedly. We can't have that, now can we?'

'He swore at you, did he? I thought he was describing your work?'

'Insult the art, insult the artist – it amounts to the same thing. I gave him the opportunity to take back what he said. He declined, leaving me with no choice but to take him to his head of year. Our scope for discipline within the classroom is limited – regrettably.'

Rosie frowned at him. What was he suggesting? Did he

regret having to take George to his head of year or regret not being able to punish the boy himself? She was met with the same inscrutable expression.

'Was he any good as an artist?'

'He had some talent, otherwise I wouldn't have wasted my time teaching him. Sadly, he did have an over-inflated opinion of himself.'

Again that cold hard stare. Rosie looked at him in disbelief. 'Sadly, he is also dead,' she said 'After you and Mr Skinner…'

Mr Haribin interrupted her. 'We'll never know what he might have achieved then, will we?'

Rosie took a couple of deep breaths, then asked, 'May I see some of his work?'

Mr Haribin flicked through a large folder and handed Rosie a fairly scruffy drawing. It was unsigned and undated. She had already seen the drawing that Tim had shown her, as well as numerous examples in George's parent's house. This piece was not by George Bremner.

'Are you sure this is his? There's no name on it. It doesn't look like anything his parents showed me.'

Mr Haribin shrugged and put the drawing back in the folder. As he bent over Rosie noticed a painting on the wall.

'That's one of his,' she said. 'Look there's his signature. It's brilliant!'

Mr Haribin looked at it. 'The boy on a good day, I suppose.'

Rosie was becoming increasingly aware of her own

emotions and the anger welling up inside her. Facts, she said to herself, stick to the facts.

'So you took him along to see Mr Skinner. Tell me what happened then.'

'Oh, I'm sure you know already. Tim Warrender will have given you a word for word account. Quite the little detective, isn't he? Five minutes with that blind copper who's never out of the papers, not to mention his guide dog. And of course that Scottish hulk – Tim's hero. I had such high hopes for him. All I get now is "when I'm a policeman." You have no idea how that makes me feel.' Mr Haribin's face had gone very pale.

'You were overheard by a member of staff. Do you deny George threatened to kill himself?'

'He could have said something like that. Children say all sorts of things they don't mean. I wasn't paying attention.'

'Don't you have any regrets?'

He pouted. 'What happened, happened. No one can turn back time.'

'And by then you and Mr Skinner were arguing?'

'We are both up for deputy head. Skinner's a fool. He doesn't understand the role – the significance of being the second-in-command. No, he only has eyes for the main chance. All he is interested in is becoming head.'

'But not you?' Rosie found herself stroking the clay figure.

'Don't touch!' Mr Haribin barked. 'Sorry, it's not fully dry and still fragile.'

'How do you keep the arms and legs in position?' Rosie asked.

'There's a supporting frame on the inside.'

The bell rang before Rosie could ask how he made the frame.

'I have to go now, I have a class to teach,' said Haribin.

CHAPTER THIRTEEN

Robbie had his head tilted to one side and was looking expectantly at Rosie Jennings. His gaze shifted from Rosie to the untouched piece of cake on her plate. He started to drool.

'Don't you feed your dog, sir?' she asked.

'Is he mooching? I blame Sergeant Grimble. He's forever slipping the dog treats,' Steadman replied. He snapped his fingers and Robbie immediately lay down.

'Those big brown eyes! He looks so sad, sir.'

'At least I'm spared that,' Steadman said. He bent down and gave the dog's head a friendly scratch. Robbie's tail wagged in appreciation.

'Maybe I'm not cut out to be a family liaison officer, sir. I almost broke down in front of George's parents. Not very professional, but I can't help feeling for them.'

Rosie had gone straight from the school to the Bremners' house. She had tried to stick to the facts, but it was impossible not to let her feelings show.

She sipped her cappuccino. It had grown cold. The

frothy milk stuck to her upper lip, giving her a ridiculous moustache. She dived into her pocket, desperate to find a tissue before... before what? DI Steadman wouldn't see it, she thought. In fact, she could be sitting here stark naked and it wouldn't make any difference. Life just didn't seem fair. She heaved a small sigh.

'Come on Rosie, tell me how you got on at the school. I want a vivid account,' Steadman said in a reassuring voice.

'Do you know Helmsmouth Merchant Comprehensive, sir?'

'Only too well! Ben, my son, went there for a couple of years after leaving primary school.'

Steadman clearly recalled Ben's first day. He had been so proud of his son in his new blazer that was a size too big for him, a tie that Ben thought was strangling him and a smart new haircut. Holly, on the other hand, with her Bohemian streak, had wrinkled her nose in disapproval.

'Be my eyes, Rosie. Describe your morning in detail.' Steadman sat back in his chair and without thinking removed his dark glasses and cleaned them with a handkerchief.

Rosie was a good narrator and in his mind's eye Steadman walked the corridors with her. He had forgotten about the prefects' uniform but had retained a vivid image of the ghastly cabinet with its collection of stuffed animals.

'Did you say the headmaster was called Rotherhyde? If it's the same chap I knew he must over a hundred by now.

Does he still speak in half sentences as though no one is listening?'

'That's him. He says he's just over seventy. How do you know him, sir?'

'He expelled my son, or at least tried to. Ben has always been a bit of a rebel and he decided, at the age of twelve, not to get his hair cut. By the time he was thirteen he had a pony tail. I think Holly encouraged him. Anyway, Rotherhyde was most unhappy.' Steadman pulled a face and did a passable impersonation. 'not in keeping, you see… standards to maintain… best all round… so glad you agree.' He shook his head. 'Holly was having none of it,' he continued. 'After pointing out, in no uncertain terms, that he was a sexist, narrow-minded bigot we were left with no alternative but to move Ben to another school. I'll bet that Rotherhyde will do all he can to keep the school at arm's length from anything to do with George Bremner.'

Steadman didn't know Mr Wilkes, Mr Skinner or Mr Haribin, but Rosie described them so well he felt he would recognise them if he ever encountered them.

'I liked Mr Wilkes but I didn't care much for the other two,' Rosie admitted. 'Skinner's stage sets are very clever and very realistic but I have no idea how he is as a teacher. And Haribin is not without talent. He had made an amazing sculpture of a man staring into the distance. I nearly got sent to the corner for touching it. Apparently there is some sort of frame inside it but it's all very fragile until it dries. They both knew Tim Warrender had been eavesdropping and worked out that he had spoken with you. I'm sorry to say neither you, Robbie nor Sergeant Munro are flavour of the month. Skinner had set his sights on an acting career for Tim, and Haribin had high hopes he would follow in his footsteps. Now, all Tim talks about is when he becomes a policeman. Unlike Mr Wilkes, both Skinner and Haribin showed little emotion, almost cold-blooded, as regards George Bremner. And there is no love lost between Skinner and Haribin either. They're both going for the deputy head's post and I guess they're trying to distance themselves from the tragedy. I would go as far as to say that Haribin in particular didn't like George Bremner. Certainly he was jealous of his talent. Skinner also hinted at other rivalries, but I'm not exactly sure what he was getting at.'

Steadman grunted and stroked his chin with his thumbnail.

'I think I know,' he said. 'Skinner and Haribin visited Tim Warrender yesterday evening. His mother phoned to tell me.'

'What? They never mentioned that!'

'No, I bet they didn't. In essence they told Tim not to blame himself too much.'

Rosie gasped in disbelief.

'It appears the two boys played a game where they tallied up their marks and at the end of each week whoever had the most had to buy the other a bar of chocolate. Tim had won for the last four weeks in a row. It was, according to Tim's mother, all very good natured. Skinner and

Haribin tried to make out that George had taken it very personally.'

'What a pair of...'

'Quite. Tim is now more confused than ever. I've asked Alan Munro to go and see him. I believe there's a big rugby match on tonight. Hopefully Alan will persuade Tim to go with him.'

Rosie looked at her watch.

'I have a bit of time. Do you want me to take Robbie for a walk before I go, sir?'

'That's kind. I could with a stretch of my legs myself. Do you fancy walking round the block with me?'

It was almost dark when they set off and the sea mist had rolled in again. The foghorn was moaning in the distance. Steadman could taste the tang of salt in the damp evening air.

'What do you think George's parents will do?' Steadman asked.

'They're going to meet the chair of school governors tonight. I think Rotherhyde will have to suspend Skinner and Haribin, however much it upsets him.'

'He would be a fool not to. And if either of them had any sense they would withdraw their applications for the deputy head post. I can't see that happening somehow.'

They stopped at a crossroads and let Robbie guide them over.

'What about the case you're involved in, sir. Any progress?'

Steadman told her about acting DCI 'Beaky' Nesbitt and his decision to arrest Harry Eeles.

'You don't believe Harry Eeles killed those two people, do you, sir?'

'No, but I admit I am struggling to tie up any of the loose ends.'

He stopped quite suddenly and a worried frown appeared on his face.

'What is it, sir?'

Steadman wanted to tell her about the dream with Tim's name flashing next to the word 'VICTIM' and Maurice Eeles's blood-spattered bike, but it just seemed so foolish. It was only a dream after all.

'I have some vague ideas, Rosie. They are all very tenuous – circumstantial, if you like. I don't even know if I'm on the right track, but... well, you know how I hate coincidences. I need something more concrete, something to tell me at least that I am thinking in the right direction. I worry, too, that I've only been brought into the investigation because people feel sorry for me. Nesbitt would chuck me out in a minute if he could.'

They walked on in silence, Steadman lost in his own thoughts. 'Unless I'm mistaken, we are back home,' he said at last.

'How did you work that out?'

'I count the steps subconsciously.'

Steadman didn't feel like going back indoors. Even Robbie seemed restless.

'Are you up for another lap?' he asked the dog after

Rosie had taken her leave. Robbie gave a small, low bark. 'I take it that's a yes. Let's go.'

The sounds of the night were muffled yet seemed close, like someone whispering in a darkened room. Only the occasional car crawled past with dipped headlights probing the murky gloom. Could he make out the lights? Steadman pushed his glasses onto his forehead and covered one eye. He listened for an approaching car and tried to peer in the direction of the sound. It was not easy. Since losing his sight his eyes tended to swivel round in their sockets in a haphazard manner. The car slowed down as it passed. Was there just a flicker of light? Steadman couldn't be sure. He replaced his glasses and started counting his steps again.

He tried to refocus on the two murders. Again and again his thoughts kept jumping back to Tim Warrender and the school. 'Concentrate, concentrate,' he muttered to himself. But every time he picked up a strand and tried to run with it, something would interrupt the train of thought – Beaky Nesbitt's squeaky shoes or, and in some ways more disturbing, Dr Sam Griffiths's tinkling laugh.

One of his old bosses had once told him, 'If you're not sure where you are going, go back to the beginning and start again.'

How had it started? A phone call from Frank Rufus – what precisely had he asked him? Steadman paused. 'Wait Robbie.'

Dr Rufus hadn't asked him who had killed Crenshaw Tipley, had he? No, he wanted to know why someone had injected his lungs with whisky, a detail Nesbitt had brushed aside. Then, of course, Velda Meemes had been doused in sparkling water. What the hell was going on there?

Despite Robbie tugging at the harness, Steadman had stepped perilously close to the kerb. He stumbled and almost lost his footing. He never heard the car. The blow to his ribs took his breath away and sent him sprawling on the pavement. The dog was fretting, desperately prodding Steadman's face with his nose.

'I'm fine, Robbie,' he gasped. Each breath was agony. He tried to move. The pain in his chest was excruciating. He let go of Robbie's harness and, after groping in his pocket, found his mobile phone. Frank Rufus answered almost immediately. All he could hear was Steadman gasping on the other end.

'What's happened, John?'

'I've been clipped by some idiot's wing mirror. I can barely breathe.'

'Where are you?'

Steadman knew exactly where he was.

'Don't move,' Dr Rufus said unnecessarily. 'I'll be right there.'

Steadman eased himself up onto his knees with a curse; it was too painful to stand. Without conscious effort, the recent events replayed in his head, only this time in slow motion. He remembered being lost in his own thoughts and Robbie tugging him. Had he taken a step away from the edge? Yes, he was certain that he had. In which case...

no, he couldn't recall hearing the car's approach. The blow, the fall… was there a squeal of brakes? Definitely not, he would have remembered that. Then the car sped off. Was there something before that? He played the sequence again in his mind. Yes! There was the unmistakable clunk of a car running off a raised kerb. Whoever had hit him had mounted the pavement. Was it deliberate?

Another car pulled up. Steadman tried to raise himself. He clutched his chest and swayed.

'I think you can be fined for being drunk in charge of a guide dog, you know,' said Dr Rufus.

'Don't joke, Frank. I can barely breathe.'

'Come on, let's get you into the car and down to the hospital for an x-ray.'

Dr Rufus put a burly arm round his colleague and gently lifted him onto his feet. Steadman groaned.

'No, I'm not going back to the hospital unless it's absolutely necessary, that's why I called you. You're a doctor – you can check me over. I'm sure I'm only bruised.' He winced again.

'I'm a forensic pathologist – my patients are mostly dead,' Dr Rufus protested.

'Well that's fine, I feel half dead. All I'm asking is that you check my chest to see if anything's broken.'

'I've got a stethoscope somewhere, but if I think your lung is punctured…'

'Then I'll go to the hospital.'

'Don't interrupt! Whatever else, you're going to spend

the night in my house so I can keep an eye on you. Agreed?'

Steadman agreed.

Another car pulled up and a tall man with a pale face and curly hair got out.

'Is anything the matter? Has there been an accident? Do you want me to call an ambulance or the police?'

Under his breath, Dr Rufus muttered something about 'rubberneckers' before replying.

'I'm a doctor, he's the police. We'll be fine.'

'Oh – do you want a lift to the hospital?'

Dr Rufus was getting exasperated.

'No, as you can see, I've got my own car. He's coming home with me.'

'What about the dog?'

Dr Rufus had barely noticed the black shape of Robbie spreadeagled at Steadman's side. In truth, he hadn't thought about the dog.

'The dog is coming as well. What did you think we were going to do, abandon it?' It was impossible for Dr Rufus to keep the annoyance out of his voice.

'I'm only trying to help.'

'Well, open the passenger door and chuck those folders off the seat, if you want to help.'

The inside of the car smelt slightly sweet and sickly, as though Dr Rufus had brought something of the police mortuary with him. Gently he manoeuvred John Steadman into the car. His colleague was pale and sweating.

'Will you tolerate the seat belt?'

Steadman nodded and Dr Rufus buckled him in. With a sweep of his arm he cleared the contents of the back seat on to the floor.

'Robbie – in the car!'

Without hesitation the dog jumped on to the back seat. Dr Rufus closed the door and looked round. For a moment he was dazzled by the stranger's headlights. The car revved up and drove off into the night.

'Weird bugger, that one, if you ask me,' he grumbled as he climbed in beside Steadman.

'I'm glad you arrived first, Frank. What is it about accidents, crime scenes and fires that attracts the oddest of spectators, do you think? They just seem to materialise out of thin air.'

'They are sent to make our miserable lives even more unbearable – a bit like this fog. It's a real pea-souper tonight.'

They trundled through the deserted streets at a snail's pace.

'I'm not sure the headlights don't make things worse, I can't see a thing. If it wasn't for the pain in your ribs, I'd let you drive!'

'You know, Frank, it's about the only thing I don't miss. I never liked driving, never was into cars the way some men are – all that nonsense about acceleration and top speed when, for the most part, you're stuck doing thirty miles per hour behind a tractor.'

'Or barely ten miles an hour in this fog,' Dr Rufus added.

Eventually they pulled up outside Dr Rufus's home. It was a rather shabby Victorian house with an overgrown garden. He let Robbie out first before cautiously easing Steadman out of the front seat.

'That's it, you go and water the roses. I'm sure there are some in there somewhere,' Dr Rufus called to the dog. 'John, are you fit to walk to the door?'

'I think so. The pain is beginning to ease.'

'I really must do something about this garden,' said Dr Rufus as another branch brushed against his colleague. 'Mind the step, that's it – we're there.'

The inside of the house was deliciously warm. Dr Rufus helped Steadman out of his damp coat and hung up his scarf and hat.

'At least you're a better colour. Let's find you a comfortable seat while I go and look for my stethoscope. I think I last saw it in the study.'

Steadman could hear his colleague rummaging in the adjoining room.

'Ah, here it is!'

Struggling to his feet, Steadman lifted his shirt.

'I'm pleased to see that Lloyd's are not letting you starve' remarked Rufus. 'Mind, there's still not much of you – I've seen more meat on a butcher's pencil.'

At Frank's request Steadman breathed in and out as deeply as he dared.

'Chest seems to be moving normally,' he mumbled.

'Nasty bruises though. Is it sore when I press?'

It was sore, exquisitely so, but only in one spot.

'One rib cracked, I would say.'

'Is that good?' Steadman asked.

'Better than two, worse than none.'

Dr Rufus laid the flat of one hand on Steadman's chest and tapped the middle finger of that hand with the middle finger of the other.

'What are you doing?'

'I am percussing your chest.'

'What will that tell you?'

'Probably nothing, but if a doctor doesn't do it the punters feel cheated. Say ninety-nine in a deep voice – that completes the dark magic.'

Steadman did as he was told, but confessed he did not feel any better.

'The trouble with you is that you don't believe in magic. For an extra shilling I will use the guessing tubes,' said Dr Rufus as he placed the stethoscope in his ears. 'Now breathe gently through your mouth.'

Dr Rufus listened intently to both sides of Steadman's chest.

'I don't think you have damaged your lung,' he concluded. 'However, I am insistent that you stay the night. I'll find you some painkillers, order a pizza and open a bottle of wine.'

'I thought you weren't meant to take tablets and drink?'

'Ah, but you will be drinking under medical supervision – an entirely different proposition.' Dr Rufus turned to

Robbie. 'I suppose you'll need feeding as well?'

'Frank, if you drive to my flat you'll find under the bed in the spare room a small case already packed with overnight essentials for me. And in the tall cupboard in the kitchen a carrier bag with emergency supplies for Robbie. Before you ask, Linda's doing, not mine. Could you bring Robbie's mat, food and water bowls as well?'

'Should I tell your neighbours?'

'No need, they have gone off for a few days. The café will be shut by now. I'll let the Lloyds know in the morning.'

Steadman swallowed the pills that Dr Rufus handed him and settled back into the easy chair. The front door slammed shut and Dr Rufus set off once again into the fog. The pain was definitely more bearable now. Robbie had decided to rest his head on Steadman's lap.

'Well, what do you think? Accident or bad luck?' He ruffled the fur between Robbie's ears. 'Is somebody trying to tell us something, Robbie? First you and now me. Whatever next?'

CHAPTER FOURTEEN

Lloyd's Café and the flats above were eerily dark. From the moment he got out of the car, Dr Rufus could sense there was something wrong. He slipped the key into the outer door. The door fell open before he turned the key. Something metallic was lying at his feet. He found the light switch and, looking down, saw the remains of the lock.

His sense of foreboding was replaced by intense anger. He stormed up the stairs. The door to old Mr and Mrs Lloyd's flat was firmly shut. Up another flight. He knew what he would find before he got there. Steadman's door was ajar and the frame splintered.

Rufus was incandescent with rage. For a moment, he simply stared at the splintered door frame and fumed.

The pockets of his voluminous tweed coat were stuffed with all sorts of things, including a copious supply of vinyl gloves and plastic overshoes. Slipping on a pair of each, he pushed the door open and switched on the light. It did occur to him that the intruder might still be in Steadman's apartment and in a way, he half-hoped he would be. Such was his outrage that he would have happily tackled anyone without a second thought. But the flat was empty and silent.

Broken glass lay on the corridor carpet. The two Pre-Raphaelite pictures, so carefully screwed to the wall, had been smashed and the prints repeatedly slashed. It was exactly the same in the lounge: shattered glass everywhere and what was left of the prints hanging out of the frames like streamers.

Rufus frowned; it all seemed rather odd. He looked round the rest of the flat: Steadman's bedroom, the spare bedroom, the kitchen and bathroom. There was nothing out of place and no sign of damage. He shrugged his thickset shoulders, picked up the phone and called the Eyesore. He was disappointed that Sergeant Grimble didn't answer. Ah well, he had to have some time off.

Sergeant Fielding, who answered, was balding like Grimble but in marked contrast was thin and reserved. He also sported an unfashionable moustache. Dr Rufus always thought he resembled something from a fishmonger's counter.

'I'll send a couple of uniformed officers round straight away.'

Rufus retraced his steps back to the spare room and retrieved Steadman's suitcase. He stuffed Robbie's bowls into the dog's 'emergency supplies' bag Linda had made up.

'That woman thinks of everything,' the doctor said to

himself as he made his way down the stairs with the case and bag and went out to his car. The flat would be sealed off and he knew if he did not take them now he would have to spend the rest of the evening traipsing round the shops, his least favourite occupation.

Steadman took some time to answer the phone.

'Is everything all right?'

'No,' replied Dr Rufus bluntly. 'Your flat has been burgled, or at least broken into, I'm sorry to say.'

Steadman swore softly under his breath.

'Is there much damage? Has anything been taken? Not that there is much to take,' he added.

'All your pictures have been trashed. Broken glass everywhere and the prints themselves cut to ribbons.'

'Damn! Anything else? What about my netsuke collection?'

Dr Rufus looked over towards the small glass topped table in the corner.

'Hang on a minute... well, it's not broken. How many figures should be in it?'

'Seventeen.'

Dr Rufus quickly scanned the contents.

'All present and correct.'

'What about my piano and the CD player?'

Dr Rufus lifted the lid of the piano and tinkled a few of the keys.

'Seems to be in order,' he said. 'And it doesn't look like your CD player has been touched either.'

'That about sums up anything of value, unless our

intruder fancied a bottle of single malt whisky. Have you phoned the Eyesore?'

'Yes, in fact I think that's them arriving now. And, before you ask, I've got your things in the car before they seal everything up.'

Steadman would have liked to have been there, but what was the use? He would only get in the way. Dr Rufus probably knew his flat better than he did, in many ways. And now his ribs were hurting like hell again. He lay back in his chair and tried to relax. It was an odd sort of break-in, he thought. Half a dozen, albeit expensive, Pre-Raphaelite pictures with their glass smashed and the prints slashed, yet nothing taken and no other sign of vandalism. Steadman had been to break-ins where all the furnishings had been wrecked and, even worse, where the perpetrators had urinated or defecated on the owner's property. At least he had been spared that insult. It was, perhaps, fortunate that his neighbours were away. They would have been terrified.

Steadman's long fingers drummed softly on his thighs and a piece of music started playing quietly in his head: a nocturne by Chopin. And then it occurred to him that whoever had broken into his flat must have known he was not there. The downstairs door was left open during the day but locked at night. Whoever it was, he thought, must simply have rung the doorbell, and on getting no reply... the music in his head drifted on, gracefully running over the keyboard. He tried to work out the sequence of events.

'Of course,' he said out aloud, 'the building would be

in darkness. And then… yes, ring the Lloyd's doorbell… no reply… try my bell… no reply… safe to enter!'

The piano playing in his head got louder. He wanted to get up and pace the floor, but the pain in his chest was too intense. Besides, he was unfamiliar with the layout of the room and as likely as not would trip and fall.

His thoughts turned back to the break-in. The downstairs door had a fairly commonplace lock. It would not take much force to lean heavily on the door and… yes, but that had implications. It suggested that it was probably a man. What would he do then? Steadman imagined someone treading lightly up the stairs, stopping at the Lloyd's door and listening intently. What would be going through his mind? Could it be that the Lloyd's bell was not working or they were watching television and did not hear? It would be dark. No! The intruder would have a torch; a heavy torch, heavy enough to smash glass. Not a sound from the Lloyd's flat, so on up the stairs.

'Now my door,' Steadman said under his breath. He visualised the man standing there, playing the beam of his torch over the door, not daring to make a sound. Would he knock just to make sure? No, he knew the flat was empty, Steadman concluded. This time the lock was more robust. The intruder heaved with his shoulder – no luck. Steadman could see him clearly, a tall man wearing heavy boots.

'That's it!' he said out loud. 'He would kick the door down.'

Steadman fell silent again. Would he risk putting the

lights on? Why not - the only person who knew he was definitely not at home was Dr Rufus.

Something troubled him. He paused the scene in his head and bit the inside of his lip. The music stopped. Somebody else knew – the 'rubbernecker' as Dr Rufus called him. Could it be...? Steadman was able to recall in detail what he said and sounded like; hopefully Dr Rufus got a good look at him.

The piano in his head started playing again. Now the lights in his flat were on. Steadman could only imagine how his flat appeared. He knew the walls were all magnolia and the carpets beige, Linda had told him. He recalled what his piano and CD player looked like and, of course, every detail of his netsuke collection, but as for the pictures, he had only a vague idea. The frames had raised, beaded edges. He knew that as he had run his fingers over them. They were probably gold, he decided. As for the subject matter, he remembered images from a book; girls with long white dresses and flowing manes of red hair, handsome men and romanticised landscapes but little else.

The heavy torch swung and the glass shattered – one blow, two blows, three blows. He could almost hear the sound of breaking glass and feel the sharp splinters under his feet. And then, and then... hadn't Dr Rufus said the prints themselves had been slashed? So the intruder must have had a knife. What sort of knife? As if in answer to his question, Robbie stirred and put his head on his lap. Steadman reached down and very gently stroked the long gash on the dog's flank.

'I know exactly what sort of knife, Robbie, I know exactly – but why did he slash my pictures and nothing else?'

★ ★ ★

Dr Rufus greeted the two officers with a cursory nod. 'Nothing taken as far as I can tell, only the door broken and the pictures smashed.'

'Can I ask what you were doing here, sir, and where is DI Steadman?'

Dr Rufus grunted. 'Steadman was out walking and got clipped by a wing mirror. Nothing serious, but he's staying the night at my place. I called round to get a few things for him and some food for his dog.'

'I don't suppose you saw anyone acting suspiciously?'

'In this fog? Good grief, I could barely see beyond my front bumper! Look, I had better push off. I've left Steadman by himself. You know where I am if you need me.'

The officer nodded. 'Looks like kids up to no good, if you ask me. I suppose we should get forensics in. It seems a bit trivial for half a dozen broken pictures.'

Dr Rufus gave the man a cold, hard stare.

'Steadman's dog has been attacked, he's been hit by a car and now his flat has been broken into – too damned right you'll get forensics in.'

The flashing light on the police car had been left on. Dr Rufus stood mesmerised as the blue beams cut arc after arc in the impenetrable fog. Someone was approaching; a woman, he guessed, by the tapping heels. It was a familiar sound. He couldn't place it until a soft Welsh voice spoke.

'Dr Rufus – is that you?'

'Sam? What are you doing out on a night like this?'

'I'm staying at the Equinox Hotel just down the road. I was checking some files at the Eyesore and saw the police car on my way back. Isn't this where John Steadman lives? Is there anything wrong?'

Dr Rufus assured her that it was indeed where Steadman lived and gave an outline of the night's events. The forensic psychologist looked worried.

'How is he?' she asked.

'Sore, but the rib will heal in a few weeks.'

'I didn't mean physically.'

'I know what you meant. Why don't you come back with me and see for yourself? I was going to order a pizza. You'd be welcome to join us.'

Dr Sam Griffiths didn't fancy a pizza. Nor did she care for the smell in Dr Rufus's old Volvo. However, there was something about the pleading look the doctor had given her that made it difficult to refuse. She was also aware that Steadman fascinated her. She felt sympathy for him, of course, yet she knew sympathy was the last thing he wanted. No, it was more than that. She was a psychologist and she liked people who could think. At their meeting in the Eyesore she had observed him closely. She had watched how, after the embarrassing start, he had taken on board each new concept, how he had twisted and turned them round in his mind, as though they were the fragments of coloured glass in a child's kaleidoscope. Was there something more? For the briefest of moments, she imagined his long, delicate fingers touching her hand.

'I don't know how you can drive in this fog,' she said, pulling herself back into the present with some effort.

Dr Rufus was flattered. 'Oh, it's not so bad. I know the road very well. Daresay I could drive it in my sleep, if I had to.' But much to his annoyance he knocked over the wheelie bin as he pulled into his drive.

'Thank goodness you're back, Frank,' said Steadman. 'I'm desperate for a pee.'

'Ah… I've brought Sam Griffiths back with me,' Dr Rufus whispered.

Steadman turned bright red and started to splutter an apology.

'It's fine,' Sam said soothingly. 'Off you go.'

She could hear Steadman castigating his friend as they went down the corridor.

'If I didn't know you better, Frank, I'd swear you did that deliberately. You could have warned me.'

Dr Griffiths was distressed by the change in Steadman. He was ashen and clearly in some discomfort. His trousers and shoes were muddy and his hair dishevelled. Not my place, she said to herself as she fought down the urge to interfere.

She looked round Dr Rufus's sitting room. It was cluttered but not untidy and, she noted, remarkably clean.

There were old black and white photos of medical classes on the wall. She was struck by how young and hopeful all the students looked. Dr Rufus was easy to pick out, for even in those days he had sported an impressive beard. On the wall above the fireplace hung a large modern painting. It was of a jazz band and skilfully executed using big blocks of colour. Sam stood up to take a closer look.

'I was just admiring your painting,' she said as the two men returned.

'Oh, that old thing! Saw it in a junk shop and thought it looked rather cheerful,' he replied in an offhand manner

Sam noticed "F. Rufus 1984" neatly signed in one corner. She raised a questioning eyebrow, but said nothing.

'I'll order the pizzas,' continued Rufus. 'Red wine all round, I think.' He disappeared in the direction of the kitchen before anyone could object.

'You've been in the wars again, John. Do you think it was an accident?'

Steadman felt decidedly awkward. It was the first time he had been alone with Dr Sam Griffiths. His chest was hurting again.

'I can't say for certain. I gather it was dark and foggy, and I think I had strayed too near the kerb. I do know the car mounted the pavement, which does suggest...' His voice trailed away and his fingers started tapping on the arms of the chair.

'What are you thinking?'

'Whoever broke into my flat knew I was out. Not

counting Robbie, that leaves only Dr Rufus and an odd chap who stopped to help. I wonder if Frank got a good look at him.'

Dr Rufus returned bearing a bottle and three glasses

'The rubbernecker? Can't say that I really took much notice. Queer fellow – tall, curly hair – doubt if I would recognise him again. He had the sort of face you easily forget.' He gave a glass to Sam. 'I've poured you a drop of wine, John.'

Steadman held out a hand and Dr Rufus placed the glass in his grasp. He sniffed the wine.

'Pushing the boat out tonight, Frank.'

'Why not? It's not often I have guests. Cheers.'

'*Iechyd da,*' replied Dr Griffiths. Seeing the look on Frank's face she added, 'Welsh, that is, for good health.'

'To get back to the rubbernecker, Frank, did you notice if he was wearing gloves?'

Dr Rufus screwed up his eyes. 'Let me think. No, I don't believe he was. He opened the passenger door and I'm fairly certain I noticed he had dirt under his nails. Why? What's on your mind?'

'I was wondering if it could be the same person who broke into my flat. It may be worth asking Kim Ho to check for fingerprints. Only, of course, the passenger door has been used since.' Steadman sipped some wine. 'What about the car, Frank?'

'It was white, I can tell you that, but not the make, and as he left the lights on I have no idea of the number. I was more concerned with getting you safely back here.'

'What do you make of the picture smashing, Sam?'

'You're sure there was no other damage?'

'Absolutely,' replied Dr Rufus.

Dr Sam Griffiths took her time in replying. Steadman liked that.

'It's an odd thing to do on its own, and that in itself is worrying for it suggests somebody who is neither thinking nor behaving rationally. The fact that it was only the pictures that were damaged also troubles me. It could be opportunistic, but more likely he knew they were there. How long have you had them?'

'Not long at all, a couple of weeks at most. In that time, I can't have had many visitors.' He started to count them off on his long, elegant fingers. 'My sister Linda and her husband, Dominic, who put them up, the Lloyds, Frank and Alan Munro, Mr Barnes from the guide dogs, Doreen Meemes, Tim Warrender and his mother, of course. I'm sure there are more. Oh yes, an annoying American agent, Arnie Yateman. Can you think of anyone else, Frank?'

'Didn't Mr Martindale, the vet, call round?'

'Yes, I'd forgotten about him.'

'What about people like postmen?' asked Sam.

'I don't think they've been in the flat. The only other caller was Rosie Jennings, the family liaison officer. She called this afternoon.' Steadman shook his head. 'I can't imagine any of those being involved, but you did say it was an irrational thing to do.'

'Irrational and threatening,' Sam replied.

'Why not just spray graffiti on the wall?' suggested Rufus.

'Meaningless, if the intended victim is blind,' said Sam.

'I agree,' added Steadman.

He imagined himself coming home, trying to find the keyhole, feeling the splintered wood, pushing open the broken door then stepping on the broken glass.

'And, of course, an awful hazard for Robbie,' he continued as he realised the dog would have gone inside first.

'I wonder why he only smashed the pictures. Frank tells me you have a nice netsuke collection in a display cabinet. You would think someone intent on mayhem would have broken that as well.'

The doorbell rang.

'That'll be the pizzas. I'm starving,' said Rufus.

The pizza was not as bad as Sam Griffiths had feared. She watched Steadman eating. Every mouthful was slow and deliberate. Even so some of the topping had spilled onto his tie. She desperately wanted to mop it up. Dr Rufus intervened.

'Saving a bit for later, are you?' he said as he wiped it off with a paper serviette.

'Getting back to what you were saying, Sam, the pictures were all Pre-Raphaelite prints. They are not to everyone's liking. Do you think whoever did this is, in some way, questioning my taste in art?'

Rufus snorted. 'You're getting carried away, John. Some hooligan kicked your door down, couldn't find anything worth nicking, so he smashed a few pictures, that's all.'

'You don't believe that for a minute, Frank. I know you're trying to be reassuring. You said yourself that not only was the glass smashed but each print was repeatedly slashed, not torn or ripped, but cut with a sharp knife. You're forgetting about the dog.'

Sam's and Frank's eyes fixed on the long gash on Robbie's flank.

'You know I don't like coincidences.'

The room seemed suddenly colder. No one spoke. Steadman eventually broke the silence.

'I don't get it. Someone is harassing me, or threatening me, or warning me… I don't know how to describe it, and I have no idea why.'

'I'll make coffee,' suggested Dr Rufus. The phone rang as he stood up. 'Hello… yes, he's here… it's Kim Ho from forensics for you,' he said placing the receiver in Steadman's hand.

'We were just speaking about you, Kim. Before I forget, would you come round in the morning and check Dr Rufus's car for fingerprints? It's a long shot and I'll explain when you're here. Have you turned up anything in my flat?'

'You probably know most of it already. The intruder wore gloves, the glass was broken with something solid, maybe a hammer, and the prints slashed with something very sharp, a razor blade or a scalpel perhaps. Only one other finding – have you had any electrical work done recently?'

'No. Why?'

'I've found a small piece of twisted copper wire in amongst the shards of glass.'

CHAPTER FIFTEEN

The three of them talked long into the night. Dr Rufus was adamant that Steadman was reading too much into the piece of twisted wire.

'I mean to say, it could have been there for ages, come from the back of the picture or simply have fallen out of somebody's pocket,' he said.

'And how often do you have bits of wire in your pockets, Frank?' Steadman asked.

'That's not the point. Listen, I once had a patient who had a birthmark on his back which, from a certain angle, looked unbelievably like Winston Churchill. Quite remarkable really.'

Dr Griffiths frowned.

'And the point of your story is exactly what, Frank?'

'The point? Well, you would think that a birthmark looking like Winston Churchill would be significant, wouldn't you? But it wasn't relevant at all.'

'A bit like your story, then.'

'I suppose so,' Dr Rufus replied with a sniff. 'But it was

a remarkable likeness – even had a cigar in his mouth.'

John Steadman pushed his dark glasses up onto his forehead and rubbed his sightless eyes.

'Frank, I know you're trying to be kind and allay my fears. The trouble is, it won't wash. Either the man who smashed my pictures left the wire there deliberately as a warning or a calling-card. Or else it fell out of his pocket accidentally, which of course begs the question, why did he have a piece of wire in his pocket? Given that we are investigating two murders where the victims were wired up, it is not unreasonable to conclude that it is more than coincidence.'

'Are you suggesting that the murderer is the same person who smashed your pictures?'

Steadman shrugged his shoulders and spread out his elegant hands.

'That's one possible interpretation,' said Sam Griffiths. 'However, the gory details of the killings have been in the press for all to see. Whoever left the wire in your flat may just be malicious.'

Steadman yawned and pressed the button on the side of his watch. The metallic voice informed him it was nearly midnight.

'Come on, John – more painkillers and bed, I think. I'll help you,' said Rufus.

'And I'll tidy up,' Sam added.

The two men went upstairs, preceded by Robbie.

'Do you remember the layout, John? First door on your left – that's it – that's your room. Next door down is my room and the door facing you at the end of the corridor is the bathroom. I've moved most of the furniture in your room against the wall. There's only a bedside table on the right of the bed.'

Steadman reached forward and found the table.

'The bed is hard against the wall so you can only get out on this side. I've put Robbie's mat at the end your bed. Next to that there's a large armchair where I've put your case.'

Dr Rufus watched his friend as he paced round the room, touching the walls and the various pieces of furniture. Once Steadman was satisfied that he had fixed in his mind where everything was, he nodded.

'Got it, now the bathroom, Frank. Robbie, lie down.'

The dog dutifully lay on his mat.

'I'll grab your soap bag and pyjamas.'

They went down the corridor. Steadman counted the steps and trailed a hand against the wall. They went through the same routine in the bathroom.

'I'll get those painkillers for you. Will you manage by yourself?'

'I think so. Would you let Robbie out for me?'

Steadman closed the door. He could hear Frank calling the dog and the rumble as Robbie ran down the stairs. He undressed, neatly folding each item of clothing in turn. His ribs still hurt, especially when he moved. He fumbled in his soap bag for his toothbrush and toothpaste. Damn, he said to himself, I forgot to ask for a towel.

There was a gentle knock at the door.

'Are you decent?' Dr Rufus enquired.

'Come in, Frank. I'm looking for a towel.'

Dr Rufus handed him a towel, the painkillers and a tumbler.

'Will you be all right while I drive Sam home?'

Damn again, Steadman thought, I never said thank-you or goodnight.

'I'll be fine. Would you thank her for me?'

'I could send her up,' Frank replied. 'Only joking,' he hastily added seeing the look of terror on his friend's face.

In marked contrast to Robbie, who was gently snoring within seconds, Steadman lay on his bed, wide awake and struggling to get comfortable. He heard Rufus crunch the gears as he reversed out into the fog. His thoughts were racing. Try as he might he couldn't chase the disturbing images out of his mind. He had spent the last three hours trying to disentangle the events of the last few hours and days. As tiredness gained the upper hand they became even more jumbled.

There was something else niggling him, something he couldn't place. He would have liked to get up and pace the floor, but there was hardly any room and he didn't want to disturb Robbie. Poor animal, he thought, he must be more confused than me, although if Robbie was, he was certainly showing no sign of it. Better than pacing the floor, Steadman felt, would be to sit at a piano and let the music lead the mental meanderings. Did Dr Rufus have a piano? He couldn't remember.

The niggle was beginning to annoy him. He knew that

if he tried to place it, it would elude him. Distraction, that was what he needed. Was there a bedside light? His hand probed the darkness. Yes – his hand felt cold porcelain, a smooth round shape with a lid. His fingers crept over the object. Was it a ginger jar? There was a push button switch below the bulb. It was stiff. After several attempts, it moved with a loud click. Robbie stirred. Steadman closed one eye then the other, peering in the direction of the lamp. Nothing; not even the faintest glimmer of light. He lay back disappointed. Sometimes he could see faint shapes, blurred shadows and bright lights, or so he fancied, but not tonight. 'Probably switched off at the wall,' he mumbled.

He tried to empty his mind; no use. The annoying thought was starting to give him a sick feeling in the pit of his stomach.

Slowly it began to take shape. It was to do with Frank Rufus. Don't try and find it or it will sink beyond reach; let it float to the surface, he said to himself. It was like trying to remember the name of a long-lost uncle's wife. And then, quite suddenly it broke the surface, a bloated corpse freed from its watery moorings. It hit him with a stinging slap across the face. He was jealous. Jealous of his friend driving Dr Sam Griffiths back to her hotel, jealous of him being alone with her in his car and having her to himself...

No, no, no – this was all wrong. How could he think this, how could he be so disloyal to the memory of his wife? He knew Frank Rufus had shown not the slightest inclination or interest in the opposite sex since losing his wife on their honeymoon many years ago. And yet, here he was with all sorts of unnamed desires scrambling round in his brain. It was as though someone had kicked an ants' nest in his head: first realisation, then guilt and now embarrassment. Sightless and feeble, what could he offer her? For once he allowed himself a brief moment of self-pity.

The painkillers were starting to kick in. Steadman felt his eyes prickle and that odd sensation at the back of his nose he knew was the precursor to sleep. The last thing he was aware of was the slamming of a car door marking Dr Rufus's return. At least he hadn't spent the night at the Equinox Hotel…

'You had better get in there quick, Inspector Steadman,' said Sergeant Grimble. 'God alone knows what Beaky Nesbitt is doing to Harry Eeles.'

Restless images formed in Steadman's sleeping brain. He looked round the waiting room of the Eyesore. It was empty and dark. The only light was a small desk lamp in front of Sergeant Grimble casting weird and terrifying shadows on his podgy face.

'Which room?' Steadman asked.

'Room six,' Grimble replied.

They exchanged anxious looks. Nobody used room six. It was a windowless box at far end of the corridor more suited to a large cupboard than an interview room. But it was quiet and conveniently out of the way.

Steadman pushed open the doors leading out of the

waiting room and ran down the corridor. The police officers in the photographs on the wall all seemed to be frowning at him. He could hear the screams before he reached room six.

'That's the bleeding truth. I wasn't there. I didn't do anything,' pleaded Harry Eeles. 'You ask Inspector Steadman. He'll vouch for me. I'm no saint, but I'm not a murderer.'

'You're a lying bastard, Harry. A dirty little criminal. You've hoodwinked Steadman but you're not fooling me. I'll get an honest answer out of you if it's the last thing I do. You killed Crenshaw Tipley and Velda Meemes then wired them up.'

Steadman heard what sounded like a drawer being tugged open. He turned the handle of the door, but it only opened a couple of inches, no matter how hard he pushed.

'Let's see how you like it,' Nesbitt said, brandishing a coil of copper wire in front of Harry's sweating face.

'Here, what are you going to do with that?'

Nesbitt sprang up from his seat and leapt behind Harry Eeles, who sat frozen with fear. The loop of wire tightened round Harry's neck.

'Gordon Bennett, you can't do this – you're strangling me!'

'The truth, Harry,' Nesbitt roared pulling the ends of the wire.

'Help me, Inspector Steadman. He's killing me. Help me…eee!'

The final 'me' trailed off into a high-pitched squeal…

Steadman sat bolt upright in bed, sweat pouring down his face. The squeal was still ringing in his ears. Gradually the realisation of where he was dawned on him. In the kitchen Dr Rufus took the kettle off the stove and the squealing subsided. Steadman could hear the clatter of crockery, and a minute later there was a gentle knock at the door.

'Oh, you're awake then. Do you want breakfast in bed or down in the kitchen? It's lovely and warm downstairs.'

'Good grief, Frank, I've just had the most awful nightmare…'

Dr Rufus interrupted him before he could finish.

'Well, you shouldn't mix painkillers with alcohol. I could have told you that. Do you want a hand dressing? No – come on Robbie, you can go and water my roses and I'll give you your breakfast while Rip Van Winkle here sorts himself out.'

Steadman shook his head at the retreating figure. Frank really is the best sort of friend; how could he possibly have been jealous of him?

Breakfast was porridge, served with brown sugar and cream.

'Just what you need on a raw foggy day,' said Dr Rufus. 'Kim Ho has been. She may have lifted a fingerprint from the top inside edge of the passenger door. We'll see.'

Steadman nodded appreciatively.

'You managed to get Sam Griffiths back to her hotel safely, then?'

'Yes. She did ask me in for an unbridled night of passion, but I resisted.'

Steadman jerked his head.

'No, of course she didn't! For all I know she may be married with a squad of kids.' That thought had never occurred to Steadman. 'Anyway, despite my undoubted charm and charisma,' continued Dr Rufus, 'she was far more concerned with your well-being than anything else.'

Steadman could resist no longer. 'What does she look like, Frank?' he asked.

'You mean apart from the squint and buck teeth?'

'Frank, are you ever serious?'

'It has been known. Sam Griffiths, let me see – petite, slim, bobbed brown hair, dark eyes, smiles a lot. Age? Hard to tell – early forties I would guess.'

Try as he might Steadman struggled to conjure up a mental image.

'I don't think she's married,' Rufus said as an afterthought. 'I've just remembered - she doesn't wear any rings.'

Before Steadman had time to contemplate whether this made his life any more or less complicated, the mobile in his pocket went off. It was DS Alan Munro.

'How are you, sir? I gather you haven't had your troubles to seek, as we would say back home,' he asked in a broad Scots accent.

'Apart from a cracked rib and a break-in I'm quite well. Dr Rufus has been looking after me. What can I do for you, Alan?'

'First is simply to let you know forensics have finished in your flat. Marco and the family are cleaning as we speak and the locks will be repaired by lunchtime. Second, the interview between our acting DCI and Harry Eeles did not go well. Harry has again refused to speak to anyone other than you. As you can imagine that went down like a lead balloon.'

'Nesbitt didn't try to strangle him, did he?'

'No, why do you ask?'

'Just curious, but please go on. I interrupted you.'

'Nesbitt came over all hard. Harry laughed in his face. I can't remember his exact words but he did refer to Nesbitt as a "cocky, big-nosed, short-arsed git who should go back where he came from, if they'd have him." I suggested you re-interview Harry. Initially Nesbitt was having none of it, however as he didn't have any other suggestions, he reluctantly agreed before storming off.'

'Will you be there, and if so what time would suit?'

'Come at ten-thirty and we can have a coffee first.'

'Would you like me to bring some cake?'

'What a splendid idea – just don't tell Maureen.'

* * *

After breakfast Dr Rufus and John Steadman went for a brief walk. It was still very damp and cold.

'How's your chest feeling now?' asked Rufus.

'Much better than last night, thanks.'

'It will get worse again in about a week as the rib heals.

I couldn't help but overhear what Alan was saying about your flat. You know, you'd be welcome to stay with me.'

'I know. However, I'm not going to be intimidated. Frank, you're very kind but I need my own space, otherwise I will completely forget who I am. Do you understand? I'm not being ungrateful.'

Dr Rufus understood only too well. 'Come on, I'll drive you to the Eyesore. Remind me to stop so we can get some sustenance for that starving detective sergeant.'

DS Munro was waiting for Steadman. Sergeant Grimble struggled to hide his disappointment that Robbie was not being handed over to his care immediately.

'You can have him when we interview Harry.'

'Very good, sir,' replied Grimble as he slipped the dog a biscuit.

Munro and Steadman went through to one of the interview rooms. After finding his former boss a chair, Munro went and fetched the coffee.

'I've brought you some cake, Alan. I think it's possibly a Victoria sponge. Dr Rufus chose it.'

'Not bad at all,' Alan said through a mouthful of cake. 'Are you not having some?'

'The good doctor filled me so full of porridge this morning I doubt I will feel like eating until tomorrow. Have you any other news?'

'The Yank, Arnie Yateman, phoned. Surprise, surprise, he would neither confirm nor deny any knowledge of Velda Meemes. Not his decision of course.'

'Why don't we get DS Fairfax to ask Doreen if her aunt

has ever been to America? I'll bet you anything you like that she hasn't. Interesting though Crenshaw Tipley's double identity undoubtedly is, I'm convinced it has nothing to do with his murder. Shall we get in our chum, Harry, and see if he's changed his tune?'

As if by magic, Sergeant Grimble knocked on the door. 'Is Robbie ready for a walkie with his Uncle Bertie?'

★ ★ ★

'OK Harry, this is how we're going to play it. In a minute or two DS Munro is going to switch on the tape recorder and we are going to formally interview you. We will go over your statement and I want you to think long and hard about your alibis for the two nights in question. Got that?'

Harry Eeles grunted.

'You don't believe I murdered those two people do you, Inspector Steadman? That bastard Nesbitt has got it in for me. And he doesn't care too much for you either.'

'What I believe is neither here nor there, Harry. It is, however an inconvenient coincidence that you were recently working at both properties and both victims were strung up with electrical cable. More than inconvenient for you, but maybe not so for someone else…'

He stopped mid-sentence. His long fingers drummed on the table. A melody began to play in his head: Beethoven, dark and brooding.

Harry started to say something. Munro shook his head

and put a finger to his lips. He knew the signs. Steadman was deep in thought.

'Maybe, maybe...' he muttered to himself. 'But that means our every move is being watched. Of course, it would explain...'

'Explain what?' Harry Eeles could contain himself no longer.

'Sorry, I was... considering another possibility,' Steadman replied hesitantly. 'Alan, are you ready with the tape recorder?'

DS Munro switched on the machine and went through the formalities. Line by line they dissected Harry's statement. Nothing had changed.

'Which pubs were you in on the two nights?'

'Only the one, The Crown and Anchor.'

'The one down by the docks?'

'That's the place. Been a regular there for years – except when I've been otherwise detained, if you know what I mean.'

'You gave us some names last time.' DS Munro read out the list.

'Well, you can forget most of them,' said Harry. 'Even I wouldn't trust them. There's two on the list that are a bit more respectable and, if needs must, would scrub up for the occasion.'

Munro circled the two names Harry mentioned.

'What about the landlord. It used to be that big Irish fellow, O'Connell. Is he still there?'

'Yeah, Declan O'Connell was there both nights. He

might remember me. He doesn't like the police much, that's the only thing.'

The formal interview was over.

'Can I go home now?'

'Not my shout I'm afraid, Harry. Have you thought about getting a solicitor?'

'A fat lot of good it's done me in the past. It's more serious this time, I suppose. Got anyone in mind?'

If Steadman could have seen, he would have noticed an evil grin spread over Munro's face.

'I've been thinking about that,' he said. 'I was wondering if Sven Jensen would be appropriate. What do you think, sir?'

'You have a mean streak in you, Alan, but on the whole I think he would be an excellent choice.'

Harry looked from one officer to the other. 'Here, what's going on? Are you two trying to stitch me up or something?'

'No, no – Mr Jensen is young, very bright and Scandinavian. He also happens to be the most pedantic and fastidious solicitor I've met for a long time,' Steadman replied.

'And he would get right up Inspector Nesbitt's nose,' added Munro.

Harry was about to say something about there being plenty of room. The door burst open before he could open his mouth.

'Looks like he has struck again,' said an out-of-breath Sergeant Grimble. 'Alan, Inspector Nesbitt wants you in his office now. DS Fairfax is already there.'

'Well, he can't pin this one on me, can he?' said Harry Eeles.

Steadman sat completely motionless. This has got to stop, he thought. What am I missing?

CHAPTER SIXTEEN

Steadman closed his eyes, not that it made any difference other than helping him to focus. Munro shot out of his chair and, with the same look of determination normally reserved for pursuing a loose rugby ball, he left the room. Sergeant Grimble escorted Harry Eeles back to the care of the custody sergeant.

'Remember to sort out that Scandinavian solicitor for me, Inspector Steadman,' he said.

Steadman appeared not to hear him. An orchestra had started playing in his head: this time it was Mozart Concerto no. 20 – deep and troubling. His right hand traced a few of the opening bars. The melody wound on, getting ever more complex. What was going on? Who was out there? Certainly not Harry Eeles, at least not this time. It never was Harry Eeles, he knew that. What possible motives could the killer have? Something linked the murders – what though? Think, think. And why wire them up? A display? A show maybe – a show of what exactly? What was somebody trying to prove? And who attacked his dog? Was it the same person as in the car or even who broke into his flat? No – it made no sense.

He pushed his dark glasses on to his forehead and rubbed his eyes. Planned murders, opportunistic attacks – someone was scheming, watching their every move.

And who stole the wire from Harry's van? Was that just another coincidence? What was it that Sam Griffiths had said? - "Maybe he's just malicious" – that was it. Could there be more than one person involved? Possibly, he thought. Working alone or together? Steadman sighed in exasperation.

He desperately wanted to go to Crenshaw Tipley's house and Velda Meemes' shop, breathe in the air and absorb the atmosphere.

And now a third murder – a murder from which he was clearly being excluded. No mention of, "and Inspector Nesbitt would like your opinion." He was disappointed but not surprised. What half-baked conclusions would Nesbitt jump to this time?

The door opened. Robbie padded in and dropped his large, furry head on to Steadman's lap.

'Oh, it's you, is it. I wondered what Uncle Bertie had done with you,' he said giving the dog a scratch behind the ears. 'What do you think about it all, then? Can you tell me what's happening? No? Ah well, I'm sure if you're here Sergeant Grimble won't be far behind.'

And he wasn't.

'Sorry about leaving you like that, sir. Inspector Nesbitt

is going ballistic.' Grimble turned to Robbie. 'And you are a very clever dog finding your master all by yourself.'

Robbie looked expectantly at the bulge in Grimble's pocket where the treats were kept.

'As I'm not invited to Inspector Nesbitt's office party, perhaps you could tell me what you've gleaned so far?'

'Not a huge amount, I'm afraid. A call came in from a PC who had answered a treble nine from Da Gama Towers.'

Steadman pulled a face. Despite its grand-sounding name, Da Gama Towers was three modern concrete high-rise apartment blocks in what was probably the most deprived area of Helmsmouth. Even on a bright day poverty, desperation and a sense of hopelessness seemed to block out the sun.

'A friend of the victim called to see him as he hadn't turned up to man his pitch at the local street market,' Grimble went on. 'Apparently, the door was open and the victim – I'm sorry I don't have a name yet – was sat on the loo with his head bashed in and wired up to look as though... well, I don't know for certain. Dr Rufus is on the scene, and I expect Inspector Nesbitt will be sending DS Munro to lead the investigation.'

'Not DS Fairfax? She's more senior.'

Sergeant Grimble snorted. 'Not quite the right sex for our acting DCI, I fear.' A phone rang in the distance. 'Damn, that's for me. I'd better go and answer it. I'll try and find out some more. I'll be back soon.'

Robbie had spreadeagled on the floor and was lying

heavily on Steadman's feet. A third murder and not much to go on, Steadman mused. From the cossetted comfort of Upper Bridgetown to the grim Da Gama Towers by way of a twee antique shop in the marina. 'Come on Robbie, you're supposed to be clever – what's the link?' he said out loud.

'Sorry sir, I thought for a moment you had someone with you. The door was open. I should have knocked.'

Steadman had not heard DS Fairfax enter the room and blushed with embarrassment.

'Just thinking out loud… consulting the dog… I blame Sergeant Grimble…' he faltered.

'May I have a quiet word with you, sir?'

'Of course.'

DS Fairfax closed the door and sat in what had been Harry's chair, well away from the dog, which she still viewed with some trepidation.

'I gather you are not leading the latest investigation.'

'No sir. I didn't really expect DCI Nesbitt to ask me. In fact, I know very little other than it does appear to be similar to the other two. But that is not why I'm here. DCI Nesbitt has asked me to go and arrest Maurice Eeles on suspicion of murder. He still reckons Harry Eeles is guilty. Now he believes father and son are in it together.'

Steadman frowned and bit his thumb nail.

'What a fool,' he said under his breath. 'I'm sorry Fiona, you will have to obey an order. Personally, I think Maurice is even less likely than his dad. At least Harry has got a track record for violence. But Maurice… handling stolen goods, cannabis and driving without insurance, if I remember correctly.'

'That's about it, sir. I think he has a pending charge for shop-lifting – a computer game. Do you think he will come in quietly?'

'He might try and do a runner because he's stupid. I would be surprised if he tries anything else. You never can tell, I suppose.'

Steadman's dream came back to him in a flash.

'There is one thing you could do for me, Fiona. Would you check if Maurice has a bicycle?'

'A bicycle? Why?'

Steadman turned red again. He never liked discussing his dreams.

'Don't laugh,' he said, 'it's just that…'

He outlined only the smallest part of his dream, omitting completely to mention anything of the fairground and the strange arcade game, although he did shudder slightly when he recalled 'VICTIM' flashing next to Tim Warrender's name.

'Oh, by the way, Fiona, I don't suppose you have had time to check if Velda Meemes had ever been to America?'

'Not only had she never been to America, sir, she has never held a passport. She once went to the Isle of Man and that is as far afield as she travelled in her life.'

'Well, that's one loose end tidied up. Please don't mention my silly dream to anyone. I'd be so embarrassed.'

DS Fairfax agreed to keep her lips sealed.

★ ★ ★

Steadman bent down and gave the dog a friendly scratch under his chin.

'Right then, Robbie, let's get your harness on. I think we're walking home.'

'That's what you think, sir,' said a loud Scottish voice. 'You are coming with me. We've got a murder to solve.'

Steadman brightened.

'Are you sure you won't get into trouble? I got the impression that Inspector Nesbitt had cut me out of all further investigations.'

'He hasn't. Well, not exactly, sir. Firstly, what he doesn't know won't harm him and secondly, what he actually said was, "I don't think there is any need to involve Steadman", which is not quite the same as saying, "don't involve Steadman", at least not in my book. Anyway, I've bought two pork pies and Maureen will kill me if I eat both of them. Come on, the Audi is parked by the main door.'

They walked along the corridor past the frowning photographs. Would they all be frowning, Steadman asked himself? He knew one of them wouldn't be: his first boss, a man whose approach to crime solving was both unconventional and remarkable. If he could, he would have given an encouraging smile and winked at Steadman and Munro as they passed.

'Here, let me help you with the wrapper, sir. It's a bit fiddly,' said Munro once they were in the car.

'Thanks,' Steadman replied. 'Aren't you going to eat yours before we set off?'

'I ate mine as we were walking out of the Eyesore,' Munro confessed. 'Let's go.'

'As you've finished eating, why don't you fill me in? Sergeant Grimble had surprisingly few details.'

'The victim is called Dennis Knotting, thirty-five, bachelor and runs a market stall selling reconditioned wind-up gramophones and old 78s.'

'I wouldn't have thought there was a living to be made in that,' Steadman interjected.

'There can't be. I suspect he is as a poor as a church mouse. I don't know yet if he does anything else like bar work or stacking supermarket shelves – I'll find out. He's been living in a flat in one of the Da Gama Towers for about five years. Do you know Da Gama Towers, sir?'

Steadman could clearly recall the grim, graffiti-covered concrete, the discarded mattresses and burnt-out cars. That was not what troubled him: it was the people who had to live there. They all looked sad and abandoned.

'I gather he was found by a friend. Do we know when?'

'Yes, just after eleven this morning. Kevin Creasey has the next stall to his. He sells Dinky and Corgi toy cars as well as old cigarette lighters. They regularly share a morning coffee. It was most unusual for Dennis not to show up. Kevin asked someone to keep an eye on his stall and went round to Dennis's flat. We will meet Kevin when we get there.'

'What about the body?'

'Massive blow to the back of the head, then wired up sitting on the loo.'

Steadman tried hard to imagine the scene.

'Have you caught up with this morning's papers, sir?' Normally Marco or Roberto Lloyd would read out anything that was noteworthy over his morning coffee.

'No, not yet. Anything interesting?'

'Your friend Jack is clearly unimpressed by our acting DCI. He described Nesbitt as being impulsive and a man who never knowingly lets facts get in the way of a quick arrest.'

'Inspector Nesbitt will probably take that as a compliment,' Steadman replied. 'What about Harry Eeles? Is he mentioned?'

'Not by name, sir, which is just as well.'

'Absolutely – whatever his past Harry, on the face of it, does appear to be trying something other than crime. Of course, Nesbitt now wants his son arrested as well...' Steadman shook his head.

'I had heard,' Munro replied.

It was still very murky outside. All the vehicles had their lights on and were crawling along the road as though part of an interminable funeral cortege.

'When do you think this fog will lift, sir?'

'I suspect it will be rather like Mary Poppins and be with us until the wind changes and comes in from a new quarter.'

'That reminds me, Maureen has invited you for supper.

If the girls don't get to meet Robbie soon my life won't be worth living.'

Steadman thought that would be a good idea. He was very fond of Maureen and the two girls.

'Do we know anything else about Dennis Knotting? It all seems very sketchy so far,' he asked.

'They are doing routine background checks back at the Eyesore. Hopefully I'll get a call within the hour. Odd name, Dennis – I don't think I've ever come across a criminal called Dennis, unless you count that juvenile delinquent Dennis the Menace in the Beano. I wonder where the name comes from.'

'I believe it's Greek – a follower of Dionysius, the Greek god of wine. There was also a Saint Dennis, the patron saint of Paris. He is believed to have picked up his head after having it chopped off and went on to preach a sermon of repentance.'

Munro shot a questioning look at his colleague.

'How do you know all that stuff?'

Steadman shrugged. 'I think I heard it on a radio quiz programme. You know, before I lost my sight I used to love looking things like that up. You may remember I had loads of books and then, of course, there was the internet. My world is very bare now, Alan, I'm so reliant on others, which reminds me...'

It suddenly occurred to him that he had not found out why the names Reg Butler and Gordon Greig were familiar. Should he ask Munro? No, damn it he was going to find that out himself, somehow.

Munro did not have time to ask him what he was reminded of as Da Gama Towers loomed out of the fog. A posse of police cars were parked outside Tower 3; their blue flashing lights had attracted a small crowd despite the weather.

'We had better leave Robbie in the car. Inspector Nesbitt would have a fit if he found his crime scene contaminated with dog hair.'

As they passed through the on-lookers Steadman could hear his name being whispered. A uniformed officer touched his cap to the two detectives.

'Fifth floor. The photographers have just left,' he added. Doubtless he was thinking there would not have been enough room for Munro if they were still there.

The lift reeked of stale tobacco. Another officer was standing by the door.

'Do you remember the layout of the flats, sir?' Munro asked.

'Only vaguely. They are fairly pokey, I recall.' Steadman suddenly felt very awkward. 'Alan, maybe I should wait in the car. I'll only be a hindrance and…'

'Nonsense – you always could read a crime scene with your eyes closed. There's no difference now.'

It was not strictly true. Both Steadman and Munro knew it.

'I'll try not to get in the way,' said Steadman.

They slipped on plastic gloves and overshoes. The door opened onto a short corridor. To their left was a small sitting room and off that a tiny kitchen. On their right was a bedroom and, at the end of the corridor, the bathroom. Munro discreetly gave an outline. Steadman nodded.

'A real bachelor existence, I would say,' Munro added. 'The place hasn't had a lick of paint for years and the carpet is long overdue its annual vacuuming.'

Munro pushed open the door to the sitting room and guided his colleague through. Steadman stood motionless, aware of the people milling about him and the distinct smell of curry.

Kim Ho emerged from the small kitchen and greeted the two men.

'What's the picture so far?' Munro asked.

'No sign of forced entry, but you probably noticed that on your way in.' Immediately she glanced at Steadman. 'I'm sorry, I keep forgetting...'

'No need to apologise. It would help me if you described the room we're in.'

Kim thought for a moment.

'Well, it's about twelve foot by twelve foot. There's a window on your left and in front of that there's a dining table and two mismatched chairs. On the table there's an old gramophone in bits and the remains of an Indian take-away meal. There are two shabby armchairs and a small round coffee table with another gramophone, an ash tray and a half-empty tin of beer. One wall is completely taken over by shelves containing several hundred old records, all neatly catalogued. In the corner there's a Swiss cheese plant dying of thirst. There's a clock on the wall and a couple of framed posters advertising the Golden Age of

Steam Travel. Apart from that there is only an old radio and some magazines.'

Steadman painted the scene in his mind's eye.

'The place is fairly filthy,' Kim continued. 'Lots of fingerprints, but they all seem to be the same and probably from the deceased. It looks like he was struck from behind while sitting at the dining table. Be careful - there is a pool of congealed blood on the carpet about six feet in front of you.'

'No sign of a weapon?' Steadman asked.

'No, but there are a couple of odd things.'

Steadman raised his head; he liked odd things.

'On the table, there is an expensive bottle of wine, Nuits-Saint-Georges. There are no prints and no dust on the bottle. It is also on top of the take-away wrappers. Dennis Knotting could have bought it last night but I think it was brought by his attacker. What little food there is in the kitchen is all budget brand and low cost – not really in keeping with wine of that quality.'

Steadman was intrigued. Why would anyone buy Dennis Knotting a bottle of expensive wine? It suggested his attacker knew him and would explain why the door had not been forced. Maybe someone else knew the Greek origin of the name Dennis.

Kim Ho was speaking again. Steadman missed what she said and it was his turn to apologise.

'Come through to the bedroom, sir,' she said. 'It will be quieter there.'

The bedroom was equally spartan and squalid. It smelt

of sweat and sleep. Steadman could imagine dirty clothes piled on the floor and an unmade bed with grubby sheets.

'We found an envelope on his bedside table,' Kim continued. 'It's good quality and had been carefully opened but...'

'The contents are missing.' Steadman finished the sentence for her.

'What are you thinking, sir?' asked Munro.

'The glimmer of a motive, that's all,' Steadman replied. 'Anything else we should know, Kim?'

'Yes, his boots are interesting me. They're covered in a layer of white dust.'

'Talcum powder?' Munro suggested.

'No, it's not as fine as that and not perfumed. The dust is impregnated into the leather and on the soles, which suggests it's not just a one-off. The boots have also got steel toe-caps. Unless he has another job, I don't see how that fits with someone who mends and sells old gramophones and records.'

Munro was flicking through the books on a small shelf by the bed. 'There's no tax on steel toe-capped boots. Maybe our Dennis is just watching his pennies,' he said. 'A keen armchair traveller, judging by his reading selection.'

Steadman was always fascinated by other people's books. 'What else does he read in bed?' he asked.

'DIY, brew your own beer, some books on art and a well-thumbed illustrated version of the Kama Sutra.'

Munro's mobile rang.

'Damn, just as it was getting interesting!' he said as he put the Kama Sutra back on the shelf.

'Hello, hello… hold on, I'll go outside to see if there is better reception. Excuse me a minute, sir.'

A voice from the sitting room summoned Kim Ho. As she left, and for no obvious reason, she pulled the door closed behind her. Steadman could not have wished for anything better. For a moment, he simply stood still, aware that he was breathing the same air that had sustained the living Dennis Knotting. This was his bedroom, a place where he had spent a third of his life, his sanctuary and place of repose. It bore his unique smell. What did he think about before he went to sleep, Steadman wondered? What hopes and dreams did he have? What was so precious about the contents of that envelope that he had kept it by his bed? Too often, Steadman thought, the victim is just ignored, unless of course it was a celebrity. "Celebrity" – how he loathed that word. It was as though all other life was insignificant. Poor Dennis Knotting – who would miss him?

The room was small. Cautiously Steadman turned round. He stretched out his arms and took a step in the direction of what he hoped would be the door. He found the knob, but his hand brushed against something soft hanging behind the door. Was it a dressing gown? Steadman patted the garment. No, it was too short and coarse and had a zip down the front. It was Dennis's jacket. Curiosity got the better of him. He went through the pockets: a comb, a tissue, a wallet, some small change and a soft packet. Steadman sniffed – rolling tobacco. And finally, a bunch of keys; four keys to be precise. Through the thin plastic gloves Steadman was fairly sure he could make out a front door key and a car key. The other two were similar in size and similar in design. Padlock keys perhaps? He held them together and ran a finger-tip over the serrated edges. Similar they may be, but definitely not identical.

CHAPTER SEVENTEEN

Whether it was excitement or nerves, Munro's Scottish accent always became more pronounced during an investigation.

'Where have you hidden DI Steadman?' he asked.

'I'm still in the bedroom, Alan.'

Munro pushed open the door and could tell from the expression on Steadman's face that he had found something.

'What have you got there, sir?'

Steadman opened his hand, revealing the keys. 'I found them in the jacket behind the door. There's also a wallet, but I've left that for you. I think this one is a car key and this could be his front door key. These two are of the same design, but I think they are different keys.'

Munro took the keys and with a glance confirmed Steadman's deductions.

'You're right, sir, they are not the same. I think they might be garage keys, but why would he have two garages?'

'Precisely,' Steadman replied.

'Half a moment, sir.'

Munro pushed open the sitting room door.

'Kim, have you found a front door key?'

'On a nail behind the door. Why?'

'Inspector Steadman has found another set of keys in the bedroom.'

Munro compared the door keys: they were the same.

'I'm going to hang on to these, Kim,' he said and slipped them into a plastic bag before pocketing them.

'You probably heard all that,' Munro said as he re-entered the bedroom. 'Let's have a look at Dennis's wallet.'

The wallet was made of black leather and worn at the corners. There were a couple of credit cards, a supermarket loyalty card, a driver's licence with a faded picture and some cheap business cards. Munro laid them neatly on the bed.

'How much money is in there?' Steadman inquired. 'I'll bet it's not very much.'

'Only fifteen pounds. Even with the small change our Dennis was carrying less than twenty pounds on him.'

'Presumably he must have other cash in the flat, otherwise how would he be able to run his stall?'

'I said you could read a crime scene with your eyes closed. Kim has found a petty cash box under the lid of the gramophone,' replied Munro as he continued to empty the wallet. 'There are some receipts in here. Let's have a look – petrol two days ago, some groceries at the beginning of the week, last night's curry – chicken bhuna, rice and a naan bread.' Munro paused. 'I could murder a curry right now. And finally,' he said unfolding the last piece of paper, 'oh, it appears Dennis has just banked a cheque for five hundred pounds.'

'Probably what was in the empty envelope,' Steadman suggested. 'It shouldn't be too hard to trace. I wonder what has happened to the accompanying letter. No one sends a cheque for that amount without some correspondence.'

Munro grunted. He had turned the wallet upside down and was shaking it. A small photograph fluttered on to the bed. He picked it up and examined it closely.

'What is it?' Steadman asked.

'Sorry, sir. An old photo taken seventeen years ago, according to the date on the back. It shows three rather scruffy, smiling men. Students I would guess.'

'Could one of them be the deceased?'

'I don't know, sir. One of them looks a bit like the picture on the driver's licence. I haven't been able to see the body yet. I was waiting until...'

He didn't have to finish the sentence.

'The doctor will see you now.' Frank Rufus's voice boomed down the corridor.

From the sitting room came a loud crackle and a hiss. Someone had wound up the old gramophone and put on a 78. An orchestra started playing, then the distinctive voice of Nat King Cole:

Last night I had a dream of you, my heart began to cry.
I saw you kissing someone new, but dreams can tell a lie.

'Will I ask them to turn it off, sir?'

'No, no,' replied Steadman. He was bemused by the lyrics.

For where there's smoke you'll find a fire
And in my dreams I saw the gleam of your desire.
Tonight we'll meet along the street and all my fears will fly.
Your loving arms will hold me and as they soon enfold me
Your kiss will soon have told me that dreams can tell a lie.

Steadman pursed his lips. 'Hmm…'

'Anything the matter, sir?'

'Not really,' he replied, although he was having some regrets about asking DS Fairfax to look for a bike in Maurice Eeles's garage. 'Well, to tell the truth, Alan, I may have made a fool of myself. I had a very vivid dream the other night – all nonsense of course – but at the end of the dream Maurice Eeles cycled off on a blood-spattered bike. I've asked DS Fairfax to check if Maurice has a bike. I'm sure he hasn't.'

'And if she finds one, sir?'

'Then that, Alan, would make life very complicated.'

The record had come to an end. Munro led Steadman down the corridor and into the cramped bathroom.

'Dear God alive!' Munro exclaimed.

'Not a pretty sight, I grant you,' replied Dr Rufus, who seemed to be enjoying himself immensely.

Another loud hiss and crackle, then Nat King Cole burst into song again. This time his voice sounded much higher; either it was a much younger Nat King Cole or the record was turning too fast.

Smile though your heart is aching
Smile even though it's breaking

'Remarkably loud, isn't it?' commented Rufus.

'I can easily get them to stop, if you like,' offered Munro.

'No, let them have their fun.'

Dr Rufus cast a sideways glance at John Steadman and thought he looked lost.

'Pay attention at the back! What we have here is a small windowless bathroom, John. On your right is the bath, on the left a large airing cupboard and in front of you is the loo and a wash-hand basin. Sitting on the loo, as naked as the day he was born, is the earthly remains, or what is left of them, of Dennis Knotting. He is wired up to look like that statue The Thinker – you know the one, by that randy bearded Belgium, whose name escapes me.'

'Auguste Rodin, and I believe he was French,' Steadman explained.

Dr Rufus shrugged, as if to imply that it was much the same thing. 'Whatever,' he said. 'Anyway, it looks all very theatrical.'

'Theatrical?' Steadman was surprised by the choice of words. 'In what way?'

'I don't know – it just seems very staged, I suppose. What killed him was a massive single blow to the back of the head. Very nearly decapitated him.'

'A bit like Dennis, the patron saint of Paris,' Munro ventured. 'Shame the head can't talk.'

Dr Rufus stared quizzically at Munro, who in turn went bright red.

'You ought to get out more, Alan.'

DS Munro pointed at Steadman.

'I might have guessed. That's just the sort of rubbish Inspector Steadman has been filling his brains with for years. Be wary, Alan, I've heard it's catching.'

Steadman ignored the aside. 'What sort of weapon are we looking for?' he asked.

'A cannon ball,' suggested Dr Rufus.

'Are you being serious, Frank?'

'Oh yes – at least we should be looking for something that is large, round and heavy. The back of the skull is neatly dished in. Look Alan.'

'I'd rather not if you don't mind. Where are his clothes?'

'They were in the bath. Kim has bagged them up.'

The record had changed again. Now it was Louis Armstrong singing:

Red sails in the sunset
Way out on the sea
Oh, carry my loved one
Home safely to me

Steadman was frowning. Something was troubling him.

'Is there a lot of blood, Frank?'

'There's a puddle in the sitting room.'

'What about in the corridor and in here?'

'Now you come to mention it, surprisingly little. A few smears on the floor, that's about it.'

Steadman scratched the back of his head. He turned towards the door, screwed up his face and tried hard to visualise the scene. Louis Armstrong was blowing for all he was worth. Turning back to where he thought Dr Rufus was standing, he asked:

'Are there any towels in the bathroom?'

'None lying about,' Rufus replied.

Munro opened the airing cupboard.

'There are some clean ones in here, sir.'

'And no dirty ones in the bin,' added Kim Ho, who had joined the men in the bathroom. 'What are you thinking, sir?'

'I'm thinking the killer must have used something to staunch the flow of blood before, or even while, he moved Dennis's body. The most obvious thing would be towels. If they are not here, he surely took them away with him.'

'How bizarre,' Kim remarked.

Steadman raised an eyebrow. 'What sort of person was he, Frank?'

'What do you mean?'

'Physically – you have the advantage over me. Can you describe him?'

'Well, he is not very tall. Of course he is sitting down, but judging by the length of his forearm I would suggest that he is no more than five foot six inches.'

Steadman was aware that by measuring from the elbow to the wrist you could get a very good estimate of height.

'He's thin, but quite muscle-bound, especially his right arm. Not really in keeping with someone who mends and sells old gramophones. His hands, or at least what I can see of them, are quite calloused and the fingernails are badly chipped.'

Steadman nodded appreciatively. 'What about his toenails? Are they badly bruised?'

Dr Rufus was taken aback.

'How the devil did you work that out?'

'Kim said he had steel toe-capped boots. Most people, I suspect, only wear protective gear when they are obliged to or if circumstances remind them of the necessity. Kim also said his boots were covered in some sort of dust. Is there anything in his hair?'

Dr Rufus lifted up a clump of Dennis's hair.

'Impossible to say. What's left of his hair is matted in blood.'

Munro bumped awkwardly into John Steadman.

'Excuse me, sir, I just need a wee bit of fresh air.'

Kim Ho stood aside to let an ashen-faced DS Munro past.

'It's always the big ones who have no stomach,' remarked Dr Rufus.

Louis Armstrong had now been joined by Bing Crosby:

On my door I'd hang a sign
Gone fishin' instead of just a-wishin'

'You know, I might just get one of those wind-up gramophones,' Frank continued. 'It would sound good in the mortuary. I could sing along to the tunes when I'm doing a post-mortem.'

Steadman sighed. 'I wonder if Dr Griffiths sees private patients, Frank. I really think you ought to talk to someone.'

Munro bustled back into the room. He still looked rather pale.

'Sorry about that, maybe my blood sugar got a bit low.'

Steadman was frowning again.

'There's something else bothering you, isn't there, John?' asked Dr Rufus.

'Yes, but I'm sure there is a simple explanation. Can anyone else smell chocolate?'

'Not guilty,' said Munro.

Both he and Kim Ho sniffed. Dr Rufus didn't bother; he knew his nose had been rendered immune to all bar the most pungent of smells.

'I agree,' said Kim. 'What is that brown trickle at the corner of Dennis Knotting's mouth?'

Dr Rufus tried to poke a gloved finger between Dennis's lips.

'It would be easier if these blasted wires were not in the way. We are going to have to cut them anyway before we move the body.'

With a flourish, Dr Rufus opened his bag and produced a pair of wire cutters.

'Excuse me, I'm just going to pop outside again and

check if there is any word from Kevin Creasey,' said Munro, who had turned an ominous shade of green.

Dr Rufus snipped the wires and freed the hand from under Dennis's jaw. Rigor mortis had set in and the arm remained defiantly in position.

'Where is a big strong man when you want one?' he remarked. After a few tugs he pulled the hand free of the jaw, which obligingly opened sufficiently to allow him to insert an enquiring finger. The smell of chocolate was now unmistakable.

'Well blow me, there are several in here,' he said. 'Any particular flavour you fancy, John?'

'You are a revolting character at times, Frank. Don't mash them up, I'm sure Kim will want to accurately identify them. First whisky, then sparkling water and now chocolates... very odd.'

'Oh look,' said Dr Rufus as he peered between Dennis's legs, 'there are some more floating in the toilet. I wonder if the killer threw them in or stuck them up Dennis's...'

'I think, Frank, that I will leave you to your grisly task. Kim, would you be so kind as to lead me to Munro?'

The officer on the door informed Steadman that Munro had left the building. He had managed to get hold of Kevin Creasey on his mobile, but the signal was breaking up.

Steadman was quite happy to wait and lose himself in his own thoughts. He knew that at times like these a tune would often start in his head, but not today. Someone was still enjoying going through Dennis's 78s. The latest offering was "Fools Rush In". How apt, Steadman thought. He didn't recognise the artist and unfortunately the record was scratched and clicked loudly with each revolution.

So what have we got, Steadman mused: an open door suggesting the killer either had a key or, more likely, was known to Dennis Knotting, an expensive bottle of wine, an empty envelope that may have contained a cheque, dusty boots, keys that don't match, an old photo, a body whose head was bashed in and whose mouth, if not other parts of its anatomy, had been crammed with chocolates, not to mention being wired up to look like a famous statue. A body that was incongruously strong and had broken fingernails and bruised toenails.

DI John Steadman's face broke into a broad smile.

'I think I can answer at least part of the riddle,' he said in a far louder voice than he intended.

CHAPTER EIGHTEEN

Steadman had not heard the lift arrive. The doors opened and Munro squeezed out. Like a lot of big men, Munro walked quietly when not in a hurry.

'And what riddle would that be, sir?'

Steadman gave a start.

'Sorry, sir. It's that bloody gramophone. I'm surprised you can hear yourself think.'

The gramophone had begun to wind down. The singer's voice had dropped an octave and the words were now elongated and unintelligible. Someone inside the flat started to laugh.

Munro pushed open the door. 'Enough!'

The music stopped instantly.

'That's better. Now tell me what you've deduced. You are looking rather pleased with yourself.'

'I have been considering the alternatives, Alan.'

Munro smiled; considering the alternatives was another of Steadman's maxims.

'I think I can account for the steel toe-capped boots, the broken fingernails and the brawny arms. It all depends on what we find in the second garage…' Steadman's voice tailed off.

'And you're not going to tell me.'

'Not yet. I may be wrong. I can't account for everything – at least not so far. It would help to speak with Kevin Creasey.'

'That's where we're heading. There is an internet café about four hundred yards from here. I've arranged to meet him there in…' Munro consulted his watch, 'about twenty minutes.'

'Good. I need to let Robbie stretch his legs and you can tell me about your other phone call.'

Munro led Steadman towards the lift. They had to wait, as the lift had been summoned to the top of Da Gama Tower.

Steadman scratched his forehead and muttered to himself, 'Well now, it could be that.'

'Could be what, sir?'

Steadman raised his head sharply as though just realising he was talking out loud.

'I was just wondering why Dennis Knotting was wired up to look like a famous statue. Do you know that it wasn't called The Thinker originally, but The Poet and was part of a bigger sculpture called The Gates of Hell?'

'I can tell you, sir, the scene in that bathroom was like something from a hellish nightmare. All it needed was for Dr Rufus to sprout horns and start prodding me with a large toasting fork. You know, I don't think I will ever get used to murdered bodies.'

'Nor should you, Alan. The day they don't affect you is the day you should retire.'

The lift arrived and the doors opened. A scruffy youth was inside smoking a roll-up. Munro jabbed the 'No Smoking' sign with a large finger. Without saying anything the young man stubbed out the cigarette and dropped the butt on the floor. Munro shook his head and pointed at the dog-end. Reluctantly, and with a look filled with loathing, the youth picked it up. For his efforts he was rewarded with a beamy Scottish smile.

They descended in silence. As soon as the lift doors opened, the youth fled, but not before turning and sticking two fingers up to Munro.

'There's gratitude for you, sir.'

'I assume, Alan, you dissuaded whoever it was from smoking in a public space?'

'That, and looking after the environment. He'll thank me one day.'

'Do you think so?'

'No, not really.'

The air was cold and moist, but at least it was fresh. More people had gathered outside the tower block to the extent that a police cordon had been set up.

Someone stepped forward from the crowd and a camera flashed in Steadman's face. He could just perceive the sudden, dazzling brightness and instinctively raised a protecting arm.

Munro intervened. 'Where are your manners, sonny?'

'I'm only doing my job.'

'Well buy a longer lens and do it from back there,' Munro replied as he gently but forcefully shoved the photographer back behind the police cordon.

A familiar voice from the crowd shouted, 'Can you give me a statement?'

Steadman turned to Munro.

'If you wouldn't mind, sir. I don't like talking to the press.'

Munro nodded to the uniformed officer, and Jack from the *Helmsmouth Echo* and *Evening Post* fell in line with the two men as they made their way back to the Audi.

The inside of the car had steamed up and smelt distinctly of damp dog. Munro switched on the engine and the air conditioning.

'Come on Robbie, let's go for a quick walk,' he said.

Robbie bounded out of the car, almost knocking Steadman off his feet.

'Jack, it beats me how you find out about these things.'

'Trade secrets I'm afraid, Inspector Steadman,' the reporter replied, having settled himself into the back seat. 'I need something snappy if I'm to make the evening papers. Has he struck again?'

Steadman gave sufficient details for Jack to write his article.

'I'm not prepared to give you any more until the family, if he has any, have been contacted,' he said. 'What you can say is that someone entered Da Gama Towers last night carrying a bag and left carrying a bag. We desperately need to speak with that person.'

'What was in the bag?'

Steadman breathed deeply. Should he give Jack any more information?

'On the way in, the bag contained an expensive bottle of wine, wire and possibly the murder weapon. On the way out, definitely the murder weapon and probably some blood-soaked towels. Obviously we would like to find the bag.'

'Any idea what the murder weapon was?'

'Sadly it falls into the category of "heavy blunt object", that's all I can tell you.'

Steadman thought it wise not to relate Dr Rufus's speculation about it being a cannon ball.

* * *

Munro tapped gently on the window. 'Are you fit to go, sir?'

Steadman nodded and got out of the car. He slipped Robbie into his harness and the dog's demeanour transformed in an instant.

'What is it about Robbie that everyone wants to pat him? Melanie and Annie can't wait to see him. Are you still on for coming over tonight? Maureen has been on the phone again.'

Steadman confirmed he would definitely be there. It would be nice, he thought, to be with a normal family away from the carnage of Da Gama Towers.

The two men started walking.

'Speaking of phone calls, I presume you have some more information on Dennis Knotting?' asked Steadman.

'Yes, and all rather sad. He was an only child, a talented artist who went to study at Helmsmouth College. His parents were killed in a car crash in his second year and he dropped out. The parents were not wealthy. The only things of value he inherited were his father's collections of old records and gramophones. Shortly afterwards, he set up the market stall. The business is more successful than I would have thought. His bank balance is reasonably healthy.'

'Any idea where the five-hundred-pound cheque came from?'

'I should hear tomorrow. There are a lot of gaps. I'm hoping Kevin Creasey will be able to help.'

A cold wind whistled round the corner of Da Gama Towers and Steadman regretted leaving his fedora in the car.

Betty's Internet Café was not far, but not quite as close as Munro had been led to believe. Robbie was clearly enjoying working again. Munro marvelled at how the dog seemed to know intuitively where they were heading, how he stopped at every kerbside and gave all obstacles a wide berth.

A gush of warm air laced with the delicious aroma of frying bacon greeted the two men as they entered the café. Behind the counter stood a large, moustached matriarch. The badge on her ample bosom declared that she was

Betty. She scowled at Robbie.

'Is that a guide dog?'

Munro assured her that it was.

'I suppose that's all right then,' Betty replied. Her scowl turned on Munro. He was so obviously a policeman that he might have been wearing a uniform and twirling a truncheon. 'Trouble in Da Gama Towers, is there?'

Munro was only half-listening. The smell of the bacon had stirred his gastric juices and his stomach was rumbling.

A tall, thin man with bulging eyes and swept back, wavy hair stood up. He had been sitting in the corner. Munro, being too absorbed with the menu chalked on the wall, had failed to notice him.

'DS Munro?'

'The very same. You must be Mr Creasey.'

Munro held out a great paw and almost crushed the life out of Kevin Creasey's hand.

'Call me Kevin. Nobody calls me Mr Creasey,' he replied, glad to retrieve his hand in one piece.

'OK Kevin, this is Inspector…'

'I know who Inspector Steadman is,' interrupted Kevin.

Steadman wondered how he knew. He could not recall anyone of that name.

'I've seen your picture in the papers,' Kevin explained.

'Let's have a seat. I'm going to have the all-day breakfast. Who will join me?' said Munro.

Kevin stared nervously from side to side and flattened down his hair with a tremulous hand. His eyes bulged even more. He reminded Munro of a startled rabbit.

'I'm paying,' offered Munro.

Kevin agreed to join him.

'What about you, sir? What do you fancy?'

'A coffee and something sweet, please. Are there any home-made cakes or biscuits?'

Steadman settled for a piece of shortbread.

'It must have been an awful shock for you finding your friend like that,' Munro said by way of an opener. Kevin's reply surprised both men.

'Friend? I wouldn't describe Dennis as a friend.'

'How would you describe him?' Steadman enquired.

'Kevin thought for a moment. 'I don't really know.'

'Chum? Pal? Mate?' Munro suggested.

'Mate, I suppose,' Kevin replied with a shrug.

'How long have you known him?' Steadman asked.

'Dennis? Let me see – about ten years or so. I already had a stand. The old girl next to me went a bit doolally and they carted her off somewhere. Dennis took over her pitch. The market shifts about the town but the layout is generally the same. I'm always next to Dennis.'

'So you must have known him quite well?'

Kevin gave the two men an incredulous stare.

'You don't understand market folk, do you? We're all a bit odd, at least the regulars are. Loners, misfits that's what we are. Some people think that we sit there day in and day out dreaming of owning a nice cosy shop, but we don't.

We choose to work in the market because it suits us. No staff, no premises to worry about and what we make is ours. Have you been to any of the markets?'

Both men confirmed they had.

'In that case you must know the butcher on the end, the one that never stops talking from the moment the market opens until we're taking down the last stand. The one that's always shouting things to the ladies like, "I'll give you a bigger piece of pork than your husband ever has" or "Has anyone seen my chopper? You can't miss it – it's a whopper." Let me tell you, he never speaks to a soul from the time he leaves the market until the next day. And, despite his banter, I'd lay a pound to a penny he has never been with a woman in his life. He's typical. Mind, he brings the punters in. I sometimes think we are like a bunch of anglers sitting round a lake and the customers are like fish circling round the stands. We make small talk and we notice who's hooking the customers, but we'd never ask each other how much they took that day, no more than an angler would ask his neighbour how many fish he caught.'

Kevin paused as Betty brought over two all-day breakfasts and Steadman's shortbread. Much to Munro's surprise she slipped Robbie a cold sausage, which vanished in an instant. She gave Munro a look that defied him to comment.

'Mug is to your right, shortbread to your left,' Munro murmured quietly.

'Dennis's records brought people in as well,' Kevin

continued. 'He always had something playing. That's why I liked having a stand next to his. Of course, we both had our regulars, collectors that is, but you would be surprised how many people buy on a whim. With me, maybe they see a model car that reminds them of their youth or they pick up a lighter that has a nice feel to it. These days we make most of our money in Betty's.'

'You mean selling on-line?' Munro said through a mouthful of bacon.

'Yeah, I have two sites, one for the cars and one for the cigarette lighters. Dennis sold 78s all over the world. People paid good money for a rare recording.'

'Can we take you back to this morning?' asked Steadman.

Kevin's cutlery rattled on the plate, his appetite suddenly gone.

'He hadn't turned up, which was unusual. We always share a coffee at eleven. I asked Marie, my other neighbour, to keep an eye on my stall and nipped round to his flat. I rang the bell, but there was no answer. Seeing as the door was ajar I pushed it open. I shouted a couple of times, had a peek in the sitting room and the kitchen. I even had a look in the bedroom. It was only then that I noticed a light from under the bathroom door. I knocked and pushed the door open. I thought he might have had a heart attack or something...' Kevin had turned pale and his hands started to shake.

'Take your time,' said Munro reassuringly.

'I don't want to think about it. I closed my eyes, went

back to sitting room and dialled 999. I nearly stepped in a puddle of blood. I felt sick and just had to get out.'

'Did you notice anything odd or out of place?' Steadman asked.

Kevin paused. He picked up his fork and gave what was left of his egg a desultory prod.

'You mean the bottle of wine?'

'Was Dennis a wine drinker?'

'We've had a couple beers over the years. I don't think he drank anything else.'

Munro finished his meal and signalled for another coffee.

'Did Dennis say anything to you about coming into some money?' Steadman enquired.

'He was dead excited at the beginning of the week, now you mention it. He did say something about money.' Kevin frowned. 'Did he say he was left it in a will? No, I think he said he'd won it in a competition. I didn't ask how much – you wouldn't, would you? Do you think he was murdered for the money?'

Munro gave him one of his wide-eyed innocent stares.

'I shouldn't ask, should I?'

'We found some keys in Dennis's flat that are puzzling us,' Steadman continued. Munro produced the clear plastic bag from his pocket and laid it on the table with a soft clunk. 'One of the keys is to his front door and another is for a car or van, but there are two smaller keys – similar but not identical.'

Kevin turned to Steadman.

'They're for his lock-ups, numbers 42 and 43. He keeps his old van in one and the other he uses as a workshop for his hobby.'

'I don't suppose you know what his hobby is?' asked Munro.

Before Kevin had time to answer, Steadman replied, 'I think he did stone carvings.'

Kevin and DS Munro exchanged glances. A smile broke out over Kevin's face.

'Blimey, you're good. How did you work that one out?'

Munro leant back in his seat. The chair groaned in protest.

'The callouses, the broken nails, the brawny arms and the dusty steel toe-capped boots – it all fits. I would never have thought of it,' Munro said with an air of defeat.

'Nonsense, Alan. You have not had the time. All afternoon you've been running around, organising people and answering phone calls. I have the perverse luxury of very few distractions – in other words, time to think. If you're finished, I think we should visit the lock-ups.'

'Do you still need me?' Kevin asked.

'I'll need you to come to the Eyesore to sign a statement and have your fingerprints taken. And if you know where the lock-ups are, it would save us time hunting for them,' replied Munro.

Kevin started to shake again. 'What if there's another...' He couldn't finish the sentence.

'Body? No, I don't think we will find anything like that,' said Steadman.

'What do you think we will find, sir?' asked Munro.

'I think it may be a question of what we won't find,' Steadman replied somewhat enigmatically.

Munro went up to the counter and paid. Robbie looked half-expectantly at Betty. No more sausages appeared and his disappointment was almost palpable.

The fog had descended again. The tops of Da Gama Towers had disappeared in the wet gloom. Steadman turned up the collar of his coat and regretted not having anything more substantial to eat than a piece of shortbread.

The lock-ups were in a series of parallel alleys running from the base of Da Gama Towers. Most of the doors had graffiti sprayed on them. Litter swirled round in the cold damp breeze. A mangy dog barked at Robbie, who totally ignored it.

Forty-two was where Dennis kept his van, Kevin explained. Munro slipped on a pair of plastic gloves, unlocked the door and heaved it up and over, revealing a small white van that was starting to rust.

'Yeah, that's his,' Kevin confirmed.

More boxes of records were stacked in front of the van. There was not much room in the garage. Munro switched on his torch and peered into the van.

'Nothing obvious, sir.' He pulled down the door and locked it.

Forty-three was on the opposite side of the alleyway.

'Would you look at that!' Munro exclaimed.

'What is it, Alan?"

'Sorry, sir – the lock's broken. The handle is lying on the ground next to a convenient half brick.'

Munro pushed the door. It opened easily on well-oiled runners. The inside of the lock-up had been transformed into an immaculately tidy workshop. There was even an electric light. Munro whistled as the full extent of Dennis Knotting's talent became apparent.

'Describe, please,' said Steadman.

'You were absolutely right, sir. He does work in stone and, although I'm no expert, I reckon he was pretty good. Unlike his flat there isn't anything out of place. At the back, there are some blocks of sandstone and what could be some marble. On one wall, there are pictures of statues, a large drawing, some books and what I think is a dust extractor. On the other side, there is a cabinet screwed to the wall with all his chisels neatly laid out, a workbench with more drawings and an assortment of small carvings – animals mostly, but also lots of hands. In the centre, there is the piece he was working on. Hard to tell at this stage what it is – possibly mermaids and dolphins?' Munro looked more closely at the drawings. 'Yes, here are the sketches. Some sort of sea fantasy, I would guess.'

Steadman tried to visualise the scene. 'Have you been here before, Kevin?' he asked.

'Only once. I never realised he was this good.'

Steadman fished out a pair of plastic gloves. Munro remembered about his netsuke collection and without being asked passed him a pair of carved hands. Steadman held them gently and stroked the intricate fingers. They were delicate; clearly woman's hands. Quite suddenly he found himself imagining what it would be like to stroke Sam Griffiths's hands.

'No,' he said out loud and let go of the carved hands.

'Careful, sir,' said Munro as he caught them in his own out-sized hand. 'Are you OK?'

'I'm fine, just a bit cold that's all,' he lied. 'Yes, the carving is excellent,' Steadman continued pulling himself together. 'Come on, Alan, what is missing? I'm blind, but even I can see it.'

Munro and Kevin both looked round the workshop. Everything seemed in place.

'You're going to have to help me out, sir'

'Can you see a stonemason's maul?'

'A maul? What's that when it's at home?'

'A very heavy round stone hammer, Alan. A bit like a small cannon ball on a wooden handle.'

Munro looked round the workshop.

'I'll call forensics,' he replied.

CHAPTER NINETEEN

The Audi bumped over the cobbles. Steadman grimaced and grasped the edge of his seat. His ribs were hurting again.

'Can you slow down a bit, Alan?'

Munro glanced at his colleague, noted his sickly pallor and gently eased off the accelerator. 'We're almost there. Maureen was right – you should have come to our house. You could easily have freshened up there.'

'I know, and she is very kind, but I need to go home, if only to convince myself I'm not intimidated by what's happened.' Steadman paused and scratched his forehead. 'It's a very hard thing to explain.'

'I think I understand. A bit like playing rugby, I guess. You take an awful clout to the head that needs stitching up. Common sense dictates you should watch the rest of the match from the bench. But, oh no, something inside you is determined to get back on the pitch to prove you're not going to be beaten. Aye, and maybe give the other fellow a wee jab in retaliation, if the opportunity arises.'

Steadman smiled; he would not like to play rugby against DS Alan Munro.

The car stopped outside Lloyd's café. Only then did Munro notice the figure standing in Steadman's doorway.

'Looks like you've got company, sir'

Steadman felt his body tense and the hairs on his neck prickle. His assailant would not be so stupid as to try something in the open street even if it was foggy, he thought. Or perhaps it's Sam Griffiths come to see if I'm still alive? He knew which one he would rather face.

'Ah – it's only young Tim Warrender reporting for dog walking duties,' said Munro. 'He looks frozen.'

Tim rushed forward and opened the car door. Robbie thumped his tail, very excited at seeing him. Steadman eased himself out of the car, wincing as he straightened up.

'Are you OK, Inspector Steadman?' asked Tim.

'Bruised ribs after a bit of a tumble, that's all.'

'Here, let me help you.' He slipped an arm through the inspector's. His hand was icy cold.

'Mind the kerb.'

'Tim, you need warming up. Let's go into the café first.'

'I'll call back in a couple of hours, sir. Look after him for me, Tim,' Munro shouted as he drove off into the mist.

It was the slack time before the evening rush and only a couple of tables were occupied. Tim steered Inspector Steadman to a table near the counter. Robbie spreadeagled on the floor at his feet. The aroma of coffee and cooking was tantalising.

'Are you hungry, Tim?' said Steadman. 'Of course you

are. I remember being your age. I could eat six meals a day and still have room for more.'

Luigi came to take their order. He was Marco's cousin, a short, swarthy man whose surly expression hid a kind heart.

'What do you say to some hot chocolate, Tim?'

Tim agreed.

'And I recommend the panini – especially the ham and cheese.'

'What about yourself, Inspector Steadman?' asked Luigi.

'I'll have a hot chocolate too, but nothing to eat. DS Munro's wife is feeding me tonight and she'll doubtless try and give me an Alan-sized portion.'

Luigi came back with the hot chocolate. He had piled Tim's drink with whipped cream and mini-marshmallows.

'Cool!' exclaimed Tim.

'No problem – glad you like it,' replied Luigi. 'Inspector Steadman, I've brought you a new key for the downstairs door. Maybe we should keep it locked all the time until we catch whoever broke into your flat.'

'Your flat's been broken into? When? Why?' exclaimed Tim.

'The "when" is easy to answer – last night. The "why" is much harder.' Steadman's brow furrowed. Should he tell Tim the whole story? He was young, he had just lost a school friend and yet, and yet… Steadman pondered. Tim was possibly mixed up in the whole business. Munro would not always be there to protect him. In fact, knowledge is what protects people, or at least ignorance puts them at risk, he concluded. He took a deep breath.

'I took Robbie for a walk last night and was clipped by a car's wing mirror – I suspect quite deliberately. My friend Dr Rufus, the Home Office pathologist, picked me up and insisted I stay the night with him. I've got bruised ribs, maybe a crack in one of them – nothing serious. He came back here to collect some things for me and found the downstairs door forced and my own front door kicked in. Whoever it was smashed all the pictures in my flat.' Steadman omitted mentioning the piece of twisted wire.

'Was anything stolen? What about your Japanese carvings?'

'The netsuke figures? No, they were undamaged. And fortunately old Mr and Mrs Lloyd in the flat below were not at home.'

Tim remained thoughtful. 'Whoever it was must have known you were out. Could it have been the driver of the car?'

'We will make a detective of you yet, Tim. Not unless the driver waited to see what happened to me or came back, and that is a possibility. A very odd character stopped and offered to help.'

'Did you get a look at him?' asked Tim, carried away by his own enthusiasm. He blushed bright red. 'Sorry,' he mumbled, 'I forgot…'

'I think I might recognise his voice,' Steadman replied hastily. 'Unfortunately, Dr Rufus was too busy tending to my needs to notice much. He may have left a fingerprint on Dr Rufus's car. Unless he is known to the police it is not much to go on.'

Luigi returned with Tim's panini and a bowl of chips.

'Mamma Lloyd says you both need fattening up – *buon appetito*. I expect you will want ketchup, young man. It seems kids these days can't eat anything unless it is smothered in ketchup.'

Luigi fetched a small bowl of tomato sauce. 'Inspector Steadman, if you give me your keys I will swap them round. It is easy to tell the new key; it is much bigger.'

Steadman fished in his pocket and produced his set of keys. A thought occurred to him.

'Is there a spare? If so, could Tim have a key?'

Luigi shrugged. 'I don't see why not. Mind you don't lose it.' He went behind the bar and came back flourishing a key on a chunky white and red fob. 'There, you are now an official AC Milan supporter.'

Very slowly and delicately Steadman swept his hand over the table until he found his mug of hot chocolate. It was velvety smooth, sweet and scalding hot. The smell of the chips wafted over the table. He had resisted Betty's all-day breakfast; this was too much for him.

'Can you spare a chip or two, Tim?' he asked.

'Sure – there's a huge bowl right in front of you.'

Tim watched fascinated as Steadman transferred the mug to his left hand and with the same slow deliberation stretched his right hand forward until his fingertips found the bowl. He pulled out two chips. Unfortunately, one was much longer than the other. Tim wanted to say something.

The long chip missed Steadman's mouth and poked him in the cheek. To Tim's surprise Steadman laughed.

'I'll bet that was the biggest chip in the bowl,' he said after successfully manoeuvring it into his mouth. 'My, but they're good.'

'Would you like any tomato sauce?' Tim asked.

Steadman shook his head. It was difficult enough finding his mouth with plain chips, let alone those smeared with ketchup.

'Is it true there's been another murder? Mum says it was on the news.'

Steadman confirmed that this was the case but did not elaborate.

'When do think you'll catch him?'

Steadman took another sip of his hot chocolate. 'Soon I hope, Tim, very soon. How was your day at school?' he asked, deliberately changing the subject.

'Not good. Everybody is dead quiet. There's a rumour Skinner and Haribin are going to be suspended, and to top it all I've lost my games kit. Mum's gone mental. I know I took it to school yesterday morning. Sometimes the sixth form girls pinch your games bag for a laugh. It's not turned up yet.'

Robbie stirred at Steadman's feet.

'I think he needs his walk. Can I take him now?'

Steadman drummed his long fingers on the table. That damned dream kept coming back to him.

'Maybe I should come with you, Tim,' Steadman replied hesitantly, knowing full well that he would be useless should Tim be attacked.

'Excuse me, sir,' said a man's voice. 'I couldn't help but overhear, perhaps I could walk with the young man seeing as how it's so foggy.'

Steadman turned his head in the direction of the voice. 'I'm sorry – who are you?'

'PC Dyer, sir. We've not worked together. I've only been with the force for six months. Luigi will vouch for me.'

Luigi gave a grunt of approval from behind the counter where he was counting the day's takings.

'Are you related to DS Munro?' Tim asked.

'No - we are the same height I believe. I would need to fill out a bit more if we were to be taken for twins, and grow some hair,' he replied running his hand over his shaven head.

Steadman slipped off Robbie's harness and handed Tim the lead. There was a cold rush of air as Tim and PC Dyer left the café. Steadman reached out over the table and found the chip bowl. Alas, it was empty.

* * *

The flat was cold and smelt of new paint. Steadman's fingers crawled over the wall, located the thermostat and turned it up. The switch for the water heater was outside the bathroom. To his relief, it had not been switched off. He wanted desperately to have a long soak in the bath. He fumbled with the plug and turned on the taps. Timing was critical. On one occasion he had overfilled the bath. Old Mr and Mrs Lloyd assured him there had been no damage, but in his mind's eye he could see the stain on their ceiling.

Having run the bath, he made his way through to the bedroom, trailing a guiding hand along the corridor wall. It was odd to think that less than twenty-four hours before some stranger had been standing exactly where he was now, smashing the glass in his pictures and cutting the prints to shreds. Steadman shook his head.

'Coward,' he muttered under his breath.

Carefully he undressed, emptied the pockets of his suit and hung it back up in the wardrobe. He rolled up his tie and put it back in the drawer. The rest went in the laundry basket. Tonight, he thought, I will be casual. He laid out a fresh shirt, cords and a jumper. It did not really matter which one for Linda had chosen his wardrobe and they all, more or less, coordinated. He realised his bath would be getting cold if he did not hurry up. In his haste, he jerked the sock drawer too far and it fell on the floor, spilling its contents. Damn, another delay while he retrieved his socks.

He lowered himself slowly into the bath. The right side of his chest ached and he was sure it was swollen. The temperature was just right. He lay back and let the events of the day swirl round in his brain. Harry Eeles... Da Gama Towers... the smell of the lift... the 78s playing... he could visualise clearly Kim Ho and the dried up Swiss cheese plant. A bottle of wine and a puddle of blood... the keys… and of course the photo in Dennis Knotting's wallet.

He could feel himself starting to drift off to sleep. The images in his brain became sharper. A naked man sitting on the toilet, chocolate dribbling out of his dead mouth… why chocolate of all things?… and wired to look like a statue. Steadman stared at the man. To his astonishment, Dennis Knotting looked up at him and through clenched teeth muttered, 'You were right about the stonemason's maul, Inspector Steadman, but where are all my other carvings? They are not in the flat, nor in the lock-up. You never thought about that, did you?'

Steadman woke with a start. No, he had not thought about Dennis Knotting's work. Maybe Kevin Creasey would know. He made a mental note to ask Munro.

The water was getting cold. With a moan he hoisted himself out of the bath and towelled himself down. Tim will be back soon, he thought, as he buttoned up his shirt. Blast, he miscounted his shirt buttons and found he had one too many at the collar. Patiently, he undid them and started again. His socks had fallen off the bed. He ran a bare foot over the carpet until he found them – one sock, two socks. The doorbell rang: TW in Morse code.

'I'll be there in a second,' he shouted, slipping on a pair of shoes. He brushed himself down. 'There, that will have to do,' he said to himself.

Tim thanked PC Dyer, wiped Robbie's paws and fetched the dog bowl.

'Help yourself to a chocolate biscuit, Tim, while you are at it,' encouraged Steadman.

'I'd better go,' said Tim through a mouthful of crumbs. 'I've got masses of homework and Mum's still mad at me about losing my games kit. Will you be OK?'

'I'm sure I'll be fine. Sergeant Munro will be here fairly soon.'

Dennis Knotting's sentimental 78s must have got stuck in his head as, for no other reason, he found himself sitting at his piano playing 'Smoke Gets in Your Eyes' followed by 'Red Sails in the Sunset'. He was just coming to the end of 'As Time Goes By' when there was a loud knock at the door. The black and white images of Ingrid Bergman and Humphrey Bogart disappeared in an instant, to be replaced by an altogether more earthly picture of DS Alan Munro.

'Taxi for DI Steadman,' he said in an appallingly bad attempt at a Cockney accent. 'Can I give you a hand on with your coat, sir? It's raw outside. Melanie and Annie have bought Robbie a chew bone. I hope that's all right. They are so excited.'

Steadman took his hat from the peg behind the door.

'Come on, Robbie, I have feeling you are going to be spoiled tonight.'

The Audi was still warm. Steadman and Robbie settled themselves in the front of the car. Munro leant over, grasped Steadman's seat belt and buckled it for him. It was too painful for Steadman to twist. After a minute's drive Steadman frowned and turned to Munro.

'Aren't you going the wrong way?'

'Just picking up our other guest,' Munro replied. He could feel his cheeks burning. 'When Maureen heard that Dr Griffiths was staying all by herself at the Equinox, and having to eat hotel food all the time, she insisted I invite her. I didn't think you would mind.'

Of course he didn't mind, but he would have made more of an effort dressing if he had known.

'Before I forget, Alan, where do you think Dennis Knotting kept his carvings? Other than the samples and the piece he was working on you didn't notice anything else, did you?'

'Good point, sir. I'll check with Kevin, maybe he'll know. Talking of stone carvings, I looked at images of a stonemason's maul on the internet and mentioned it to Dr Rufus. It would certainly fit the bill. Do you think we'll find it?'

'I doubt it. If I were the murderer I would have chucked it in the sea.'

The car pulled up in front of the Equinox Hotel. Sam Griffiths was waiting under the awning.

'Good evening, Alan. Good evening, John. And hello, Robbie – I didn't see you nestled down there.'

She got into the car, which immediately filled with her fragrance; something fresh, floral and expensive. Automatically Steadman removed his fedora. Damn, he thought, all she is going to see now is my bald patch and dented skull.

'It's very good of your wife to invite me,' she said. 'I

can't wait to meet her and your children. I gather you gents have been busy today. You had better tell me all about it now as, if what the papers say is true, it's not a topic for the dinner table.'

Munro and Steadman gave her a detailed account.

'I agree,' she said at last, 'Knotting must have known his killer. I would also add that of the three victims this is the one he despised most.'

'Why?' asked Munro.

'The planning, the choice of weapon, the staging of the scene and the desecration of the body. Why chocolates, I wonder?'

The same question had been troubling Steadman.

'If they knew each other then it may make our life easier. Any luck with the photo, Alan?'

'I'm going to Helmsmouth College of Art tomorrow. Hopefully someone will recognise the other two individuals, it's a little while ago though - people change.'

* * *

Melanie and Annie could barely contain their excitement. They gave their Uncle John a perfunctory kiss and shyly shook hands with Sam Griffiths. Steadman slipped off Robbie's harness and handed Melanie the lead.

'Go on, take him out in the garden. Then you can play with him.'

'He won't bite, will he?' asked Annie. She looked diminutive next to the dog.

'No, you'll be fine,' Steadman reassured her.

'That will be the next thing,' Maureen said with a sigh. 'I can just hear them. "When can we have a dog? Oh please, we promise we'll look after it."'

'I'm sure they can borrow Robbie for the odd day. I suspect he will need a break from guide dog duties now and again.'

The meal passed without incident. Maureen had neatly arranged Steadman's plate and cut his steak into bite-sized pieces.

'Forgive me fingering my food,' Steadman said to Sam with his fork poised in his right hand. 'It takes the guesswork out of eating.'

Just in time she moved his wine glass as he swept his left hand over the table.

'It is all the things a sighted person takes for granted, isn't it? I never realised...' Her voice trailed off.

'I can assure you, Sam, neither did I until I became blind. Robbie will transform my life, that's if these two girls haven't worn him out.'

Robbie could be heard snoring gently under the table. Melanie lifted the tablecloth and peeked at the dog. When she emerged she was struggling to keep a straight face. She whispered in Annie's ear and both girls dived under the table. This time they reappeared giggling.

'What's so funny?' asked Munro.

'Uncle John is wearing odd socks!'

Maureen was affronted.

'You will apologise immediately, both of you.'

'There's absolutely no need,' Steadman replied. 'What we do need however, is a second opinion.'

Steadman turned towards Sam Griffiths and hitched up his trousers.

'I am afraid I'll have to agree with the girls, John. Definitely one grey and blue spotted sock and the other red with black stripes. Quite fetching – it could become a new fashion.'

'And what's more,' Steadman continued, 'I have another pair exactly the same back in my flat.'

'Have you really?' asked Annie and Melanie simultaneously.

Before they could work it out, the phone rang in the hall.

'No peace for the wicked,' muttered Munro.

Maureen was still remonstrating with the girls. Steadman thought he heard Alan mention his name. His ears pricked up.

'Yes, he's here... No! – You have got to be kidding... Well, I don't know how he knew... You're right, Nesbit is not going to be pleased... I'll tell him.'

Maureen sensed danger in her husband's voice.

'Right, you two – kitchen duties as a penance for embarrassing our guest. Melanie, you can wash and Annie, you're drying.'

Without protest the girls followed their mother into the kitchen.

'You are not going to like this,' said Alan as he re-entered the room. 'That was DS Fairfax on the phone. She got a search warrant authorised this evening. Sitting in the garage next to Harry Eeles's van was a bicycle spattered in blood.'

CHAPTER TWENTY

Steadman slept fitfully. Dreams, if he had any, were beyond his recall. He did remember waking twice thinking he heard footsteps in the hall. Robbie's total lack of concern on each occasion reassured him that they were only figments of his imagination.

His watch informed him in its metallic voice that it was seven fifteen, too early to call for coffee and too late to go back to sleep. He lay back with a groan. A dreadful sense of foreboding washed over him. Today, he thought, was not going to be a good day.

Tim arrived late and out of breath. He too had slept poorly. There was to be a special assembly this morning in memory of George Bremner and Tim had to do one of the readings. He was sure he was going to mess it up.

Only Robbie appeared to have any enthusiasm for the day. He raced down the stairs and sat panting at the bottom waiting for Tim.

Steadman was too distracted to sit down. He paced the floor nursing his coffee and drumming his long fingers on the side of the mug. Should he phone the Eyesore? Or should he wait until they phoned him? That blasted bike! Why had he mentioned it to DS Fairfax? And more to the point, who had planted it in Harry Eeles's garage? For he was certain that Maurice Eeles had about as much to do with it as he had with running a fantasy carnival games arcade.

The doorbell brought him back to reality.

'What's the weather doing, Tim?' Steadman asked.

'Still cold and foggy. Robbie doesn't seem to mind though,' Tim replied as he wiped the dog's paws. 'I'd better be going. Can't be late today.'

'Will you leave the downstairs door unlocked?'

'What about the burglar? Shouldn't you...?' Tim stopped in mid-sentence when he saw the look on Steadman's face. Even with the dark glasses Tim could tell by the clenched jaw and raised eyebrows that his questioning was out of order. It was a harder, more determined side of John Steadman than he had observed before. Quite suddenly Tim felt very small. He would not, he thought, like to be interrogated by DI Steadman.

'Sorry - I'll leave the door unlocked. See you this evening.'

'Phone before you come round. I have a feeling I may be out.'

★ ★ ★

Steadman found the silence stifling. Twice he reached for

the phone but decided against calling. Robbie barked as the doorbell rang. Steadman could not decide if it was a relief or a disappointment when the caller proved to be Mr Barnes.

'Just wanted to see how you and Robbie are getting on. I thought maybe we could catch the bus into town and go into one of the big stores.'

Poor Mr Barnes; he too saw the black look on Steadman's face.

'Of course, if it's not convenient we could go another day.'

'Do you read the papers?' Steadman asked.

'I glance at the headlines... Oh! I see, the murders. You are involved in the investigations, aren't you?'

'I am,' replied Steadman. In his head a small voice said, 'At least for the time being.'

'I'm expecting a phone call at any minute. I'm sorry, I didn't mean to be abrupt, only I'm a bit preoccupied, that's all.'

'Perfectly understandable. I must say, they sound so bizarre.' That wretched word again. 'At least you and Robbie seem to be working well together.'

'I can't imagine life without him.' Steadman bent down and ruffled the dog's head. Robbie nuzzled into his thigh.

Mr Barnes turned and headed back down the stairs. Steadman hadn't fully closed the door when he heard Mr Barnes talking to someone. He heard a female voice. Steadman listened intently. It wasn't Mrs Lloyd or DS Fairfax or Dr Sam Griffiths. Puzzled, he opened the door wider. Damn, he said to himself as he realised it was Miss Elliot, his piano tutor. He had completely forgotten that he had arranged a lesson for this morning.

'A guide dog, how wonderful!' she enthused. 'Oh dear, has he had an operation?'

'No, just met with a little accident.'

Miss Elliot had brought some new pieces. She played them through several times. Steadman's ear was good, but they were challenging and required all his concentration. All thoughts of murder, Maurice Eeles and blood-spattered bikes were put to the back of his mind. The hour raced by.

'You need to keep practising the left hand. It is still a bit heavy,' said Miss Elliot. Steadman agreed that he would. He closed the door and retraced his steps back to the living room. What to do now, he asked himself. Subconsciously he found himself opening the netsuke display cabinet and picking up a small carved figure of a hunched, cloaked man. The man's head spun in his hood, revealing either a happy or a sad face. With his fingernail Steadman could just discern the two. He flicked the head.

'Happy face, we call Sergeant Grimble, Robbie. Sad face, we wait.'

The phone rang before the head stopped spinning.

'Inspector Steadman? It's Kim Ho here. I expect you've heard about the bicycle.'

News at last!

'Yes. What have you found out?'

'Other than the blood, the bike has been thoroughly

cleaned with white spirit. I've only managed to get one fragment of a smudged fingerprint.'

'Can you match it?'

'Not with any degree of certainty. Possibly...'

Steadman held his breath.

'Well, the fragment is similar to the print found on Dr Rufus's car, but by no means conclusive. And that print is not on any of our databases.'

'You say the bike has been cleaned – deliberately?'

'Without a doubt. The seat, the underside of the seat, the handlebars – all scrubbed.'

'And the blood?'

'Definitely not human. That's why I'm phoning. I would like a sample of Robbie's blood to compare.'

'Does it have to be fresh? Despite my sister's best endeavours, he still has some matted tufts round his hind legs.'

'Those would be fine. Can I call round now?'

'By all means. I don't suppose you know how Inspector Nesbitt got on with Maurice Eeles?'

'I had to speak with Sergeant Grimble to get your number. I gather Inspector Nesbitt let Maurice stew in his own juice overnight... is that the correct phrase?' Kim asked.

'Not a pretty phrase, but correct. Go on.'

'He is interviewing him as we speak.'

★ ★ ★

It was not clear who was the more surprised: Maurice Eeles for finding himself with a solicitor or Inspector Nesbitt finding him accompanied by one. Sven Jensen was a thin, slight man with fair hair, a close-cropped beard and round gold-framed spectacles. He was wearing a dove-grey suit, a white shirt starched with military precision and an elegant silk tie. His shoes and briefcase were of matching nubuck. He looked suave and sophisticated. Inspector Nesbitt despised him on sight.

'Who the hell are you?' he demanded.

The solicitor smiled, his grey-blue eyes twinkled behind their gold frames. He cleared his throat with a slight chuckle. His English was perfect, despite his strong Scandinavian accent.

'I am Sven Jensen, solicitor representing my clients Mr Maurice Eeles and Mr Harry Eeles. Might I assume you are acting Detective Inspector Nesbitt?'

Nesbitt puffed out his chest and stuck his chin in the air like some tin-pot dictator.

'Acting Detective *Chief* Inspector, sonny.'

'Ah yes, I was forgetting DCI Long's brother was taken ill, was he not?'

Nesbitt ignored the question. 'Who sent for you?'

The solicitor chuckled again and wagged a finger.

'Ha! – My clients have a right to legal representation according to section…'

'I know they have,' Nesbitt butted in. 'And I don't care what goddamned section of the book it's in.'

'Very good, I am glad we are in agreement. Shall we commence?'

Nesbitt's jaw fell open. He was taken aback. The dapper solicitor appeared to be taking control. Nesbitt fixed him with a withering look. Sven Jensen smiled, took out a single, crisp white sheet of paper and laid an expensive silver pen by its side.

'Do the formalities, Lofthouse,' Nesbitt barked over his shoulder.

DS Fiona Fairfax gave a slight cough.

'DC Lofthouse has been taken ill, sir. I'm his replacement.'

It was not exactly a lie, but was certainly not entirely true. Everyone knew that as the arresting officer Fairfax should have been present. But Nesbitt disliked women and had asked Will Lofthouse instead. Lofthouse had no choice. Initially he thought it might be fun especially as word had got out that the most pedantic solicitor in Helmsmouth would be representing Maurice Eeles. Nobody knew who had organised it, although everyone suspected Sergeant Grimble. At the last minute Will Lofthouse thought there was more amusement to be had by asking DS Fairfax to take his place. He feigned stomach cramps, thrust the file into her hands and dived into the gents.

Beaky Nesbitt's top lip twitched. He smelt a rat.

'Get on with it, then.'

Fairfax switched on the tape recorder and stated the time, date and those present.

Nesbitt stared long and hard at Maurice Eeles.

'Why are you looking at me like that? I haven't done anything!'

'We'll see about that, laddie. Where were you two nights ago?'

'I dunno – nowhere.'

'You must have been somewhere. It is not possible to be nowhere. I even know where your dad was. He was in the cells, leaving you the opportunity to get up to some wickedness by yourself.'

Maurice turned to his solicitor. 'What's he on about?'

Again Sven Jensen gave a little chuckle.

'I think the officer, in a most circuitous route, would like you to tell him where you were – not last night, but the night before that.'

'I was at home – Grand Theft Auto on the pooter.'

'What's he saying?' Nesbitt rasped.

'I believe my client is trying to tell you, in the vernacular of the day, that he was playing a popular and absorbing game on his computer.'

'Oh yeah? All night?'

'Maybe – 'spect so.'

'So when did you go round to Dennis Knotting's flat, bash his head in then wire him up?'

Maurice looked bewildered.

'My client has already informed you that he was at home all night.'

'Is that a fact, Mr Jensen?' Nesbitt looked triumphant. 'I have it on good authority that your client went to the

Golden Fry chip shop at eight o'clock.'

'The Golden Fry! Yeah, I went there. Dad does all the cooking and seeing as he wasn't at home I nipped out for a sausage and chips. Ask the girls there – they'll tell you.'

'Oh, we have Maurice, don't worry, we have. That's how we know. Now if you can lie about that, who is to say you're not lying about going round and doing in Dennis Knotting.'

'Really, Inspector Nesbitt, it is more than a leap of faith, one might say, to suggest that a momentary lapse in memory is tantamount to committing murder. My client denies all involvement.'

'Murder? I haven't killed anyone! What are you on about?' Maurice turned a sickly shade of grey and beads of sweat ran down his temples.

The interview was not going the way Nesbitt had planned. He tried several more times, but Jensen merely wagged a finger and stated that his client had already answered.

Nesbitt stood up and with his hands clasped behind his back paced the floor with exaggerated strides. Suddenly he turned round, slammed both hands on the desk and stuck his large nose into Maurice's face. Maurice bleated.

'Ha! That old trick Inspector Nesbitt. I do hope you are not trying to intimidate my client.'

'OK, laddie, tell me about your bike and how it got covered in blood?' Nesbitt shot a sideways glance at the solicitor. Sven Jensen was unmoved. He appeared to be doodling on the sheet of paper.

'I don't have a bike.'

'So it's Harry's bike?'

'Dad doesn't have a bike. An old man like him would look stupid on a bike.'

'You admit it's yours, then.'

'My client has told you once that he has not got a bike. That should suffice.'

'Then how the hell does your client account for a bike that's covered in blood being inside his garage?'

'Quite simple, inspector – my client does not account for it.'

The room was getting hot and stuffy. Huge damp patches had appeared under Maurice's arms. Nesbitt ran a finger round his collar. Even DS Fairfax was starting to glow. Only Sven Jensen seemed unperturbed by the turn of events. Nesbitt tried again and again to get Maurice to confess. Jensen objected to every question. Eventually, in exasperation Nesbitt turned to the solicitor.

'Exactly what questions am I allowed to ask your client?'

Sven Jensen chuckled again, a sound that was starting to really annoy Inspector Nesbitt.

'My dear inspector,' Sven Jensen responded in his most charming manner, 'you may ask anything you like. I am not here to guide your questions; my duty is to advise my client when and how to answer.'

Nesbitt's top lip twitched violently.

'May I put a question to your client?' asked DS Fairfax.

'By all means,' Jensen replied.

'If you must,' Nesbitt grumbled.

'Can you ride a bike, Maurice?'

Maurice Eeles shuffled his feet and looked at the floor.

'Never learnt,' he mumbled. 'Mam ran off when I was little and dad wasn't always around. Never even had a bike.'

'Thank you, that's all I wanted to ask,' said DS Fairfax.

Nesbitt was puce with rage.

'Interview terminated at eleven forty-five,' he shouted at the machine and angrily switched it off.

He opened the interview room door and bellowed down the corridor to the custody sergeant.

'And before you ask,' he said turning towards the solicitor, 'no bail. I'm not finished with Sunny Jim here, not finished by a long chalk.'

He swept up the file from the desk.

'And as for you, sergeant,' he glared at DS Fairfax, 'I want you in my office in five minutes.'

He strode out of the room, slamming the door behind him.

'I think you may have upset your acting detective chief inspector,' Sven Jensen observed. 'I don't think he likes you.'

DS Fairfax was tempted to reply that Inspector Nesbitt did not appear to like anybody. She confined herself to a shrug and removed the cassettes from the tape recorder. Only then did she notice that Sven Jensen had drawn a caricature of Beaky Nesbitt, complete with outsize nose, on his sheet of paper.

'A fair resemblance, don't you think?' he said with a chuckle. 'I would not like to be in your shoes, sergeant. Good luck!'

* * *

Nesbitt screwed up his eyes and gave Fiona Fairfax a filthy look. 'I don't like being made a fool of, sergeant, especially in front of scum like Maurice Eeles and his poncey solicitor.'

'Sir?'

'I think you understand me perfectly well, Miss Goody Two-Shoes… How long have you known that Maurice Eeles couldn't ride a bike?'

'I didn't know, sir.'

'I don't believe you. You waited until I had dug a hole for myself, didn't you?'

'That's not true, sir.'

'So why did you ask the question?'

DS Fairfax tried to look at Inspector Nesbitt, but he had turned his back to her.

'I don't think Maurice Eeles is very bright, sir, and I suspect he lies as often as he tells the truth. He must have spent years concocting stories for his classmates about where his mother was or indeed, where his father was half the time. But like most men, he is vulnerable.'

Nesbitt swung round to stare at her. 'What do you mean by vulnerable?'

'Ask any man about something he should be able to do but can't, and he will either exaggerate wildly or do what

Maurice did – shuffle his feet, look at the floor and honestly admit his failings in a whisper. That's why I asked the question, sir. I hoped to get the truth.'

Nesbitt strutted up and down, staring at the ceiling.

'They told me you were sharp. Now let's see how sharp you really are.' Nesbitt thrust his face into hers. His breath smelt of stale garlic. 'Who tipped you off about the bike in the garage?'

DS Fairfax could feel her cheeks burning. She hesitated.

'No one tipped me off, sir.'

'Don't think I got where I am today by not knowing when someone is lying to me, especially a junior officer. And you are lying your cotton socks off! You may be easy on the eye, Fairfax, but don't delude yourself for one minute that I wouldn't bust you back to a constable walking the beat. You got a search warrant without a nod to me, your superior officer. The first thing you did was open the garage. Don't deny it – I've read your report. And surprise, surprise – what was lurking in there – a blood-caked bike! So, Joan of Arc, who tipped you off?'

The room fell silent bar the ticking of the wall clock that suddenly sounded very loud and ominous. DS Fairfax's eyes filled with tears and her voice became tremulous.

'It wasn't a tip off. It was more of a suggestion, sir.'

Nesbitt made a deprecatory gesture.

'Suggestion, tip off, all the same in my book, sergeant.

You have twenty seconds to tell me who it was, or you're busted.'

The ticking of the clock grew even louder. DS Fairfax bit her lip and held back her tears. At last she spoke.

'You won't believe me even if I tell you, sir.'

'Try me.'

'DI Steadman.'

'Your blind chum? You've got to be joking.'

'I knew you wouldn't believe me, but hear me out. Since his accident, I know that Inspector Steadman has very vivid dreams. I've overheard him saying that they are his last hold on the visual world. Well, rightly or wrongly, I spoke with him after you had ordered me to arrest Maurice Eeles. He had just finished re-interviewing Harry. He doesn't believe Maurice or his father have anything to do with the killings.'

Nesbitt snorted loudly.

'Inspector Steadman asked me to check if Maurice had a bike. In one of his dreams, Maurice had been riding a bike covered in blood.'

'And you believed him? You may be sharp, Fairfax, but, by Christ you are gullible.'

'He seemed very embarrassed telling me about his dream and made me vow not tell anyone.'

Nesbitt was jubilant. 'I should say he was embarrassed, spinning you a yarn like that. Dreams – pah! He's got an informant, that's what he's got. And he's not letting on. Withholding information – oh dear, life is just going to get a whole tougher for your blind detective pal.'

'I don't think…'

'Listen, blondie, I don't care what you think. You're either a fool or possibly the two of you are in it together.'

Tears ran down DS Fairfax's face.

'And don't bother with the Versailles Fountain act, it won't wash with me. God knows I hate working with women – poor judgement, the lot of you. Now, it's high time I had a little chat with ex-inspector Steadman. Go bring him in – now!'

If Nesbitt thought he had broken DS Fairfax he was sadly mistaken, for her tears were neither sadness nor self-pity but frustration and anger.

CHAPTER TWENTY ONE

Munro was looking forward to his visit to Helmsmouth College of Art. He remembered clearly his own first day at university, entering the portals of the physics department that still bore the engraving "Natural Philosophy" over the bronze doors, the solemnity of the atrium with its marvellous collection of old instruments: the telescopes, clocks, astrolabes and the wonderful clockwork model of the solar system. The walls were hung with portraits of eminent scientists, mathematicians and past professors. The air was dry and dusty and smelt of learning. The students all seemed scrubbed and eager.

Maybe it was the dank weather that caused the students at Helmsmouth College of Art to look so miserable. They certainly were not like the cheery bunch of Munro's youth. And there were so many of them. Smokers huddled in groups outside the main entrance, their thin shoulders hunched against the cold and damp. No one seemed to be talking. Inside it was bedlam. The foyer was large and packed with students of every size and shape, but Munro was at least half a head taller than the tallest. It was not just his height that set him apart; his neat haircut, shirt and tie and sensible overcoat made him look like a different species.

Munro was amazed by how young everyone appeared. Most ignored him. Those that bothered gave him suspicious looks. He felt old, awkward and out of place.

He had expected to find old masters hanging on the walls. In fact, everywhere was festooned in paint-soaked rags and bits of rubbish that made no sense to him. He had once been called to a jumble sale in a church hall where a gas cylinder had exploded, and the scene before him was vaguely similar.

Risking a snub, he asked one of the passing students where he could find the reception desk. The student pointed wordlessly to Munro's left. Sure enough, under a version of the Union Jack painted in orange, green and pink, Munro made out a small sign that read: 'All Visitors Report Here'.

He waded through the thinning crowd. The person behind the glass partition seemed no older than the students and had dyed jet-black hair, earrings in the shape of two skulls and dark purple lipstick. It was only when he spoke that Munro realised it was a man.

'Detective Sergeant Munro,' he said holding out his ID. 'I am wanting information about some former students.'

The man was singularly unimpressed.

'Sign the visitors' book,' he replied, pushing a ledger with a pen attached by a piece of string in his direction.

Munro noticed that no one had signed the book for over two months. He scrawled his name and in return was given an adhesive label with the word "visitor" printed in bold red capitals.

'Stick that on your coat,' the voice said.

Munro obliged and waited in vain for any form of spontaneous help.

'Can you suggest who I should speak to?' he asked eventually.

'Try admin.'

'Admin?'

'Yes – administration.' The voice drew out each syllable as though Munro were a two-year-old.

'Funnily enough, I know what admin stands for - I was actually hoping for directions.' Munro tried a smile to no avail.

'Office directly above this one.' The voice turned his back on Munro.

Munro rapped the glass.

'And where are the stairs, if it is not too much trouble?'

The voice turned and looked at him as though he were stupid.

'On your right, end of the corridor.'

Munro did not bother to say thank you as the voice had made it abundantly clear that he had something far more important to do than speak to police officers.

Munro trudged along the corridor, climbed the stairs, and then double backed on himself, hoping to find the admin office. He glanced at the pictures that covered every inch of the walls. Munro thought he recognised some of the subjects. However, on closer inspection, what he took to be a bowl of bananas and peaches proved to be something quite different.

Despite her green hair and numerous piercings, the young lady in admin who greeted Munro was friendly and cheerful and not overawed by an enormous policeman.

Munro showed her the photograph. 'I am trying to identify two of the men in this picture,' he said.

'But it's ancient!' the girl exclaimed. 'I mean, look at the clothes – and the hair.'

'It's only seventeen years ago.' Munro blushed as he realised the girl with the green hair had probably still been in nappies when the photo was taken.

'Like I said, ancient. Why do you only want to know who two of the men are?'

'Good question,' Munro replied. He was warming to the girl. 'I know who the man in the middle is, or should I say, was. I found this photo in his wallet. He has been murdered.'

'Murdered!' The girl's eyes widened in astonishment. Hastily she handed the photo back to Munro and wiped her hands on her jeans as though they had somehow been contaminated.

'Did the other two men…?' She stopped short of asking the question.

'They need to be eliminated from our enquiries,' said Munro. 'I believe the picture may have been taken here at the college. Can you think of anyone who might be able to recognise the people in this photograph?'

The girl was silent for a minute. She looked so vacant that Munro almost waved a hand in front of her face. At last she spoke.

'The trouble here is that everything changes so quickly. The staff move on as frequently as the students.' She bit her lip. 'You could try Deirdre in admissions – she must be nearly forty.'

'Deirdre it is, then,' Munro replied. 'Now, where will I find admissions?'

'I'll show you,' the girl with the green hair replied. She opened the door and joined Munro in the corridor.

Munro was surprised at how diminutive she was despite her platform shoes. She was also rather chubby and had squeezed herself into very tight jeans and a top which was so tight that she wobbled when she moved.

'Follow me,' she instructed, setting off rapidly. Munro had never seen anyone move quite like her before. It was somewhere between a skip, a hop and a run. She positively bounced along the corridor. Munro had to walk briskly to keep up with her. It was even harder not to smile.

'Here we are,' she said at last.

'Thank you, you have been very helpful. I'm sorry I didn't catch your name.' She might have been wearing a name badge, but Munro was too embarrassed to scrutinise her quivering bosom for it. Instead he held out a huge hand. She seemed surprised and shook Munro's hand clumsily.

'Oh! I am called Leaf.'

'Leaf?' Munro was not sure if he had heard correctly.

'Yes, Leaf. My parents wanted to call me Petal. Can you imagine how excruciating that would have been? If you need anything else, you know where to find me.' She bounced off down the corridor. Munro shook his head. Extraordinary, he thought.

Deirdre proved to be quite a different character: no dyed hair, no piercings. However her hair was pulled back into a tight bun held in place by what Munro presumed were a variety of large crochet hooks.

Again he went through the routine of showing his ID and explaining about the photograph. Deirdre too looked at the picture with alarm.

'What is his name? You know, the one who was...'

'Murdered.' Munro finished the sentence for her. 'Dennis Knotting – he is the one in the middle.'

'Knotting? I think I read about him in the *Echo*. Wasn't he wired up or something?'

'Something like that,' Munro replied cautiously.

'Well, let me see.' She stood up and went over to a very large bookcase full of dusty ledgers. 'Seventeen years ago, you reckon?'

Munro nodded. He wanted to say something, but Deirdre was already running keen fingers over the old tomes. She took down a book, blew dust off the top and started flicking through the pages.

'G, H, I, J, K – here we are,' she said more to herself than to Munro. 'Knight, Knobbs, Knox – no Knotting I'm afraid. I'll try the previous year.'

Munro felt exasperated. He really wasn't interested in finding Dennis Knotting in the records. But Deirdre was not to be stopped.

'King, Kirby, Knotting Dennis – found him! Now, if entered the college then he ought to have graduated…'

Munro interrupted her.

'He didn't graduate. His parents died and he dropped out after two years.'

Deirdre looked disappointed. 'Oh, I see.'

'You could tell me what course he was signed up to?'

Deirdre ran a finger down the page.

'Fine arts.'

Munro shrugged his shoulders.

'What does that involve?'

'In the first year, students are exposed to a variety of media and forms of expression. The college strives to let students find and explore their own creative outlets.'

Munro had studied physics and mathematics in his first year. He had no idea what Deirdre was talking about; she might have been speaking a foreign language.

'What about the other two men in the picture? Does the college take year photos, or even better, class photos?'

'Oh no, we don't believe in anything like that here, sergeant.' She gave Munro a disapproving look.

'How about a list of people in his class?'

'I doubt if that would help you. You see, we actively encourage students to make friends across the spectrum of disciplines that we teach. It inspires creative synergy and diversity.'

Munro looked blank.

'We also encourage older students to look after younger students, so the other two gentlemen in your picture could be anybody in the college. They may even be from one of our sister colleges. We have affiliates throughout the country. What did you say their names were? I could try and find them in our records.'

Munro felt like hitting his head on the wall. How could he put this without sounding rude?

'Deirdre, you have been very kind, but if I knew their blooming names I wouldn't be here wasting your time.'

Deirdre looked more than a little put out.

'Are any of the lecturers who taught Dennis Knotting still working in the college? Maybe I could try them?' asked Munro.

Deirdre pouted and was about to say something which Munro felt sure she would regret.

'Can I remind you, I am investigating a murder.'

'Yes, well, the only one would be Mr Benson,' she replied huffily.

'And where will I find Mr Benson?'

Deirdre led the way. Disappointingly, her gait was unremarkable.

* * *

'Knotting, you say? Can't recall anyone of that name. What has he done?'

Mr Benson had wavy, brushed-back white hair and

very thick glasses. His fingers, Munro noticed, were heavily stained with nicotine. He appeared irritable. Probably desperate for a smoke, Munro thought.

'He has been murdered,' he explained.

'Ah – nasty!' Mr Benson pulled a face.

'He was at college for barely two years. His parents died.' Munro gave him a questioning look.

'Sorry, still doesn't ring any bells. Listen, sergeant, we get hundreds of students through our doors every year – undergraduates, postgraduates, exchange students.' He pursed his lips. 'I remember a few of them, of course. The ones that went on to achieve something. The ones that made a name for themselves, you know. My memory, like time itself, confines the second-bests to the dustbin of history.' Mr Benson looked rather pleased with himself at this last sentence.

'Very profound, sir,' Munro replied. 'This photo was found on the deceased. We believe it was taken at the college. Dennis Knotting is the one in the middle. Do you recognise either of the other two men?'

Mr Benson took the photograph and held it very close to his glasses, then took off his glasses and moved over to the window.

'How long ago did you say, sergeant?'

'Seventeen years.'

Mr Benson shook his head.

'I'm afraid neither of these men mean anything to me.'

The studio door opened with a loud bang and a gaggle

of noisy students rushed in, paying not the slightest attention to Benson or Munro.

'Look at that, sergeant. That is what passes as the talent I am expected to nurture. I would do more good teaching them how to serve burgers or make a skinny latte, whatever that is. Is it any wonder I smoke?'

Some of Mr Benson's despondency had rubbed off on Munro and it was with a heavy tread he found himself leaving Helmsmouth College of Art. He unpeeled his visitor's badge, screwed it up and threw it in the bin by reception. He did not bother signing out. He doubted if anyone would notice.

* * *

Kim Ho arrived as Steadman was struggling to make himself coffee. He did have a gadget which supposedly alerted him if his mug was too full, but it was fiddly to use and twice he had managed to tip coffee everywhere. It was easier, although a little more hazardous, simply to stick your finger over the lip of the mug and stop pouring, hopefully before getting scalded.

Kim preferred tea and, at Steadman's suggestion, made it herself.

'There may be some biscuits if Munro and young Tim Warrender haven't eaten them all,' said Steadman.

Kim looked round the flat. She could not help but notice the bare walls. 'They were very quick at tidying up the mess, sir. Are you going to replace the pictures?'

'My sister Linda is adamant that I should, and I have learnt over the years that it is much easier simply to agree. Her husband is in the antiques business and he's keeping an eye out for anything suitable. I don't think I'll go for Pre-Raphaelite prints again.'

'What about something oriental to complement your netsuke collection?' Kim suggested.

Steadman considered this with his head cocked on one side. 'Sounds like an excellent idea, Kim. I'll phone Linda this afternoon. Talking of Linda, she spent an age trying to get the blood off Robbie, but, unless I am mistaken, there are still some matted tufts of fur between his hind legs.'

Kim looked at the large dog spreadeagled at Steadman's feet.

'Do you think he will let me take some clippings?' She looked most dubious.

'Oh, that will be no problem, wait and see.'

Kim opened a small attaché case and slipped on a pair of vinyl gloves. Meanwhile Steadman undid Robbie's harness.

'If there is one thing this dog likes, it is a good belly rub,' he said.

Robbie immediately rolled on to his back. Steadman bent down. He let out a small groan; his ribs were still hurting. Vigorously he rubbed the dog's belly. Robbie closed his eyes and Kim would have sworn the dog was smiling. The matted hair was obvious and in no time she had collected four samples and placed them in small pots which she neatly labelled. She held one of them up to the light. It glistened dark maroon.

'Yes, it is definitely blood.'

Robbie, on realising the belly rub was over, stood up and gave himself a shake before sloping off to the kitchen for a drink.

'When do you think you'll have the results, Kim?' Steadman asked.

'Possibly late this afternoon or early tomorrow. By the way, I have managed to trace the sparkling mineral water. It was more difficult than I thought as several have similar mineral content. It's a local brand, Helmsmouth Upper Reaches – very expensive for what it is. You may remember seeing it as it comes in a distinctive purple bottle. You can buy it in a handful of shops, but mostly it is distributed to hotels and clubs frequented by people with more money than sense.'

'So not something that Velda or Doreen Meemes would be likely to buy?'

'I wouldn't have thought so, sir. DS Fairfax will confirm.'

'And what does our acting DCI make of it?'

Kim sniffed. 'I have no idea, sir. He no longer speaks to me. I send him a report and if he wants to know anything he contacts one of my male colleagues. I do however get the impression he thinks it is irrelevant to the investigation.'

'What about the chocolates recovered from Dennis Knotting?'

'Well, they're proving tricky too. They are not an everyday make. Like the whisky and the mineral water, I suspect they will turn out to be an exclusive brand.'

Steadman rubbed his temples with his thumbs as though massaging the information into place.

'And the wire?' he asked.

'Stripped electrical cable again. The same gauge as was stolen from Harry's van... If you don't mind me asking, sir, what do you make of the bike found in the Eeles's garage?'

Steadman sighed.

'I would be willing to bet every last penny of my police pension, Kim, that the blood on the bike will match Robbie's. As to how the bike got into their garage, that is another riddle altogether.'

'You don't believe Harry or Maurice have anything to do with it, do you, sir?'

'No. I'm not even sure as yet that the person on the bike who slashed Robbie is the same person that committed the murders. Somehow, I am fairly certain that it's the same person who broke into my flat and smashed my pictures... But there was that piece of twisted wire in amongst all the broken glass, and you know how I hate coincidences. What I do believe is that we are being watched and, if you like, being played with, and the game is not over.'

'Then are we dealing with a madman, sir?'

'Probably, but not in the sense of somebody who is raving. No, this is someone who holds down a job and otherwise leads a normal life, if anybody's life can be described as that. I suspect he's got an idea fixed in his head, an idea that has taken over his life.'

'Have you any notion what it could be, sir?'

Robbie came back into the room and plonked his head on Steadman's lap. Steadman gave him a friendly pat.

'We're working on it, aren't we Robbie?' Steadman replied.

CHAPTER TWENTY TWO

DS Fairfax strode out of the Eyesore, her face burning. She marched past Sergeant Grimble's desk without even glancing in his direction. Sergeant Grimble had already guessed something was up and pretended not to notice her departure. He would find out soon enough, he mused to himself. He always did.

Fairfax got into one of the police cars and slammed the door. Her teeth were clenched, she breathed deeply and slowly counted to ten. She was more angry with herself than with Nesbitt. He was a fool, she told herself repeatedly. But she had been forced to break her promise to John Steadman, and that was what really irked her. How was she going to explain that to him without feeling even more stupid and disloyal? She crunched angrily into gear and crawled out of the car park into the fog.

The visibility was appalling. The headlights only made things worse; two solid white cones that seemed to stop no more than a few yards from the front of the car. At least they picked out the cat's eyes in the centre of the road, and cautiously she followed these, going at no more than ten miles an hour. Within minutes she had someone stuck on her tail. Under normal circumstances she would have pulled in and let them pass. Today she was too preoccupied rehearsing what, if anything, she would say to DI Steadman. No matter how hard she tried, she could not find the words to express how she had felt so bullied and intimidated. So much so that she had ended up spilling the beans.

Maybe it had been cowardice on her part. Maybe she had thought her career was more important than promises to a colleague. And then, after a having a full confession wrung from her, the humiliation of not being believed. She felt anger mixed with shame boiling up inside. Her cheeks were burning again.

Despite going at a snail's pace it did not take long to reach Lloyd's café. Somewhere on the way she had lost the tailgater.

The downstairs door to Steadman's flat was unlocked, which surprised her. Half way up the stairs she remembered that Steadman had a dog – a big black one. What if it was territorial? Couldn't animals sense when someone was afraid of them?

With a shaking hand she rang the doorbell. Steadman opened the door almost at once.

'Come in, Fiona,' he said.

DS Fairfax looked perplexed.

'I hope you don't mind me asking, sir, but how did you know it was me?'

Steadman smiled.

'The clever answer would be that I could tell from your distinctive perfume. Alas, the truth is more mundane - Sergeant Grimble forewarned me. Our acting DCI couldn't resist the temptation to gloat over browbeating you into revealing your sources. He also delighted in telling Sergeant Grimble, in no uncertain terms, how he intends to take me down a peg or two before dismissing me from the case. Inspector Nesbitt should choose his confidants more wisely. As soon as he was gone, Sergeant Grimble phoned me.'

Robbie led the two of them to the sitting room. DS Fairfax still felt very uneasy.

'I'm so sorry, sir. He knew I was lying and threatened me with demotion if I didn't answer him. Even then he didn't believe me. The man is a fool.'

Steadman dismissed her apology with a wave of his hand.

'There is no need to feel sorry. You did absolutely the right thing. Your future in the force is far more important than my feelings. The man is a bully and a misogynist, of that there is no doubt. I don't believe he is entirely stupid, though. He just doesn't have any depth to his thinking. His world is black and white. He will make the facts fit his theory and ignore anything that contradicts.'

'He's still convinced that Harry and Maurice Eeles are guilty, sir.'

'I know, and I fear that is where he and I are going to fall out.' Steadman drummed his fingers on the arm of the chair. Robbie sat up, looking expectant. DS Fairfax stared at the dog with alarm.

'Are you sure the dog's safe, sir?'

Steadman did not hear her. He was lost in his own thoughts.

'I know Nesbitt wants to question me... under what conditions am I being summoned?' he asked.

'How do you mean, sir?'

'Well, am I under arrest?'

DS Fairfax pursed her lips.

'He just said, "Bring him in now".'

'Good. In that case you have time to tell me about this morning's interview and have a bite of lunch before leaving. I believe Inspector Nesbitt likes letting people stew in their own juice – let's see how he likes it.'

DS Fairfax gave a detailed account of the morning's proceedings. Steadman raised a questioning eyebrow at Will Lofthouse's subterfuge.

'An odd young man. I suspect he will go far, though in what direction is anybody's guess,' he remarked.

'Did you have anything to do with the appointment of the Scandinavian solicitor?'

Steadman shrugged. 'I may have mentioned something to Sergeant Grimble.'

'Sven Jensen really annoyed Inspector Nesbitt, sir, although I'm sure that was never your intention.'

'Quite.'

'I think Inspector Nesbitt thought he would catch Jensen out by bringing up the bike.'

'If my memory serves me correctly, the man is unflappable.'

'He was, sir, but Maurice got into a terrible state. Inspector Nesbitt tried coming down heavy on him. Jensen was having none of it.'

'Is that when you cleverly asked if Maurice could ride a bike? I'm afraid your intuition has not endeared you to our acting DCI, according to Sergeant Grimble.'

'I gathered as much. That pretty much terminated the interview. Then it was my turn, only I didn't...'

'Don't be too hard on yourself. You told him the truth. It's his problem if he doesn't believe you. I doubt if I will fare much better.'

Steadman saw little point in putting DS Fairfax through the ordeal of reliving her encounter with Nesbitt. 'Come on, let's eat,' he said.

Robbie stood up. Steadman was aware of another movement.

'Does the dog still trouble you, Fiona?'

'I'm afraid he does, sir.'

Steadman pointed to the floor. Immediately the dog sat down.

'Give me your hand,' he said.

DS Fairfax put her hand in Steadman's. It was cold and clammy. Together they stroked the dog on the top of his head and then under his chin. Robbie closed his eyes and thumped his tail on the floor.

'Why, he's nothing but a big softie, sir!'

'A softie yes, but highly intelligent. And as you have just

found out, nothing to be frightened of. All you have to do now is conquer your fear of Inspector Nesbitt.'

'I doubt if he would respond to a pat on the head or a tickle under the chin.'

★ ★ ★

Marco Lloyd served them lunch. Old Mrs Lloyd had made some fresh tortellini stuffed with spinach and ricotta.

'It's a miracle. Mamma must have known you were coming!' Marco exclaimed to DS Fairfax who didn't eat meat. 'Today's speciality is a vegetarian dish, just for you. How did Mamma know, eh?'

DS Fairfax was not feeling in the least bit hungry. However, she had to admit that the pasta was delicious. It was served simply in a bowl with a little grated cheese and no sauce, much to Steadman's relief. DS Fairfax may have overcome her fear of dogs, but Steadman remained terrified of eating in public.

He wanted to linger over a coffee. DS Fairfax declined and Steadman sensed her growing anxiety.

'I'll pass too, Marco,' he said. 'We have work to do.'

Steadman slipped Robbie out of his harness once they were back in the flat. 'Fiona, would you mind taking Robbie out into the garden while I change?'

'I don't see why not, sir, now that Robbie and I are the best of friends.'

There was no question in Steadman's mind that this

was a day for a white shirt. What tie to wear? Damn it, he said to himself, why not? His son Ben had bought him a tie with a cartoon policeman on it for one of his birthdays. This afternoon was going to be a farce anyway, he mused, and he might as well get in the spirit of the occasion.

To stop her brother selecting it accidentally, Linda had put a safety pin in the tail of the tie. He found the tie without too much difficulty. He was fully dressed with his heavy coat, scarf and hat on when DS Fairfax returned. She was out of breath.

'He's just a big puppy,' she remarked.

'Oh, he's that all right until he has to work. Now Robbie, it is time you earned your keep.'

Steadman fastened the dog's harness and closed the door behind them.

It was not the green Audi, but an ordinary and rather small patrol car. DS Fairfax pushed the front seat as far back as it would go and guided Steadman in. The door was at a different height from the Audi and he cracked his head on the ledge, knocking his fedora askew.

'Are you OK, sir?'

'Fine thanks. I'll just add it to my ever-increasing collection of bruises.'

Robbie jumped in and curled himself into a ball at Steadman's feet. He fitted in so perfectly it was as though the space had been specially designed for him.

'I'm afraid I'll have to go dead slow, sir. The fog is as thick as ever.'

Steadman grunted. Something had triggered a new

train of thought. Perhaps it was Robbie fitting in so precisely at his feet. A tune started playing in his head; a simple duet for flute and oboe by Bach. The two instruments wove in and out in perfect counterpoint. His head nodded ever so slightly in time to the music. He had not been able to make these three murders fit together. Yes, of course, all had been wired up, but that on the face of it was the only similarity. Or was it, he asked himself? Each body had been violated – whisky, sparkling water and lastly chocolates. These were not random choices, yet so far nobody had come up with any plausible explanation. What he desperately wanted to do was to go back to the beginning and start again with a blank sheet of paper, or at least in this case, with an open mind free from the distraction of an irascible and irrational acting DCI.

'Why is it, sir, that the worse the weather the closer the driver behind you feels compelled to sit on your bumper?'

Steadman had to pull himself back into the here and now. The music stopped. He paused, rewinding Fiona's last comment in his head.

'Oh... I suppose it is easier to follow someone's tail lights than try to find the road yourself,' he replied. 'What sort of car is it?'

'Could be anything in this fog. I can't even tell if there's a passenger in the car. Look out! The idiot's overtaking us.'

At last they arrived at the Eyesore. The only parking space DS Fairfax could find was at the back of the building.

'Mind your head, sir,' she said as she assisted Steadman out of the car.

'You'd better give me your arm. Robbie doesn't know his way from here.'

Sergeant Grimble was looking out for them. 'Thank goodness you've arrived. I'm surprised your ears aren't burning – both of you. Nesbitt is pacing up and down like a caged lion, albeit one with very large nose. He's none too happy about being kept waiting.'

Steadman was aware of some movement behind him.

'Are we alone?'

'A drunk stumbled in just before you entered. He's parked in a corner. I'll make him a coffee in a minute and let him sober up, then see if wants anything. I doubt it – probably only needs a sleep and a warm-up.'

The drunk suddenly sat up.

'Are you the blind detective? Well, I'm blind drunk!' And with that he fell back into a stupor.

'What beats me,' Sergeant Grimble continued, 'is how anyone can get so inebriated so early in the day. Look, I don't mean to hurry you, but I don't think Nesbitt has had his lunch and...'

'I can't say my heart bleeds for him. Is he interviewing me in DCI Long's office or in one of the downstairs rooms?' Steadman asked.

'Upstairs. I suspect he wants to emphasise the point that he is an acting DCI whereas, in his eyes, you are only a former DI. Pathetic, when you think about it. Will I keep Robbie for you, sir?'

'Probably just as well, if you don't mind.'

Steadman undid Robbie's harness and handed him over to Sergeant Grimble. 'Not too many doggie treats. Bring him up if he gets restless. Fiona, your arm please. "Lay on, Macduff, and damned be him who first cries Hold! Enough!"'

The Shakespearean reference was not lost on DS Fairfax who, linking arms with her former boss, gently steered him upstairs and knocked on what had once been DCI Long's door.

* * *

Grimble was right; the acting DCI was not a happy man.

'And about bloody time too,' Nesbitt exploded.

'Good afternoon, Inspector Nesbitt. I gather you wanted to see me.'

DS Fairfax guided Steadman to a seat.

'OK, Doris Day, you can make yourself scarce. I want a private word man-to-man with *Mr* Steadman.'

It was as though he underlined the word 'mister' out of spite.

'Let's have it, Steadman. I know the game as well as you or anyone else round here. You may not be a real policeman now, but I bet you still have your little band of informers. The riff-raff willing to whisper in your ear for a few quid or hoping you will turn a blind eye...' He stopped, he even stammered. 'Well, you know what I mean.'

For a brief moment Steadman almost felt sorry for him. He must have spent several hours rehearsing what he was going to say and had still managed to make a hash of things.

'I'm a busy man, Steadman, and I don't have all day. I don't believe a word of what you told Fairfax. Dreams? Pull the other one. In fact, I'm surprised she fell for it. She's quite sharp, for a woman. Look, I could come down on you like a ton of bricks for deliberately withholding evidence, but I'll give you one chance. If your informant knew about the bike, I'll bet he knows something else. He and I need to have a cosy little chat. Understand? So out with it – I want a name,' Nesbitt jumped up on to the desk and the infernal shoe squeaking started again as he swung his short legs back and forth.

'Morpheus,' Steadman replied.

'Morpheus? Odd sort of name – foreigner is he?'

'Greek, I believe.'

'And what does this Morpheus do and where can I get my hands on him?'

'What does he do?' Steadman replied with a wry smile. 'Well, he was the son of Hypnos, the Greek god of sleep. Morpheus is more usually known as the Greek god of dreams. If you want to find him, I am afraid you will have to read Ovid.'

Nesbitt stopped swinging his legs. The silence was as chilly and impenetrable as the fog outside.

'Don't piss about with me, Steadman. You'll regret it.'

Steadman tapped his hand on the arm of the chair. 'For

once in your life, why don't you listen? You are like a cat in a roomful of mice. You pounce on one and once it's in your claws, you ignore the rest. But they are still there scampering around while you chew the head off that one poor mouse. Let's start with the bike that DS Fairfax found. Whether you like it or not, the fact is that the image of Maurice Eeles, or at least someone who sounded like him, on a blood-spattered bike came to me in a dream.'

Nesbitt tried to butt in. Steadman held his ground.

'Hear me out, damn it! I have always had very vivid dreams, even more so now that I've lost my sight.'

Nesbitt snorted.

'Now, I no more believe in prophetic dreams than you do, Nesbitt, and I wish in retrospect that I had never mentioned my dream to Fiona. What I believe is that when I'm wrestling with a problem, my brain simply doesn't switch off. Even while I'm asleep it continues to consider all the possibilities, all the alternatives. The pieces of information are juggled round until they all appear to fit neatly, even if it makes no sense in the cold light of day. This puzzle is incomplete. There are still some important pieces missing...'

'There's nothing missing! Harry Eeles was working at both houses with electric cable. Harry is a violent ne'er-do-well. Case closed.'

Steadman sighed.

'How long are you going to play with that same mouse and ignore the rest? Ask yourself this – why were all the victims wired up? Why were the bodies all violated? A forensic psychologist has been brought in for very good reasons and you deliberately snub her. Whisky, sparkling mineral water and now some fancy chocolates. What links them? And you are nothing but rude to Kim Ho.'

Nesbitt put his face very close to Steadman and hissed at him.

'OK, clever clogs, I still don't buy your bullshit about a dream. Explain to me how that bike came to be in the Eeles's garage. A bike that I have just confirmed is covered in your dog's blood.'

'Let me answer you by posing another question. Why was the bike wiped clean of all fingerprints?'

Nesbitt jumped back on his desk and started swinging his legs again.

'Because Maurice Eeles is a smart bastard.'

It was Steadman's turn to get irritated.

'I've interviewed Maurice – you've interviewed Maurice. Surely the one thing we can agree on is that Maurice Eeles is by no stretch of the imagination smart.'

'You've gone soft, Steadman.'

Steadman frowned and shook his head.

'Whisky, sparkling water, chocolates and wired up – why?'

'All irrelevant. Three murders and we can place your friend Harry at the scenes of the first two. As for the third murder, like father, like son I say – I'll make it stick. And if you don't want to press charges against Maurice Eeles for attacking your dog, then that's your lookout.'

Steadman stood up.

'For the last time, I'm telling you, Inspector Nesbitt. Harry and Maurice Eeles are entirely innocent. Innocent of murder and innocent of attacking Robbie. I may be blind but even I can see that the wretched bike was planted in their garage. We are dealing with someone devious and cold-blooded. Someone who is watching our every move and what's more, probably laughing at us right now.'

'You know I think you're right – you are nothing more than a dreamer. If you think I am going to chase up all your fancy distractions, you have another think coming. Let me remind you who is in charge of this investigation.'

'I need no reminding, Nesbitt. Would you like to charge me with obstruction or withholding information?'

Inspector Nesbitt's lip twitched. Steadman stood motionless in front of him, his chin tilted slightly upwards and his fists clenched by his sides. In that instant Nesbitt hesitated: a fatal error. It was as though he knew he had met a man who was more than his match.

'I've got better things to do,' he said. 'But you are off the case, Steadman.'

'Let me get this quite clear – you no longer want me to work with you?'

'Got it in one, Steadman.'

'That suits me just fine.'

There was a muffled knock on the door.

'Come in, blast you,' bellowed Nesbitt.

'Sorry to interrupt,' said Sergeant Grimble. 'Robbie is getting a bit fretful.'

Nesbitt glowered at Sergeant Grimble and the dog.

Robbie appeared quite unconcerned.

'That's quite all right,' Steadman replied. 'I don't think Inspector Nesbitt and I have anything left to say to each other.'

Robbie padded over to join him and waited patiently while Steadman replaced his harness. Sergeant Grimble moved the chair to one side and without being asked, took Steadman's arm and led him from the room. Nesbitt slammed the door.

'How much of that did you hear?' Steadman asked.

Sergeant Grimble was unabashed.

'About the last ten minutes or so, sir.'

'I'm beginning to think Fiona may have been right after all. The man is a fool.'

They arrived back in the waiting room.

'Is there anyone else in here?' Steadman asked.

'Only our drunk friend, who is now fast asleep in his corner.'

'I think we need an alternative investigative team. Could you organise a meeting for seven thirty this evening, for me?'

'Delighted to oblige, sir. Where do you suggest and who would you like to invite?'

Steadman hummed a little tune to himself. 'Let's go back to where it all started. Try and book a large table at the Three Grasshoppers in Upper Bridgetown. Sandwiches and chips, I think. Of course, I will pay. See how many of the following are free: DS Fairfax, DS Munro, Dr Rufus, Kim Ho and Sam Griffiths.' Steadman paused. 'And DC Lofthouse. If nothing else, it might amuse him. I needn't tell you to do it discreetly. If anybody asks, tell them it's my leaving do. Maybe Alan Munro could pick me up if he's free.'

'Did someone mention my name?' It was the unmistakable Scottish voice of DS Munro.

'Perfect timing, Alan,' Steadman said. 'Have a word with Sergeant Grimble. He'll fill you in. I must be off.'

'Don't you want a lift, sir?'

'No, I need the exercise and the time to think.'

The drunk in the corner stirred as the door closed behind DI John Steadman.

'Is it true he's off the case? That's what everyone is saying upstairs.'

'Don't you believe it for a minute, Alan,' Sergeant Grimble replied. 'He's just getting his teeth into it.'

CHAPTER TWENTY THREE

The cold, wet, late afternoon air hit Steadman as he stepped out of the Eyesore. He gasped and immediately clutched his ribs as a spasm shot through his chest. He knew that if he stopped Munro would come bounding out and force him to accept a lift. He needed to be alone with his thoughts, so he stuck his right hand into his coat pocket to stop his arm from swinging and cautiously continued on his way. Each step was painful.

For some reason, Robbie seemed eager to get him home and was pulling on the leash.

'Easy, Robbie, easy,' Steadman said.

Robbie looked round and instantly slowed his pace. The pain in Steadman's ribs was becoming a nagging, persistent ache. By the time he had walked two hundred yards he regretted not accepting Munro's offer.

His toe caught on a raised paving slab. He lurched and stumbled, clutching his chest again.

'Are you all right?'

It was a man's voice; vaguely familiar. He felt like

answering, 'No – I'm blind, cold, wet, my ribs are hurting like hell and I've just been kicked off a case by a pompous, narrow-minded, jumped-up acting DCI.' Instead he replied, 'I'm fine, just a little trip.'

'Will you manage?'

'Yes, thank you. The dog will look after me.'

'Well, if you're sure.'

The man crossed the road. Steadman listened to his retreating footsteps. Was the voice really familiar? A car passed. Then there was silence. Steadman thought it odd but presumed the man must have gone into one of the flats opposite.

'Go forward, Robbie.'

They had walked another fifty yards or so before Steadman realised he had lost count of the number of paces. He did not stop. He knew Robbie would lead him home, yet he felt angry with himself and vulnerable.

They came to a road junction. The dog turned and led Steadman down to a safe crossing point. If the kerb edge had raised bumps, he would know exactly where he was. Robbie stopped and Steadman brushed his foot over the pavement. Sure enough, there were the tactile markers. He could even say how many paces he was from his front door.

Another two cars passed before Robbie led him safely to the other side. He still got a thrill out of crossing a road by himself and for the first time that day he allowed himself a little smile.

His good humour was short lived. He heard more

footsteps behind him, and his heart started to race. Don't be stupid, he told himself, it's a free country, people are allowed to walk where they like. There was no point in going any faster; a child could outpace him, and, besides his ribs were really starting to hurt. Instead he stopped. It was an old trick. If you thought you were being followed and you stopped, so would your pursuer. The footsteps continued, and someone walked past him. Whoever it was gave Steadman and the dog a wide berth. He breathed a sigh of relief.

'Go forward, Robbie.'

The dog obeyed and they walked on.

Behind him footsteps started again. He swore under his breath. There was nothing for it but to keep going. Another two hundred yards and there were shops with bright lights. He passed an Indian restaurant. It was not open yet, but someone inside was busy cooking and a pleasing aroma of spices and garlic wafted through the air. Not much further. He crossed another road. The fog muffled all noises in a way that made it impossible for him to tell how far behind him the footsteps were. Ten yards, twenty perhaps? No more than that, he guessed.

Lloyd's café at last. Should he walk in? He would be safe there. An image of the Lloyd brothers and Mamma Lloyd coming out of the kitchen brandishing knives flashed through his brain. But the argument with Beaky Nesbitt had made him obstinate, pig-headed even, and he was damned if he was going to be prevented from going home.

The downstairs door was locked. He pulled out his bunch of keys, fumbling desperately to find the right one. The footsteps were getting louder. Steadman gave a start as a voice behind him asked:

'Are you all right?'

A shiver ran down Steadman's spine. The same man's voice. Alarm bells rang.

'I'll manage,' he said, far more brusquely than he meant to.

'I'm only trying to help,' said the voice.

The new key was stiff, but the door unlocked and with a shaking hand Steadman stepped inside.

★ ★ ★

'Is that you, Inspector Steadman?'

It was Tim Warrender. He was sitting at the top of the stairs outside Steadman's flat.

'Have you been here long, Tim?'

'No. I've only just got here. I did mean to phone but I dropped my mobile in school and broke it.'

Steadman took off Robbie's harness and the dog raced up the stairs. He followed slowly.

'Crikey, you look awful!'

'It is only my ribs hurting and I'm a bit cold, that's all. I suspect you're cold too. You should have got yourself a hot drink in the café. You know you won't have to pay as long as you're helping me.'

'I'm OK, honest. I'll make you a cup of tea as soon as we get in,' Tim replied.

The flat was warm. Steadman hung up his coat, scarf and hat. Tim gave Robbie a rub down and set about making the tea. He even remembered to put in less milk than last time.

'I've helped myself to squash and a biscuit. Is that OK?' Steadman smiled

'Of course. How was school today?'

'The assembly was a bit gloomy,' he replied through a mouthful of biscuit. 'Loads of the girls were in tears. At least I didn't muck up my bit. But wait till I tell you – Haribin and Skinner have been suspended! Which is a shame really as I was meant to be going on a school trip, not tomorrow but the next day. There's a new exhibition on in the Art Gallery and some of us were supposed to go after school. I forgot to mention it. I'll be about an hour late in coming round for Robbie, if it's still on.'

'That's fine. What are you going to do about your phone?' It was difficult for Steadman to keep the anxiety out of his voice.

'Don't know yet. Mum is still mad at me for losing my games kit. She'll go nuts when I tell her I've smashed my phone.'

Steadman fished his wallet out of his back pocket.

'You're not allowed to work for me without a phone. Remember?' Slowly he unfolded the notes and counted out a sum that made Tim's eyes almost pop out of his head.

'I can't take all that,' he protested.

'I insist. It is imperative that you can phone at all times. There should be enough there to buy a tough, protective case as well. If your parents object, I'll have a word with them.'

Reluctantly Tim took the money.

'I won't be able to get anything until Thursday when the shops open late.'

A worried look spread over Steadman's face.

'Is that a problem?' Tim asked.

'I think it might be. Robbie doesn't need a walk tonight as we've just come from the Eyesore. Perhaps Alan could go with you tomorrow if he's free. You would like that, wouldn't you?'

'Cool.'

'After that, well... maybe you will have your new phone.'

'How is the case going? Have you caught the murderer yet?'

'Not yet. There have been some interesting developments, but everything is top secret.' Steadman sensed Tim's disappointment. 'Would you feed Robbie for me, then take him out to the garden? After that, if you have time, he could do with a really good brush.'

Tim was grateful for something to do. He put out the dog's food and made Robbie sit and wait until he blew three blasts on the whistle.

'Can I clean your shoes for you while Robbie's dinner is settling? They are covered in mud.'

Steadman had had no idea about the state of his shoes. 'That would be very kind of you, Tim. Do you know where the polish and brushes are kept?'

Tim had already found them when he had been looking for biscuits one day. 'There you are,' he said, giving the shoes a final buff. 'They look as good as new. I'll take Robbie out now.'

Steadman felt his way over to the piano, sat down and lifted the lid. He played a few scales, then ran through the pieces Miss Elliot had asked him to practise.

'Now what?' he mumbled to himself.

His fingers randomly fell on the keys. Bach? No, not Bach – something light-hearted, something relaxing. Without thinking he found himself playing a piece he had composed years ago. It was a simple melody and it had been one of Holly's favourites. Tears filled his sightless eyes. What would Holly have thought about Beaky Nesbitt? He knew full well that she would simply have laughed at his antics and in the end he would have laughed too. A thought sprang into his mind. What was Sam Griffiths' favourite tune? He lost his place. The chord jarred.

Just then, fortunately, the doorbell rang with the now familiar pattern of TW in Morse code. He stood up, wiped his eyes and blew his nose.

'What was that tune, Inspector Steadman?' It sounded lovely.'

'Oh, just a piece that my wife Holly liked. I made it up myself.'

Tim noticed a tear on Steadman's cheek, but didn't comment. 'I'll give Robbie a brush, then I had better go.'

'You will give me a quick call to let me know you are safe, won't you?'

* * *

Steadman took off his ridiculous tie, replaced the safety pin with some difficulty and put it back in the drawer. He pulled on a jumper, partly because he felt the cold but mainly because he wanted this evening to be as informal as possible. He knew that if even a whisper of tonight's meeting reached Inspector Nesbitt it would mean trouble for his colleagues.

The phone rang: Tim was safely home.

'Now Robbie, what loose ends do we need to tidy up? He ruffled the dog's ears. 'I suppose the only mystery you're interested in is where does Sergeant Grimble get all those doggie treats, isn't that right?' He tickled the dog under the chin.

Whether it was in response to Grimble's name or the mention of doggie treats, Robbie began to drool. Steadman's hands became sticky.

'Come on Robbie, before you dribble all over my trousers.'

Steadman walked through to the kitchen, found some kitchen roll, wiped the dog's muzzle and washed his hands. His watch informed him that he had more than half an hour before Munro was due to arrive. He sat in his favourite chair with Robbie not so much lying at his feet but on them, and mentally counted up the unanswered questions. They were questions that vexed him, yet were being studiously ignored by Inspector Nesbitt. One by one he ticked them off.

He was roused from his reverie by a growl from Robbie and a loud pounding on his front door. He was tempted to add to his list the mystery of why Alan Munro never used the doorbell.

'Good evening, sir. Sorry if I'm a wee bit early. Heaven knows how long it will take us in this weather. I took the liberty of coming through the café rather than make you walk down the stairs. I'm glad the street door's got a proper lock on it.'

Steadman sniffed. 'You know as well as I do, Alan, that it will only slow somebody down. If my memory serves me correctly the door's got stained glass in it. Still, if it keeps everyone else happy...'

Steadman sniffed again.

'Are you wearing aftershave, Alan?'

Munro turned scarlet. 'Me? No, absolutely not. Why do you ask?'

'Something's fragrant, and it's definitely not Robbie.'

'Ah - that would be Dr Griffiths. I picked her up before calling for you. I gather Kim Ho is giving the others a lift.'

'Well, we'd better not keep the lady waiting. Would you pass me my coat and hat?'

Steadman pulled the door behind them. His hand crept over the wall until he found the light switch. With a click the stairs were illuminated.

'For Robbie's benefit,' he explained.

'And mine,' added Munro.

The car was filled with Sam Griffiths' perfume. A small thrill ran down Steadman's spine. 'Good evening, Dr Griffiths,' he said.

'Well, if we're going to be all formal – good evening Detective Inspector Steadman, and good evening to you Mr Robbie,' she replied mischievously.

Steadman could imagine the twinkle in her eye and it unsettled him, though not in an unpleasant way.

The fog in Helmsmouth was as thick as ever. Munro crawled forward warily. He gripped the steering wheel tightly and peered into the gloom.

'It will be a slow drive, sir,' he said apologetically.

'No problem, Alan. Have you updated Sam?'

'He has,' Dr Griffiths replied. 'On the face of it, it gets even more bizarre.'

Steadman frowned: he wasn't so sure.

'But only on the face of it. I've been thinking,' Sam continued.

'Go on,' said Steadman.

'This time, I think we can all agree, the killer knew his victim and vice versa.'

'All except Beaky Nesbitt,' Munro growled.

Sam ignored his remark.

'Also, he must have known where his workshop was and probably had a good idea what he was looking for. Interestingly, he did not smash any of Dennis's carvings.'

Steadman nodded approvingly. He had not thought of that.

'He gives him a fancy bottle of wine. I presume it's not his birthday. Alan has told me about Saint Dennis. I'm impressed, but not convinced. I think it was on account of him winning the competition. I don't suppose we know what the competition was yet?'

Alan shook his head.

'What do you think happened next?' she asked.

'I suspect he suggested to Dennis that he should finish his meal,' Steadman replied. 'Dennis sat back at the table. The killer possibly went to look at some of the records. Once he was behind Dennis... You know the rest.'

Munro and Dr Griffiths let out simultaneous gasps.

'What is it?' Steadman asked anxiously.

'The fog, sir – it's vanished!' exclaimed Munro. 'We've been climbing steadily since we left Helmsmouth. I guess we've risen above it.'

'It was quite dramatic,' Sam added. 'Like a diver breaking the surface for air. I don't think I've ever seen anything like it. And now the stars – living in London, I'd forgotten how beautiful they are.'

They parked and got out of the car. Robbie, realising he was not needed, went off to explore the undergrowth at the side of the road.

'Paint me the picture,' said Steadman. 'Ladies first.'

Dr Griffiths looked thoughtfully at the scene before her. 'We must be a hundred feet or so above Helmsmouth. It looks like someone has dropped the entire town into a sea of very thin milk whose edges are lapping the road fifty yards down the hill.'

Sam looked at Steadman, who was standing silently, drinking in her every word.

'You can still see the street lights. The nearest ones form a hazy chain, but in the centre of the town it's just an indistinct mass of shifting lights. There are blocks of illumination which I suspect are buildings, intertwined with moving red and white lines of cars and twinkling specks of green and red from the traffic lights. And a blue flashing light has just appeared on my left. It's impossible to say if it's an ambulance or police car. To my right there are possibly three dark buildings rising above the fog. They must be quite tall as they have red beacons on their roofs.'

'Those would be Da Gama Towers,' Munro explained.

'And then in the far distance I can just make out the sweeping arc from the lighthouse,' Sam continued. 'You can't see where the land meets the sea. The milky white simply melts into blue, then inky black.'

'Very good,' said Steadman. He did not try to visualise the scene. He simply let Sam Griffiths' words paint the images themselves.

'And the night sky is awesome, sir,' ventured Munro.

'Tell me about it, Alan, in words that I can understand.' Turning to Dr Griffiths, he continued, 'I'm not sure if you know – our detective sergeant has a degree in physics and an encyclopaedic knowledge of astronomy.'

Munro was as red as the beacons on top of Da Gama Towers.

'I wouldn't go that far, sir. Here goes…'

Steadman tried in vain to imagine the night sky. Perhaps he was only half listening. The lilting voice of Dr Sam Griffiths was playing over and over in his mind like a catchy tune that gets stuck in your head.

Robbie nudged his leg and broke the spell.

'How are we doing for time?' Steadman asked.

'We've got plenty of time, sir. Upper Bridgetown is only about a mile away.'

'Could we drive past Crenshaw Tipley's house?'

'We could do better than that, sir. I've got the key in my pocket. I'll give you a guided tour.'

★ ★ ★

The house smelt stale and musty. And it was silent; too silent, like the enforced quiet of a funeral parlour. Without thinking they found themselves talking in whispers.

They passed through the vestibule, where Crenshaw Tipley's coat was still hanging above his outdoor shoes. Nothing had been moved. It felt as though they were trespassing and Crenshaw Tipley would step out of his study to lambast them at any moment. Steadman was glad he had left Robbie in the car.

There was another odour here; slightly sweet and sickly. An odour Steadman could not place. They moved forward.

'This is the main room,' Munro explained. 'I suspect it was two rooms and a corridor once upon a time, now knocked into one. On your left is a large oak refectory table and on your right is a fireplace with some comfy chairs. All the walls are covered in book cases. There are even smaller bookcases set at right angles to the wall.'

Steadman tried to visualise the room. As Munro described the various items he thought he could smell the wax polish on the table, the vague whiff of wood smoke from the fire and the dry, dusty aroma of old paper. He would have liked to take out his cane and carefully pace round the room, touching the tables and chairs and running his fingers over the books. He felt somehow that if he could only absorb the atmosphere of the place he might understand better the awful events that had taken place in this house. But wouldn't it look pretentious – ridiculous, even – to go bumping round the room fingering objects in the off chance they would provide inspiration? Munro might understand, but what would Sam Griffiths think?

Munro touched his arm. 'Tipley's study is through here, sir.'

The odd, sickly sweet odour was even stronger in the study. Steadman could resist no longer.

'Alan, have you any idea what the smell is in here?'

'Oh that. Yes, it is still fairly strong. It's some sort of gentleman's eau de cologne that Tipley was fond of. He reeked of the stuff. I think there's a bottle in his lavatory... Here we are.'

Munro opened the bottle and wafted it under Steadman's nose. The aroma was pungent and not particularly pleasant. Steadman grimaced.

'Do you think he wore it to fend off people?' he asked. 'It's certainly not attractive. What do you think, Sam?'

'It reminds me of my great-uncle – a most unsavoury character.'

Steadman took a pace forward and bumped into a piece of furniture. Instinctively his hands reached out and he ran his fingers over the surface.

'Is this Tipley's desk?'

Sam Griffiths and Munro watched as Steadman traced his way round the desk until he found Tipley's chair. He sat down rather heavily. His face was expressionless. It would have been difficult to know what he was thinking. In point of fact, he was not thinking about anything in particular. Ideas and random thoughts drifted in and out of his consciousness. His fingers explored the desk top. They found the ivory paperknife, and he picked it up and started to tap a gentle rhythm on Tipley's blotter. Dr Griffiths and Munro exchanged glances. Sam was about to say something, but Munro put a finger to his lips.

At last Steadman spoke.

'You know, Dr Rufus has been right all along. It all hinges on why somebody filled his lungs full of Debantry's Deluxe Blended Whisky.'

Before either Dr Griffiths or Munro could ask him to elaborate, the front door opened.

CHAPTER TWENTY FOUR

'Here, you lot – clear off quick before I call the police!'

It was the unmistakable rasp of Juliet Winterby. Munro opened the study door. She was standing in the centre of the library, brandishing a poker.

'Calm yourself, Mrs Winterby, we are the police.'

Juliet Winterby glowered at the enormous bulk of DS Munro. She was not in the least put out.

'Oh, it's you again. Where's your sidekick?' she said, replacing the poker by the fire.

'DI Steadman is in the study. Come and join us.'

'I hope he hasn't brought that ruddy dog in here. I've enough work to do without cleaning up muddy paw prints on top of everything else.'

Steadman stood up and extended his hand. 'You are just the person to help us, Mrs Winterby,' he said warmly. She shook the hand reluctantly. 'Alan, is there another chair for Mrs Winterby?'

'I'll stand. I know my place.'

Dr Griffiths gave a little cough.

'Where are my manners?' Steadman said. 'Mrs Winterby, this is Dr Samantha Griffiths, a forensic psychologist who is helping with the case.'

Juliet Winterby looked her up and down. 'I didn't think you were a copper – you look too soft by half.'

'I'll take that as a compliment,' Sam replied.

'Take it any way you want dearie, it's all the same to me. Anyway, what are you lot doing back here?'

Steadman eased himself down into Tipley's seat and much to Juliet Winterby's annoyance, started playing with the ivory paperknife.

'Something in this case remains quite…' Steadman was about to say "bizarre". At the last moment he substituted "puzzling". 'Puzzling, yes, and that is where you might be able to help us, Mrs Winterby.' He dared not refer to her by her first name. 'Tell me, was Crenshaw Tipley fond of whisky?'

'Him? Whisky? No, he couldn't abide the stuff. You won't find any spirits in this house. Nothing stronger than a dry sherry.'

This snippet of information appeared to please Steadman.

'You know his lungs had been filled with whisky after he was killed. I'm surprised you didn't smell it when you found him that morning.'

Juliet Winterby wondered if this was a trap. She looked round the room before answering.

'Mr Tipley was partial to a generous splash of

gentlemen's fragrance. I didn't notice any whisky. Should I have?'

Steadman sensed the rising hostility in her voice.

'You have been most helpful. Don't worry, we will lock up.'

'Just make sure you turn off all the lights. I don't know who's going to pay the bill now he's gone.'

'I'll attend to the lights,' replied Munro. 'Can we give you a lift home?'

'No thank you. I walked here and I can walk back.'

Munro busied himself switching off the lights and closing the doors. Without fuss, Dr Griffiths slipped her arm through Steadman's and started leading him towards the car.

'Well, fancy that,' cackled Juliet Winterby. 'Don't you two make a pretty pair?'

Steadman's cheeks burned. He could think of nothing to say.

* * *

The Three Grasshoppers was only a short drive away. The car park was deserted.

'Looks like we're the first here,' Munro remarked.

The inn was old and large and had retained many of the original features, including numerous changes in floor level. Steadman was not concentrating, and had it not been for Munro's quick reaction he would have been sent sprawling on the floor.

'Thanks, Alan. Not my finest entrance,' he said with an apologetic smile.

Munro led him to the bar where a large man, not as tall as Munro but more heavy set, was dusting the bottles in front of an antique mirror advertising a brewery that had long since closed down.

'Good evening, Inspector Steadman. Welcome to The Three Grasshoppers.'

Steadman frowned. He was irritated by the man's apparent familiarity. He thought he recognised the voice, but without being able to see his face he could not place him.

'Should I know you?' he asked peevishly.

'You interrogated me several times after the drugs raid at Pinkerton's Yard some years back. You were convinced that there was someone working on the inside. I admit I looked the part and I don't hold it against you. Weren't we all surprised when it turned out to be that slip of a girl in the office? No more than seventeen and not long left school.'

Steadman slapped his hand on the bar. 'Zoltan Parker!'

The man smiled, revealing missing teeth.

'Yes, it's all coming back to me,' Steadman continued. 'It was indeed a few years ago and... well, quite a lot has happened in between times. Wait a minute though – Zoltan is not your real name, is it?'

'Please don't try too hard to remember.'

'It's Cedric.'

'Ssh! I wouldn't want the world to know. Do I look like a Cedric to you?' he asked, turning to Sam Griffiths.

'No, you are definitely more suited to Zoltan,' she replied.

'Thank you. Now, what can I get you? I've laid out the big table in what we call the snug. It's partitioned off from the main lounge and there's a nice fire lit. I can't imagine there'll be anybody else in until about nine, when half a dozen of the lads will step in for a game of darts. I doubt if they'll disturb you.'

'The evening is entirely on me. Do you want my credit card?' Steadman asked.

'No, no – I think I can trust you. We'll settle up at the end. Here comes the rest of your party by the sounds of it.'

Dr Rufus was leading the way, lustily singing 'By the Light of the Silvery Moon'. 'What a spectacle,' he said at the end of the chorus. 'Shame you missed it, John. I suspect you saw enough stars this afternoon when you had your bust-up with Beaky Nesbitt. Grimble told me all about it.'

DS Fairfax and Kim Ho exchanged embarrassed glances. DC Lofthouse grinned.

'What?' spluttered Dr Rufus. 'What have I said now?'

Sam Griffiths steered Steadman to the table.

'Is he always like that?' she asked.

'Frank? Oh no! Sometimes he is much worse. I guess that's maybe why I'm so fond of him.'

They all sat down and Robbie stretched himself out at

Steadman's feet. Zoltan lumbered over with the drinks.

'Thank you all for coming to my leaving party, because that's what it is if anybody asks,' said Steadman. 'There are chips and sandwiches ordered and, of course, vegetarian options. Where are you, Fiona?'

'Sitting opposite you, sir, at the other end of the table,' DS Fairfax replied.

'And for those of you wishing a pudding, I'm assured that Zoltan will provide. Alan, will you make sure everyone has drinks?'

'No problem,' answered Munro.

'It appears to be common knowledge that our acting DCI and I had a major disagreement this afternoon and he has removed me from the case.'

'Can he do that, sir?' asked DC Lofthouse.

'I have no idea, but he has. Here comes the food. Let's eat first and talk afterwards.'

Robbie cast a hopeful eye up at the chips as they passed over his head.

'Don't even think about it, Robbie. I may be blind but I know how your mind works.'

Not surprisingly Munro and Rufus opted for pudding as well. Zoltan brought coffee, then retired behind the bar, where he proceeded to polish glasses.

'Seeing as it's a party I thought we might play a game,' Steadman suggested.

'Does it involve spinning a bottle?' asked Rufus.

Steadman shook his head in mock dismay. 'No, Frank. The game is called 'Loose Ends' and it involves going over the three murders and trying to tie up... well, the loose ends, if we can. I'll start. My involvement began when I was rudely awakened by Dr Rufus in the small hours. He didn't ask me who killed Crenshaw Tipley, or even why. No, he asked me why someone had gone to the bother of injecting his lungs with whisky. Now Dr Griffiths, DS Munro and I had a chance meeting with Juliet Winterby earlier this evening. Apparently Tipley disliked whisky and never had anything stronger than sherry in the house. Tell me, Sam, in your experience, when a body is violated would whatever is used be of more significance to the perpetrator or the victim?'

Dr Griffiths thought for a moment.

'In this instance we have three murders in which the three bodies were violated in different ways. It is almost certain that the whisky, sparkling water and chocolates were relevant to the victims. Of course, the same cannot be said about wiring them up. I think that is something significant to the killer.'

'Thank you,' Steadman replied. 'So loose end number one is to find out the whisky link. A book was borrowed under an alias from Tipley's library. Do we know what the book was?

DC Lofthouse answered, 'It was a book on stage design in the theatre, sir.'

Steadman pursed his lips.

'Was it, now? That's interesting. What about the alias?'

'Gordon Greig? I've checked everybody in the phone book and on the electoral register, sir, without any success.

The same goes for Reg Butler, the name used at Velda Meemes' shop to reserve the Buddha.'

A statue and a book on stage design, Steadman mused, and two names that somehow felt familiar. He was struck by an idea.

'Let us call that loose end number two. I'll be honest, I'm sure I've heard those names before and I've just thought of someone who may help me. Let me do some digging. What's next?'

'Richard Armstrong?' suggested DC Lofthouse.

'I think we can forget that one,' answered Munro. 'Too far back, we know what it's about and we've been told not to pursue it.'

'Loose end number three has to be the sparkling water,' suggested DS Fairfax. There was a murmur of approval.

'All agreed, then' said Steadman. 'An expensive, unnecessary item that we know Velda Meemes never had in the house. Which brings us on to the last murder. Frank, what can you tell us from the post-mortem?'

Dr Rufus cleared his throat. 'Cause of death was obviously the blow to the head. His mouth and backside had been stuffed with chocolates – two hundred and fifty grams worth, to be precise.'

'And we know what they are, sir,' added Kim Ho. 'Saturnalia Special Selection – another luxury brand.'

'I make that loose end number four,' announced Dr Rufus.

'If you like,' Steadman replied. 'Dennis Knotting has

left us several other loose ends. Any luck identifying the two men in the photograph, Alan?'

'I went to the Art College today and to cut a long story short, no joy.'

Steadman pressed the button on his watch. 'Eight twenty-one' chirped the metallic voice. 'You know, we have time to get it printed in the morning paper if you have it with you, Alan,' he said.

Munro produced the photo.

'Get them to blank out Knotting's face and print the usual stuff about urgently needing to identify and eliminate from police investigation. I'm sure Jack would come and collect it. He lives not far away. His number is on my phone under *Helmsmouth Echo and Evening News*.'

'I'll see to it,' offered DC Lofthouse. He took Steadman's phone and the photo from Munro.

'If we're publishing the photo, shouldn't we tell Inspector Nesbitt?' Fiona Fairfax queried.

'It had better come from me,' grunted Munro. 'You know what he's like.'

'Back to Dennis Knotting,' Steadman continued. 'There are the cheque and the empty envelope that still need explaining.'

'The cheque came from a wholesale grocer' said Munro. 'I only found out late this afternoon. I'll contact them tomorrow.'

Steadman was willing to bet that the grocer supplied Saturnalia Special Selection.

'The envelope is high quality and widely available. The

only prints on it were those of the deceased,' added Kim Ho.

Will Lofthouse rejoined them. 'Jack's gone off with the picture. It'll be tight, but he thinks he can get it there in time.'

'Do we know what happened to Knotting's sculptures?' asked Steadman.

'I spoke with his mate, Kevin,' Lofthouse replied. 'A gallery in London takes everything he makes and sells them on commission.'

'They've probably been ripping the poor man off for years,' said Munro.

'They were expecting a new piece any day now,' continued Lofthouse.

But there was nothing nearing completion in his workshop, Steadman mused, unless...

'Could he have entered a sculpture into a competition?' he asked.

'It's a possibility,' said Munro. 'And if he had won some money then he would have put one over on the greedy gallery owners, and possibly been able to charge a wee bit more for his work.'

'Anything from the bottle of wine, Kim?'

'No, the bottle had been wiped clean. Although it is an expensive wine, at least thirty shops in Helmsmouth sell exactly the same bottle.'

'I think that about sums up the loose ends for the third murder,' Steadman concluded.

'You've forgotten about the missing blood,' Dr Rufus

reminded him. 'The body was pretty much exsanguinated – lost most of its blood, if you like. Whoever killed him must have mopped it up and taken it away with him, although I have no idea why.'

'Sir, sir,' Fairfax interjected in a hushed voice.

'What is it, Fiona?' Steadman asked.

'Someone is watching us.'

'Where?'

'In the mirror.'

Only Fiona's seat was facing the bar. Zoltan had disappeared, and reflected in the faded mirror behind the bar she could make out a man with piercing blue eyes who was staring at them from the other side of the partition. The others, except Steadman, turned to look, but whoever it was had raised a newspaper in front of his face.

'We had better keep our voices down,' suggested Steadman. 'I think we've come to the end of our game anyway.'

'Not so fast,' said Dr Rufus. 'Or so coy. You seem to have skipped over the fact that you were deliberately hit by a car and had your flat trashed.'

'And right at the start of this, someone photographed you at the traffic lights,' added Munro.

Steadman had not forgotten. Nor had he forgotten that someone had chased Tim Warrender in the park, stolen cable from Harry Eeles's place, attacked his dog and planted the blood-splattered bike in Harry Eeles' garage. Frustration mounted inside him. These were all asides. Were they relevant? Possibly, but they were distractions, at least for the moment. He was a policeman. Three murders had been committed, three innocent lives taken. Would the killer stop at three? Suddenly he remembered DCI Long's words. Hadn't the only previous serial killer in Helmsmouth killed three times? And if so, would there not be the temptation to strike again? Fame, notoriety, celebrity status – wasn't that what so many people craved?

He frowned and bit his lip. This was getting nowhere. He knew what had to be done. They all had to…

'Focus!' he said in a voice far louder than he intended. 'If we don't keep our minds fixed on the murders we will lose sight of our goal.'

An odd turn of phrase, thought Sam Griffiths, for a blind person to use.

Robbie stirred at Steadman's feet, sat up and gently butted him in the thigh. Steadman stroked the dog's head.

'What is it, Robbie? Are you needing out?'

DS Fairfax immediately stood up. 'I'll take him, sir.'

'I thought you were terrified of dogs,' Dr Rufus remarked.

'I can't think what gave you that idea. Robbie and I are great pals, aren't we Robbie?'

Steadman slipped off his harness and handed DS Fairfax the leash. Robbie was skittish and, instead of making for the door, he dragged DS Fairfax round the partition to where the man with the piercing eyes had been sitting.

'There is nothing there for you, Robbie,' she said, for Zoltan had cleared up and wiped the table.

Robbie persisted. He knocked over the chair and pushed his nose under the bench seat that ran along the wall.

'What have you got there?' DS Fairfax bent down and peered under the bench. There was a dark shape wedged up against the wall. She pulled Robbie back, his paws skating over the polished wood. Will Lofthouse and Alan Munro joined her.

'What is it, Fiona?'

'Robbie has found something under the seat, I think.'

'I'm the smallest, I'll have a look,' said Will Lofthouse. He took out a pocket torch and lay on the floor.

'You're not going to believe this!' he exclaimed.

Dr Rufus and Kim Ho leapt out of their seats to join them.

Steadman sat perfectly motionless and silent. There was not a trace of emotion on his face. Sam Griffiths gently touched his arm.

'This must be very trying for you, John. I think I would get very angry if I were in your shoes. How do you cope?'

Steadman raised an eyebrow.

'I play a little game with myself.'

'Oh really?'

'Yes, I bet who will be the first to come and tell me what is happening and then I try to guess what they have found.'

'So who is your money on?'

'Frank will come and tell me. He is my oldest friend and, despite his apparent insensitive manner, understands me better than the others. What have they found? Logically it is most likely to be a bag of some description. And judging by the hubbub I wonder if it could possibly be...'

'John, you won't believe what was jammed under the bench,' said a very excited Dr Rufus.

'Let me guess, Frank. A small rucksack containing blood-soaked towels.'

CHAPTER TWENTY FIVE

Dr Rufus looked stunned.

'I swear you're psychic. Don't tell me how you worked it out, I couldn't cope with you looking smug. Kim Ho is bagging them up. She's got some of her paraphernalia in the car and she'll dust for fingerprints. I suspect Zoltan has probably done a thorough job and wiped everything clean.'

'And he's already washed the man's glass,' added Munro who had joined them.

'I don't suppose Zoltan recognised the man?' Steadman asked.

'Never seen him before,' replied Munro.

'Does he have CCTV?'

'Only in the car park. However, our chum was wearing a baseball cap, so no useful pictures. He was carrying the wee rucksack when he came in and left without it. Do you reckon it was our killer?' If it was, he's taking an awful chance.'

Sam Griffiths looked at the three men in turn. 'He wants to be caught,' she said.

'Caught?' queried Munro.

'It's not as unusual as people believe. I wonder if he's annoyed with Nesbitt's insistence that Harry and Maurice Eeles are the guilty party.'

'Do you think that makes him more or less likely to strike again?' asked Steadman.

'I think it is very likely he will try again, and I wouldn't be surprised if he doesn't make a show of it,' Sam replied.

Dr Rufus and DS Munro swore softly under their breaths.

'How do you think we ought to handle all of this, sir?' asked Munro.

'With honesty, Alan. I would suggest you lead on the investigation. Tell Nesbitt the truth, that I invited you all out for a drink. We don't have to mention our conversation.'

'If the man is our killer, how do we account for him knowing we would all be here?' Dr Rufus asked.

'I've been wondering that myself. He could have followed one of our cars, I suppose. Unless...'

'Unless what, sir?'

'There was a supposed drunk sobering up in the waiting room of the Eyesore when I was there this afternoon. He recognised me and probably overheard my conversation with Grimble. I am fairly certain he was still there when I left.'

Steadman omitted to mention that he had been followed home. He felt foolish, particularly as Munro had offered him a lift.

'I'll check with Grimble,' Munro suggested.

Steadman sagged in his chair. It had been a long day. 'Did Fiona get a good look at the man's reflection, I wonder?'

'I'm here, sir. I've just brought Robbie back in. No, I'm afraid I didn't. The mirror is old and has writing on it. All I could see were his piercing blue eyes staring at us.'

The darts players had arrived. Steadman could hear the rhythmic thwunk, thwunk, thwunk of the darts, the clink of glasses and the laughter. Would they be so jolly if they knew that only minutes before a serial killer had been sitting not yards from them having a quiet pint? One of them might even be drinking out of the same beer glass.

'I'm tired,' he said. 'Would one of you take me over to the bar so I can settle up?'

They drove home in sombre silence. Munro was concentrating hard on driving, for as soon as they had driven out of Upper Bridgetown the fog had descended. At last Munro said, 'When Grimble finds out that Robbie discovered the bag, he'll buy him a bone as big as a tree trunk.'

'You're very quiet, John' Sam Griffiths observed.

'Sorry. I was just thinking, and I don't know why, but I wish Rosie Jennings had been there tonight.'

★ ★ ★

Steadman slept fitfully. His sleep was disturbed by nightmarish images of piercing blue eyes staring at him in a mirror. Every time he tried to get a better look, whoever it was would pull a hat down over his face or else raise a newspaper. Yet as soon as he looked away he knew those eyes would be staring malevolently at him again.

Steadman woke to his doorbell sounding TW in Morse code. He pressed the button on his watch. Tim was early; never a good sign.

'Are you all right, lad?' Steadman asked in a fatherly tone. He really was growing quite fond of Tim.

'Suppose so. Mum is still mad at me for breaking my phone and now she's none too happy about me taking so much money from you.'

'I'll give her a call if you like.'

'That would be great. She's out all day so it will have to be this evening.'

'When will you get another phone?'

'Tomorrow night, I hope. Come on, Robbie. Let's go for a walk.'

Steadman had washed and dressed by the time Tim and the dog returned.

'Are you still going to be late tonight, Tim?' Steadman asked.

'Dunno for certain. If I'm not here at the usual time, you'll know that one of the other teachers will have taken us to the exhibition.'

'Hopefully, Alan Munro will be here.'

'Great.'

'I thought that would cheer you up.'

★ ★ ★

Steadman called down for a coffee. He was aware of the delicious aroma long before Marco reached his door. He sipped it eagerly and smiled for the first time that day.

'While you are here, Marco, would you help me find a phone number?'

'Sure. Who do you want to call?'

'The main office of the *Helmsmouth Echo and Evening News*.'

Marco called the number and handed the phone to Steadman. Rather than listen in, he busied himself taking Steadman's cup and saucer through to the kitchen. He could not help overhearing the end of the conversation: 'Excellent... I look forward to meeting her at eleven thirty.'

'Have you got a date?' Marco asked with a twinkle in his eye.

'In a manner of speaking, yes. Except that the lady in question must be in her mid-seventies.'

Marco waited for more details. As none were forthcoming he took the cup and saucer and made for the door.

'Good luck, anyway,' he said over his shoulder as he left.

Steadman's phone rang. It was Mr Barnes. 'Your timing is impeccable,' said Steadman. 'I need to go into town and, if it is convenient, go to the Marks and Spencer's on Victoria Street.'

The journey on the bus was not a great success.

Steadman found it very hard to gauge where the platform was and caught his toe in the gap. He struggled to find the right change and when the bus moved off with a jerk, he lost his balance. If Mr Barnes had not been with him he would have fallen into the lap of one of the other passengers. A lady offered him her seat. He had no idea whether it was on his right or left. He was hoping Mr Barnes would come to his assistance, but he remained silent.

'Thank you. Which side of the aisle is it on?' Steadman eventually asked.

Even Robbie did not appear to be enjoying the experience. Whoever was sitting beside Steadman asked where he was planning to get off.

He panicked. 'I had a colleague with me. I don't know where he's gone. I was going to get off at Marks and Spencer's.'

'That's the next stop.'

Mr Barnes was not being unkind. He was sitting only a couple of rows behind Steadman and was ready to intervene.

'It was quite deliberate,' he explained. 'I won't always be with you. You should have told the driver and he would have given you a shout at the right stop.'

Of course, thought Steadman, how simple.

'It is not likely you'll be doing this journey on your own, but you never know. What do you want from Marks?'

Steadman had given this some thought. The lady he was seeing had a sweet tooth. He had considered chocolates, but Dr Rufus's description of the post-mortem had put him off the idea. There was only one thing for it, he decided – macaroons.

The store was busy and Steadman was bumped and jostled. The noise was almost unbearable. Despite this he could hear derogatory comments about the dog, especially when they entered the food hall. For two pins, Steadman would have left and taken a taxi home. Then a shop assistant came to his rescue and without making a fuss, helped Steadman with his purchase.

At last they were back on the street.

'How was it?' Mr Barnes asked.

It was difficult for Steadman to find the right words. 'Unnerving,' he said at last, although he would have like to have added 'terrifying' and 'humiliating'.

'Next time will be much easier,' Mr Barnes reassured him. 'What do you want to do now?'

'I have an appointment in the offices of the *Helmsmouth Echo and Evening News*, which I believe are directly opposite. If you could guide me there I will make my own way home, though not by bus.'

* * *

The newspapers were no longer printed in the centre of town. The presses had been moved to a large industrial unit close to the railway station. However, the building still smelled strongly of printer's ink, oil and cheap paper.

The girl on reception recognised him. 'I'll give Miss

Bartholomew a call, Inspector Steadman. She is expecting you.'

Miss Irene Bartholomew was the newspaper's archivist and had been doing the job since leaving school almost sixty years ago. Her memory was legendary, so much so that in latter years she had been nicknamed 'the human computer'. Steadman remembered her as a small lady with short grey hair and large round glasses who was always serious and always seemed to be in a hurry.

'Here she comes now,' said the receptionist.

Steadman listened. There was something wrong. The approaching footsteps were out of time: one footfall was slower than the other. She stopped in front of Steadman.

'It is good to see you again,' she said.

The voice was unmistakably hers, but it was slightly slurred and the hand that shook Steadman's was quite weak.

'Are you well, Miss Bartholomew?' Steadman asked.

She could tell from the concerned look on his face that this was more than a mere pleasantry.

'I wondered if you would notice,' she replied. 'I had a small stroke three months ago. I'm afraid the human computer is not as reliable as it once was, particularly for anything recent. Hopefully, I can still help you. Let's go and have a cup of tea. Will I take your arm?'

'If you lead, Robbie will follow you.'

They reached her inner sanctuary and she helped Steadman into a seat. There were flowers in the room. Possibly freesias, Steadman thought.

'I've brought you some macaroons,' he said, handing her the bag.

'My favourites – how kind!'

She placed a mug in Steadman's hand. He nibbled on a macaroon. It was sickly sweet. Miss Bartholomew ate three in quick succession.

'Sugar for the brain,' she said. 'Now, how can I help you?'

'Did you know Crenshaw Tipley?'

'Of course – a strange, arrogant man who was not nearly as clever as he thought he was. He often made blatant factual errors and he hated being corrected. He made a lot of enemies and, much as I deplore violence, his murder did not surprise me.'

'We believe whoever killed him borrowed a book from his library giving a false name and address. The name is bothering me. I think I have heard it before, or something very similar. The writing was not easy to decipher. Does Gordon Greig mean anything to you?'

'The only Gordon Greig I knew was at school with me,' she replied without hesitation. 'A very good footballer who died tragically in a skiing accident. I doubt if that's who you mean. What was the book he borrowed?'

'A book on stage design.'

'In that case, I wonder if the alias was Gordon Craig. More correctly it should have been Edward Gordon Craig, although he seldom used the Edward. He was a famous British actor, director and theatre designer. I think he died in the sixties. You see what I mean about Tipley being an impostor. If he really knew his stuff he should have spotted the deception.'

'Crenshaw Tipley wrote a book himself, Miss Bartholomew. Did you ever get round to reading it?'

'I read it six months ago, before I had my stroke.'

'Was it any good?'

'I hate to admit it, but it was well written and displayed remarkable insight into a field I would not have thought Tipley was acquainted with.'

'It wasn't about political intrigue and espionage, by any chance?'

Miss Bartholomew glanced at Steadman's face, which remained as inscrutable as ever.

'It was. I am right, am I not? He was an impostor.'

'Possibly,' Steadman replied vaguely. 'Did you know his book won a competition?'

'To be pedantic, Inspector Steadman, the book did not win, although that was what Tipley would have liked you to believe. No, it was awarded second prize. I knew months before it was announced. Tipley told anyone who would listen. Would you like more tea?'

Steadman waved away the tea. 'We have a similar conundrum with Velda Meemes' murder. Someone, possibly the killer, reserved a small statue of the Buddha under the assumed name of Reg Butler.'

Miss Bartholomew clapped her hands together.

'Now that one is easy. If your wife had still been with us, I'm sure she could have told you. He was an English sculptor who rose to fame in the fifties. Some of his work is on display in the Tate.'

Steadman nodded. He knew he had heard the name before. Now it was all coming back to him. Holly had been very enthusiastic about art and had dragged her husband round what seemed to him like every gallery in London. He must have come across Reg Butler on his travels.

He frowned. Was it just coincidence that the two aliases were a sculptor and someone whose life was the stage? Miss Bartholomew noted his troubled expression.

'What's puzzling you, Inspector Steadman?' she asked.

'Coincidences – that's all. I never like coincidences.'

'I'm afraid I have thought of another one,' said Miss Bartholomew. 'Velda Meemes also won a second prize – in the *Helmsmouth Echo* annual watercolour competition. I thought her work was a bit garish, but the judges appeared to like it.'

Could this be relevant? Steadman's brow furrowed. Would someone really get murderously jealous of anyone coming second? He would have to ask Sam Griffiths. Something else was troubling him, something about second place...

'Of course, the prize was not to be sniffed at,' continued Miss Bartholomew, interrupting his thoughts. 'I believe the runner-up pocketed a cheque for nine hundred pounds.'

'I'm surprised the *Echo* can afford that sort of money,' Steadman commented.

'Oh, the paper doesn't pay. The competition is always sponsored. This year it was that snooty mineral water company. They make Helmsmouth Upper Reaches – have you heard of it?'

Steadman was stunned.

'Is something the matter? You have gone very pale.'

'No, it's just...' He paused and screwed up his eyes behind his dark glasses. 'You wouldn't happen to know who sponsored Tipley's book prize?'

'Not off hand, but I can find out.'

Miss Bartholomew switched on a computer in the corner of her office.

'Password? Password? I have to change it every month. It was never a problem before I had this blasted stroke. Where's my diary? I have to write so many things down now. Here it is.'

Steadman was lost in thought. He started tapping his fingers on the table. A tune began to play in his head – a Bach fugue. Cadence and rhythm weaved in and out. Loose ends were beginning to tie up. The music stopped. He desperately needed to speak with Alan Munro and Fiona Fairfax.

'Got it!' Miss Bartholomew exclaimed. 'A posh whisky label.'

'Debantry's Deluxe Blend, by any chance?' Steadman enquired.

'I thought you didn't know.' Miss Bartholomew sounded disappointed.

'I didn't until just now,' Steadman conceded.

There was a sudden noise in the adjoining room. Both Steadman and Robbie stood up.

'It will only be some schoolchildren wanting information for their projects. I was half-expecting them.' She limped through to the next room. Steadman could only make out part of the conversations.

'First man on the moon? July twenty-first 1969 – top shelf on the left... no, your left!'

Another whispered request.

'Well, the Berlin Wall... Now, do you mean when people were allowed to cross or when they started pulling it down? You're not sure. Start with November the ninth 1989... the shelf below your colleague.'

More whispering.

'What odd things you children study at school! Ruth Ellis was hanged on the thirteenth of July 1955, which was a Wednesday... There is an excellent editorial in the Saturday edition... you'll find those in the third room on your right.'

She really is a human computer, thought Steadman. How sad she should have suffered a stroke.

She bustled back into her little office. 'Sorry about that. However, I'm glad the schools still encourage the little dears to do some original research.'

A thought struck Steadman. It was a long shot.

'Do you get members of the public asking to look up articles in the archives?'

'Frequently. Never a week goes by without five or six people coming in. Why do you ask?'

'Helmsmouth once boasted a notorious serial killer.'

'I know,' Miss Bartholomew replied. 'He was even before my time. Mr Alfred Sheridan bumped off three of his domestic staff in 1923. When I first started here, it was one of the most popular articles people wanted to read. Now you come to mention it, someone did come in the other day and asked about it. It was fairly recently. Everything is a bit hazy…'

Steadman held his breath.

'It was a man… yes, definitely a man. Now, what was his name? You see, that's the effect of the stroke. If he had come in six months ago or even six years ago, I would have remembered. It may come back to me.'

'If it does, will you let me know straight away.' Steadman fumbled in his pocket and produced his card. 'Can you remember anything about him – anything at all?'

MIs Bartholomew took off her glasses and closed her eyes.

'There was something unusual about his appearance. Sticking out ears? No. it wasn't that. A big nose? No, not that either. Did he have a beard? Well, they all have scruffy beards these days, don't they? An earring? Possibly, I'm not sure. Something about his eyes? Yes! That's it – he had the most unsettling piercing blue eyes.'

CHAPTER TWENTY SIX

Sergeant Grimble was shuffling round the papers on his desk. It was his time for tidying up, although to the untrained eye, and in this case everyone else's except Sergeant Grimble's, he appeared only to be adding to the confusion. He looked at the clock; it was nine twenty. Usually he liked this hour of the morning. The waiting room had been cleared, and all the officers were either busy with their own paperwork, attending meetings or doing one of the countless myriad of tasks required to keep a semblance of law and order in Helmsmouth and its surrounds. There was no excuse for anyone to be loitering by his desk. Even the criminals were quiet.

Today, however, had not started well. DS Fairfax had tackled him early; so early that he had not had time to finish his first coffee of the day. He clearly remembered the drunk entering the Eyesore, then edging along the wall as he had made for the toilets. Grimble pulled a face as he recalled the noise of someone retching, then being violently and copiously sick. The drunk had not reported to the desk. Grimble knew he should have challenged him, but police stations were full of anonymous drunks, weren't they? He had planned to give him an hour, then a strong coffee and a friendly chat before showing him the door. From experience he knew this was the best way of dealing with the situation. A drunk in a police station was far safer than one out in the streets.

Grimble was naturally a good observer. He could have told DS Fairfax the colour of his trousers, the cut of his anorak and even the logo on his baseball cap. What he could not give was any indication of what his face looked like. Sergeant Grimble was stung. It took a lot to make an officer of his standing feel foolish, but foolish was exactly how he felt now.

They had gone over the CCTV footage frame by frame. How clever to have stumbled round the edge of the waiting room looking for the toilets. How clever to have slumped in a chair in the farthermost corner. How damnably clever not to go up to the desk. Whoever he was had played a masterful hand. With his head down, all the camera had picked up was the baseball cap. Only one frame on his exit showed part of his face. Even then it was indistinct. All that could be said was that he did not have a beard.

He had definitely left after John Steadman, that much was clear. Had he heard Steadman's plans? Impossible to say. If it was any consolation, Munro's memories were even more vague.

Sergeant Grimble had no doubt Beaky Nesbitt would

milk the situation for all it was worth. Damn it, he thought, Nesbitt may even succeed in getting rid of me as well as Inspector Steadman.

The door of the Eyesore banged open. 'Speak of the devil,' Grimble muttered.

In came a very angry Acting DCI Nesbitt. His whole body exuded outrage. His top lip was twitching uncontrollably.

'Tell me, Grimble, what filthy, unspeakable low-life does Helmsmouth Police Force allow to prowl these wretched, miserable streets at night? Not just any streets, but those less than half a mile from what you lot pretend to be a police headquarters. Come on, answer me. Speak up Grimble, I can't hear you!'

'I would imagine, sir, it is pretty much the same filthy, unspeakable low-life that prowls the streets of any British city, including your own.'

'That's where you're wrong, Grimble. Someone in this fog-infested dump chucked this through my windscreen last night.' Nesbitt dropped an exhibits bag on to Grimble's desk. It contained what looked like a large round stone.

'I would imagine something like that could do a lot of damage to an old car like yours, sir.'

'Old car? Old car?' Nesbitt spluttered. 'I'll have you know, Grimble, it is not any old car but a 1974 two-litre Ford Capri Ghia finished in flame orange with a black vinyl roof. It is a classic. I love that car, Grimble, it is like family to me.'

Well, it certainly shares the family characteristic of a long ugly nose, thought Grimble.

'Was there much damage done, sir?'

'A broken windscreen's enough, isn't it? I've spent nearly two hours cleaning out my car. I'm still not sure I've got all the glass from under the front seat.'

Grimble glanced at the clock again. 'I was wondering what had kept you this morning. There's been a development. DS Munro has put a report on your desk. In fact, I think I can hear him coming...'

It was difficult to mistake the crashing footsteps of DS Munro racing down the stairs.

'Morning, sir. Everything OK? Good grief, Grimble, what have you got there?'

Munro grasped the round stone in the exhibits bag in one enormous hand and lifted it up for closer inspection.

'I'll be damned – it's a stonemason's maul. Look, there's a short wooden handle at the flat end.'

Nesbitt glared suspiciously at Munro. 'Well, well, fancy you knowing what that is, Munro,' he said with a sneer. 'That thing, whatever you called it, was thrown through the windscreen of my beloved Ford Capri last night. Where were you last night, sergeant?'

Munro's face turned scarlet. 'I was just about to explain...'

'I see, laddie, like that is it?' Nesbitt puffed out his chest and stuck his chin in the air. 'Got a grudge because your blind hero is off the case, have you? I think you need to come to my office for a little chat.'

'It is not what you think, sir. The only reason I know what a stonemason's maul looks like is because it is highly likely to have been the weapon used to kill Dennis Knotting. In all probability it was Knotting's own maul.' Munro lifted the bag again. 'Look there, sir, that dark smudge could be blood.'

Nesbitt was still not convinced. 'You still haven't told me where you were last night, Munro.'

'Easily explained,' replied a soft Welsh voice. Grimble winked at Dr Sam Griffiths, who had quietly slipped into the Eyesore.

'I wasn't speaking to you, Griffiths,' Nesbitt snapped.

'Nothing new there, then' she replied, quite unabashed. 'Alan Munro was with me yesterday evening along with Inspector Steadman, DS Fairfax, Kim Ho, DC Lofthouse and, of course, Dr Rufus. We were having a little gathering at The Three Grasshoppers to mark John Steadman's departure. Not so much a celebration as a wake.' She paused as she caught sight of the stonemason's maul. '*Bobl bach!*' she exclaimed in Welsh. 'Who found the murder weapon?'

Nesbitt's eyes narrowed as his gaze flitted between Sam Griffiths and Alan Munro.

'There's no proof it's the murder weapon,' he declared. 'Some piece of excrement tossed it through the windscreen of my car last night.'

'Call Autoglass,' Griffiths suggested in an offhand manner as she inspected the maul.

'They won't stock a replacement. Mine is a classic car.'

'Oh? What have you got? A Ferrari? A Porsche?' Sam Griffiths knew perfectly well that it was neither.

'No dearie, it is a two-litre 1974 Ford Capri Ghia. Not that you would know what that was.'

'On the contrary, my uncle had the John Player Special Mark II 3000 GT. The Midnight Special, I believe it was called, finished in black and gold.'

Nesbitt's stared wide in disbelief.

'A JPS Capri – 3000 GT. It's what every Capri owner dreams of.'

'I wouldn't know about that. From a psychologist's point of view, I have always worried what sort of male inadequacy is being compensated for by a car with such a long bonnet.'

Grimble snorted, stifling a laugh.

'Something to say, sergeant?' thundered Nesbitt.

'Me? No, nothing – coffee went down the wrong way that's all.'

'Of course,' continued Sam Griffiths, 'it would tie in with the man in The Three Grasshoppers and the blood-soaked towels.'

'What blood-soaked towels? What are you on about?' Nesbitt asked. For once he looked worried.

'I've been trying to tell you, sir,' said Munro. 'The report is on your desk.'

Just then an elderly couple came into the waiting room. They looked cold and damp. The old man's spectacles had misted over. He took out a handkerchief and, blinking in the unaccustomed brightness, proceeded to wipe them clean. The lady went over to Grimble's desk and stole a nervous glance at Nesbitt, Munro and Griffiths. Sergeant Grimble was at least wearing a uniform shirt and tie. His hat was on a hook behind him.

'Is this the police station?' she asked.

'Indeed it is, madam. And I am a genuine police sergeant. Now, how may I help you?'

Nesbitt beckoned to Griffiths and Munro. 'My office,' he said nodding in the direction of the stairs. 'Grimble, get that thing over to forensics.'

* * *

Slowly and deliberately Nesbitt read Munro's report. He took out a red pen and underlined a word here and there. At last he looked up.

'Kim Ho has confirmed, sir, the blood on the towels is definitely from Dennis Knotting,' said Munro.

Nesbitt shook his head in mock disbelief.

'And if it hadn't been for Steadman's dog, none of you lot would have noticed the bag.'

'I'm sure Zoltan, the owner, would have found it and…'

Nesbitt held up a silencing hand to Munro.

'I don't believe what I've just read. Three fully operational police officers – two detective sergeants and a detective constable – have our murderer in their grasp and they fail to arrest him.'

Munro turned red again and looked at his feet. Sam Griffiths was having none of it.

'Tell me, Acting Detective Chief Inspector, exactly what the charge would have been? I don't believe staring at a police officer through a tarnished bar room mirror constitutes an offence. Apart from anything else, you have told us in no uncertain terms that Harry and Maurice Eeles are the guilty parties and you have them safely locked up.'

Nesbit slammed his hands on the desk and turned to Munro.

'Hear that? Typical of a woman – always jumping to conclusions.'

'Me? Jump to conclusions? God give me strength! If you hadn't locked up Harry and Maurice Eeles and declared to the world and his wife that you'd caught the killers he would never have turned up at The Three Grasshoppers, nor would he have chucked the murder weapon through your car windscreen – not anyone else's car windscreen, *your* car windscreen, Nesbitt. Don't you see what it's all about?' Her face had gone deathly pale.

Nesbitt lay back in his chair, staring first at the ceiling then at his fingernails.

'OK, Sigmund Freud, the floor is yours – explain.'

'Freud was a psychoanalyst, I'm a forensic psychologist – I won't waste my breath explaining the difference. Our killer is a highly intelligent and devious sociopath with very little regard for anybody's feelings other than his own. The fact that you stopped looking for him has really offended him. He needs the attention. He has to feel important.'

Nesbitt tried to give Munro a conspiratorial glance and half-opened his mouth to say something.

'The floor's mine, Nesbitt. I'll tell you when I'm finished,' said Sam.

Munro could not take his eyes off the psychologist. He had never seen anyone hold their ground so forcefully, especially when up against someone like Beaky Nesbitt. He was in awe.

'All the way along we have been left little clues. Why? Because he relishes the chase. He wants, or at least wanted, to outsmart us. His masterstroke was planting the bike in the Eeles' garage. Maybe it was a step too far, because after that you stopped pursuing him. Don't look so shocked. The man who attacked Robbie, trashed Steadman's flat and killed three people are one and the same person.'

'You have no evidence,' Nesbitt interjected.

'True, I haven't – not anything that would stand up in court. And I can't tell you why he has picked on John Steadman and not Alan Munro or Fiona Fairfax, although Steadman did suggest our killer is a coward. Beyond any shadow of a doubt Steadman is the most vulnerable unless, somehow, he is closer to the killer than we have realised.

'Let's get back to last night. I agree with you for once, we missed the opportunity to make an arrest. How did he know we were there? Again speculation, but it would not be hard to follow a blind man. Why did he bring the blood-soaked towels, evidence that would incriminate him, and leave them for us to find? He probably even anticipated that Robbie would sniff them out. There are only two possible conclusions. Firstly, he wants us to realise we have got the wrong men and secondly, he wants to be caught.'

'Caught? That's madness!' exclaimed Nesbitt.

'After a fashion, I suppose. That's why a forensic psychologist was brought in. I can see you don't believe me. Listen, it gets better. After he leaves us our bloody package, he goes on to deliver the murder weapon. He knows it's your car, everybody does, it's bright enough. I'll bet he also knows how much you cherish it. You have royally upset him by calling off the search so, by God, is he going to upset you in return. Smash! The stonemason's maul used to kill Dennis Knotting right through your windscreen.'

Nesbitt winced. 'Supposing you're right, and I'm not saying for a moment you are, you reckon he wants to be caught. Why doesn't he just pitch up and hand himself in?'

Sam Griffiths breathed a sigh of relief. At last Nesbitt was thinking.

'That, DCI Nesbitt, is what I fear the most. I think he is going to go out with a bang – the ultimate ego-trip, and I think it will be soon.' Sam Griffiths looked at her watch. 'I have to go. Don't say you haven't been warned.'

She left the door open and both men watched as her figure retreated down the corridor.

'Does she annoy you, Munro? She gets right under my skin.'

Munro did not respond.

'Do you think her uncle has still got the JPS Capri? You wouldn't ask her for me?' Munro stared at Beaky Nesbitt in disbelief. 'No, perhaps you're right – maybe later.'

Nesbitt turned back to the report and tapped it with his pen.

'I'm still not happy, Munro. A clandestine meeting, eh? I wonder what else you were scheming. Doubtless I was the main topic of conversation.'

Munro suddenly remembered about the photo in the morning paper. Fortunately, Nesbitt would have been too busy cleaning out his car to have seen a copy yet. Munro thought fast. He turned to Nesbitt, wearing his most innocent expression.

'Not exactly, sir, but I did think of you and decided to take a leaf out of your book. Follow your lead, as it were.'

Nesbitt remained doubtful. 'I'm not sure I'm going to like this, Munro.'

'Oh, I'm sure you will.' A boy scout having done his good deed for the day could not have looked more angelic. 'In fact, sir, I'm certain you would have thought of it much sooner than I did.'

Munro could not believe he was spouting all this nonsense. Nesbitt, on the other hand, was beginning to lap it up.

'You recall the photo we found in Dennis Knotting's wallet – the one taken seventeen years ago, when he was at Art College? We're certain Dennis knew his killer and let him in. He has no family. This was the only photo in his flat. Now, the two men in the picture may have nothing to do with his murder. However, we need to eliminate them from our enquiries. I spent a wasted morning at the college trying to identify them. The college is not very strong on formality and record-keeping.'

'Bunch of hippie anarchists, more than likely,' suggested Nesbitt.

'A wee bit alternative, yes,' Munro hastily agreed. 'Well sir, remembering how keen you are to foster relationships with the press, I decided to follow your example and see if I could get the photo published in the morning paper appealing for anyone to come forward and identify Knotting's two friends. It was a near thing and I only just made the print run. I didn't have time to contact you. Of course, I guess you would have thought of doing it straight away and made yesterday evening's paper.' He didn't dare mention that the whole thing had been Steadman's idea.

Nesbitt puffed himself up like a turkey cock. A triumphant smile spread over his face. Munro worried for a moment he had overplayed his hand.

'Well done, laddie, that is exactly what I would have done except, as you say, a bit earlier in the day.' He gave Munro a patronising nod.

If he comes over and claps me on the shoulder, so help me I'll clock him one, thought Munro.

'Thank you, sir, I'm glad you approve. I haven't heard anything yet. I guess most people around that age will be working. Hopefully someone will come forward during their coffee break or over lunchtime. We'll see.'

Nesbitt beamed. 'You're the only one round here with any sense, Munro. Watch my methods and learn!'

Munro was struggling to keep up the pretence.

'The Eeles, sir – shall I arrange with the custody sergeant for their release?'

A hint of doubt flickered over Nesbitt's face and his lip twitched again. He looked down at his desk and the three Post-it notes requesting him to phone Sven Jensen urgently.

'Get rid of them, Munro. And while you are at it,' he said, thrusting the notes into Munro's huge hands, 'let Noggin-the-Nog know.'

Munro was grateful for an excuse to leave. He spoke with the custody sergeant and left a message with Sven Jensen's secretary. Before returning to his office he looked in on Sergeant Grimble.

'Patience, young Alan. I'll make sure you know as soon as I hear anything,' Grimble said without looking up from his desk which seemed in even more disarray.

The heating in the office had been turned up and the room was stifling. Munro took off his jacket and left the door open. It was time to chase Dennis Knotting's cheque.

* * *

The phone was eventually answered. Munro explained the nature of his call without giving away too many details.

'I'll put you through to accounts. They may be able to help you.'

Another interminable wait.

'May I take your account number?'

Again Munro went through his prepared speech.

'But have you an account number? I'm sorry, we only deal with account holders. How much was the cheque for?'

'Five hundred pounds.'

'Sounds like returned goods. I'll transfer your call.'

'Wait...' Munro protested. It was too late.

'Very unlikely to be from us,' explained the lady in the returns section. 'Our cheques are never for nice round numbers. A figure like that is more likely to come from the claims department. If you hold, I'll transfer your call.'

'I don't believe this,' Munro muttered.

'Not us, I'm afraid,' said the cheery voice from claims. 'Have you got the cheque number?'

Munro assured him he had.

'Oh, in that case it should be easy enough to trace. I'll transfer you to accounts.'

Munro banged his head on the table.

'You again? I'm not sure I can give out that information without speaking to my manager.'

'Well go and speak to him!' Munro barked down the phone.

'He's in a meeting.'

'And I'm investigating a serious crime.'

There was a pause of several minutes.

'Mr Rupert, my manager, says to phone back in two hours.'

'Go and tell Mr Rupert that if he doesn't come to the phone now, he may be charged with obstruction, and if you don't tell him I'll charge you as well.'

Mr Rupert proved to be as pompous as Munro imagined he would be.

'I don't like your attitude, sergeant, not at all. I'm a very busy man.'

'I'm not paid to be liked, sir. Here is the cheque number. It was made payable to, and cashed by, Dennis Knotting shortly before he was murdered. I'm sure you have read about it in the papers.'

'Murdered? I see...' There was a furious rustling of paper. Munro swore he could hear sweat dripping onto Mr Rupert's precious ledgers.

'Here it is. It was issued on behalf of Saturnalia Chocolates. We handle all their finances.'

Munro could barely keep the excitement out of his voice.

'And their phone number is?'

Mr Rupert gladly gave out the number and Munro thanked him for his cooperation with just a hint of sarcasm.

Saturnalia Chocolates could not have been more helpful.

'Dennis Knotting? The sculptor? Sure – he came second in this year's arts competition. His carving is gorgeous. I would love to buy it, but I'm not paid enough! There's a picture of him and his work on our website.'

'You have a website?'

'Of course.'

Damn and blast it, thought Munro.

'Is there a problem?'

'Yes. Dennis Knotting has been murdered.'

'Good heavens! Do you think it has anything to do with Saturnalia Chocolates?'

Munro remembered Dr Rufus fishing the chocolates out of Knotting's mouth and his delight at finding more in the toilet pan.

'I'm afraid it might have,' he replied.

DS Fairfax was standing at the open door trying to get his attention. Munro added a few placatory remarks, promised to keep them informed and put the phone down.

'We've got positive identification of the two men from three different callers,' she said. 'The one on the right is called Jeff Skinner and the one on the left is Edwin Haribin.'

Skinner and Haribin? Munro's brow furrowed. Weren't they the names of two of Tim Warrender's teachers? He needed to speak with John Steadman.

CHAPTER TWENTY SEVEN

Steadman walked back down the corridor with Miss Bartholomew limping beside him.

'How are you going to get home?' she asked.

Steadman had already taken his mobile phone out of his pocket. 'I was about to call HQ – trade some information for a lift,' he said with a smile.

'The mobile signal is not very good in the building. If you give me the number our receptionist will call for you.'

He rattled off the number. 'It was good to meet with you again, Miss Bartholomew. As always, you are a fount of knowledge. Or should that be font? I never can remember'

'You can use either, I believe. You always knew how to flatter, Inspector Steadman. When that man's name comes back to me, I'll let you know. Here's your call.'

She placed the receiver in Steadman's hand and limped back to her office.

Sergeant Grimble's familiar voice answered.

'Is it convenient to speak with Alan Munro?' Steadman asked.

'Should be,' Grimble replied. 'Nesbitt's gone to grab himself a coffee. Lots of developments – I won't spoil young Munro's fun.'

DS Munro was indeed very excited.

'Before you say a thing, sir, can I just check something with you? Skinner and Haribin – aren't they two of Tim Warrender's teachers?'

'Yes – why?'

'Well, sir, they are the two gentlemen in Dennis Knotting's photo. Hang on a second.' He placed his hand over the mouthpiece and relayed the information to DS Fairfax. 'And there's more, sir.'

'Can it wait, Alan? I also have some information. I'm stuck in town at the old offices of the *Echo and Evening News*. What are the chances of you giving me a lift? We could chat in the car on the way home.'

'I'll check with DS Fairfax.' He put his hand over the receiver again. 'Fiona, is it OK if I pick up the boss from town? I'll only be thirty minutes max.'

'Sure, as long as you let Nesbitt know we have a positive ID on the two men before you go. He won't believe me,' replied DS Fairfax.

Munro took his hand off the receiver.

'Be with you in ten minutes, sir.'

He scribbled a hasty note – "Two men identified – Jeff Skinner and Edwin Haribin. Being tracked down and will be brought in for immediate questioning."

Fairfax took the note, read it, and handed it to Will Lofthouse. 'Run along to our acting DCI, would you Will?'

Lofthouse took the folded paper and returned a few minutes later with a dreamy look in his eyes.

'I don't think Inspector Nesbitt knows what to make of me,' he said.

'No one does, Will,' Fairfax replied.

'Does that mean we can go out on a date?'

'Not a chance. If you want to do something useful, get some background on Haribin and Skinner while I phone the school.'

* * *

Miss Smythe was none too pleased to get the call. 'Who did you say you were? The police? Again? If it's about Mr Skinner and Mr Haribin, neither of them are here. They have both been suspended.'

'I'm sorry, I'm a bit confused. What do you say again? And why have they been suspended?'

'Well, you should know! One of your WPCs has already been here, stirring up trouble. Jennings, I think she called herself. She interviewed both of them after that silly boy Bremner jumped in front of the train.'

DS Fairfax did not stay long on the phone. She got their home addresses and hung up.

* * *

Munro sped through the town despite the fog. What was the point in having a fast car with blue flashing lights if you couldn't use them sometimes?

Steadman and Robbie were sitting in the foyer keeping out of the cold. As the Audi pulled in at the kerb, Robbie stood up and nudged Steadman's knee with his muzzle.

'You reckon that's our lift, Robbie?' Steadman said as he too got to his feet.

A sharp, wet blast rushed in as Munro opened the door. Steadman gasped and immediately clutched his chest.

'Ribs still hurting, sir? The car's nice and warm,' said Munro, steering Steadman gently into the front seat. Robbie had already hopped in and curled up into a ball in the footwell.

'You made good time, Alan,' Steadman observed.

'I think the blue lights may have got turned on accidentally. I've got awfully fat fingers. Never mind about that, I've got loads of news.'

Steadman sensed the barely suppressed excitement in his colleague's voice. His news could wait.

Without apparently pausing for breath, Munro told him about the blood on the towels and the stonemason's maul.

'Nesbitt thought I had chucked it through his windscreen at first. Can you credit the man? Sam Griffiths put him in his place!'

Steadman listened attentively as Munro gave a blow-by-blow account of their exchanges.

'How did you explain getting the photo in the paper?' Steadman asked.

'Oh, you know – a lot of flannel and soft soap,' Munro replied with a blush. 'I think he fell for it.'

Steadman had a clear image of Munro looking saintly.

'That's not all, sir. After a bit of probing, I've managed to track down the source of Dennis Knotting's cheque.'

'Let me guess, Alan. I would say he received it from Saturnalia Chocolates as second prize for the sculpture we failed to find in his workshop.'

As soon as Steadman had spoken, he regretted it. Despite his blindness, he could immediately detect Munro's deflation.

'Sorry, Alan. Miss Bartholomew and I have been busy as well. You see, Debantry's Whisky sponsored the literary prize Crenshaw Tipley won and Upper Reaches Sparkling Water, so liberally doused on Velda Meemes, put up the prize money for the newspaper art competition. I say 'won' – in point of fact all three victims actually came second. Doesn't that strike you as odd?'

'Bizarre,' Munro replied.

Steadman had gone silent. Munro noticed his fingers tapping rhythmically on his thighs. He's going to start humming any second, Munro said to himself. He was right.

Something had sparked in Steadman's brain. A reference to being second in a competition. He could not place it. An obsession with being second? It didn't make sense. Maybe Sam Griffiths could enlighten him.

Quite suddenly he became aware of his own silence.

'I've found out some other things, Alan,' he said at last. 'The two aliases – the one used to borrow the book from Tipley was a famous theatre designer, and the other, used to reserve the statue of the Buddha, an eminent British sculptor. And now you have identified the two men in Knotting's photo. Two teachers – an art teacher who does sculpture and a drama teacher who loves stage design. I hate coincidences, Alan.'

The car had pulled up at a set of lights. Munro turned to his former boss.

'Do you think either of them could be our killer?'

'Rosie Jennings has interviewed them both over George Bremner's death. I would like to speak with her,' he replied. Although he knew which one he would put money on.

They stopped outside Steadman's flat.

'I know you're ridiculously busy, Alan, but is there any chance you could call back later in the afternoon? I feel uneasy about Tim walking Robbie alone.'

'I'll be there,' Munro assured him.

'Oh, and there's one last thing. Miss Bartholomew said that last week someone came to the archives looking for information on Helmsmouth's only other serial killer. She can't recall his name. However, she did remember his piercing blue eyes.'

★ ★ ★

Steadman opened the downstairs door and made his way through to the garden at the back of Lloyd's café. He slipped off Robbie's harness and listened as the dog snuffled round the bushes. His watch informed him it was nearly one o'clock. He could still taste the sickly sweet macaroon and could not face any lunch.

It was not until he sat down in his own flat that he realised how tired he had become. He thought about playing the piano, putting on a CD or, at the least, turning on the radio, but with Robbie curled at his feet he lay back, closed his eyes and drifted off to sleep.

'Look at the state of you. Mother will be furious,' said a girl with pigtails and missing front teeth.

Steadman instantly recognised the younger version of his sister. He looked down at his bare knees, which were stained green with grass. His shoes were covered in mud and there was a rip in his shorts.

'It's the last day of term – it's sports day' he replied. 'She'll understand. Anyway, I'll need a new uniform in the autumn because I'm going to grow over the holidays,' he replied manfully.

Linda shook her head and smiled. 'Come on, it's the teachers' race. We don't want to miss that.'

She took hold of her brother's hand and the two of them ran up the hill to where the race was starting. A mist had descended and there was sudden chill in the air.

'On your marks – get set – go!'

Fifteen grown-ups huffed and puffed their way up the slope. As was tradition, the schoolchildren ran behind, shouting encouragement at their favourites or howling in protest at the flagrant cheating of others. The course was steep and the race ended at the top of the hill now shrouded in dense fog. As Linda and her brother neared the finishing tape, it was clear that something was wrong. Two of the teachers were arguing loudly.

'You were first – I saw it clearly.'

'No, you were. I let you pass me.'

'Gentlemen, please! Not in front of the children,' said the familiar voice of Steadman's old headmaster. 'I declare it a tie. You are first equal.'

'Can't we be second equal?' protested one of the men.

Steadman couldn't see who was arguing. A tall, thin red-haired boy was blocking his view.

'It's all your fault, Warrender,' the man continued, turning on the boy.

'Yes, if you had entered the competition, Tim, you could have come second,' the other man retorted.

Steadman was standing on tiptoes. 'Who is arguing? Can you lift me up, Linda?' he pleaded, but the headmaster had started to blow his whistle to mark the end of the day. It was an odd sound: more like a door bell than a whistle…

Steadman woke with a start. Robbie was gently tugging at his cuff. The doorbell rang again. He made his way along the corridor and opened the door a crack.

'It's me, Marco, Inspector Steadman.'

Steadman opened the door.

'I'm sorry to keep you waiting. I must have nodded off in the chair.'

There was a hint of fragrance in the air: floral, expensive and familiar.

'I've brought you a guest,' Marco continued.

'I hope you don't mind, John, but as neither of us are particularly welcome at the Eyesore I thought I would call round and, well... keep you up-to-date and see how you are...' Sam Griffiths' voice faltered.

'You're very welcome. Have you had any lunch?'

She confessed that she hadn't and gratefully accepted the offer of coffee and sandwiches.

'Come through to the lounge and find yourself a seat. There is only one house rule – try not to move the furniture.'

Dr Griffiths had no need to ask why. She noted how bare the flat looked without ornaments or plants, not even a clock, and only marks on the walls where the pictures had been.

'It must be very difficult living on your own,' she observed.

'Oh, it would be impossible without the Lloyds to look after me. They arrange the cleaning and are always willing to provide me with food and drink. My sister looks after my laundry and stocks the fridge and freezer. I'm very fortunate.'

No, you're not, Sam thought. Your wife was murdered and you were blinded in the same attack. She looked at John Steadman and caught a fleeting glimpse of a man far sadder than she had ever noticed before.

'I see you've got a piano. Do you play much?'

'I get lessons. I played a bit when I was younger. It's coming back slowly.'

Marco arrived with a large tray.

'John, tell me what to do or what not to do,' Sam said bluntly. 'I'd rather be told than do the wrong thing.'

Steadman admired her frankness. 'Some sandwiches on a plate would be nice, and if you would put the coffee on the table to my right, I should manage, thank you.'

Robbie stirred and looked hopeful.

'Sorry, dog – none for you. You're worse than Alan Munro when it comes to food,' he said.

'I gather you and Alan met up earlier, so you know about this morning's developments and my run-in with Inspector Nesbitt.'

Steadman nodded.

'Luckily I made my escape before things got really heated. I was only going to collect my shoes from the cobbler's.' She giggled, and Steadman's stomach did a small somersault.

'I called back before I came here,' she continued. 'They haven't managed to track down either Haribin or Skinner, although DC Lofthouse was very quick off the mark. While some of the uniformed officers were knocking on doors he contacted the ferry terminal. Jeff Skinner is already in France as we speak. Of course, our acting DCI has immediately concluded that his departure is as good as a confession.'

Steadman stopped chewing his sandwich and raised an eyebrow.

'No sign of Mr Haribin?' he asked.

'Not even a trace. He's well and truly gone to ground.'

Steadman wondered what sort of car he had, but did not like to interrupt.

'Inspector Nesbitt demanded all efforts be concentrated on finding Skinner. He was determined to contact the French authorities, but he doesn't speak a word of the language himself. Is it true that Fiona Fairfax is the only officer who speaks French?'

'It's true that she's bilingual; her mother is French. Sergeant Grimble is also fairly fluent and Munro speaks passable French. Why do you ask?'

'The lads made out that none of them knew a word of French! Nesbitt couldn't complain as he was similarly ignorant. They told him Fairfax would only do it if requested by a senior officer. I gather it was a sickening spectacle watching Nesbitt trying to be charming. The upshot was the French police would keep an eye out for him, but unless Nesbitt produced the appropriate arrest warrant they would, under no circumstances, detain him. You can imagine, Nesbitt threw all the toys out of the pram.'

'Did Alan Munro tell you about my morning's detective work?'

'He did. I would like to meet Miss Bartholomew – she sounds amazing.'

'She is indeed. In one fell swoop we have sorted out the aliases and the reason for the whisky, sparkling water and chocolates. What strikes me as odd is that none of the three victims were actual winners. They either came second or were runners-up. Does that tell us anything?'

'Alan did mention it. I've been thinking long and hard. It's not something I've come across before. I remember you saying you thought the killer was a coward and maybe it ties in. Someone who is too frightened to lead may well be very happy always to be second. It could also be to do with attention-seeking behaviour – I mean, everybody loves the underdog and people feel a bit sorry for the loser.'

'Yes,' Steadman agreed. 'It has often struck me as odd how frequently people say to anyone who doesn't win "bad luck" – as if to suggest the winner arrived there by chance rather than anything else.'

'I have one other thought,' Sam continued, 'and that is someone who seeks to be the power behind the throne. The one who whispers in the king's ear, the one who holds the power, but without the ultimate responsibility.'

'Somewhat like the deputy head of a large comprehensive school,' Steadman suggested.

Robbie sat up and gave a small bark, rather like an old man clearing his throat before saying something important. Voices could be heard on the stairs. Someone knocked loudly on the door.

'That will be Alan Munro,' said Steadman. 'For reasons best known to himself he never uses the bell.'

'I've brought Rosie Jennings with me, sir,' Munro announced. 'She insisted in coming in her own car – says I drive too fast.'

'I've been in conference with the coroner most of day,' Rosie explained. 'Trying to work out the best way to handle George Bremner's case, bearing in mind the family's distress.'

'Not easy,' Steadman replied with a shake of his head. 'But don't stand there. Come in and meet Dr Sam Griffiths, a forensic psychologist on loan from the Met.'

'You make me sound like a library book,' Sam protested.

Munro's eyes fell on the remains of their lunch. 'Are those sandwiches going spare? It would be a shame to waste them. I'll go and put the kettle on.'

Steadman turned to Rosie. 'Have you spoken with Inspector Nesbitt?' There was a hint of anxiety in his voice. Procedure had to be followed.

'Only briefly, sir. He didn't seem particularly interested. I would have liked to speak with DS Fairfax, but she was busy with the French authorities.'

Munro came in with four mugs of tea.

'On your usual table, sir,' he said putting the mug down with a deliberate clatter next to Steadman's empty coffee cup.

'Rosie, I assume Alan has briefed you. You're the only person who has spoken with both Skinner and Haribin. If I recall, you didn't care for either of them.'

Rosie cradled the mug in her hands.

'No, sir. Skinner was offhand to the point of rudeness. He showed little compassion for the boy's death. I got the impression he was a very angry man. Haribin was no better – cold and unfeeling. I wouldn't like to get on the wrong side of him.'

'Wasn't one of them doing something with wire?'

'Skinner was making stage sets. They were very realistic.'

'Didn't Dr Rufus describe the way Dennis Knotting had been positioned as theatrical?' Munro suggested.

Steadman frowned. He was sure there was something else, something he had forgotten.

'I suppose the million-dollar question is, which one of them has piercing blue eyes?' said Sam.

Before Rosie could answer, Steadman's phone rang. He fished it out of his pocket and, with what seemed like painful slowness to the other three, located the 'accept' button.

'Miss Bartholomew... no, you are not disturbing me.'

'I have remembered the first name of the man who was enquiring about the serial killer. It was Harold.'

'Harold? Are you certain?'

'Probably another alias,' Munro muttered.

'Now you come to mention it, he called himself Harry, not Harold,' Miss Bartholomew corrected herself.

'Harry! You can't recall his surname?' Steadman asked.

'It was something very short, that's all I can remember. Let me think...'

Steadman held his breath. Munro and Rosie Jennings exchanged puzzled frowns. Harry Eeles had dark brown eyes.

'Something like Flynn or Fin, perhaps... I'm sorry, I can't be sure.'

'Could it have been Bin?' Steadman suggested.

'Yes! How did you guess?' Miss Bartholomew exclaimed.

Steadman put the phone back in his pocket.

'And the man with the piercing blues eyes was also Haribin,' Rosie said in a quiet voice.

'No news of his whereabouts, I suppose, Alan?' Steadman asked with a sigh.

'Neither of him nor of his car.'

'Is the car a light-coloured estate?'

Munro slammed the arm of his chair. 'The man who took your photo!' he exclaimed.

'And probably the man who helped me into Dr Rufus's car after clipping me with his wing mirror,' Steadman continued.

'Not to mention attacking Robbie and trashing your flat,' added Sam Griffiths.

No one spoke for a while. The silence in the room was ominous. Eventually it was broken by Alan Munro's phone ringing.

'Yes... hang on Kim, I'm with Inspector Steadman, Sam Griffiths and Rosie Jennings. Can I put you on speaker-phone?'

Kim Ho always sounded nervous, more so when she had unearthed something important.

'I've been working on the small rucksack, the one the towels were in,' she said. 'There was a name tag on the inside. It was soaked in blood and at first I thought it was blank. I did some tests and in the name section there was a long dash followed by a dot and two dashes.'

The colour drained from Steadman's face. Sam thought he might faint.

'What's the matter, John?'

'Dash, dot dash dash – it's the Morse code for TW. The bag belonged to Tim Warrender.'

CHAPTER TWENTY EIGHT

'What time is it? He should have been here by now.' Steadman's voice wavered.

He pressed the button on his watch. It was four thirty. With a shaking hand he passed his own phone to Munro. 'His mother's number is stored – Ann Warrender. Can you find it? I'll speak.'

Munro called the number and handed the phone back to his colleague.

'If it's about the money,' said Ann, 'I really think you're being too generous, especially as Tim is so careless.'

'It's not that at all,' Steadman replied, trying desperately to keep the unease out of his voice.

'What is it? Is something wrong?'

'Is Tim with you?'

'I thought he was with you. He was meant to be going to an exhibition, but the school called to say it had been cancelled…'

Munro's phone rang loudly.

'What? Holy shit! I'll be right there.' He leapt out of his chair.

Steadman quietly said, 'Hang on a second, Ann,' and put his phone on his lap.

'What is it, Alan?'

'The bastard's got Tim Warrender on the roof of the Art Gallery. He's threatening to push him off.'

'Go! Take Sam Griffiths with you,' Steadman replied quite calmly. In that moment he once again became Detective Inspector John Steadman. He lifted his phone off his lap.

'Ann, who is at home with you?'

'I'm alone. Something's wrong, isn't it? It's Tim.'

'He's been taken hostage. We will pick you up in less than five minutes.'

'Hostage? No, it can't be true. He is going to be OK, isn't he?'

Steadman could not give a straight answer.

'Just get ready and wait for us.'

* * *

A single street light cast an oblique shaft of white outside the Warrenders' house. As though confined by the beam, Ann paced up and down shooting nervous glances into the fog, stopping suddenly at every sound while her fingers feverishly shredded paper tissue after paper tissue.

Eventually the small police car turned into the street. She pulled open the door before it had time to stop.

'Where is he? Where's my Tim?' Her voice was breaking. 'Who would want to harm him?'

Steadman had tried to rehearse the situation, tried to find the right words, the right tone, but he too was finding it hard to maintain his composure. In as flat a voice as possible he replied, 'He's at the Art Gallery with Mr Haribin, his art teacher.'

'Mr Haribin? Then he's all right. Tim likes Mr Haribin and Tim is one of his favourites.'

Steadman struggled to respond.

'What is it? What are you not telling me?' Ann pleaded.

'He and Tim are on the Art Gallery roof. Mr Haribin is not what he seems...' was all that he could bring himself to say.

Ann let out a shriek.

'Is he the killer? Oh, dear God, please tell me he's not! What does he want with my Tim? Why would he harm him?' She put her head in her hands and sobbed.

'It's impossible to say for certain. Haribin's grip on reality is tenuous. In order to make any sense of what's happening I've been trying to get into Haribin's mind. It's not easy as he doesn't think like you and me.' Steadman paused. Something was not right. The pattern was being broken. Could he...?

Ann interrupted his thoughts.

'But why Tim, Inspector Steadman?'

'I blame myself. Boys of that age very quickly transfer affection and allegiance...' His voice faltered.

'Maybe I can help explain,' Rosie offered. 'I interviewed Haribin over George Bremner's death. I got the impression that he thought your Tim would follow in his footsteps and was flattered. And then Tim met DI Steadman and DS Munro. Here was a whole new possibility. A career as a detective appeared a lot more exciting than being stuck in a classroom.'

'And I encouraged him,' Steadman continued. 'I asked him to think like a policeman. I insisted he should carry a phone at all times. I even suspect he followed George Bremner and Mr Haribin, acting like a detective.'

'I am afraid, Mrs Warrender,' Rosie added, 'Mr Haribin took an unreasonable dislike to Tim and may well hold your son responsible for scuppering his chances of becoming deputy head.'

'But it doesn't make any sense,' Ann protested, tears flowing down her cheeks.

'No, it doesn't,' Steadman agreed.

'Can't you stop him? There must be something you can do.'

'As long as they are both still on the roof, there is some hope. I need to think.'

Steadman rested his chin in his hands. He shoulders sank, as though the burden of responsibility was too great for him to bear. Thoughts raced back and forth in his head. The pattern was not being followed. Could this be the chink in Haribin's armour?

Quite suddenly he turned to Ann. 'Has Tim heard how he got on in the art competition?'

'No, why?'

'Good,' was all that Steadman replied.

Ann wanted to say more, but Rosie caught her eye in

the rear-view mirror and put a finger to her lips. She could see that Steadman was not to be disturbed.

Steadman was muttering in a barely audible voice. 'That might work... but only if... and would he believe me? Then what? I can't think of any alternative...' His mind was reeling this way and that. It was as though he was trying to crack open a safe, each thought spinning like a dial until the tumblers, with the smallest of clicks, fell into place.

'What do you think, Robbie?' he said at last. 'I doubt if you will be able to help me this time.'

The dog eased himself up and placed his head in Steadman's lap.

'You have a plan? You've worked something out, haven't you?' Ann asked.

'I wouldn't go so far as to call it a plan. I have an idea, that's all. Heaven alone knows if it will work.'

Rosie Jennings nosed the car through the fog. Eventually she turned into the broad sweep of Gladstone Circle. It was not strictly a circle, rather an oval formed by two arching, elegant crescents. In the centre was a small islet of fenced-off garden. From the air, thought Steadman, it must look like an eye. And in a pang of self-doubt his thoughts continued, a useless eye, not unlike my own.

The Art Gallery stood in the middle of one of the crescents, flanked by a museum on one side and the City Chambers on the other. The rear of the building was secure. The only means of entrance was by the enormous front doors. The whole area had been cordoned off with police tape.

An officer shone a torch into Rosie's car. He recognised DI Steadman instantly.

'Tim's mother,' explained Rosie hastily before he could ask who the other passenger was.

'Pull over by the other side of the garden,' he said gruffly.

Rosie parked next to DS Munro's Audi. A familiar figure was waiting for them.

'I've been looking out for you, John,' said Dr Rufus. He nodded to Rosie Jennings, who had already got out of the car.

'This is Tim's mother,' she said.

Dr Rufus did not know what to say to her. Instead he patted her clumsily on the shoulder.

Steadman got out of the car awkwardly and fumbled with Robbie's harness.

'This way is quieter – less chance of running into Beaky Nesbitt,' said Dr Rufus as he led Steadman round the grassy island.

Rosie put a comforting arm round Ann's shoulders and followed the two men. A fire engine was positioned to the right of the Art Gallery, its large searchlight trained on the roof. Next to it were two ambulances. Several police cars with their blue lights flashing were parked close by. Over twenty officers were standing silently staring at a small parapet high up on the roof and barely discernible in the gloom.

In a whisper, Frank Rufus outlined the scene to Steadman. 'Sam Griffiths is doing an excellent job talking to Haribin,' he added.

They rounded the garden. Steadman noticed a slight breeze had picked up. It was coming from the east and bitingly cold. The mist swirled round Gladstone Circle and in an instant parted, revealing the two figures. Ann let out a gasp.

'What is it?' asked Steadman.

'We can see them clearly,' Frank explained. 'They're standing right on the edge of the parapet.'

Tim somehow looked smaller, as if fear had shrunk him. Haribin stood proudly, a step behind the boy with his hands placed firmly on his shoulders.

'Nobody within fifty yards of the building or the boy goes over!' Haribin's voice boomed and echoed over their heads.

Steadman was now standing behind Sam Griffiths and Alan Munro. Sam raised the megaphone to her lips.

'Nobody is coming near the building, Mr Haribin,' she said soothingly. 'The television cameras you requested are expected to arrive any minute, I promise. Why don't you just take a step away from the edge? I'm sure the breeze is a little stronger up on the roof than down here.'

Haribin didn't move. Raised voices could be heard a little way off to their left.

'Someone tell them to keep quiet,' Sam hissed.

Frank Rufus ambled off and returned a few moments later. 'You won't credit this. Crouchley has arrived with armed back-up and wants to take a pot-shot at Haribin. For once Nesbitt is showing a bit of sense. Crouchley is not backing down easily.'

Steadman shook his head in disbelief.

'Are you making any progress, Sam?' he asked in a whisper.

'Well, he's still there. He has demanded to be on TV. However, I think he is stalling. I get the impression that he can't decide whether to jump himself or not. He realises it's almost over. Does he end it in spectacular fashion, or would he prefer the notoriety of a high-profile trial only to be followed by an ignominious end in a high-security hospital? I don't know how much longer he's going to last.'

'It's Tim I feel sorry for, he didn't ask for any of this,' added Munro.

Ann was sobbing in Rosie's arms. In that instant Steadman's mind was made up.

'May I speak with Haribin?' he asked.

Before Sam Griffiths could pass over the megaphone, Beaky Nesbitt barged in between them.

'Steadman, I thought I made it clear you were no longer on the case. You, speak with Haribin? I don't think that's a good idea.'

'I, on the other hand, think it is an excellent idea,' said a deep rumbling voice. A very tall man stepped out of the shadows.

'And who the hell are you?' barked Nesbitt.

'I am DCI Long and I am resuming charge of the investigation with immediate effect. Thank you for filling in for me, Inspector Nesbitt. Dr Griffiths, you may pass the megaphone to DI Steadman.'

'Wait a minute – you've been off somewhere. You don't know a thing that's going on.'

'On the contrary, I have had twice daily bulletins from none other than Sergeant Grimble. I'm sorry to hear about your car,' he added to make the point. 'John, I think time is of the essence.'

Nesbitt cursed, mumbled something about ingratitude and shoved past the officers standing behind DCI Long. Nobody gave him a second look.

Steadman took the megaphone and with Robbie at his side, stepped forward.

'Mr Haribin, I'm sure you know who I am. I know how much you dislike me, but hear me out. I want to talk about Tim. He is only a boy at an awkward age who, whatever you may think, is wholly without fault. In fact, I blame myself entirely for his present predicament. If I had not asked him to walk my dog he would never have met me, or Robbie, or Sergeant Munro. For the moment, his heart is set on being a policeman. He is young and will change his mind countless times. He may yet become an artist, if given the chance. So, I have a proposal to make to you – let me take Tim's place. There is also another very good reason why this would make a lot more sense to you.'

There was a murmur behind Steadman and several of the officers exchanged puzzled looks. A television van with a large satellite dish pulled up. Other than that there was silence. Steadman waited.

'More sense to me, you say – how?' Haribin's voice sounded ghostly and far away. The fog had descended again and only vague shadows could be seen from the ground.

'You know that I was up for Helmsmouth Citizen of the Year. Well, I have just been informed that I came second. You, of all people, understand the significance of second place. If it makes it any easier, I also know you entered one of Tim's carvings into a competition. Sadly, it didn't make it through to the finals.'

'What is he on about?' whispered Dr Rufus.

Alan Munro shrugged his enormous shoulders. Dr Sam Griffiths smiled wistfully; she understood.

A gust cleared the fog again. Haribin was no longer standing tall. One hand was raking through his hair in agitation, the other was still firmly placed on Tim.

'How can I trust you?' he said eventually.

'Name your terms,' Steadman replied.

'No dog.'

'Agreed.'

'Unarmed.'

'Agreed.'

'You come alone.'

'I will need someone to guide me, unlock the Gallery and escort Tim back. I presume there is a lift, then stairs and a door leading to the roof. They will accompany me no further than that door.'

'I don't trust you, Steadman.'

'Tim can stay with you on the ledge until I take his place.'

'Are the television cameras here?'

Steadman turned round for assistance.

'They're up and running,' said Sam Griffiths.

'Apparently so – have we a deal?'

Alan Munro had turned bright red. He turned, scanned the officers behind him and disappeared into the throng.

Dr Rufus came up to John Steadman.

'You realise he'll kill you. He's totally insane.'

'Can you think of another way of saving Tim?'

'No, but... anyway, what's all this nonsense about second place? I don't understand.'

'Ask Sam Griffiths, she knows. Where is Sam?'

'I'm here,' she replied, staring intently at her feet. She could not bring herself to look at John Steadman.

'Any advice, Sam?'

'Keep him talking as long as you can.'

'I need someone to look after Robbie?'

DS Fairfax stepped forward. She could not look at Steadman either. 'I'll take care of him,' she said.

'I presume you want me to come with you on this fool's errand?' said Dr Rufus.

'No, Frank. I need someone who knows Tim. Where's Alan Munro?'

'Here, sir.'

'Do you know how we will get in?'

'I have the key, the code for the alarm and instructions on how to switch on the electricity.'

'Are you sure you want to go ahead with this, John?' asked DCI Long.

'I could never live with myself if I didn't. Give me your arm, Alan, before Haribin changes his mind.'

The fog closed in again as they made their way to the Art Gallery steps. They could hear Sam Griffiths gently reassuring Mr Haribin.

A sudden gust whipped off Steadman's fedora. Munro bent down and retrieved it. He paused before handing it over.

'Do you mind if I borrow your hat, sir?'

'Borrow? You think there's a chance I may need it again, Alan?'

'Always a hope, sir.'

'You have a scheme, haven't you? Don't tell me what it is. All I ask is you don't do anything risky until Tim is safely out of harm's way. Do I have your word, Alan?'

'Of course.'

They reached the flight of steps and ascended slowly. There was a new sound to their left. In the distance he could hear the clipped tones of a commentator doing a piece to camera.

'By the way, sir, when did you hear about the Helmsmouth Citizen of the Year?'

'I haven't – I lied. It's simply that all his other victims…'

'Won second prize!' Munro finished the sentence for him. 'And Tim?'

'No, I made that up as well.'

Alan Munro unlocked the huge door, shone a torch on

the control panel, disarmed the alarm and switched on the electricity. In an instant the building was bathed in light.

Steadman was getting impatient. 'Come on, Alan, before it's too late.'

They entered the lift. Neither spoke until it jolted to a halt.

'The stairs are on our right, apparently,' said Munro, 'behind a door marked 'No Access'. Here it is.'

He opened the door and was met by a draught of cold night air.

'I'm not comfortable doing this, sir,' he said suddenly.

'Damn it, Alan, I can't do it by myself. Just get me onto the roof and point me in the right direction.'

The door onto the roof was already ajar. The roof itself was flat, broken only by several large chimney stacks. Munro could see the outlines of Haribin and Tim standing on the parapet. Steadman took out his cane and unfolded it.

'They're straight in front of you, sir. There are two chimney stacks immediately on your right. They're standing on a low wall no more than twenty yards away.'

'Thank you for everything, Alan.'

'I don't know what to say, John.'

'Better to say nothing, then.'

Steadman swept his cane over the flat roof and, scuffing his feet, cautiously picked his way to where he thought Haribin and Tim were standing. At last his cane hit the parapet wall.

'Are you there, Mr Haribin?'

'Right beside you, Steadman.' The voice was almost in his ear.

'Let the boy go.'

Haribin released Tim's shoulders.

'Scram, kid!'

Tim jumped down from the wall. 'He's mad, Inspector Steadman. He's going to kill you. He said so!'

'Run, Tim. Alan Munro is waiting behind the door. Go now – not another word.'

Tim raced towards the half-open door. Haribin watched him go, then turned his piercingly blue eyes on Steadman.

'So, we meet properly - face to face at last,' he said.

CHAPTER TWENTY NINE

Tim ran as fast as he could on shaking legs. Munro's voice could be heard, deep and reassuring. It was not possible to make out the words. The sound faded as they made their way down the stairs. Then there was silence.

'You agreed to take Tim's place, Steadman, which means on the parapet, not behind it,' said Haribin.

At the sound of Tim and DS Munro's retreating footsteps Steadman was quite suddenly filled with an overwhelming sense of serenity. He no longer cared what happened. Ever since the phone call he had directed all his energy, every grain of strength and every inch of resource into saving Tim Warrender. And he had succeeded. Whatever the price demanded of him, he was willing to pay.

'As you wish,' he replied.

He leaned forward and touched the top of the wall. It was only a foot high. The stone was cold and wet. A strong hand grabbed him under the armpit. For a brief instant he believed Haribin was going to throw him over there and then. No, he thought, he'll want his moment in the limelight. Maybe he'll wait until Tim is out of the building. Pray God Tim doesn't see me fall.

'Not afraid of heights, are you, Steadman?'

'Heights, like sunsets and the night sky, are now only memories. I'm sorry to disappoint you, but the height of a kerb or the depth of a pothole is far more worrying.'

As he spoke he ran his cane, apparently aimlessly, over the top of the wall. It was wider than he had imagined, at least eighteen inches.

'Up here,' Steadman continued, 'I can hear the distant rumble of the traffic, the wind in the branches. I can taste the fog with its hint of salt. I can tell you there is an easterly breeze and by tomorrow the sun will be shining. It's not that my senses are any better than yours, it's simply that I have no visual distractions.'

Haribin did not appear to be listening. He was still holding tightly, almost painfully, onto Steadman's arm.

'Me, I love heights, always have,' he said. 'When I was a child I used to stand on the very edge of the cliffs. My mother would scream at me, but she was too terrified to come near me. I would stand there until she was sobbing. When I got home I knew I would get a beating from my father. He would beat my mother too. It didn't stop me. My father couldn't stand heights either. Even if he was with us, I would find a chance to stand on the edge. It was like having my own little kingdom, my own realm where I was untouchable.' His grip tightened on Steadman's arm. 'I don't know why I'm telling you all of this.'

He turned and stared at Steadman. 'Are you really blind?'

'Virtually – sometimes I can make out bright lights.'

Haribin seemed intrigued.

'Can you tell which side the searchlight is coming from?'

Steadman obliged him by raising his dark glasses and peering into the darkness with one eye then the other.

'I think it's brighter on my left.'

A ragged cheer broke out from the crowd below.

'Oh look!' said Haribin. 'There goes Tim with your lanky sergeant. Why, he's even wearing your hat. Did you give it to him as a keepsake?'

Steadman shrugged. 'Thank you for letting Tim go.'

Something was not quite right. He rewound the conversation in his head. Lanky sergeant? Whatever else Munro was, he was definitely not lanky. Tall, yes, but massively broad with it. The hairs prickled on the back of Steadman's neck. He knew that somehow Munro was still in the building. At all costs he must keep Haribin talking.

'Tell me, when did you decide to kill Crenshaw Tipley?'

Haribin gave a derisory laugh. 'I've had thoughts of killing him for years. On numerous occasions he has damned my work and ruined my exhibitions with his sneering comments. He once claimed to have seen a bit of copper wire poking through the clay on one of my sculptures. It was a lie. The clay model wasn't part of the exhibition. It was there only to illustrate the process before the bronze casting is made. He suggested the wire frame might have been more interesting than the final figure. I wonder how Crenshaw Tipley liked copper wire poking out of him.'

Steadman nodded; so that's why the victims were wired up.

'You do realise the man was a complete charlatan,' Haribin continued. 'I borrowed a book from his precious library on stage design giving the name of a famous theatre designer and he never batted an eyelid.'

'I thought you might have done that to cast suspicion on your rival, Jeff Skinner,' Steadman queried.

'That too! You asked me when I actually decided to kill him. It was when his book won second prize. Have you read it?'

Steadman shook his head.

'That was what annoyed me. I hoped it would be rubbish. It wasn't. In fact, it was brilliant. Of course, it should have won first prize. But everybody knows in the arts world the best entry is always given second place. Look at the Turner prize or the Booker prize. The judges set out to shock and provoke, that's all. It's just a big game, a pantomime. No, if you enter any of these competitions, as you know full well yourself, the aim is always to come second.'

Steadman nodded again. Things were beginning to fall into place, albeit in a bizarre fashion.

'Yes,' Haribin continued, 'my aim in life is always to be second. That's where the real power lies.'

Like being deputy head of a school, Steadman mused.

'Now Velda Meemes simply annoyed me because she broke the rule. I entered that competition and, by rights, second place should have been mine.'

He is mad, Steadman said to himself, and getting madder by the minute.

'And then there was Tim. My star pupil, my successor before you stole him from me. I didn't know you existed until then, but I soon heard all about you, your wretched dog and DS Munro.'

'It was you who took my photograph.'

'Correct – I needed to know what you looked like. And I followed Tim and your dog in the park. I think I scared him.'

'I can forgive that, but not the attack on Robbie.'

'It was a warning – you chose to ignore it.'

'And the wing mirror? And trashing my flat?'

'A stronger warning and, quite fortuitously once I knew what Rufus was going to do with you, the opportunity to visit your flat. You have a nice netsuke collection.'

'You didn't care for the Pre-Raphaelite prints?'

'Oh please! Spare me chocolate box art. Destroying them was doing you a favour, believe me.'

'Harry and Maurice Eeles almost spoilt it for you, didn't they?'

'That was pure chance. To begin with I enjoyed it, especially Inspector Nesbitt running round like a headless chicken announcing to anyone who would listen how he had solved the crime. It is true I use old electrical cable. It's cheap. Even cheaper if you cycle up to Harry's van, open the door and help yourself. You know, I sometimes think cyclists are invisible. How did Nesbitt account for the stolen wire?'

'He didn't even try,' Steadman replied. 'Nor for the bike you left in Harry's garage after you killed Dennis Knotting. I thought he was your friend.'

'Knotting was a failure and a dropout.'

'His parents died when he was at college.'

'And so? Artists are meant to suffer. It was an opportunity missed. A stall in the market place selling old records and wind-up gramophones – I ask you!'

'He made a living. He also sold sculptures in a fancy gallery in London.'

Haribin swung round violently, shaking with rage. Steadman stumbled, almost losing his balance. There was a gasp from the people below.

'Just stay calm, Mr Haribin.' Sam's voice drifted up. 'Why don't you take a small step back onto the roof?'

'Bloody woman,' Haribin muttered under his breath. 'Tell her to shut up, Steadman.'

'It's all right, Sam. Mr Haribin and I are having an interesting conversation,' Steadman shouted.

'You say he made a living. Even as a second-rate art teacher I could buy and sell the likes of Dennis Knotting ten times over. That is, until he was runner-up in the competition. Do you know what that would have done to his work? Do you?' The aggression was mounting in his voice. 'Let me tell you. Everyone will now want a Dennis

Knotting sculpture. And the price? Add a zero – no make that two zeroes!' Haribin was seething.

'You know,' Steadman said in a soft voice, 'you may have been the one person he cared about. We found a photo in his wallet, the only photo in his possession it would appear. It was taken at college. He was smiling, and he was with you and Jeff Skinner. That's how we tracked you down.'

Haribin's grip slackened on Steadman's arm. The breeze dropped and again the two men were enveloped in mist. After a long pause Haribin let out an enormous sigh.

'I know,' he said. 'Perhaps that only made it worse.'

'Is that what made you decide you had done enough?'

'I needed to be caught. It had to stop. But Nesbitt wasn't going to do it. I sat in the waiting room of the police station for ages. I make a good drunk! Twice I almost gave myself up to Sergeant Grimble.'

The door on the roof creaked. Haribin froze. 'Who's there? Come one step closer and Steadman goes over. I'm warning you.'

'I think it was just the wind,' said Steadman. 'We would have heard the lift, and I doubt if anyone would enter the building as long as we are standing here.'

A couple of seagulls perched on one of the chimneys took off with a loud squawk. Haribin swung round, still clutching Steadman's arm. He stared into the fog which was again shrouding the roof. All he could make out were the ghostly shapes of the chimney stacks. His grip relaxed a fraction.

Steadman knew he must keep him talking.

'Now, of course, you realise you can have your place in history.'

There was a long pause.

'I don't know what you're talking about, Steadman,' Haribin replied.

'Fame at last, public recognition – isn't that what all artists crave? The opportunity to be first at something, as it were.'

If Steadman hadn't been blind he would have seen Haribin gazing wide-eyed at the crowd gathered below him as it drifted in and out of view in the swirling mist.

'What do you know?' he said at last.

'I know you visited a very old friend of mine, Miss Bartholomew, the newspaper archivist. She remembered your blue eyes. Eventually she recalled your name, or at least she thought you were called Harry. She told me you had read all about Alfred Sheridan, Helmsmouth's only other serial killer. I gather he killed three of his parlour maids. So you have tied with him. One more, and your name will be remembered for ever.'

'Yes,' Haribin replied with relish. 'And that person is you, John Steadman.'

Something cold and thin slipped over Steadman's head and tightened round his neck. It was a copper wire noose. Instinctively Steadman raised his free arm and prised a finger under the wire circle.

'Oh, don't worry. It is only for show – my trademark, so to speak. It will be the fall that kills you.'

Time was running out.

'Have you decided?' Steadman asked.

'Decided what?'

'The most important thing, of course.'

'And what exactly would that be?' Haribin's voice hesitated.

'Is it just me or are we going over together?'

This time there was no hesitation.

'Only you, Steadman, only you – as soon as the mist lifts again.'

A breeze rustled through the trees in the garden opposite. Haribin placed his hand on Steadman's back.

'Just one little push,' he whispered in Steadman's ear.

'Oh no you don't, you monster!' roared Alan Munro as he charged from behind the nearest chimney stack.

Haribin turned, paused, then pushed. Munro dived. An enormous arm wrapped round Steadman's waist and the two men tumbled backwards onto the flat roof with a resounding thump.

'Are you all right, sir?'

'You took your time, Alan. I don't think I could have kept him talking much longer. God, but my ribs hurt. I can barely get my breath... where's Haribin?'

Munro looked round. Haribin was nowhere to be seen. Suddenly he became aware of the clamour rising up from the street. He ventured to look over the parapet. The fog had cleared and a gibbous moon illuminated the scene beneath him. The twisted body of Edwin Haribin lay lifeless on the ground. Dr Rufus was kneeling beside it.

Even from Munro's lofty perch, it was obvious that there was nothing to be done. All eyes turned upwards towards the parapet. Munro's massive frame was outlined by the searchlight. He felt sick.

'I think he's dead, sir.'

Steadman did not respond. He lay motionless on the cold roof. His breathing was coming in short gasps.

Munro gently shook his shoulder. Steadman rolled over. His lips were blue. The copper wire glinted in the moonlight. Munro swore under his breath, slackened the noose and slipped it over Steadman's head. It made no difference: still he was scarcely breathing. Munro swore again.

'Don't do this to me, John, please,' he said out loud as tears welled up in his eyes.

He lifted the limp body and raced towards the half-open door.

★ ★ ★

One of the ambulances circled over to where the crumpled remains of Edwin Haribin lay. The paramedics leapt out; one opened the back doors while the other made for the body. Dr Rufus placed a restraining hand on his shoulder and shook his head.

'There's nothing to be done, lad. At a guess, albeit one based on years of experience, I would say his neck is well and truly broken.'

Both men looked up as the large doors of the Art

Gallery burst open with a resounding crash. Munro, with Steadman cradled in his arms, bounded down the steps. He was yelling at the top of his voice. The only discernible words were 'Where's Rufus?'

Dr Rufus waved his arms and ran to meet them. He took one look at Steadman.

'Into the ambulance!' he shouted.

Dr Rufus could not recall if it was he or the paramedic who had ripped open Steadman's shirt. He rather fancied it must have been him as someone, in the confusion, had managed to slip an oxygen mask onto Steadman's face.

'Please tell me he's still alive,' asked Munro.

'Barely,' Dr Rufus replied. 'What happened? We couldn't see clearly.'

'I grabbed him as Haribin was about to push him over. We went down with a tremendous wallop. He said he could barely breathe. The bastard had put a wire noose around his neck. I got that off, but by then he was blue and unconscious.'

Dr Rufus grunted. His nimble fingers ran gently over Steadman's chest and neck.

'Tension pneumothorax,' he declared. 'Give me a large cannula.'

The other paramedic was a step ahead of him. She had a large bore needle already in her hand.

'What's a tension whatever-you-called it?' asked Munro.

'His lung has collapsed, probably punctured by his broken rib when the two of you toppled over. The problem is, every time he takes a breath, air escapes from the hole in his lung. The air has nowhere to go, so it builds up under his ribs, causing the lung to collapse even further.'

Munro didn't really follow. All he could see was Steadman gasping under the mask.

'Look – it's pushed his windpipe way over to the left.'

As Dr Rufus was explaining all this, his fingers were counting the gaps between Steadman's ribs. He pointed at a particular spot. The paramedic wiped the area with an antiseptic swab and Frank Rufus plunged the needle in. There was a hiss, like a bicycle with a puncture, followed by a loud thump as Munro passed out on the ambulance floor.

'He's probably just hungry,' Dr Rufus observed. He fished about in his pocket and found a half-eaten bar of chocolate. 'Here – give him that when he comes round.'

Munro was already beginning to stir when the ambulance doors opened. It was the crew from the second ambulance.

'Need a hand?' asked the first paramedic.

'Help our sergeant to his feet. We need to be going to hospital,' replied Dr Rufus, who appeared to have taken charge of the situation.

Munro protested. 'I just need a blow of fresh air, that's all.'

Through the open doors Dr Rufus could see DCI Long giving detailed instructions to DS Fairfax. Some of the blue and white police tape had come loose and was flapping in the breeze. A flash from a police camera briefly illuminated Haribin's twisted body. In that instant, Dr Rufus noted that Munro was desperately pale and physically shaking.

DCI Long strode over to the ambulance. 'How is Steadman?' he asked.

'Alive and breathing a bit easier. But he's not conscious. We really need to go.'

DCI Long nodded and closed the door. With its siren wailing, the ambulance sped off. Dr Rufus noticed that the half-eaten bar of chocolate was still lying on the floor.

★ ★ ★

Munro stood silently staring up at the wisps of cloud racing past the face of the moon. He barely noticed the officer who handed him back his coat and Steadman's hat.

'Do you have a car, Alan?' DCI Long asked.

Munro turned a pale face towards him. 'The Audi's parked on the other side of the gardens, sir. I don't think I'm up to driving.'

'Give me the keys, Alan. We should go back to the Eyesore. There's nothing more for us to do here.'

'Where's Tim?' asked Munro.

'Don't worry. Rosie Jennings is looking after Tim and his mother.'

The two men did not speak on the journey. The streets were eerily quiet, as was the Eyesore.

Sergeant Grimble looked up from his desk. 'Evening sir. Evening, Alan.'

DCI Long nodded in his direction. One look at Alan Munro and Grimble thought it best to keep quiet.

'Coffee or tea?' said DCI Long when they at last reached his office. Munro merely shrugged. 'Coffee it is then, Alan. Help yourself to sugar, and there should be a packet of biscuits in here,' he added, producing a tin from a drawer.

Munro mechanically shovelled sugar into his coffee.

'You understand, Alan, I need a full statement,' said Long.

'Where do you want me to begin, sir?'

'I gather you were at Steadman's flat with Dr Griffiths and Rosie Jennings when you got the news. Why don't you start there?'

'Actually it started before that, sir.'

Munro recounted picking Steadman up from the offices of the *Echo and Evening News*, the meeting with Miss Bartholomew, the phone calls at the flat and then the mad dash to the Art Gallery. DCI Long was noting it all down in meticulous copperplate writing.

'Dr Griffiths did her best to reason with Haribin. Then Inspector Steadman arrived. Everything seemed to move so fast. I didn't understand the significance of second place, but one thing was certain – if Steadman was to take Tim's place and be left alone on the roof, Haribin would undoubtedly push him off. That's when I thought of PC Dyer.'

'Go on.'

'Well, barring yourself, sir, PC Dyer is the only other

officer approaching my height. I asked him to edge around behind the fire engine and when Haribin was distracted, to make his way to the doorway of the art gallery. I had planned simply to give Tim my coat to take down to him, then I remembered he was bald, which would be pretty obvious to anybody looking down from above. Steadman's hat had blown off as we made our way to the Gallery, and that gave me the idea of borrowing it.'

'Quick thinking on your part, Alan. Tell me about the scene on the roof.'

'I took Tim down to the lift, gave him my coat and the hat and explained PC Dyer would be waiting for him. He's a bright kid and, fortunately knows PC Dyer. I made my way back to door leading to the roof. I couldn't hear what Inspector Steadman and Haribin were talking about. I had promised not to do anything until Tim was safe. When I heard the cheer, I knew the boy had made it. All I had to do then was creep up behind Haribin. I picked my way across the roof, taking cover behind the chimney stacks every time the fog came down. A couple of seagulls nearly gave the game away. Suddenly, it became obvious that Haribin wasn't going to wait any longer. I may have shouted something as I rushed forward. It was all over so quickly. I managed to get an arm around Steadman just as Haribin gave him a push. We fell heavily...' Munro paused and wiped the sweat from his brow. 'Do you think we could phone the hospital, sir?'

'In a minute, once we've finished.'

'It was Inspector Steadman who asked where Haribin

was. You probably saw me standing on the ledge.' DCI Long nodded. 'When I turned back to Inspector Steadman, he was unconscious and barely breathing. Haribin had slipped a wire noose around his neck. I removed it, but it didn't help. The rest you know.'

DCI Long drew a line under the last paragraph.

'Let's phone the hospital and find out how he is.'

* * *

Dr Rufus had made himself thoroughly at home in the hospital. Such was his air of authority that nobody questioned his presence. He had supervised the insertion of the chest drain, which was now bubbling away at the side of the bed. He had allowed Steadman's sister and Sam Griffiths the briefest of visits before shooing them away and was now reading a copy of the *British Medical Journal* which he had found in the resident doctor's office. He cast a concerned eye over his patient every few seconds. Steadman had spoken briefly, and only to ask after Tim and Alan Munro.

In truth, Dr Rufus was only glancing at the journal. If someone had snatched it from him, he would have been hard pushed to say whether he was reading the article on high blood pressure or diabetes.

'You're wanted on the phone, Dr Rufus,' a nurse informed him.

He gave Steadman another anxious look before following the nurse.

'How is doing?' asked DCI Long.

'He'll survive. The collapsed lung appears to be expanding. He's sleeping peacefully. I'm going to stay here tonight. Tell the Coroner I'll do the post-mortem on Haribin tomorrow.'

* * *

DCI Long did his best to reassure Munro, who still looked awful.

'More coffee? No – well, here's your statement. I hope you can read my writing. Take a seat next door and read it carefully while I write up my own report.'

No sooner had DCI Long sat down when his phone rang. It was the Assistant Chief Constable.

'Potential disaster, Long. Are you listening?' The ACC was a man very much concerned with his position.

'Yes, sir. I can hear you.'

'Have you got DS Munro with you?'

'He is checking his statement as we speak, sir.'

'Good. Get him to check it very carefully – very carefully indeed. You understand?'

'Not really, sir. Is there a problem?'

'There most certainly is, Long. I've just been shown some of the TV footage. They've blown it up a bit, awkward angle and not one hundred per cent clear, but it does look like your sergeant may well have pushed Haribin off before he grabbed Steadman. Are you still there?'

'Yes, sir. I'm taken aback, that's all.'

'Well, it can't be helped. Of course, I've reported it to the Independent Police Complaints Commission for further investigation. They'll be dealing with it from now on. Obviously, Munro is to be suspended with immediate effect.'

'Is that necessary, sir?'

'Damn it, Long – there is no question about it! The picture has already been sold to the press. It will be all over the morning's paper. I'll leave you to it. Oh, and make a room available for the investigating team – a nice one.'

DCI Long put the phone down and contemplated the backs of his hands. He was not a man given to uncouth language, nonetheless he muttered an oath under his breath.

There was a tap on the door.

'I've finished reading it, sir. Do you want me to sign it?' asked Munro.

'Take a seat, Alan. Are you quite sure there's nothing you want to add?'

Munro sensed there was something wrong. 'Quite sure. Is there a problem?'

DCI Long leaned back in his chair and stared hard at Munro's anxious face. He took a deep breath and puffed out his cheeks. Eventually he spoke.

'That was the ACC on the phone.'

Munro frowned.

'He has been shown some of the TV footage. It is not absolutely clear but…'

'But what, sir?'

'It suggests that you may have pushed Haribin before you grabbed Inspector Steadman.'

Munro started to protest. DCI Long shook his head.

'Don't say anything, Alan. It is now out of our hands.'

'What do you mean, sir?'

'The TV company has sold the picture to the newspapers already. The IPCC has been informed. They will be investigating the matter further from here on in.'

'And me, sir – what will happen to me?'

'I am afraid, Alan, that with immediate effect you are suspended on full pay. I must ask you to clear your desk and surrender your warrant card.'

Munro was crestfallen and stared at the floor.

'I will need to send your jacket to forensics to check for cross-contamination of fibres. You have your coat?'

Without looking up Munro replied, 'It's in the Audi.'

'I'll fetch it for you before you go.' Long looked at his watch. 'I'll arrange for a taxi to collect you in thirty minutes. You should remain available for interview at any time. I assume Sergeant Grimble will know how to get hold of you. You must have no contact with anybody involved in the case. In effect that means anyone in the force, as well as Dr Griffiths, Dr Rufus and, of course, John Steadman.'

'You believe me when I say I have no recollection, don't you, sir?'

'Sadly, Alan, it's not up to me.'

CHAPTER THIRTY

Angela Carswell was a taciturn lady of indeterminate age. Although her hair was greying, her eyes retained a youthful sparkle. She had been an investigator with the IPCC since it was formed. She was accompanied by a younger man who, if Sergeant Grimble was to be believed, spent his whole time looking flustered and whose speech comprised only two phrases: 'sorry ma'am' and 'yes ma'am'.

DCI Long had temporarily vacated his office, and behind its closed doors Angela Carswell and her colleague had pored over the television footage, the written statements and the forensic evidence. DCI Long had been interviewed at length. It was clear that from where he and the other officers had been standing Haribin's final moments had been obscured by the swirling mist. Only the TV camera had captured his fall. An expert on interpreting CCTV images had been brought in and was in conference with the two investigators. Sergeant Grimble deemed it a safe moment to give Steadman a call.

'How are you, sir? They didn't keep you in hospital for long, did they?'

'I'm better than I expected unless I cough, then it hurts like blazes. As soon as my lung expanded they removed the drain and once they were sure I was behaving myself, they booted me out, much to my relief. How are things at the Eyesore?'

'Ms Carswell doesn't give much away. She strikes me as very methodical and fair. Her opinion of Beaky Nesbitt's handling of the whole episode is pretty damning. I don't think she is going to bother interviewing him.'

'Have you any idea when I am likely to be asked to attend?' Steadman asked.

'That's one of the reasons for the call. If you are up to it, she is hoping to interview everybody tomorrow afternoon.'

'Fine by me. Do you know who will be there?'

'Tim Warrender's first. He's coming with his mum and Rosie Jennings. Then Dr Sam Griffiths followed by Dr Rufus. DCI Long has already been interviewed. You're next, and lastly, Alan Munro.'

'I don't suppose you've heard how he is?' Steadman would have been very surprised if he hadn't.

'Yes, his wife came in to collect his jacket. Kim Ho couldn't find anything on it, by the way. She says he's barely spoken and even more worryingly, he hasn't eaten since being suspended. The article in the paper didn't help.'

'I missed that,' Steadman replied.

'The *Echo* printed a grainy picture of the three of you on the Art Gallery roof under the heading "Hero or

Villain?" along with a photo of Munro. You can guess the rest.'

Steadman reflected for a moment. Despite his size, he knew his colleague was sensitive to criticism. An article like that would humiliate him even further, he thought.

'I almost forgot to ask – how's Robbie?' Grimble continued.

'Mr Barnes looked after him while I was in hospital. He's fine, a bit fretful and won't leave my side. Every time I sit down he deliberately lies on my feet. I'm not sure who fusses more, Robbie or my sister.'

'Give him a pat from me. I'll call you again, sir, when the interview times are confirmed.'

True to his word, Sergeant Grimble phoned back to confirm his presence was requested the following afternoon.

Steadman pressed the button on his watch, and the metallic voice informed him it was four twenty-five. Before he had time to wonder if Tim would arrive, the doorbell rang – one long ring followed by a short ring and two longer rings. Standing at the door beside Tim was Rosie Jennings.

'I hope you don't mind, sir, Tim insisted I come with him. He has brought you a present.'

'In that case you had both better come in.' Steadman was intrigued.

Tim was like a beetroot. 'This is for you... for saving my life.'

Steadman was somewhat taken aback as Tim forced a small parcel into his hands.

'Why… thank you, Tim. However, if you consider the alternatives, it was all really my fault. If you hadn't been helping to look after Robbie, you would never have been put through such a dreadful ordeal in the first place.'

Tim was only half listening. 'Aren't you going to open it?'

Steadman fumbled with the paper. Rosie and Tim were desperate to help. Eventually, he unwrapped the parcel. Inside was an exquisitely-carved wooden squirrel eating an acorn. Steadman's fingers gently played over its surface.

'Is this one of yours, Tim? It's absolutely wonderful. I can even tell that it's a red squirrel, not a grey, by the ears and the tail.'

'It's the one I entered in the competition. I came third, thank goodness. I think I would have thrown it in the fire if I had come second.'

'I'm very glad you didn't. I'll treasure it,' Steadman replied.

Tim mumbled something and blushed again.

'All the best people come third. I was pipped to the post as Helmsmouth's Citizen of the Year by a footballer and a local rock star,' Steadman continued. 'Not that I'm complaining.'

The dog scrambled to his feet and gave Tim a nudge.

'I think Robbie wants his walk. Come on, we'll go down the park.'

The two raced off down the stairs.

'He's a brave lad,' remarked Rosie.

'You'll be with him tomorrow, I gather,' said Steadman. 'Any news about the George Bremner inquest?'

'No date has been set, however the Coroner is happy to accept Tim's statement. He won't have to appear in court. Skinner has been tracked down in the Loire Valley. I understand he is not very keen on coming home. I've been back to the school. Mr Rotherhyde has at last agreed to retire. Mr Wilkes has taken over meantime. He is planning to have one of George Bremner's pictures professionally framed and displayed in the main corridor. His parents are touched. They have asked me to come to the unveiling with Tim.'

Steadman nodded appreciatively.

'May I ask you something, sir?'

'Sure – fire away.'

'How do you think things will go tomorrow? Tim's terribly worried that Alun Munro will lose his job – or worse.'

'I can't say for certain, Rosie. Not even Sergeant Grimble knows. Just tell Tim only to answer the questions put to him – stick to the facts and hopefully... who knows?'

★ ★ ★

Dr Rufus phoned first thing the next morning. 'Still breathing then?'

'I am, thanks to you,' Steadman replied. 'I will remain forever in your debt, Frank. Never let me forget.'

'Don't worry – I'll remind you on a regular basis. Listen, do you want a lift this afternoon? I'm picking Sam Griffiths up from the one-thirty train. If you like we could all go in my car.'

A shiver ran down Steadman's spine at the mention of Sam Griffiths's name. He hadn't forgotten she would be coming. He had, however, deliberately tried not to think about it, at least, not too often.

★ ★ ★

Dr Rufus opened the car door and Steadman squeezed in with Robbie at his feet. Sam Griffiths's perfume filled the car.

'You're looking better than when I saw you last, John,' she said.

Before Steadman could think of an appropriate response, Dr Rufus interjected, 'I wouldn't take that as a compliment. You looked so bloody awful in the hospital, it would have taken some effort not to look any better.'

Steadman shook his head and smiled.

'How are you, Sam?'

'I'll be fine once this afternoon is over. I gather Alan has taken it very badly, which of course, is perfectly understandable. Is Tim well?'

'Remarkably resilient, as boys of his age can be. He is back on dog-walking duties. He gave me one of his carvings – it is quite astonishing. I hope he will not be too upset by the proceedings.'

They continued to make small talk until Dr Rufus pulled up in front of the Eyesore. Sergeant Grimble ushered them into one of the interview rooms and told them to wait. As usual, Grimble made a fuss over Robbie.

'Who's a clever dog, getting all those nasty staples out? I don't care what your daddy says, you're going to get a special treat from your Uncle Bertie.'

'Do you think there's any hope for him, Sam?' asked Dr Rufus.

'None at all – too far gone in my opinion,' she replied.

'Has Tim been in yet?' Steadman asked.

'Just taken him in now,' answered Sergeant Grimble.

* * *

Angela Carswell stood up as Tim, his mother and Rosie Jennings entered the room.

'Please take a seat,' she said. 'My colleague, David Greene, will be taking notes. Tim, are you happy to talk about what happened?'

Tim nodded.

'Good. If you want to stop at any time, you only have to raise your hand. I've read your statement, however, I would like you to tell me yourself what happened. I gather Mr Haribin picked you up in his car? Maybe you could start there.'

Tim took a deep breath. 'I'd just got off the bus and

turned into my street. I recognised his car – it's a white estate car with a dent on the passenger door. He wound down the window and smiled. He said something like, "Coming to the exhibition, Tim? I've squared it with the school and your mum." It was a lie, but I didn't know that.'

'How did he seem in the car?' Ms Carswell enquired.

'He didn't say much, mind, he's always a bit quiet. It was also difficult to see where we were going because of the fog. We parked a little way from the Art Gallery. The exhibition was on the top floor. Another school party were already looking around when we arrived. We mingled with them. I didn't think much of the pieces on display. Haribin said we were to get a better view later on. I noticed he kept glancing at his watch, and at times he was muttering to himself. At quarter to five they rang a bell to say that the gallery would be closing in fifteen minutes. He said, "Quick, we've just got time." He pushed me through the door by the lift and then through another door and up some stairs. The next thing I knew we were on the roof. I asked him what did he think he was doing and he said, "Getting the best view." Do you think I could have a drink of water?'

Mr Greene jumped up and poured him a glass.

'Are you happy to carry on?' asked Ms Carswell.

'Yeah, I'm fine. It all gets a bit confused after that as he started rambling. He placed his hands on my shoulders and walked me round and round the flat roof between the chimney stacks. I was getting scared by this time as I couldn't understand what he was saying. He kept mumbling about being second and how nobody took his work seriously. Then he said, "This time I'm going to be famous." He spun me so I was facing him and he stared really hard into my eyes. He said, "And you'll be famous too, Tim." Well, I could tell he was bonkers. I said that I didn't want to be famous, I wanted to be a detective. That set him right off. He grabbed both my arms and marched me over to the little wall and made me stand on it. The only other thing he said was, "Alfred Sheridan killed three, Tim, but I'm going to beat him. You are going to be number four."'

Tim's mother, who had been screwing up a hankie, now bit her knuckles to stop herself crying out.

'It wasn't long before a small crowd had gathered and then the police arrived. I was too terrified to move or say anything. Haribin didn't speak to me again until Inspector Steadman appeared on the roof.'

'What do you think he meant when he talked about Sheridan killing three and you were going to be number four?' Ms Carswell said softly.

'I figured out he was the murderer Inspector Steadman was looking for. I thought he was going to kill me as well.'

★ ★ ★

Sam Griffiths winked at Tim as they passed in the corridor.

'I have read your statement, Dr Griffiths. It is very thorough. Have you anything you wish to add?'

Sam shook her head.

'I have only three questions to ask you,' continued Ms Carswell. 'Firstly, do you think Haribin would have killed the boy without Inspector Steadman's intervention?'

'Beyond any shadow of a doubt,' Sam replied.

Greene scribbled away feverishly.

'Secondly, do you think Haribin was insane?'

'That is much harder to answer. I only spoke with him for a relatively short period of time in very unusual circumstances. I would say he was very disturbed, but I would have needed longer to ascertain his sanity and degree of responsibility for his actions.'

'Last question, did you see him fall from the parapet?'

'No, I don't think any of us saw from where we were standing on account of the fog.'

Dr Rufus hadn't seen anything either. He confirmed that Haribin had sustained multiple fractures to his neck and a significant brain injury. Death, in his opinion, had been instantaneous. He did add, however, that if he had accompanied Steadman on to the roof instead of Munro, he would have had no qualms in pushing Haribin off and that his timely death had saved the taxpayer a fortune.

Ms Carswell thanked him hastily and, under her breath, instructed Mr Greene not to record his last remarks.

Sergeant Grimble escorted Steadman into the room and helped him find his seat. 'I'll take Robbie out so he can stretch his legs,' he said, slipping off the dog's harness before Steadman had time to protest.

'You are to be congratulated, Inspector Steadman,' said Ms Carswell. 'I have no doubt your quick thinking and actions saved Tim Warrender.'

'Perhaps, although it was because of me Tim's life was put in danger. It was fortunate that Haribin was fixated with coming second. I didn't fully appreciate the depth of his obsession myself until I was on the roof.'

'Yes, I have read your very detailed statement. I have one question to ask you.'

'Only one?' queried Steadman.

'Only one, and it's this – were you actually pushed before Munro grabbed you?'

Steadman thought for a moment before realising the enormous importance of the question. The scene replayed in his mind in slow motion. He remembered Haribin placing a hand on his back, whispering in his ear, Munro roaring then...

'Yes, he pushed me – he definitely pushed me before Munro grabbed me. I had lost my balance and...' His voice tailed off.

'Thank you, Inspector Steadman. I have no further questions.'

★ ★ ★

Maureen Munro had driven her husband to the Eyesore. They waited in the car until Sergeant Grimble called him in.

'You realise, Maureen, this might be my last visit to the Eyesore,' said Munro.

Maureen squeezed his enormous hand. 'Hush, pet, you'll be fine. I know you will.' But she could not keep the tremble out of her voice.

Grimble led him in by way of a side entrance. 'I doubt if you would appreciate an audience even if they are all one hundred per cent behind you,' he said.

'Thanks. What are they like?'

'Angela Carswell and David Greene? Well, she seems very thorough – keeps her cards close to her chest, definitely a Ms. As for her colleague, Mr Greene, he lives up to his name – wet behind the ears and seems out of his depth most of the time. I'm sure he'd rather be somewhere else.'

'I know that feeling only too well,' Munro replied.

Grimble tapped on the door. 'DS Munro, ma'am.'

'Thank you, Sergeant Grimble. Please take a seat, Mr Munro. Let me remind you of the gravity of the situation and the fact that you are being interviewed under caution.'

Munro was bright red. 'I understand, ma'am,' he replied.

'There is no question your actions helped save the lives of Tim Warrender and John Steadman. For that you are to be commended.'

'Thank you, ma'am.'

'You are aware, however, of the allegation made against you?'

'Yes, ma'am.'

'Can you recount in precise detail the last few minutes when you, Haribin and Inspector Steadman were on the roof?'

'I have thought of nothing else for the last week, ma'am. I will do my best, but the events went so fast and emotions were running high.' He swallowed. 'When I knew that Tim was safe I made my way on to the roof. I couldn't hear what they were saying and could only catch glimpses of them in the swirling mist. I knew Haribin was standing to the left of Inspector Steadman. I picked my way behind the chimney stacks until I was about ten or twelve paces behind them – not directly behind them, but at something of an angle, ma'am. I saw Haribin put a hand on Steadman's back. I knew I had to act quickly. I raced towards them. I think I was shouting. I flung my arms around Steadman and we both toppled on to the roof. It all happened so quickly.'

'I will ask you this only once, Mr Munro. Did you push Haribin to his death?'

Munro stiffened. He looked straight ahead not focussing on Ms Carswell or Mr Greene, but at some distant point. He moistened his lips with the tip of his tongue.

'I have no recollection of having done so, ma'am. My sole intention was to save John Steadman.'

'Thank you, Mr Munro. I realise this has not been easy for you. You know that I have now to prepare a file with my recommendation to the IPCC. In my experience, the recommendation will not be challenged.'

Munro held his breath, as did Sergeant Grimble who was listening at the door.

'My recommendation is that there is insufficient evidence to pursue any form of conviction against you.'

The room was silent bar the retreating footsteps of Sergeant Grimble.

'Does that mean...' Munro could not finish the sentence.

'It means, DS Munro, once the bureaucrats have rubber-stamped all their pieces of paper you will be reinstated.'

A smile the size of a boomerang broke out on Munro's face.

'Thank you, ma'am.'

* * *

'Now, I didn't tell you lot anything,' hissed Grimble, as Munro's ponderous footsteps thundered down the stairs. Munro pushed open the door and beamed at his colleagues.

'I'm to be cleared – insufficient evidence.'

Spontaneous applause broke out. Maureen flung her arms about his neck. DCI Long shook his hand. Tim was dancing around the waiting room.

Grimble's phone rang. He waddled over and picked up the receiver. 'Yes, he's here. Dr Rufus – call for you.'

Munro sidled up to John Steadman and Dr Griffiths. 'I don't know what you said in there, but thanks anyway,' he said.

'I'm so relieved,' Steadman replied. 'I would rather have died than have your career ruined on my behalf.'

'I think, John Steadman, you are getting a bit blasé about putting your life on the line,' said Sam Griffiths.

'I agree,' Munro added.

Dr Rufus joined their group. 'Will you be able to make your own way home? They've just pulled a body out of the harbour.'

'I rather fancy a walk, if it's dry,' Steadman replied.

'The sun has come out. I'll chum you home if you'd like,' Sam added. 'My train is not till later this evening and I can always get a taxi to the station.'

Sergeant Grimble clipped Robbie back into his harness. 'Now, you come back and see your Uncle Bertie soon,' he said. 'There's always a bag of you-know-what in my desk.'

'Come on,' said Sam, 'I worry Sergeant Grimble's affliction might be catching.'

They stepped out into the watery autumnal sunlight. Steadman pushed his dark glasses onto his forehead and felt the warmth on his eyelids. Sam slipped her arm into his, and again Steadman felt his stomach lurch.

They didn't chat much on the way back to Steadman's flat. As they approached, he ventured: 'Would you like to come up and see Tim's carving?'

'Is that the same as asking a girl to look at your etchings?' Sam replied teasingly.

'If you would rather not,' Steadman stammered.

'Don't be silly. Besides, I've got you a present.'

Tim's wooden squirrel was duly admired.

'He's got a lot of talent,' Sam commented. 'I've brought you a bottle of whisky to add to your collection,' she added. 'It's Penderyn, Welsh malt whisky.'

'That's very kind of you. I've heard of it, but never tried it.'

'No time like the present. I'll fetch a couple of glasses.'

'You will have to help me by opening the bottle as well, I'm afraid,' Steadman said ruefully.

Sam poured two generous measures. Steadman sniffed the glass and slowly rolled the whisky appreciatively round his mouth.

'It is very good,' he said.

'I'm glad you like it.'

Steadman could feel her breath on his cheek. Without realising what he was doing, he put out a hand, touched her shoulder and leant forward.

Sam put a finger on his lips.

'Don't think I'm not tempted, John, but you're not ready yet. You wouldn't know whether you were kissing me or Holly's ghost.'

'I'm sorry – how stupid of me. I know you're right,' he sighed.

'There's no need to apologise,' she replied. 'Anyway, tell me John, do you think Alan Munro really did push Haribin off the roof?'

'I really have no idea, Sam. Being blind, my recollection is even more hazy than Alan's and I would never ask him. He did, after all, save my life.'